Dedalus Europe 2015
General Editor: Timothy

What Became
of the
White Savage

François Garde

What Became of the White Savage

Translated by Aneesa Abbas Higgins

Dedalus

This book has been selected to receive financial assistance from English PEN's translation programme. English PEN exists to promote literature and our understanding of it, to uphold writers' freedoms around the world, to campaign against the persecution and imprisonment of writers for stating their views, and to promote the friendly co-operation of writers and the exchange of ideas.

This book is supported by the Institut français (Royaume-Uni) as part of the Burgess programme. (www.frenchbooknews.com)

Published in the UK by Dedalus Limited,
24-26, St Judith's Lane, Sawtry, Cambs, PE28 5XE
email: info@dedalusbooks.com   www.dedalusbooks.com

ISBN printed book 978 1 910213 08 7
ISBN ebook 978 1 910213 29 2

Dedalus is distributed in the USA & Canada by SCB Distributors,
15608 South New Century Drive, Gardena, CA 90248
email: info@scbdistributors.com   www.scbdistributors.com

Dedalus is distributed in Australia by Peribo Pty Ltd.
58, Beaumont Road, Mount Kuring-gai, N.S.W. 2080
email: info@peribo.com.au

First published by Dedalus in 2015

Printed in Finland by Bookwell   Typeset by Marie Lane

The Author

Born in 1959, François Garde grew up in Aix-en-Provence and studied at the prestigious Ecole Nationale d'Administration before embarking upon a career as a senior civil servant. He worked for many years in the French Overseas Territories in the Southern Pacific and Indian Oceans, before becoming a novelist.

Published in 2012, *What Became of the White Savage*, is Garde's first novel. Inspired by a true story, it won nine literary prizes, including the prestigious Prix Goncourt in the first novel category for 2012.

The Translator

Born in London, Aneesa Abbas Higgins studied Sociology, French and Russian at the University of Sussex and later obtained her MA in Romance Languages and Literatures from the University of London. She taught French for many years before becoming a freelance literary translator.

For Laurence

1

When he reached the top of the small cliff he realised that he was alone. There was no sign of the dinghy drawn up on the beach, no sign of a boat floating on the blue-green water. The schooner lying at anchor in the entrance to the bay was nowhere to be seen, no sails visible on the horizon. He closed his eyes, shook his head. Nothing. They had left.

Absurdly, he felt guilty. When the dinghy had landed on the beach, the second mate had divided the sailors into three groups to increase their chances of finding water. Three men went towards the trees, vaguely outlined at the far end of the beach; three towards the other side of the bay, rocky and uninviting; the rest were sent to search through rock holes and look for a cave at the base of the limestone cliff. At first, he'd turned over coral blocks with his shipmates but soon decided that their efforts were in vain: any rain that fell on this terrain would seep into the sand. Rather than digging at random, surely it would be better to try and find signs of life: men or animals would lead him to water. A light offshore breeze was blowing, softening the burning rays of the tropical sun.

He'd climbed straight up, finding purchase on roots and holes in the rock. Moving with athletic skill, he reached the top within a few minutes. Unnoticed by the crew, he waved his arms in a wide motion, signalling to the boat before heading inland. A vast, almost flat plain spread out before him: a dusty, parched landscape, with tufts of grass and sparse, meagre trees, all of the same metallic green. No buildings. No smoke. In this arid steppe, they would surely search in vain for a spring.

Looking again at this discouraging landscape he noticed a small channel that began near where he was standing and ran towards the interior of the plateau, widening out into a valley. He followed the path of this furrow with his gaze, and realised that it became deeper as well as wider. Trees growing along the side became gradually bigger and greener than the others, eventually forming an emerald green grove that stood out against the muted colours of the forest. When the rains came, water must run into this natural depression. Perhaps there was still a pool somewhere in a shady hollow. The smallest, muddiest pool would be enough to fill a cask, and save the sick on the ship.

He struck out straight ahead towards the hollow, following it to the bottom of the slope. Walking was difficult, the vegetation different from that on the plateau: now he had to make his way through tangled woody scrub, edging his way through the waxy leaves of spindly bushes. He noticed a sort of cress that grew more densely as he advanced. Eventually he came to a small hollow a few metres lower than the plateau. He touched the ground, felt its humidity. No sign of a brooklet, not even a puddle. Crouching down, he used his knife to dig and scrape. The soil was loose and damp and he managed to dig a hole as deep as his forearm. But there was nothing to be found.

Somewhat disappointed at not proving to be the hero of the day, he stood up and headed back along the valley floor towards the beach. This walk through the cool green woods away from the grey forest above would be his secret, one small pleasure derived from their attempt to find water in this nameless bay. He moved unhurriedly and climbed at a leisurely pace back towards the modest hilltop overlooking the bay.

It was then that he realised he was alone. He let out a cry, but no ship could hear him. Frantic, unable to think, he ran like a madman down the cliff, slipping and sliding, the bushes scratching him, twice almost breaking his neck. He leapt onto the sand, raced along the shore and ran into the water up to his chest in an effort to get as close as he could to the vanished ship. Howling with rage, he shouted and cried out for help. His cries were no more audible from the sea than from the cliff. A wave wet his neck and he moved back, staring out to sea.

He had to get up high to survey the horizon. Trembling with confused emotions, he climbed back up the cliff.

What had happened? How long had he been gone on his solitary exploration of the interior? An hour, at the most. Enough time for the dinghy to be called back: he hadn't seen the flag signalling the order to return to the ship, hadn't heard the warning gunfire. The *Saint-Paul* had weighed anchor, cast off and set sail. But why? Why in such a rush? Why had they gone without him?

He sat down in the shade of a scrawny, twisted tree. Memories came back to him: seafaring knowledge, a few phrases exchanged between officers and petty officers. The bosun had reported that the ship was anchored in coarse sand on rock; it wouldn't hold firm. With the full moon two days before, there would be high waters. The captain had only agreed to enter this unknown bay to seek fresh water for the sick on board. The offshore winds seemed to be picking up.

At the entrance to the bay, he could see the water beginning to swirl and eddy. The sea had been smooth as a lake when they entered the bay. Now he could see what the lookout at the masthead must have spotted earlier: most of the bay was bounded by a coral reef that was gradually becoming visible. There were only two narrow channels. Arriving at high tide, they had entered the bay without incident, passing through the main channel by chance, unaware of the danger now revealed by the ebbing tide. With an unreliable anchorage and this strengthening wind, the captain could not risk getting trapped in the bay. He had to get out as quickly as possible while he could still manoeuvre the ship. Perhaps the second mate had mentioned that there was a man missing. But it could take another hour to return to shore, find the missing man and re-embark. They had to get out to sea and save the ship.

He found some reassurance in picturing the scene, imagining the conversations and the orders being given. The captain was right, he'd made the only choice possible to a sailor. It wasn't a deliberate abandonment or a personal betrayal, but simply the consequence of a perilous situation. By leaving the group, he had disobeyed orders and deserved to be punished. He wasn't too worried about a thrashing from the second mate – he'd had plenty of thrashings at school or in his father's shoe workshop, and then on the ship – but he hoped to avoid being fined. And two or three months from now, they would all be laughing together about the whole episode.

The wind was picking up, and out at sea, beyond the bay, swells were beginning to form, the rollers breaking on the coral reef. He picked up a stone, and without thinking, threw it towards a pile of dead branches, one of which turned out to be a rather large, silvery-coloured lizard. It scurried towards the undergrowth, stopped for a moment nodding its snake-like head, and disappeared.

Only then did he grasp the reality of his situation. He was seized by fear. Abandoned on these barren shores, surrounded perhaps by wild animals or savage cannibals ready to devour him as soon as night fell, he had no food, no water, nothing with which to start a fire. He had nothing in the world but the knife in his belt and the clothes he stood up in.

He would have to prepare to sleep on the ground. The rough seas meant there was little hope of the ship coming back before nightfall, but he was reluctant to leave his lookout point with the clear view of the whole bay. To pass the time, and with a vague idea of defending himself, he cut a few more or less straight branches from a nearby tree, stripped off the bark and shaped the ends to a point. Now he had a bundle of sharp sticks, like short spears or thick arrows; armed with these rather primitive weapons he felt somewhat reassured.

His solitude and growing hunger weighed on him like a heavy tiredness. The sun was sinking and he calculated that he probably had an hour of daylight left, two hours at most of being able to see. He wondered where to settle down for the night. The strengthening wind might be a warning of rain and he decided not to sleep at the top of the cliff. He headed back down towards the valley floor and walked on until he found a sandy spot under the trees where he went about building a shelter. He broke off a few branches, intertwined them and stood them up against two adjoining trees. Then he gathered a few armfuls of tall fern growing nearby to use as walls and bedding. This makeshift hut would afford him some protection from bad weather, and if an animal or a savage were to attack him in the night, the shelter would collapse and alert him to their presence. He'd grab his spears and fight for his life.

Before the light faded completely, he went back again to his lookout point. Huge clouds scudded across the dark sky.

The sea was a simmering black mass, silvery waves slicing across its surface. The roar of the surf crashing on the reef was deafening. And out to sea, no sign of a lantern, not a glimmer of light.

This would be his first night on land since they had put in at the Cape. He couldn't help smiling at the thought of the Cape. They had sailed from Bordeaux without incident, and during their week-long stopover at the Cape he had spent two evenings on shore. He'd explored the cosmopolitan port with three of his shipmates, savouring the white wine from the surrounding hills, doing his best to communicate in garbled English, Dutch and Spanish, and admiring the beads and fabrics that adorned the African women.

They'd spent the first night wandering aimlessly from one tavern to another, downing tankards of the local brew. In the fourth establishment, a fight broke out between some other French seamen and a group of English tars. He and his mates had sided with their compatriots, thrashing the Englishmen before going on to the next tavern with their new friends to celebrate their victory. No one remembered what happened next, and how they managed to get back on board ship remained a mystery.

Two nights later they were in town again. After dining on meat and fresh vegetables, they'd gone to an establishment with a red lantern outside, recommended by the old hands. They went in, sat down at a table and ordered something to drink, trying to look casual and at ease. The girls appeared and paraded across the floor in front of them, swaying their hips. Without too much ado, the four sailors stood up, made their choice and settled the bill.

The girls were half-caste and he ended up with the darkest

of them. As she led him towards one of the huts clustered together at the back of the courtyard he made a lewd suggestion with a broad smile on his face. She didn't understand French, but she murmured something in response as she closed the door. In the half-light he could make out a basin, a mat and a candle. He undressed and lay down beside her. He heard his shipmates' groans carried on the soft air through the holes in the walls as he turned his attention to his own pleasure.

When he'd finished, he began to doze off, sensing the warmth of her dark skin – when an insistent banging on the doors reminded them that the time paid for was up. He dressed and rejoined his mates and together they drank a last jug, boasting of their prowess.

Now, as the last rays of light faded, he went back to his makeshift shelter. He managed to edge his way in without causing the structure to collapse, and lay down on his bed of ferns. He was used to the swaying of the hammock aboard ship and the hard sand seemed strangely still and flat. He thought of all the times during the voyage when his mind had taken him back to that night with the whore from the Cape. He was sorry he hadn't asked her name. He couldn't really remember her delicate face, he had barely glimpsed it. But he could recall the smell and distinctive texture of her skin. His mates had made fun of him and joked about the blackness of her skin. In all his encounters at different ports of call, she was the darkest of the women he'd been with. But so what? It was her dark skin that had filled his thoughts during his nights in the hammock, and now, lying here alone in this alien land, he wrapped himself again in the warmth of those memories.

It was after the Cape that things had started to go wrong. The captain had chosen a southerly route to make the most of the easterly winds. They'd come up against the storm, with heavy, cross seas and snow squalls. For six days, they'd tried night and day to force a passage before finally abandoning the attempt and heading back to calmer latitudes. The ship and the crew had taken a beating: broken rigging, ripped sails, numerous bruises. One fellow, a topman from the Vendée, had broken his shoulder after falling from a topsail and the second mate had done what he could to repair the broken bone. The ship had sustained damage to the hold with several water barrels rendered useless.

In the Cape they'd taken on a man from Brittany, from Guilvinec, who claimed to be a deserter from an English ship. He didn't look too healthy, but the captain was always short of hands and had agreed to take him on. The man had ignored the abuse hurled at him by the crew and had sat out most of the storm trying to find shelter before finally declaring himself sick. The rumour was that he hadn't jumped ship but had been put ashore on account of his weakened state. The second mate tried some of his remedies, but the Breton faded away before their eyes and died ten days after they set sail. No one had taken the time to get to know him: they hadn't really felt any inclination to. But the death of a man aboard ship always leaves a lasting impression.

Their maps showed an island, Saint-Paul, in the middle of the Indian Ocean. The captain hoped they'd be able to take on some fresh water there and do something to help the injured man. From that point on, the sea was calm, occasionally disturbed by a long swell. Banks of mist drifted under a milky sky. They found the island of Saint-Paul and sailed around it: an extinct volcano, no sign of a river or a stream, nowhere to put in, nowhere to drop anchor.

They were left with no choice but to continue towards

Australia. According to the second mate, the vast west coast was treacherous and sandy, with no shelter or fresh water anywhere. The south coast was virtually unknown. On the east coast, there was the penal colony founded by the English in Sydney, with another one at Hobart Town in Tasmania. They decided to try the north coast, and from there, continue towards Java or one of the Dutch colonies in the Sunda Islands.

After the island of Saint-Paul, the wind dropped almost completely. They could go no further south in the light breeze. The sails shivered and rustled silkily as the heat and humidity became oppressive. The injured man lay on the bridge in agony. And then a cabin boy and the carpenter fell ill and took to calling incessantly for water to drink. The captain decided to ration the water. It was now two months since they had set sail from Bordeaux.

The wind picked up again but now it was a facing wind. For five days they plied windward only to realise that a reverse current was hindering their meagre progress. The seawater was warm, the air stifling; an oppressive humidity engulfed the ship. The wounded sailor and the two sick men lay groaning at the foot of the mainmast. The captain wore a grim expression on his face. In the forecastle, men talked in hushed voices, recounting earlier voyages to China and the dangers they had faced. There was no more singing in the evenings.

The cabin boy died. He was a good lad, a Breton, from Quimper. The crew were deeply affected by his suffering. Squalls streaked the horizon, but no rain came their way. And then another man fell ill, a fellow from Sète. The captain seemed more and more at a loss. Shouts were heard, angry words exchanged between the captain and the second mate. After two weeks with no wind at all, followed by a period of foul wind, a good breeze from the south finally set in and they were able to breathe again. But then, two more men fell ill; no one could understand why. Two deaths, one wounded man, three sick: there weren't enough hands to hoist full sail and the captain had no choice but to go on under reduced sail even though the winds were favourable. Water rations were reduced.

They sailed well clear of the west coast and the north-western tip of Australia. Coming into the Gulf of Carpentaria they followed the coastline at a distance. With the aid of a telescope, they could make out nothing but inhospitable mangrove swamps and long stretches of sand. The captain never dared to give the order to take a closer look, sailing further from the coast in the evening, and only approaching again in the morning. The Arafura Sea seemed to go on for ever. They spent a week navigating in this cautious manner. The islands of the Torres Strait came into view, but the captain did not want to make landfall there for fear of being attacked by savages. The heat had once more become intolerable. There was no improvement in the sick men's condition.

The schooner headed full south and tried to find a passage through the maze of sandy islands and coral reefs that rose out of the water and threatened constantly to rip open the ship's hull. On the third day, they managed to get reasonably close to shore and found a welcoming bay, bordered by a ring of trees, behind a rocky peninsular. The captain decided to explore it, telling the men that if this area proved to be as arid as the others, they would abandon Australia and head for Java. The dinghy was launched, the larboard watch called; they rowed to shore, pulling hard on the oars and landed on the beach with four empty barrels to be filled with fresh water.

Yes, it was after the Cape that things had gone from bad to worse. Now, lying on his bed of ferns, he thought longingly of water: a great jug of fresh water.

He went to sleep, forgetting his hunger. Several times in the night, he woke up with a start, expecting to be roused by an order for more sails, with the reassuring sound of bare feet on the boards and the snoring of his shipmates. But no, there was only the silence of this alien land, a bed of leaves instead of his hammock. He closed his eyes again, amazed that he was still alive.

In the morning, it took him a few moments to recall the previous day's events. He leapt up, knocking down his makeshift hut. The sun had just risen, but no birdsong had announced the dawn. He headed back along the wooded valley towards his lookout point at the top of the cliff. One glance was enough for him to realise there would be no rescue that day: heavy clouds were scudding across a lowering sky, the sea was flecked with white horses, huge rollers were breaking on the reef that bounded the bay, the surface of the water alive with waves criss-crossing it. No mariner would risk sailing his ship into this.

He felt crushed by the physical sensation of his solitude. Letting himself slide to the ground, he put his head on his knees and fought back the tears of rage that engulfed him. Thirst made his tongue stick to the roof of his mouth. On the ridge, the sand blew up in whirls, whipped up by gusts of wind into short-lived tornadoes.

He went back down to the beach and followed the bay towards the south. The trees he'd guessed at in vague outline the day before became a forest, and by the time he reached them, he realised he was in a mangrove swamp. Trunks rose out of the muddy, murky water, where there lurked God knows what kind of creatures. Turning away from the sea, he began to walk along the side of the gully. The plateau dropped down into a vague plain, the swamp stretching inland as far as the eye could see. Discouraged, he turned back and retraced his steps. Even if he had found a way through, what would he have done? Crossed the mangrove swamp to get to the next beach? The only European settlement he knew of was Sydney and that was hundreds of leagues away. Without food or water, with no map, he'd have no chance of surviving. And the rescue party would only look for him where they had last seen him.

The wind grew stronger, cracking the branches. Black clouds gathered, squalls forming somewhere out on the horizon. Long strands of seaweed littered the beach, thrown up by the roiling seas. The tide was drawing out, and he waded into the water to examine the coral blocks revealed by the receding waters. He found five shells that looked like mussels and wondered if they were edible. Without a second thought he consumed them, but these few grammes of tender salty flesh only sharpened his growing hunger and intensified his thirst.

A feeling of dizziness overcame him and he went to sit in the shade of a eucalyptus tree. To avoid thinking of his misfortunes, he slept, unperturbed by thoughts of protecting himself from danger: there were no wild beasts, no human beings living in this place.

When he awoke, the worst of the bad weather seemed to have past, leaving only the leaden skies and oppressive heat. Feeling despondent, he walked to pass the time; without any particular plan in mind, he headed for the rocky point that bounded the bay to the north, with little hope of finding anything that might be of use in this chaotic pile of sterile coral blocks. Heaving himself up to the top, he looked out at the coastline of steep cliffs and sheer drops, intercut by creeks that would be impossible to penetrate from the coast. And beyond stretched the plateau with its endless monotony of dusty green vegetation.

The tide seemed to be out and it occurred to him to build a fish trap; he'd heard talk of them and would lose nothing by trying. He spent the next hour shifting rocks and stones around, erecting a sort of low curved wall turned towards the beach. At high tide, some of the less agile fish would obligingly linger there and he'd be able to catch them with his bare hands once the tide went out.

With the trap completed he was overcome by obsessive hunger, and by an even stronger, all-consuming thirst. Water had been rationed on the ship for more than two weeks. And he hadn't passed water for more than a day now; he knew this was a bad sign. There was no fruit on the trees, no hidden reserves of moisture to be sucked from the woody branches of the bushes. He went back to sit at his lookout post at the top of the small cliff, in the shade. Dusk was gathering. Out beyond the bay, the sea seemed to be gradually smoothing out, a long swell the only remaining sign of the storm's passage. Aboard the *Saint-Paul* it would be time for the evening meal, for tales and songs after a day's work and before the night. Was there talk of him? Had the captain made known his intentions with regard to him? With water supplies low, one crew member injured and three sick men on board, the captain would surely be in a hurry to pick up the missing man, and continue the voyage to Java and China. Two days ashore without food, water or any means of communication would surely be punishment enough for his foolishness. A fitting price to pay for thinking he could flout orders and strike out alone to explore beyond the cliff. Dawn would bring high tide, the ship would be there, lying-to beyond the bay while the dinghy came ashore. The oarsmen would be worried at first, unsparing in their sarcasm when they found him, but they'd give him water to drink and offer him a biscuit to eat.

What was he thinking? With water supplies low, one wounded man and three ailing, would the captain waste precious time searching for one foolhardy individual who'd got himself left behind on shore? He would first have to think of getting help for the injured and wounded. What chance was there that he'd opt to wait out the storm, tacking into the wind until they could come ashore again. And for what? To find that the lost man had been devoured by wild beasts or eaten by savages? Four lives against one. Why try to rescue one man who was in all probability already dead? Who would take such a risk? The only reasonable choice would be to set sail for Java without delay as soon as the dinghy returned. They'd try to get ahead of the storm. By now the *Saint-Paul* had probably been heading due north for two days. And here he was, watching out for the ship from the top of his perch. No. There would be no rescue party.

But then again. Even if the captain had taken the heartless decision to abandon a man, the entire crew would have mutinied, wouldn't they? Forced the captain to let them come to his rescue? All of the men? Who would actually have spoken up in his favour? Pierre? Joseph? Yvon? He started to count off on his fingers the men who might stick up for him, hesitated, started again, and finally gave up.

Such speculations were unhealthy. They served no purpose. His only concern must be to stay alive, and first of all to find water. That was the only thing that mattered.

He stood up quickly. Dizziness overcame him again and he had to lean against the tree to regain his balance and stop himself falling to his knees. Hunger continued to gnaw away at him. He went to the edge of the cliff, faced the hard blue darkening sea, cupped his hands around his mouth and shouted: "I am Narcisse Pelletier, sailor on the schooner *Saint-Paul*."

He heard no echo, only his words fading to nothing on the boundless horizon. But the act of proclaiming them made him feel that some of his dignity had been restored.

An idea came to him as he looked at the rocks that lay scattered around on the beach. He went back down to the beach and started to arrange the bits of rock and stone to trace the outline of an arrow pointing towards the cliff and the hollow where he slept. That way, if he wasn't to be seen on the beach when his shipmates arrived, they'd know that he was alive and where to look for him. He became engrossed in the task and hauled the biggest boulders he could lift, lining them up and filling in the gaps with smaller rocks, even clearing away all the other stones around his handiwork to make it stand out from the background of pristine sand. For two hours he toiled, eager to prove to himself that he could lift these great blocks in spite of his thirst.

He looked down at his creation from the top of the cliff. The arrow was five metres long, its tip clearly shaped. It would be impossible to miss: a call for help, a sign to be followed. What ship could resist such a message? It might even point to a hidden treasure.

On the way back to his hut he broke off some branches to mark his path, no longer concerned about revealing his presence to potential attackers. And as for the rescuers, their arrival was beginning to seem more and more unlikely.

Back at his makeshift shelter, he moved the toppled sticks away from his bed making no attempt to reconstruct his would-be fortification. He lay down on his bed of ferns, his tongue dry as a stone, clinging to the roof of his mouth. His throat filled with the taste of bile. He began to feel pains in the muscles of his arms and legs. Lying there, half buried beneath the leaves, he began to weep, gently at first, silently and without tears. Racked by muffled sobs, he went to sleep.

The third day was worse. He woke up feeling weak, his mind blank, his legs shaking. The sky was blue, and although there was a light breeze, it did nothing to ease the oppressive weight of the heat and humidity. He went back up to the ridge: no sign of a ship, no sail on the horizon. He slept again, this time in the dirt, or perhaps he passed out. When he came to, the sun was high in the sky and the tide was out. He walked along the burning sand to gather his catch, but the fish trap was empty. He'd run out of ideas for finding food or water. This alien land seemed as arid and desolate as all the deserts of Arabia. He began to hallucinate, and thought he saw an enormous red rabbit bounding along on its hind legs, up there on the cliff. He blinked and it was gone.

He went back up to lie down under his tree, facing the empty bay. Incapable of making any plans, he found he could no longer even remember the faces of his shipmates on the *Saint-Paul*.

A vision appeared to him and he saw clearly his own tomb in the village church. The news of his disappearance wouldn't reach his parents for several months. They would hold mass for him. Once, in his days as a choirboy, he'd attended the mass for a young fisherman from the village who was lost at sea. He'd seen the parents' distress; the absence of a coffin made it even more poignant. In his vision, he saw his own mass. His little sister Emilie, would be there; she always loved his rare visits home and the little trinkets he brought for her. He saw his brother Lucien, the apprentice shoemaker, next to her. It was the older brother's responsibility to take over their father's workshop, and as the youngest, he'd had to try his luck elsewhere. At the age of fifteen he'd embarked as a cabin boy and had grown accustomed to life at sea. No one could have imagined that it would end like this, with a stroke of bad luck, alone and cut off from any living soul, utterly abandoned. He would leave nothing behind him. These bleak thoughts did nothing to lessen the raging thirst that scoured his throat. He felt feverish and was seized by fits of trembling.

The idea of ending it all began to torment him, of leaping head first from the top of the cliff. Was this the only choice left to him? Death by his own hand, or waiting for death to come to him? He found no solace in his memories of catechism. All that was left to him was the freedom to choose his own death. He clung to this certainty: he could choose to get up, to stand and look down on the piles of rock and coral, and then…

Sleep crept over him again with its temporary respite from anguish and suffering.

He woke up feeling a chill. The wind had picked up again and was sweeping across the ridge where he was lying. The sun was sinking, the horizon streaked with orange and red above the colourless forest. The hunger tearing at his entrails paled beside his piercing thirst. Cautiously, he stood up and made his way back to his shelter of the previous nights. His head was spinning, each flagging step demanding an effort of will. How simple it would be to just drop to the ground where he was and wait for the end. But he had to get back to his hut and his bed of ferns. He staggered on, swaying drunkenly, his mind a blank. Reaching the valley, he walked along the seemingly endless sandy path between the tree trunks and collapsed in front of his shelter. Protected from the wind, he curled up on himself, and lost consciousness.

The fourth day's travails were one long agony. Without the strength to walk back to the beach or to the cliff, he stayed where he was, lying motionless. As the cool of the evening set in, he gave himself up to the idea of dying: death would come to him there, on the sand, far away from everyone else.

LETTER I

Sydney, 5th March 1861

To the President of the Geographical Society

Monsieur le Président,

It is now more than four years since I wrote to you for the first time, expressing my desire to serve the cause of science and to make a contribution to the study of geography. Knowing nothing of me other than this wish, you did me the honour of welcoming me into your presence.

In that great hall, the birthplace of so many expeditions, I spoke to you of my plans. I informed you of my intention to use my inheritance, the fruit of two generations of frugal living by members of my family, to advance the cause of progress. I chose not to live the honourable but idle life of a country gentleman, preferring to serve science for the glory of France.

You listened with fatherly solicitude as I described my ambitions, which were at the time somewhat vague. The answer you gave was twofold. You began with the adage that travel is a full-time occupation, not a diversion. I did not then grasp the truth of this remark, and only later appreciated the extent of its significance. I had yet to learn how to travel with open eyes, to understand that one can often be mistaken, that time wasted can be time gained, and that one must sometimes remain still to observe the movement of life. All these lessons were humbly learnt. You, who have travelled so well and so much more widely than I, know too that every traveller must begin as an apprentice: that this period of initiation is of fundamental importance.

You then counselled me on my choice of destination, and whether I should journey towards Africa, the Poles, or the Pacific. These observations were to be of great importance to me then, and have been a cornerstone of all my travels.

You have no doubt forgotten this exchange, no different from those you must have had with many a young upstart. I, however, remember it with absolute clarity: your words for me were as the Ten Commandments. I can even recall perceiving a hint of irony in your kindly regard. At that time, you no doubt believed me to be another of those who would venture no further than the station at the end of the line, or the ship's last port of call. You went so far as to set before me the dangers of each of the three destinations: the cold and isolation of the Poles and the difficulties of navigating through ice; warring among African kings, Arab merchants, English adventurers and missionaries of all persuasions; the great distances across the Pacific and the realities of voyaging into the unknown.

Armed with this wisdom, I went away and weighed up the three horizons before me. For reasons I shall not dwell upon here, and which later turned out to be unfounded, I chose a polar route and began preparations for an expedition to Iceland.

I was to spend ten months on the eastern coast of Iceland, in a village of about fifty souls. I was able to explore this little known area although I did not draw up as many maps as I would have liked: my efforts were hampered by the early onset of winter, frequent storms and the difficulties of transportation. I was nevertheless able to make some progress in another area of enquiry and to give a detailed description of the way of life of these fishermen-farmers. My report on this, which I submitted to your Society, was considered worthy of forming the basis of a public lecture in a plenary session of the Society. Artefacts I brought back from Iceland, such as maps, sketches, clothing, toys and pottery, are now deposited in your archives. You graciously accorded me the title of associate member, an honour of which I was then scarcely worthy.

Some time later, you were good enough to welcome me once again into your presence and make enquiries about my projects. I informed you of my desire to continue my travels, but was wary of telling you the full truth, which was that I had discovered in Iceland that I am completely unable to tolerate cold. It robs me of the ability to think clearly and I find myself utterly at a loss, devoid of will, unable to take pleasure in life. I am content to concede the privilege of polar exploration to those who are better equipped than I to withstand the blizzards and snowstorms swirling around the cliffs, the icy winds that cut through one like a knife. The polar route is not for me.

For several months, I hesitated between Africa and the Pacific. Libraries, journals, generals and ministers alike all spoke only of Africa. I therefore determined to head for the Pacific, and one year after my return from Iceland, I set off once again.

The journey from Bordeaux to Sydney, although long, was without incident. We disembarked here in this English town built by convicts, and I made enquiries about continuing my journey towards the unexplored islands. I was both astonished and disappointed to learn that there are no longer any *terrae incognitae* yet to be charted in those regions. Moreover, one can readily obtain transport with the shipping companies to any point in the Pacific. I was thus able to journey to Lifou Island, Fiji, Espiritu Santo and Auckland. Everywhere, I found consuls, shipping companies and their agents, missionaries and even European settlers.

I did not fail to send you brief missives from each of these ports of call. My reports were later redrafted and were published last year under the title of *Scenes from the Pacific*. I spent many an evening on my terrace, writing these travel memoirs, while the eternal tropical rain drummed ceaselessly on the roof.

Every destination revealed a similar history. European presence had made its mark in the harbour with houses all around. But beyond this at a distance of two or three leagues, behind a range of hills, native tribes lived as they had always done. Making contact with them was more difficult than I had envisaged. As a Frenchman, I was regarded with suspicion by Protestant missionaries, and the rare Catholic missions I encountered were reluctant to burden themselves with the presence of a stranger. The practice of religion left little room for scientific observation. Whereas my aim was to give an account of naked savages going about their lives, the holy fathers thought only of urging them to cover their nakedness and teaching them to invoke the Holy Spirit.

My efforts invariably came to an end after several weeks or months, with very little to show. I obtained, at great cost, a modicum of information describing tribal practices, and accomplished very little mapping. Sometimes, as I walked on the beach in the morning watching the canoes depart, I found myself longing for Iceland and my conversations in German with the pastor who housed me there in his modest dwelling. It was apparent that my two years in the Pacific had yielded no tangible results; I could see this quite clearly, and harboured neither bitterness nor vain regrets.

I have of course no reason to reproach you, Monsieur le Président, on this matter. I went to the Pacific at your suggestion and found these islands and their peoples to be indeed exotic and undocumented. There is much for geographers to study here and a wealth of material yet to be discovered. But little remains for navigators of uncharted waters. Those who wish to study these lands will have to spend long periods living here, familiarising themselves with the savages' way of life. It will take time to gain the trust of the native tribes, to learn their languages and, with their assistance, to reveal the mysteries of these archipelagos. I am, alas, not equal to the rigours of this task and cannot undertake to embark upon it. Your assessment of the destination was indeed accurate; it is I who am not as you supposed.

Weary of my adventures, I decided to spend some time in Sydney to reflect upon the direction I wished my life to take. Australia may hold few charms for me as an explorer, but this new city is not without its attractions. My status as associate member of your Society opened doors for me: everywhere I went, I was welcomed by those few suitable individuals who were in a position to assist me. They all encouraged my efforts and not once reproached me for my failures. Through these contacts, I kept in touch with new developments in the wider world. At one such gathering, I met a young woman who seemed to share my inchoate notions and I believed she might become my future wife. But when, beneath her father's disdainful gaze, I declared my intentions, she informed me drily that she would never marry either a Frenchman or a Catholic. Until this moment, I had enjoyed the pleasant conversation to be had in Sydney, but this harsh rejection made me think that I should once more take to the seas. My tormentor, the lady in question, would have been amused at having chased me away. I decided to stay for a few more weeks and enable myself to leave with dignity.

One evening, sitting on the terrace at the house of Mr. Wilton-Smith, a respectable merchant, I was approached by the captain of the ship that had brought me back from Fiji fifteen months earlier. He asked me for my opinion, as an explorer, on the subject of the white savage. Believing I had misunderstood him, or that this was said in jest, I asked him to forgive the inadequacy of my English and to repeat what he had said.

The captain replied, in short, that an armed ketch had happened upon a white savage while trepang fishing. The savage spoke only gibberish and was found running about on the beach, naked and tattooed from head to foot. The man was clearly European: his hair, his height and the colour of his skin, burnt as it was by the sun, all confirmed that he was a white man. The crew had taken him by force and brought him on board, but had soon grown tired of this singular being. In Sydney, the governor had seized the man and thrown him into the city's gaol, where he had languished for the last week.

Like me, you will often have heard tales in various ports of women with the body of a fish, or men with three heads. Thinking this was just such a rumour from the taverns, I accorded the captain's remarks no more than polite attention. I replied only that I believed explorers had quite enough to do studying black savages without having to deal with a white savage. At that moment, the music struck up and put an end to our exchange.

I could not have been more mistaken, my witty riposte more misguided.

Three days later I was called to a meeting in the governor's office. I recognised some of the others present: a German merchant, an Italian priest, a Russian baron, a Dutch captain and a swarthy Hidalgo with the arrogant look of Spaniards the world over. All the principal nations of Europe, or at least speakers of all its main languages, were seated around the table.

The governor explained his difficulty to us. He had put the aforementioned white savage in his gaol and now did not know what to do with him. Having examined the man, the governor too was convinced that this man was European, that he was of white parentage and not of native or mixed blood. But where did he come from? He spoke only in gibberish and had about his person no object or symbol that might indicate his origins.

A convict dressed in servants' livery brought us some port, no doubt to lighten our spirits. The governor then set out his plan: each of us would address the savage in our own language to see if he recognised one as his mother tongue. We discussed this ingenious plan for a while. The priest then declared that he would only address the man in the Neapolitan dialect if this could be followed by some phrases in Latin. This was agreed to and the Spaniard muttered that he could also say a few words in Portuguese.

The businessman from Königsberg objected, asking why the consuls from our respective countries could not be contacted? Only an official representative of His Prussian Majesty could recognise a subject as one of his own.

The governor sighed in agreement. He could only address

the consuls in an official capacity. What would happen if two of the consuls were to disagree over the white savage? Or if one of them were to take offence at the suggestion that this naked, tattooed individual were a compatriot of his. This could give rise to diplomatic embarrassment, protestations, official despatches and reports in every capital. The confusion might continue for years, perhaps even become a subject of conflict between powers. Who knows where it might end? Mindful of these potential complications, he had invited the cream of the colony's foreigners to this unofficial audience, in the hope of finding a satisfactory way of proceeding.

Aside from a certain admiration for our host's acute political sensitivity, I will admit that I felt at the time no more than a passing curiosity towards the man they called the white savage. Sitting at the governor's table, I understood that this was not merely a fanciful hoax; I was intrigued to set eyes upon this person, and to learn a little more about him. Perhaps his story would form the subject of an entertaining anecdote in a Parisian salon at a later date. Ladies are invariably charmed by travellers' tales, and the strange tale of the white savage would be sure to amuse the gentlemen and set the ladies aquiver.

We were then introduced to a tall, somewhat shy young man, who seemed intimidated by the prospect of addressing us. The governor identified him as the assistant medical officer of the garrison and asked him to read us his report, which he proceeded to do.

"In accordance with your instructions, I have examined the stranger known as the white savage. This man is aged about fifty years and is five feet, six inches in height. He seems to be in good health, although he is somewhat thin. His chest, shoulders, arms and legs are covered in tattoos and scarrings. I observed two scars which had apparently not been properly treated: one on the left ear, where the lower part of the lobe was torn and partly ripped away, and the other on the right thigh, which could have been made from a knife or the tip of an arrow."

The young doctor seemed to gain in confidence as he progressed with his account and continued without looking at his notes:

"He belongs to neither the black nor the yellow races. This is evident from the colour of his skin, his build and the texture of his hair. Nor is he of the semitic races. This can be seen from his high forehead, straight nose, straight brown hair and full beard. I must also point out that he is circumcised, not in the way that Jews and Muslims are, but rather in the manner of the natives of this country."

This rather disconcerting detail was greeted with a few discreet coughs.

"His appearance therefore strongly suggests, indeed confirms, that this man belongs to the white race. He seems to have some intelligence: he listens when spoken to, uses gestures to express simple wishes, and obeys when given orders such as, get up, come, do not go beyond a certain point. He is very sensitive to emotion conveyed by inflections of the voice: friendship, anger, fear and pain arouse in him both interest and compassion.

He does not say a word and does not understand English. He has been heard by the crew of the *John Bell*, the ship that brought him back, lamenting in incoherent gibberish. He is dressed only in a loincloth given to him by the sailors, and spends his days squatting on his heels, knees apart, with his elbows pressed to the insides of his thighs.

He does not like our food and accepts it only to avoid starving, eating it with obvious disgust. He eats with his hands and drinks from his cupped palms, not knowing what to do with a cup or a spoon. He is not repelled by brackish water, but when a sailor gave him some wine in a spirit of jest, he spat it out."

This was the first report I heard on the subject of the white savage and I have presented it to you in its entirety, in the belief that you will find it useful. The Dutch captain objected, muttering that this could not be a portrait of a subject of His Majesty the King of the Netherlands. I found myself wondering for the first time about the life of this unfortunate soul. Others in the group saw in him a fairground oddity or a subject of controversy, but I began to think of him as someone to be pitied.

The governor invited us to step out into the garden, feeling that this would provide a less imposing setting for our discussions than the official reception room. In the shade of a large tree that swayed gently in the breeze, the white savage was squatting in the manner the doctor had described. He was guarded by two burly soldiers armed with clubs, who motioned to him to get up, but to come no closer. The man I beheld was as the doctor had described, and was indeed a member of the white race. I saw an oval face, with an aquiline nose, a well-defined chin and unremarkable mouth. There were lines on his face that told of sufferings he may have endured. His body was lean and well-muscled without an ounce of fat.

Although we had been prepared, we were all surprised by this spectacle: a white man, dressed only in a loincloth, tattooed from head to foot, mute and immobile, observing us.

I wondered which of these gentlemen would be the first

to speak. The Russian baron stepped promptly forward and uttered a few words and phrases in his tongue. I noticed the man listening to him with interest, apparently desirous of establishing some contact. But the words and phrases held no resonance for him and his disappointment seemed equal to that of the baron, who rejoined the group, a disdainful look on his face. Lighting a cigar, he declared that this was certainly not a subject of His Majesty the Tsar.

Then it was the turn of the Italian priest, who stepped forward and recited a *Pater Noster*, as much for the benefit of us all as for his interlocutor. The prayer evoked no response, but the savage continued to listen with the same alert and concentrated attention. The priest then spoke a few phrases in the Neapolitan dialect, and this change in the sonority and inflection of the voice provoked a reaction in the man that confirmed the intelligence he was reputed to possess. But he uttered not a word. After several sentences yielding no result, the priest modulated his voice again and began to sing what could only have been a lullaby or a nursery rhyme. He sang in a falsetto that was both absurd and touching, and the savage understood the change from speech to song, but showed no signs of responding in Italian.

Spanish, Portuguese, Dutch and German all failed to elicit a response, but the white savage listened to them all with the same concentrated interest.

I allowed these gentlemen to try their chances before me in order to have some time to reflect on the best way to proceed. Faced with this unfortunate soul, they undoubtedly felt as disconcerted as I. What should I say to this man who was physically so clearly a white man, but whose demeanour was so astonishingly primitive?

"So, my good fellow. Do you come from France, as I do? Did you board ship in Marseilles, or in Nantes? Dieppe perhaps? Your friends and family await you at home. Do you not wish to return to them? You must help me to help you."

It was apparent that he did not understand. I held out my hand to him, which none of the others had done. He looked intently at my hand, without seeming to think of grasping it.

"I do not know how long you have been wandering on these shores. Several years, certainly. Perhaps you were shipwrecked during the reign of Louis-Philippe? Do you know that France is once more a glorious Empire? That our destiny has been guided for ten years now by the Emperor Napoleon III?"

Why I spoke to him of our government I do not know, but to the consternation of all, he replied slowly and with great effort: "Po-lon."

Until this moment, he had not repeated a single word in any of the languages attempted; he had not even made a sound. Silence befell the group of onlookers behind me.

"Napoleon. Yes. Do you remember the name? Napoleon. The Emperor Napoleon."

He stared intently into my eyes, as if he might find there his forgotten memories.

"Po-lon."

Profoundly moved by this first exchange, we continued to repeat these sounds, absurdly united in our incomprehension of a code neither of us had the tools to decipher.

"Napoleon, Emperor of France."

"Po-leon. Po-leon."

He gazed at me with an intensity impossible to describe, while the other gentlemen, astounded and attentive, moved closer to form a semi-circle around us as we groped our way towards a dialogue.

Suddenly, the white savage leapt backwards and ran towards the wall, taking the soldiers guarding him by surprise. Never before had he moved with such swiftness. Until this moment he had seemed merely apathetic and resigned to his fate. There was no hope of escaping from this enclosed garden. He made no attempt to scale the wall or climb a tree, and showed no signs of attacking any of us. The governor gestured to the guards not to make a move, but the white savage paid them no attention. Turning his gaze towards the sea beyond the stables and the garrison, he declared in a loud voice:

"Sees-Ti-Ay-Oo-Pawl."

These strange syllables, which could perhaps have come from our language, were mingled with sounds that bore no resemblance to any recognisable idiom.

I approached him calmly, and he made no move to escape. I repeated, to the best of my ability, these nonsense syllables. He continued to look at me encouragingly, repeating them more slowly and softly to himself several times. Hearing what I thought might be a rolled R before the first syllable, an N before the last, I tried further sounds: Ra –Na – Pa – Sa. Together we arrived at the following mysterious formula:

"Arr-sees. Ti-ay. Oo-na. Pawl."

What was there in this utterance that he wished me to understand? Why had he recoiled from the group, and made this proclamation to me alone? What was he trying to tell me? What was it that he had not wanted, or perhaps not been able to communicate to the others?

When two men without a common language meet, what is the first thing they say to each other? My travels from Iceland to the Pacific had shown me that the first exchange is always of names. I placed my hand on my heart in what I hoped was a universal gesture of respect and said:

"Octave de Vallombrun."

He returned the gesture, once more mirroring my actions in a way he had not previously done, and said again:

"Arr-sees. Ti-ay. Oo-na. Pawl."

Was he trying to introduce himself, repeating his name again and again? I tried:

"Narcisse?"

"Ar-cisse!"

His joy was plain to see, but the words resisted memory, bringing tears to his eyes. I tried again, more insistently:

"Narcisse? Is that it, my good fellow? Your name is Narcisse?"

"Ar-cisse," he said in acknowledgement, placing his hand over his heart.

We stood there in silence, both overcome by the emotion of this first step towards some form of communication. I stared hard at this mystery in flesh and blood, as though his face might reveal the secret of who he was.

Speaking softly, I repeated his words: "Arr-sees. Ti-ay. Oo-na. Pawl."

It seemed that Narcisse was indeed his name, and all that had persisted in his peculiar speech was the single sound "Sees". Might one surmise that the other nonsense syllables were also fragments of whole words? Perhaps the accented syllables of words? How could I test this hypothesis? Would I need a dictionary of sailing terms? The sound "Pawl" suggested something to me. Perhaps he meant "pol". Was he trying to say that he came from Paimpol in Brittany?

I tried again: "Pol. You hail from Paimpol? You boarded ship in Paimpol?"

He looked blankly at me, and I realised this would not be sufficient. There was no magic wand: the French language would not come back to him in a flash merely because we had exchanged one or two words. It was not a question of turning on a tap. Somewhere, buried in the depths of his memory, was a wellspring of language. We would have to dig for it before we could begin to drink from it, and then, only drop by drop would we sup, over long months of effort. The well might even be completely dried up; he might never speak again.

At that point, the governor invited us to return to his office, indicating that the meeting was at an end. I paid no attention to the ensuing chatter, which consisted mostly of my fellow guests expressing their relief that this was not one of their countrymen in such a base condition. Only a Frenchman could sink so low.

But I too had come to the conclusion that this white savage was indeed French. I wondered what terrible ordeal he had survived. Who was this man Narcisse? How had he come to be in Australia? What torments had he endured? What had happened to the other members of the crew after the shipwreck? My head was spinning with questions.

Seated once again around the vast conference table, we listened as the governor expressed his thanks to all his guests for participating in this experiment. Through the French windows, I could see Narcisse, as I now assumed him to be called, squatting on his haunches at the end of the garden, completely still. The governor announced that the so-called white savage had been shown to be a Frenchman, and hoped that there were no objections to this conclusion.

He went on to stress that we would of course be at liberty to make our own reports to our respective governments. This was a case without precedent, and he would proceed in this manner, provided there was neither conflicting evidence, nor any diplomatic objections. All agreed that this was a satisfactory resolution of the difficulties. Delighted by the charms of this singular episode, the representatives of the various countries took their leave.

As I was about to depart, the governor requested that I remain to speak to him alone. He informed me that he did not know what to do with Narcisse, since there was as yet no French consul in Sydney. After some diplomatic prevarication and circumlocution, he asked me to take responsibility for Narcisse, stressing that the colony would provide funds for the return journey to Europe. In short, he wished to be relieved of responsibility for this case, with my assistance.

The first objection that occurred to me was that I possessed no authority to take responsibility for one of my compatriots. The governor appreciated my concern and assured me that a Sydney judge would confer upon me some form of guardianship for the white savage. This would be done with all due haste.

My second objection was that I was merely a traveller. I had no official function and was in no position to accept responsibility for this unfortunate soul. The governor concurred, but asked what other options he had? To whom might he have recourse? There was no Frenchman in the colony at that time who could fulfil such an official function.

I was loath to tell him that I had undertaken to travel the world alone. I had encountered agreeable companions from time to time, and had enjoyed their company for an evening or a short excursion. One or two had suggested that we travel together, as much for reasons of safety as for the pleasures of conversation. In keeping with another of your invaluable pieces of advice, I had always declined, preferring to remain alone and unfettered. And now I was being asked to take on the burden of this unknown person, a man who could neither speak nor eat like the rest of us, and who would probably require as much care as a helpless infant.

The governor seemed to share my concerns, but skilfully avoided addressing specific questions. Where else could he turn? What would become of the white savage if I were to refuse this request? If he were to be set free, he would surely starve to death here in Sydney. That is, if he were not attacked by convicts or arrested by the police. And how could the governor hold him in prison with no prospect of release, when there was no legal basis for this, no charge against him? Should he order one of the colony's vessels to take him back to the wilderness where he had been found? This would be a cruel course of action. Such callousness would surely incite protestations from the imperial government and from all respectable individuals, once it was known.

The only solution was to return him to France, and I alone was equipped to accomplish this.

Under the tree, the white savage remained, motionless. I felt somewhat lightheaded and asked the governor to accord me a few days to consider the matter, to which he readily agreed.

Two days later, I accepted. I cannot hide the fact that you played a part in this decision. The governor's arguments were reasonable enough and I felt compelled to look after my fellow countryman both for reasons of common decency and from a sense of patriotism. I could quite easily have ignored these scruples and declined, without making any attempt to justify my decision. I might also have pointed to the responsibilities I bear to you, sir, in travelling as I do under your aegis.

But I did not wish to delude myself any longer. Alone on the balcony of the hotel, looking out at the bay of Sydney in the gentle evening breeze, I contemplated my situation, and realised that I would never become the explorer I dreamt of being. The meagre spoils and written accounts from my time in Iceland and my forays in the Pacific could have been produced by any literate sailor, and no doubt with more alacrity. Becoming a great geographer would involve making sacrifices, facing greater perils. If I wished to make a significant discovery I would have to venture further afield, run greater risks. I knew I would not measure up to the task. I had put myself to the test and it was clear to me that the dream I had been pursuing for five years had evaporated. Here, in the antipodes, I knew that I must accept this reality. I shall aspire to no title more prestigious than that of Associate Member of the Society of Geographers. I shall make no great geographical discoveries.

My parting gift to the study of geography will be the case of the white savage. I shall seek to learn more about his singular adventures. My goal will be to help him rediscover our language so that he may tell us about his exile among the savages. This extraordinary story must not be lost to scholarship.

I shall chart the progress of this man Narcisse, if that is indeed his name. I hope to follow this letter with two or three further missives in which I shall recount that progress and any colourful details he may reveal to me of the customs and practices of the people amongst whom he lived. I do not know what will become of him in the long run. For myself, I have no intention of writing a book, but I trust that you will permit me the liberty of writing these letters to you. They will provide you with a record of the various stages of Narcisse's progress, and of the nature of my investigations.

When I beheld him in the garden that afternoon, something in his attitude, in the way he looked, expressed what I believed to be more than mere curiosity or surprise. I understood this only later, when I was deliberating over what to do. Looking deep into his eyes, I saw fear, a terror akin to that of a hunted animal. I wished to allay that fear, and this no doubt influenced my decision to accept the governor's proposition.

I trust you will approach this matter with the same benevolent goodwill you have shown towards all my endeavours, and that you will regard it as worthy of your interest. Any advice you may wish to give me will be invaluable, and I shall follow it to the letter. In the meantime, I herewith convey to you what I have perceived, and leave it to those better versed in these matters than I to sort through my observations and separate the wheat from the chaff.

I remain your faithful servant...

2

Water. Water on his cracked, parted lips. Water flowing into his mouth, running down his throat. A cascade of earthy-tasting water. Instinctively his lips sought the spout of the gourd and attached themselves to it. He didn't think to open his eyes to find out who was bringing him succour, he wanted only to drink, to drink his fill, drink and never stop, drink as he had not done since leaving the Cape. Water coursed through his body, flooding every channel, bringing life back to his burning torso, his throbbing head, his weary legs and lifeless arms. It rushed down his cheeks, his chin, along his neck, seeking out the parched recesses of his body.

He would have gone on drinking for ever, he would never have stopped, when all of a sudden, his thirst still not slaked, the gourd was wrenched from him. He blinked with difficulty, trying to see who his benefactor might be.

A black, wrinkled face, leaning over him. Greying, frizzy hair, streaks of red earth on the cheeks and the bridge of the nose. A searching look, no hint of a smile. Not a word. A woman, an old woman. He sank back onto his bed of leaves to get a better look at her. Yes, a woman, completely naked, black as coal, her skin leathery and wrinkled like cowhide, breasts

limp and drooping. She was squatting next to him, heedless of
the countless flies buzzing around her, settling in the corners
of her eyes. And in her hands a water pouch made from animal
hide. They looked long and hard at each other, he not knowing
what to do or say, returning her enigmatic gaze. She held out the
gourd to him again and he grabbed it and drank, in long gulps
to the last drop, little minding the bitter, dusty, animal taste.

He stood up and felt dizzy, the gnawing hunger in his belly
asserting itself now that his thirst was appeased. The woman
stayed where she was, squatting on her haunches, watching
him as he struggled to his feet, staggered and righted himself
again. He took a few steps, trying to look composed and take
in his surroundings. Not another soul in sight. Surely this old
woman must live with her family, her tribe. Now that this
ancient grandmother was here to help him, the feeling of being
completely alone should have abated. And yet, something in
her manner, her silence perhaps, left him feeling no less alone
than before. Looking at her, he thought how different her
world must be, how far removed from all that was familiar to
him. The schooner, his shipmates, the stopovers yet to come
on the voyage to China. These were the only things that could
put an end to his loneliness and make up for being abandoned.
This black woman and her ministrations changed nothing.

He walked back over to her, put his hand to his lips, pointed
to his belly, and pretended to chew on an imaginary piece of
meat. She showed no reaction, did not even look at him, as if
she had lost all interest in him.

"I'm hungry. Please. I'm hungry."

He didn't expect her to understand. His voice echoed
strangely inside his head, his ears unused to hearing its sound
in the silence of this desolate forest. Still, the woman did not

move. Now that she'd given him water and saved his life, was she going to just ignore him and leave him to die?

"I'm hungry, you old hag! Give me something to eat!"

The change in his tone was clear and unambiguous, but still she did not react. Raising his hand to the woman who'd helped him was out of the question. And resorting to violence would not make food appear out of thin air. He went back up to the edge of the plateau, expecting to encounter more savages, but there was no one. Not knowing what else to do, he came back to the motionless old woman, sat down beside her and said, more calmly this time:

"My name is Narcisse Pelletier. I'm from Saint-Gilles, in the Vendée. Over there, in France. I'm a sailor on the schooner *Saint-Paul*. My ship left without me four days ago. It'll come back, I know it will, and you'll be well rewarded for helping me. But you must give me something to eat."

This speech proved no more successful; still the woman did not respond. She seemed not to realise that he was speaking to her. At a loss to know what to do, and not knowing where else to go, he stayed where he was, at her side. At some point during the day or that evening, he reasoned, she would have to get herself something to eat. Then he'd be able to seize his chance and make sure she gave him some of her meal, by force if necessary.

The sun was at its highest. In the moist, still air the heat was once again becoming unbearable. He dozed off for a while, and woke up to find her still in the same position.

He had never seen anyone with skin so black. And yet he'd encountered many different faces on his travels, from the Cape to the quays of Saint-Louis in Senegal. Perhaps these black skinned Australians were entirely different from the African natives.

All of a sudden, the woman made an abrupt gesture in his

direction, the palm of her hand turned up vertically towards him, her eyes fixed on him, staring intensely. He responded to her command and kept still. In her other hand she held a stone, which he hadn't noticed her pick up. Raising it to shoulder level, she threw the stone sharply at a bush twenty paces away, leapt up, grabbed a fallen branch and used it to strike the bush, whacking it hard several times. Finally, she bent down, pushed aside the leaves and grabbed hold of a lizard the size of her forearm. Then she broke the beast's neck and came back carrying her trophy, its grey scales glistening. She dropped it in the dirt and went back to her old position, squatting on the ground. She made no move to gut or begin to cook her prey.

So great was his hunger he would have eaten the repellent beast raw. He could see that the woman wasn't going to make a move and decided to take matters into his own hands. He took hold of his knife, thinking he would skin the lizard, then cut off its head and legs. But just as he was about to grab it, the woman leapt up, seized the lizard and placed it behind her back, making it quite clear that he had no right to touch it.

Should he fight her for it? He was bigger, stronger, younger. He had his knife. She wouldn't stand a chance. But then what? If she ran off, if he killed her or wounded her, what would he do for water? How would he find anything to eat in this alien land? The woman had hunted and killed this lizard. Sooner or later, she would eat it. Better to wait. His physical strength was of no use to him. He had no choice but to put away his knife and lie down again on the sand.

As the sun began to sink in the sky, she stood up and headed to the end of the valley. She went over to where some pale green cress grew in the damp soil, the same spot where he had searched in vain for water. She knelt down, and using her hands, dug out a tuber. Breaking off its stem, she put it to one side and continued to dig, moving towards the left. She soon unearthed a second bulb, and then a third.

He followed her over, wanting to be useful, to help with this harvest. He wanted to have something to do, find more to eat. But when he went to kneel down close to her, she signalled to him in no uncertain terms to stay back. When he didn't move, she repeated the gesture, and barked an order in a shrill voice. So, she did talk, after all. Her words sounded like nothing he'd ever heard before, a sort of hissing noise punctuated with clicks. He didn't insist further, took a few steps back, and stood there watching her collecting her harvest. He'd spent his life obeying orders: from his father, the curate, the schoolmaster, the ship's bosun, the captain. What choice did he have but to do as this old woman commanded? How his shipmates would have laughed to see him meekly obeying her orders!

Why had she not spoken before? They had no means of understanding each other, but he would have given anything to have her answer his questions. She had said nothing, nothing until this rebuff. If he were in her position, surely he would have tried to find a way to communicate: a few simple words, a gesture, or even just a smile.

Did she not care about him at all? But why then had she saved his life?

She went on digging up tubers until she seemed satisfied that she had enough. Using a stick she picked up from the ground, she made a hole in each of the tubers, threaded them onto a length of vine and draped it over her shoulder. Still without saying anything, she went back over to the spot where she had left the lizard and threw the string of tubers down beside the carcass. He followed her, judging that it must soon be time to eat, now that there were some vegetables to go with the meat.

But she paid no more attention to her spoils. Faint with hunger, he had to wait another hour. At last, when evening began to draw in, she gathered some sticks to build a fire, and using two stones, lit the fire and arranged the tubers in the sand around it. Then she placed the whole lizard in the centre of the coals, added some dead wood, and let the fire burn until it went out.

It was dark by the time she took hold of the lizard. It had cooked in its own skin and she used a sharp rock to cut off the feet, slit open the belly and, with a few precise gestures, remove the white flesh. She held out a piece to him; he grabbed it with a trembling hand, trying not to see that it was a leg, and put it in his mouth. The meat was stringy and tasteless; it left a vague after-taste of ash. He ate his share hungrily, sucking on the bones and the cartilage. She gesticulated towards the coals, letting him know he could help himself. He took one of the charred tubers, trying not to scorch his fingers. He bit into it carefully to avoid burning his lips. It tasted almost like a lightly cooked turnip, bitter and sweet at the same time. He wished he had some salt to sprinkle on it, on the meat too. But at least this peculiar vegetable would fill his stomach. He took another and held out his hand for some more meat. She gave him another slice and let him take as many of the strange vegetables as he wanted. She ate too, in silence. Three times he asked for more meat, and three times, she served him. But when he reached for the leftovers of the lizard scattered around on the sand, she barked something at him again, to let him know that this was not allowed. He didn't argue and waited for her to offer him the last scraps of meat on the backbone.

Then, without saying a word, she stretched out on the sand and went to sleep.

In the pitch black, cloudless sky, innumerable stars twinkled, the same stars that had kept him company during his night watches aboard ship, when the schooner was slicing through the water, sailing along on a light breeze. He used to enjoy those moments when there was nothing to do but murmur in low voices, gaze at the stars, summon up visions of the last port of call or perhaps anticipate the next. Perhaps now, at this very moment, some of his shipmates on the *Saint-Paul* were awake, savouring the gentle softness of the tropical night. Were they thinking of him? Would they come to find him?

These questions were too cruel and he put them out of his mind. Lying on his back, he summed up the situation. Things were not as bad as they had been the night before. He had drunk plenty of water. He'd eaten, not enough to fully satisfy him, but enough to quell the worst of his hunger pangs and leave him with a pleasant sensation of warmth in his belly. He was at a loss to understand the old woman's behaviour, what she would accept and where she drew the line. But what did he care? He would survive, that was what mattered.

The ship would return. They were sailing to Java to save the sick men and get provisions. Then they would set sail again for the south. Two weeks at sea. He'd have to wait two weeks. Whatever the old woman gave him, he would eat: lizard, fish, shellfish, plants. And water, she would find him water.

He'd lose two weeks' pay. The second mate would give him that unpleasant smile and scribble some figures to indicate how much the whole escapade had cost, while some of the crew looked on and smirked. Sheepishly, he'd make sure that his conduct was exemplary for the rest of the voyage: he'd be the most obedient, hard-working and dedicated hand on the ship.

When he awoke, he looked around; the old woman was no longer there. He supposed she was foraging for food somewhere in the forest. He ate a few of the cold turnips and set off towards the beach without waiting for her to come back.

No sign of a ship on the horizon. He'd been prepared for this and did not allow it to upset him. But he was stunned to see that his giant arrow on the sand had vanished, the sign he'd toiled so hard to construct from rocks and blocks of coral. Now they all lay scattered around the beach, his message obliterated. A ship out at sea, or a search party on foot would see nothing but scattered stones.

It could not have been the tide that had dismantled his handiwork: he'd been careful to make sure he built it above the high tide mark, beyond the range of even the biggest waves. Nor could it be the work of the old woman: she'd have had neither the time nor the strength to move such huge boulders. The biggest of them weighed as much as a loaded cask: with a strength born of desperation he'd summoned his last reserves of energy to inch them into place, breathing heavily, back muscles tensed, legs trembling with fatigue, his arms crushed by the weight.

There must be more people living on these shores. Here was proof that the old woman was not alone. He tried to make himself believe that he'd been aware of this all along. No human being lives in complete isolation. Even animals don't live alone. This woman lived with her own people, others who spoke her language, shared the same customs. And among those people were men, strong and sturdy enough to be able to undo his work.

But where were they? They knew he was there, they'd sent the old woman to sound out his intentions. She was expendable, she no longer mattered to them, they could risk sacrificing her. They were watching him from afar. But if their intentions were friendly, why didn't they show themselves? Why didn't they all come and welcome him, all together, men and women, young and old? Why didn't they invite him to their village and help him?

Why had they destroyed his arrow? The answer, alas, was only too apparent: they'd destroyed it to prevent other white men from understanding its message and coming to take him away.

Trying to fathom these mysteries only served to increase his anxiety. All he had to protect him from hostile savages was the knife in his belt. And it wouldn't take many of them to overpower him and push him under water, knife or no knife. No, his only weapon would be his wits: he'd use his wits to get the better of them, although he couldn't quite see how. But he knew his intelligence would protect him from naked savages, and he clung on to this notion.

For now, they'd spared him: they'd let him live. He would be vigilant from now on. Should he put the arrow back together again? It would mean two hours of backbreaking toil in the heat of the sun, only to give them the pleasure of taking it apart again as soon as his back was turned. One man against a whole tribe? He wouldn't stand a chance. And if he did put it back together, it would be a sure way of telling them that he knew they were hiding nearby somewhere, watching him, that he knew they wanted to prevent him from writing his message on the beach. No, it would be better if they didn't realise he was aware of their presence.

What did he know of these people, these Pacific savages? At sea he'd heard tales told on the 'tweendecks, but they were vague and inconsistent, often impossible to believe. If only he'd paid them more attention, asked questions of the older hands who'd seen a thing or two on their voyages across this vast ocean.

One thing they all agreed on was the difference between the Eastern and Western Pacific. The Eastern Pacific and Bougainville's Tahitian Isles were the stuff of every sailor's dreams: friendly natives, obliging women, food in abundance, plentiful supplies of fresh water, excellent anchorage. Countless men had jumped ship in these isles, crews had mutinied for the sake of the earthly delights they offered. No man could resist the dancing and singing of those bare-breasted girls, their skin the colour of honey.

But the Western Pacific offered no such delights. Only barbaric tribes of warring black-skinned savages, armed with sticks and assegais, fighting every inch to defend their chickens, their vegetables and their unsightly women. They were known to attack suddenly and with great savagery. European sailors had been ambushed. And in all the tales, there would inevitably be a great *kaï-kaï* at the end. The cabin boys would always ask: "What's a *kaï-kaï*?" And the old hands would answer: " It's like a great big cauldron, where they cook up the enemies they've killed in battle."

He knew nothing about this part of Australia. But given its geographical position and the old woman's skin colour it was probably just like the Western Pacific. And then there was the mystery of the disappearance of La Pérouse and his ships: Sydney was their last port of call before they vanished soon after setting sail. It all added to the threat of hidden menace.

He felt a nagging fear, greater than the fear of dying, crueller than the prospect of being killed. Much worse than the vision of his own body abandoned in the dust for animals to prey on was the terrifying thought of savages feasting on his flesh.

He had no choice but to go back and look for the old woman. With a heavy heart, he walked back along the valley floor. Finding no sign of her in the thicket where they'd slept, he carried on to the bottom of the gorge to the spot where she'd dug up the bulbs. No one. Come to think of it, he hadn't seen her since the evening before.

Had she abandoned him? Why would she do that? It was too cruel. Why save his life, give him water and food, only to leave him alone again? Abandon him to certain death in this forest of whose secrets he knew nothing? If she and her tribe wanted him dead, why hadn't they killed him? Or left him to die of starvation or thirst?

It was futile to think about all this. He had to find her again; feeling sorry for himself wouldn't help him to get out of this black hole. One after another, great waves of despair welled up in him, followed by periods of frantic activity. He climbed up the cliff face, out of the gorge and ended up on the plateau again, in the meagre shade of the twisted trees with their grey trunks and metallic leaves. Silence. No footprints on the flat, sandy coral ground. He tried to haul himself up into one of the sturdier trees to get a better view, but succeeded only in ripping his breeches.

Wandering aimlessly amongst all these trees was a sure way of getting lost. Orienting himself by the position of the sun, he walked parallel to what he reckoned to be the coastline. After about one hour, he turned sharp right, and keeping the sun at his back, walked until he reached the northern tip of the bay and the small rocky hill he'd climbed on the second day. Still no sign of the old woman.

They were probably watching him all the time. They'd seen how he managed to get his bearings. They'd been observing him ever since he'd built his giant arrow. He'd drawn attention to himself with all that hard work that day. Perhaps he should have chosen to stay hidden in the bushes, under cover. Should he just have waited it out?

But if they hadn't been aware of his presence on the beach, they would never have sent the old crone to him with the gourd full of water. No, it hadn't been a mistake, all that effort struggling to move the boulders on the beach. The thought suddenly occurred to him that it made no difference. What did it matter if they'd seen him making his sign? They must have seen the schooner at full sail out in the bay. They'd watched as it dropped anchor. They'd seen the dinghy being launched, the crew's vain efforts to find water on the beach.

The savages had known they were there all along; they'd been watching everything. From the first sighting of the white sails coming over the horizon and the great wooden vessel entering the bay, they'd been aware of these men with their strangely pale skin, their clothes, their shouts. They'd gone to ground and watched the strangers' every move. They'd seen the nine seamen land and split up. They'd watched them searching for something, meeting up again, eight men returning to the ship. They'd looked on as the crew hoisted the jib and fore stay-sails, and seen the great ship moving off out of the bay, getting ever smaller and disappearing over the horizon. With one white man wandering deep in the forest, emerging after the ship had left. One lone white man, walking up and down on the beach, going back to the valley, making himself a shelter, spending his days keeping watch over the bay; the vessel not returning; the white man getting weaker with every passing day.

They'd watched him, and left him to suffer. They'd waited until he'd lost all his strength, sending the old woman to him when he could no longer be considered a threat. What a fool he'd been to think she wanted to help him.

For a few moments, he was pleased with himself for having understood the truth. But why had they sent her to him? Should he go in search of the rest of them? But what good would it do him to climb a tree or comb the woods? They'd show themselves when they were good and ready. They'd stay hidden if they felt like it. Either they'd send the old woman to him, or they wouldn't. She could bring him life-giving water, or she could give him a poisoned apple. He had no means of knowing the rules of the cruel game they were playing. He sat down under a tree.

When he was a boy, playing with the other lads in the courtyard before their catechism lessons, he and the other boys would sometimes play with a mouse brought there by the cat. The little creature would run around, coming up against a boot, the fence of the vegetable plot, or a plank laid across the courtyard by the boys. They'd move the obstacles around and the mouse would flail about desperately, crashing into the barriers they put up. But it would never give in, and its tormentors had to remain on their guard – woe betide the careless lad who let the little creature get away. Finally, when the curate rang the bell, they'd go in, leaving the mouse at the cat's mercy.

Now it was his turn to be that mouse.

The old woman was back. He hadn't seen her coming, but she was walking at a good pace towards the forest. He went over to join her, but she paid him no attention and continued to walk at the same pace.

"Where are you going, you old crone?"

She seemed not to hear him when he spoke. Angrily, he

called out to the trees, the hill, the bay:

"I know you're there! I know you're watching me! Come out and show yourselves! Why are you hiding? I know what you're up to!"

She carried on walking, heedless of his shouts, already disappearing into the trees that marked the edge of the forest. He ran to catch up and made to grab her wrist to stop her, but she anticipated his move and he didn't even manage to touch her. Should he throw himself to the ground, force her to stop? But then what?

He started walking beside her. Were they heading for a spring? A place where there was good hunting? His hunger was ever present, and like it or not, this woman was his only chance of getting anything to eat.

After about two hours of walking, he began to get worried. They'd left the beach and were moving inland away from the coast. Everything in this flat forest looked the same. So different from the forests of his childhood, where he'd go to collect firewood and look for mushrooms, or birds' nests. The trees here were all the same. Instead of the infinite variety of beech, ash, alder and chestnut there was only a tree that he couldn't identify. No undergrowth, no fertile compost of rotting vegetation. Only this sterile, sandy earth; no animals but lizards and flies of all kinds. There was no breath of wind in this forest, no whisper of the breeze stirring the foliage, no cracking of a branch, no rustling of unseen beasts. Here the space was filled with the emptiness of an overwhelming silence.

His shipmates would never find him if he went too far away from the shore. He could leave the old woman and retrace his steps, but he'd starve to death or die of thirst before the ship came back. He had to get her to turn back with him. He tried to block her path, standing in front of her with his arms spread to show her that he would not go any further. But she anticipated his move as before, and with an agile movement slipped under his arm and continued without slowing down or deviating from her path.

He'd have to keep going. What else could he do? She carried on walking without turning round to see if he was following. After a few moments' hesitation, he set off again, walking about twenty paces behind her.

The plain had given way to a gentle slope, getting slowly steeper; they were climbing. From the top of the hill, he'd be able to see the sea and fix his position, work out a route back to the bay.

But up on the plateau, the same trees grew in a dense formation, completely blocking the view. The old woman carried on walking. They went downhill again. He was lost, with no way to find his bearings. He felt he was being plunged into a desolate limbo, far away from the land of the living.

The sand gave way to dusty red earth. Night was approaching. Hungry and thirsty, exhausted now from the long march, he began to stagger drunkenly, leaves and branches whipping him as he stumbled blindly along.

And then, all of a sudden, the trees began to thin out and he saw a clearing, with a dark greenish pool in the centre.

On the far side of the pool, a fire was burning.

LETTER II

Monsieur le Président,

I had thought that this affair would be no more than the stuff of an amusing anecdote, but it is gradually becoming clear to me that I am embarked upon a veritable adventure. I believe that you may find some use for the singular details of this tale, which I now take the liberty of recounting to you.

The governor was true to his word. Once I agreed to accept the curious mission he wished to confer on me, he promptly gave me his full support and enquired as to my needs.

Taking a room for Narcisse at my hotel was out of the question: no respectable establishment would have accepted this speechless creature. Virtually naked, hirsute and covered in tattoos, he did indeed present a somewhat alarming spectacle. Equally inconceivable was the prospect of setting off for France immediately. For what captain would have taken on such a passenger? Narcisse would first have to learn to speak our language, how to dress, and how to conduct himself in polite society. In short, he would have to adopt our way of life.

A small house was made available to me at the far end of one of the longest inlets of Sydney Bay. This charming residence belongs to the colony and reputedly once housed the mistress of a former governor. Open on one side to the sea, and with a small river at the back, the house can be reached by dinghy or by means of a rough trail. A discreet guard was mounted at the gate and ordered to remain out of sight. It was not clear to me whether they were there to protect us or to prevent us from leaving, although this was perhaps of little import.

We were transported to the house in a dinghy along with the servant I had requested. Bill had been serving his time in the colony for the last three years, convicted of a series of thefts, precise details of which I do not know. He proved to be an obedient servant. Resourceful, intelligent and ambitious, he had previously been in service in several good families in London and understood that the report I gave of him would determine his future in Australia.

The house consists of a tastefully furnished apartment, opening onto a veranda. At the back, there is a simple kitchen and two modestly appointed bedrooms. A meadow, bordered by trees, leads down to the jetty. Beyond the river, a few flowering shrubs mark the boundary between the grounds and the sparse forest that one sees everywhere around Sydney.

It did not take long for us to move in. The crew of the dinghy deposited our possessions in front of the house, and Master Bill busied himself with organising them. I was informed by the coxswain that if I were to need assistance, I was to hoist a white flag to the top of the flagpole, or at night, a lantern, and the dinghy would come to my rescue within two hours.

After they had left, I considered my situation, not without some ambivalence. Had I thrown myself too hastily into a ridiculous experiment? What was I doing here at the back of beyond in Australia, with this white savage, and a convict for a servant?

As for Narcisse, he seemed less concerned about such matters and was clearly pleased to have regained his liberty. Freed from the confines of his prison and from the watchful scrutiny of soldiers armed with bludgeons, he wandered about at will. He went down to the river, drank deeply from it and went over to sit on the grass and gaze at the sea. He had not uttered a word since our encounter in the governor's garden. While he sat there, completely still, I took the opportunity to make some sketches of the tattoos and scarifications on his back, shoulders and torso.

My sketching was interrupted by Bill who came to ask for my instructions for dinner. I was thrown into confusion by this simple, everyday question. Narcisse had eaten almost nothing while in prison, and what little he did accept, was consumed with visible disgust. I instructed Bill to vary the dishes on a daily basis, hoping to stimulate Narcisse's appetite and learn something of his tastes. From then on our mealtimes were full of unexpected and surprising moments in which Bill did his best to provide a mixture of flavours, striving to recreate dishes from every corner of the world. It was soon apparent that neither sweets nor foods from the dairy appealed to Narcisse. He enjoys meat, but only when grilled. He loves fish and considers nuts to be an incomparable delight.

In the morning, after his swim in the river, Narcisse breakfasts on whatever is left over from the previous evening, preferring it not heated. He eats no midday meal. When the sun sets, he dines on a hot meal, but without the use of knife or fork. Not wishing to modify my own habits, I instructed Bill to serve me exactly as he would were I to be dining in company. Narcisse occasionally observes me as I sup by candlelight on the terrace, the table set with porcelain plates, crystal glasses and silver candelabras.

From the second day, I concerned myself with improving his appearance. It was a long time since his unruly hair had seen a comb and it grew over his neck and covered his shoulders. His face was concealed by a thick, dirty beard. I now instructed Bill to play Figaro to Narcisse.

I should tell you that convicts in Australia have their heads shaved once a week, and must remain clean-shaven, with neither beard nor moustache. This ingenious rule makes it easy to identify them and to recapture them if they escape. My man Bill was subject to this ruling and I feared that he would give the same treatment to my countryman, if only out of malice. I therefore stayed close at hand as he wielded the razor and scissors. He combed Narcisse's brown hair back from his face, shaved his beard and fashioned his whiskers in the English style with a thin, neatly trimmed moustache. When he had finished his barbering, I could scarcely believe my eyes. Narcisse looked ten years younger and now presented an attractive physiognomy, with the ugly scar on his left ear covered by his longish hair. Bill was to be commended on his work.

The question of attire was somewhat more delicate. In order to take Narcisse back to France, I would have to teach him to dress in the European fashion. He had been clothed, all this time, in nothing but a loincloth given to him by the crew of the *John Bell*, and it was with this rudimentary garment that we would have to begin.

In accordance with my instructions, Bill assisted Narcisse in removing the insalubrious garment and donning some drawers. Narcisse accepted this latest flight of fancy with the same resigned indifference he showed towards everything. Turning my attention towards my servant's livery, I determined that it was not fitting for this convict to so disport himself in a costume that was not at all reminiscent of the colony and its harsh discipline. That he should thus place himself above my unfortunate compatriot was not to be countenanced. Nothing should suggest that Narcisse was inferior in rank to an English convict. I therefore ordered Bill, ignoring any objections he might harbour, to restrict his own attire to his drawers.

On his left shoulder, Bill has a tattoo in the shape of a flower, which his shirt had hitherto hidden from sight. Looking at these two men, dressed in the same fashion and both sporting tattoos, I reflected on life's vicissitudes and the unexpected turns of fate. If providence had determined otherwise, Bill might have been the castaway, Narcisse a member of the crew that found him some years later.

On the afternoon of the second day, Bill came to inform me, in an obsequious tone heavy with innuendo, that my protégé had urinated in his trousers. The implication was that Narcisse was unable to control himself and did not deserve to be treated as an adult: he was no better than a child who wets the bed. I was shaken for a moment. Was it possible that Narcisse was mad, or simple? Not the simple-minded village idiot, living out his life in his village, who no captain would burden himself with for a long sea voyage. But regressed to childhood, or to infancy, perhaps as the result of a blow to the head. The doctor at the garrison, however, had found no scars to the head. Could this be the result of the sufferings of his exile, the extreme anguish of his sorrows? Had he lost his reason as the ship foundered, or a few months after the shipwreck?

And yet contrary to Bill's insinuations, Narcisse's demeanour provides daily evidence of his intelligence. In spite of the language barrier, we communicate in gestures; his efforts to improve our exchanges are as avid as mine. His reserved attitude, his interest in all that we do, his ability to learn, all this suggests an adult of sound mind, utterly foreign, but entirely normal. I hold firm in my belief that I will succeed in bringing him back to our world. I surmised that if he had embarrassed himself thus, it was simply because he had forgotten our customs with respect to such matters. The question would have to be approached with the same patience and gentleness I strove to employ in all our endeavours. I instructed Bill to provide Narcisse with fresh linen, and then to show him how to relieve himself without mishap. At a time when I had so many pressing details to take care of, I was much amused by the comical spectacle of Bill's crestfallen and incredulous expression. He nevertheless complied, although not without much indistinct muttering of an array of obscenities, and the lesson was successful: Narcisse adopted our habits in this regard with good grace.

But of greater import than all of this, is without doubt, the question of language. During the short week before we removed to our present retreat, I betook myself to the prison every morning and evening, where I undertook to speak to Narcisse in French. I had no means of knowing how best to help him rediscover his mother tongue, and he was scarcely of any assistance since he remained completely mute. I surmised that he would first need to become accustomed once again to hearing the sounds that were once so familiar to him, and that this would then enable him to recover his language more readily. Every day, I would sit down next to him, tell the guards to leave, and talk to him about anything that came into my head. I am scarcely garrulous by nature and inspiration soon deserted me. The prison governor made his entire library of French books available to me, but they numbered only three. And how could I read to Narcisse from such titles as *Elements of Mathematics for Infantry Officers* or *Italian Memoirs of a Woman of the World*?

The remaining volume offered a selection of extracts from the works of Racine, and I decided to avail myself of this. I spent the afternoons declaiming great speeches to Narcisse: the tragic death of Hyppolytus; the dream of Athalie; the sufferings of Berenice; the premonitions of Agrippina. Narcisse seemed to respond, if not to the torments of these heroic characters, at least to the rhythm of the alexandrines and the nobility of the language.

Every time I addressed him, I would say our names, Narcisse and Octave, to help him absorb them. On the first morning in our new abode, I greeted him as usual with the words: "Good morning, Narcisse."

He swallowed, looked at me at length, and muttered with great difficulty: "Tave."

To hear at last this word, "Tave", to hear this as testament to my endeavours in his regard, this was for me a precious reward. I might have included Bill in this gallery of names, but prudence restrained me. Bill did not speak a word of French. I was afraid that the two languages might confuse Narcisse who was not yet ready for the Tower of Babel. I told the convict that from then on, he must communicate with Narcisse by gestures only; he should never address him in English.

Narcisse had been able to repeat my name, not in imitation like a parrot, but because he had understood this to be my name. I then tried to show him concrete objects, naming them and encouraging him to imitate me: sky, sea, water, grass, rock. To no avail. He watched attentively, following my finger as I pointed to the items in question, and said not a word.

After lunch, the lesson resumed. What should I suggest? I uttered our names, he repeated them. This was scarcely progress. A further attempt with different aspects of our surroundings yielded no more success. Discouraged, convinced that I was talking to myself, I sighed, and in a theatrical gesture, brought my hand to my lips: "Narcisse, my poor boy, I despair of ever hearing a sentence from your mouth."

"Mouth," he said, mimicking my gesture. In the same way, he repeated: "Head" and "Arm", and with less success, "Back" and "Belly". All these details of his daily progress are recorded in the notebooks that I have been assiduously maintaining. Within a week he had uttered about twenty words.

I give you these details, Monsieur le Président, to persuade you of the worthiness of this young man. He is certainly no imbecile, of that I am now convinced. He is learning our language, not as an infant or a foreigner would: rather, he is rediscovering it within himself. He is relearning something that he always knew, but had forgotten on the Australian beaches. I am at a loss to know what conclusions to draw from all this. So singular is this case that I have wished to spare no pains. Scholars will construct theories; my role is merely to relay to them the bare facts of the case, with you as my intermediary.

I would like to believe that in a few weeks, his language and memory will have been almost completely restored, and that he will be able to tell us his tale and the story of his shipwreck. In this way, he will enable us to learn all about the life of the tribes that took him in. Here, in the tranquil setting of my study, through my unrelenting questioning, I shall be transported, without exertion or distress, to the scenes of his exile whence I shall return with a host of curious and hitherto unheard observations.

There is a further mystery confronting me. Apart from his lamentations while aboard the *John Bell*, Narcisse has not yet uttered a word in the language of the savages. And yet, during all these past years, he communicated in that language alone. He must have learnt the rudiments at least, and yet he utters not a word of it now, not even inadvertently. He either remains mute, or rediscovers a few words of French with me. Without his assistance, how shall I be able to create a dictionary of the language of the north east Australian savages? Such a project would be of use to missionaries and sailors; I had thought that it would be a simple task to accomplish, and yet I find that I cannot take the first steps.

I beg you to forgive me for the disorder of these reflections. The dinghy leaves in an hour, and a mail ship departs for Europe this very evening. I trust that I do not prevail upon you unduly in sending you this latest report; you may imagine how anxiously I await a missive from you, with perhaps some advice or instructions for the correct way to procede. You will no doubt have realised that this adventure occupies me more than I had at first envisaged.

May I take the liberty of making one final request? I find this case unique and know of no other tale, no adventure on any ocean that resembles the story of Narcisse. But perhaps it is not unique. It is possible that you, or the Council of the Geographical Society have identified a case in the archives, which could serve as a precedent or a point of reference. The smallest scrap of information, the slightest hint of a rumour pertaining to such a case would be of great value to me. How did these castaways survive? By what means did they come back to life? And with what form of assistance? Were they then able to resume the normal course of their lives or did they remain affected by their sojourns among the savages? And what became of them later? Some knowledge of their stories would assuredly be of assistance to me in my efforts to help Narcisse.

I await the results of any research you may have the kindness to see conducted; in the meantime I shall continue the lessons in manners and the French language, in the hopes of presenting my protégé to you before the end of the summer.

I remain your faithful servant...

3

The sight of the fire burning at the other side of the clearing was almost too much to bear. Weakened more by the crushing sense of isolation than by physical exhaustion, he was overcome with emotion at the promise offered by those flames.

He knelt down beside the pool, not noticing the figures gathered around the fire, and tumbled head first into the green water. Long feathery weeds caressed his sun-scorched face as he drank and drank until he was gasping for breath.

The second mate's warnings echoed in his head: use only water from a stream to fill the water barrels; if you have to use stagnant water, wait until you're back on board and be sure to boil it for a long time before you drink it. He wondered as he gulped this rank, murky water what creatures and diseases lurked in the mire. He went on drinking, beyond caring.

Finally he stood up and looked around. No sign of a village, no huts or cabins. About thirty naked savages were gathered around the area. Naked women played with babies under the trees. The men were naked too, standing around the fire, where an animal was cooking under the coals, giving off a pleasant odour of grilled fat and skin. The sun had gone down, taking the heat out of the day. Three naked children were playing in the bushes. The old woman was scuttling about seemingly at random.

He walked slowly around the stagnant pond and approached the group, keeping what he considered to be a respectful distance. He went up to an old man whom he took to be the chief, and spoke to him in what he hoped was a voice full of self-assurance:

"I am a seaman on the schooner *Saint-Paul*. My ship is coming back to find me. If you give me something to eat and take me back to the beach, you will be given gifts: necklaces, mirrors, nails, axes. And I will tell people that you are an intelligent and reasonable leader."

He knew no one would understand his little compliment, but he hoped that his bearing and tone of voice would impress them. The old man looked at him for a moment, then sat down and set to work stripping a piece of wood. People went on with their conversations and games, they seemed uninterested in him. He walked around in their midst, trying to familiarise himself with these faces, their heavy brows, and greyish black skin, their bodies naked and tattooed. The smell of grime and dust.

The natives were all smaller than him, the men by at least a head. They were solid and stocky and looked strong. The women showed no modesty and made no attempt to cover any part of their anatomy. He thought briefly of the whore from the Cape who now seemed dazzlingly beautiful in comparison. These women wore no ornaments except for a piece of bone or shell in the nose. Their tattoos were confined to arms and legs, while the men had markings all over their bodies.

Slowly, trying to appear more confident than he felt, he walked around the encampment. Here and there, in the shade of some of the sturdier trees, he could see makeshift sleeping areas. There was no apparent order to these shelters, each of which was covered by a rudimentary roof made of sticks leaning up against the trunk. Was he looking at a temporary bivouac, a stopover at a hunting ground? Or were these what passed for houses among these people? Various objects lay scattered around on the sand: gourds, green stones, sticks shaped into assegais, the tanned hide of a small animal, strings of rolled up vine. Anxious to avoid any misunderstanding, he kept his distance from the women and children, and carefully avoided touching any of the objects lying on the sand .

But no one paid him any attention: none of them came over to touch him or talk to him. Even the children had gone back to their games and seemed indifferent to his presence. He imagined what an uproar would ensue if one of these savages were to appear in his home village, in the street, in front of his house, on the way to the washhouse or the church. Was he so invisible to them? Or had they been watching him since the moment he came ashore and simply become used to his presence?

The men were all sitting around the fire engaged in animated conversation. They must be talking about him, he thought. What else could have happened that would be so worthy of discussion? He moved closer to listen to them speak, to try and make out something in their language he might recognise, some basic words. But their talk was like nothing he had ever heard before: voices rising and falling, syllables punctuated with clicks of the tongue or rasping guttural sounds.

He crouched down next to them and placing his hand on his chest said slowly:

"Good evening. I'm Narcisse. My name is Narcisse."

He wondered if he might have interrupted someone. They

71

all turned to look at him, but he could read no emotion in their faces. They showed no surprise, no sign of curiosity or displeasure, nothing that he could recognise. They went back to their conversation.

His thoughts turned to the *Saint-Paul* and he wondered where it was now. About ten days from now, it would come back. He calculated that the march through the forest had gone on for at least four hours, which meant that they were too far away from the coast for a ship to see the light-coloured smoke from the fire. Not even the lookout at the top of the mast would be able to make it out. He would just about be able to retrace his steps and get back to the shore but he'd have to have it all worked out with everything properly organised before he left. And he'd have to time his escape carefully to get back to the beach at the right time. He'd get his strength back living with these savages, he'd steal a water gourde and some scraps of meat and he'd be there for the pick-up. Their indifference was a good sign. It meant they wouldn't stop him from leaving. A plan was forming in his mind.

Scraps of meat? He'd eaten nothing since the few mouthfuls of lizard and the tubers the night before. Pangs of hunger began to grip him again now that his thirst was quenched.

He wasn't being treated as a guest – they hadn't offered him a meal or a place to sleep. The worst thing would have been to be a prisoner, under constant surveillance, his hands tied. But even prisoners were given their mess of food by their gaoler, morning and evening. So what was he to these people?

After dark, there was a commotion in the group of men. Two of the younger men were using sticks to push away the embers and rocks in the fire. Clearing away the sand they revealed the opening to a pit, covered with charred leaves. They made the opening bigger, almost burning their fingers, and removed the leaves. Inside the oven a good-sized animal had been cooking and now it released rich odours of braised meat. Using two sticks as forks, they lifted the beast out of the pit and flopped it down on the earth.

The old man that Narcisse had spoken to picked up a sharpened stone and with a few deft movements, cut off some pieces of meat. The other men came up one by one to take a piece and went back to sit down around the fire to eat it. When all the men had been served, Narcisse stepped up to get his share. The old man looked shocked and signalled him to keep away. Seeing Narcisse hesitate, he barked an order, its meaning clear, just as the old woman had done when he had tried to help himself. The younger men had stood up, ready to intervene. He knew he didn't stand a chance against them, and left it at that.

The men chewed their food tranquilly, coming back for more meat until they'd eaten their fill. Someone called out and a group of youths, fifteen to twenty-year-olds, came over to take their turn. As they mingled with the adults, Narcisse decided to try his chances with the boys, but again he was met with the same rebuff.

Next came the women's turn. By now there was not much meat left on the carcass, but he made no attempt to put himself forward. Was he supposed to wait until all the others had eaten their fill? Would he have to be satisfied with what was left at the very end? The women claimed their share and went back to sit on the sand, where they fed the waiting children. The men had finished eating and were listening as one of them recounted a story in hushed tones. He wandered around among the diners and found himself once more next to the old woman, the oldest in the tribe as it now seemed. He felt no pleasure at seeing her again and had nothing to say to her, but as he approached, she offered him a piece of meat, a good-sized hunk with a bone and well-browned skin on one side. Grabbing the meat, he devoured it, sinking his teeth into the flesh. It tasted like an overcooked cheap cut of mutton, but feeling the grease run down his chin, he felt a thrill of intense pleasure that served only to stoke his appetite. He consumed the whole thing in a few mouthfuls, chewing at length, sucking on the bone, crunching the cartilage between his teeth.

He used his knife to scrape off the last bits of flesh clinging to the bone, and with his appetite now somewhat appeased, he turned to the old woman and gestured imperiously to her that he wanted more. If he wasn't permitted to help himself, if it was up to her to serve him, she could at least be quick about it! She stood up and went over to get him another share of what was left of the shoulder. As the men continued to pile dry branches on the fire, he took more time to savour this second piece. The stars were out, the fire a warm glow. The old woman had lost interest in him again. The men were lying on the ground near the coals, chanting monotonously.

He was appalled by it all. Everything about this primitive gathering filled him with disgust.

For the first time since his trials had begun five days ago, he had eaten his fill. Selecting a tree at a distance from the others, he curled up on the ground and closed his eyes. Exhaustion overcame him and he slipped easily into the deep sleep of the young.

He was shaken roughly awake at dawn. Leaping up at a bound, he found himself surrounded by about ten men, watching him intently, in silence. Narcisse was immediately on his guard, sensing that something of great significance was about to happen. He hadn't particularly liked the previous evening's indifference, but it was better than this. They looked as if they were getting ready to attack him. Why now? Why wait till this morning? He was surrounded. He had his knife, but he'd be easily overpowered by so many sturdy assailants.

One of them advanced slowly towards him, coming close enough to touch him. Gingerly, he reached out a hand and brushed the cuff of Narcisse's grubby cotton shirt, as if to see what it felt like, to assess its texture. Was that all it was? Simple curiosity? A naked savage's desire to stroke a white man's clothing? Narcisse clung onto this hope.

"See, old chap, it's just a shirt. Look, there are two buttons here, and I can roll the sleeves up, like this."

He demonstrated, and as he did so, the watching native cautiously placed his hand to his chest.

"That's it, you understand. And there are buttons here at the front too. That's how you put it on and take it off. Watch."

He took off his shirt, revealing his muscular physique and the down on his chest where the watching men had none. He placed his shirt down on the ground beside him.

One of the natives made a little speech, nodding his head at regular intervals as the others listened with obvious interest. He ended with a sort of shout and fell silent again. No one had moved.

That was when they jumped on him. He didn't see it coming and feeling himself seized by so many hands, he thought his last moment had come. Instinctively he struggled, kicking out and trying to escape, but there were too many of them. He was pinned to the ground. He soon realised that they hadn't hit him, they just wanted to immobilise him. The pain came from the powerful arms restraining him. He carried on struggling, twisting his body, but the overwhelming sense of fear and panic was beginning to subside.

He realised with amazement that the hands imprisoning him were pulling off his trousers. He tried, in vain, to stop them. And then his drawers went the same way; he kicked and writhed but they soon pulled them down to his ankles. Naked now, he carried on struggling and saw the old woman picking up his clothes and walking towards the forest.

It all happened too fast. Why had they woken him up to strip him naked by force? He hadn't sustained a single blow. Was it some kind of game, a joke in bad taste? He had never been naked in front of anyone, not in the village nor later aboard ship. Only the girls in the bordellos of the ports had seen him naked and then only for an instant in the semi-darkness. Even though there were no women here to witness this scene, and in spite of the fact that his attackers were all naked, he felt embarrassed, humiliated, bruised.

Still held firmly by his captors, he continued his efforts to escape their clutches. If he got away, he'd be able to catch up with the old woman and get his trousers back. And the knife attached to his belt. At the very least, his trousers.

Two hands grabbed him around the temples and pushed his head to the right, holding him firmly face down in the dirt. As he tried to escape the grasp of whoever was holding him, fear overcame him again, breaking over him like a wave. Had they stripped him naked before killing him? Were they going to slit his throat and bleed him, and then devour him?

The pain came so suddenly and with such violence that he almost passed out. There were no hands to restrain him now as he howled in pain and curled up in a ball, clutching his left ear with his hand. Blood was running down his neck. He felt for the spot where the pain was coming from, groping with his finger tips as blades of fire lanced through him. They had cut off his ear, detached the earlobe where he sported the gilt earring he was so fond of.

"I'd have given it to you," he moaned despairingly through his tears. "All you had to do was ask. I'd have taken it off."

The savages had moved off. He felt broken inside. Pressing his ripped ear between his fingers to staunch the flow of blood, he carried on talking and sobbing in an effort to bear the pain.

"Why are you doing this to me?" he cried. "Why are you being so cruel? Let me go. Or else kill me now, but don't torture me like this. I want to go back to my ship. Damn you! Have you no pity? It's not even a gold earring. What have I done to hurt you?"

He cried like a child for a long time, gulping and sniffing, tears streaming down his face. As waves of searing pain coursed through him, he gave in to despair, not caring any more whether he lived or died. Nothing he had ever experienced could have prepared him for this ordeal. He could make no sense of any of it.

The gilt earring took him back to a year ago, in a narrow street in Bordeaux. He'd just been promoted to able seaman and had joined the crew of a brig shipping barrels of wine to London. On their third voyage, the ship had been caught in a storm in the Bay of Biscay. They'd battled for three days and nights against high seas and icy autumn winds. The captain ordered them to reduce sail, and with gigantic waves crashing all around them, they heaved to and prayed for their lives to the Virgin and all the saints.

On the fourth day, the sun came out, the wind dropped and the sea gradually became calmer. At last the captain set a course for the lighthouse of Cordouan. There were only three wounded men. When they docked, they found out that five ships had gone down in the storm.

When the ship was unloaded and the repairs completed, the captain handed each member of the crew a coin. Without a moment's delay, Narcisse set off with a shipmate to explore the shops around the port. They both fancied themselves wearing a gold hoop in one ear like some of the old salts on board, and went from stall to stall mulling over their choices. In the end, it was a shop-girl's smile that decided them. They took turns to have their left ear pierced and walked out of the shop both sporting a gilt ring in one ear. Thus adorned, with the pencil moustache he'd taken to wearing to make himself look a little older, a confident swagger and a quick turn of phrase, he thought he cut a fine figure. And they still had enough cash left after their purchase to go to the tavern and then on to a seamen's brothel.

He sensed a presence. The old woman was sitting beside him, waiting.

"You too. You've come back to torment me too."

She showed him a greenish paste in the palm of her hand and mimed a gesture several times of putting it on his ear. Eventually, he understood and let her spread her ointment on his wound. The mixture was cooling and gave him some relief; the pain seemed to subside a little.

"You wait till I'm half dead from thirst and starvation to give me something to eat and drink. I build an arrow on the beach and you destroy it. You rip off one of my ears and then you look after me. Are you all mad in this place?"

She held up what looked like a hairy cucumber. Obeying her gestures, he bit into it and found it watery and tasteless but not unpleasant. As he raised his hand to his mouth, he saw the dried blood on his wrist and thought that his neck must be sticky with blood too.

They weren't going to finish him off today then, or they wouldn't have sent the old woman to minister to him. He might as well go and wash himself off in the pond. As he got up, his left hand still clutching his ear, he became aware again of his nakedness; he hadn't thought about it since the pain started.

Instinctively, he covered his groin with his other hand. He would never get used to being exposed like this. Two years before when he'd crossed the Line for the first time, he'd bravely endured the various Old Father Neptune trials. But he'd balked when the old hands, disguised as devils, had ordered the young men to strip and run up and down from one end of the deck to the other, completely naked, while their shipmates made fun of them and hurled buckets of water at them. The ragging hadn't lasted more than ten seconds but those few moments had been the only part of the whole day's merry-making that he'd found hard to endure. And now he had to walk around with nothing on among all these naked savages. None of the men covered themselves as he did, none of them walked around with their arm crooked in front of them, their hand on their groin. Their lack of modesty showed just how uncivilised they were. He had no desire to be like them.

He walked across the encampment. No one looked at him or laughed at him. They weren't interested in him. Who could reproach him for being naked like them, naked because of them? He knelt down at the water's edge. The touch of the cool water was soothing and he spent a long time splashing water on the back of his neck, his throat and arms. The feeling of the sun on his bare skin so close to the water was surprising and unexpected rather than actually unpleasant. His mutilated ear was still hurting.

One of the men, the one who had given the little speech before they jumped him, came over to him. Narcisse stood up, wondering what new torture they had in store for him. The man stopped a few steps away from him, stretched out his open hand towards Narcisse and said:

"Amglo."

He pronounced it slowly, enunciating each syllable. "Amglo," he repeated and pointed with his finger towards the sky. Narcisse wondered what he wanted. What was he saying? The man had spoken calmly, without smiling. His implacable demeanour only served to enrage Narcisse, who erupted:

"Amglo? You've torn off half my ear, you brute! Give me back my trousers! And my knife! And give me some food!"

What hope did he have of intimidating with this outburst, standing there with nothing on, a young man with one hand cupped around his injured ear, the other covering his manhood? But the rage in his voice was unequivocal. Narcisse was on the verge of tears. He could take no more. Without stopping to wonder at the wisdom of this attitude, he looked at the man defiantly, wanting to make him pay the price for all that he had suffered on this soil. The savage stepped back and waited until Narcisse had finished. Then, as if he had heard nothing, he held out his hand again, palm turned up towards the sky and said once more: "Amglo."

LETTER III

Sydney, 8th April 1861

Monsieur le Président,

Upon reading my letter of 17th March you were no doubt persuaded that I had confounded the timing of events, so incoherent was my account of what transpired. I cannot deny that I write without first thinking of what I am going to say, setting down my thoughts on paper as they occur to me each day. And indeed, the progress Narcisse makes is a constant source of surprise. My feelings are akin to those of a father, observing his child grow and develop, although I have not yet had the good fortune to experience that paternal bond. Indeed Narcisse is an adult to whom I have no relationship other than the fact that I have taken him in.

In spite of my efforts to the contrary, this letter begins as inconsistently as my previous ones; I assure you that I shall strive to bring more order to my account in the future.

First to the essential questions. Narcisse has been recovering his tongue for a month now, and I never cease to be amazed by his ability to learn. He still speaks in confused sentences with little regard for syntax, and he is not yet able to distinguish between masculine and feminine articles, but we are on the right path. I cannot but notice that he makes the same mistakes as a child might, although he masters in one week what a child would take six months to absorb. He has a singular way of pronouncing words, lending them a sing-song quality and modulating his voice. At times, he embellishes his words with strange guttural sounds.

One cannot fail to perceive his keen desire to learn. Our lessons take place twice a day, for two hours, and it is never he who wishes to call an end to our tutorial. The rest of his time is spent bathing, sleeping, walking about and silently observing Bill as he goes about his tasks. Occasionally we exchange a few words.

Is he happy? I pondered this as I watched him weaving a basket. It is a question impossible to answer, for he never expresses any emotion and seems to live from one day to the next. Thrust aboard the *John Bell* by chance, thence to the governor's prison and now in this isolated house, he seems to be passively accepting of his lot. Is this a sign of wisdom, indifference to his fate or merely lack of curiosity or initiative?

I had informed the governor that I wished to speak to the captain of the *John Bell* in order to ascertain from that gentleman himself how they had come upon Narcisse. In accordance with my wishes, the governor sent the dinghy for me as soon as the schooner reappeared in Sydney Bay, and I arrived in Sydney at dusk and hastened to the room that had been reserved for me in that town's finest establishment. As the evening wore on, I found myself observing the diversions of this routine hotel soirée – gentlemen in evening attire, bare-shouldered ladies in their Paris gowns engaged in polite conversation on the terrace, a convict expertly playing dance airs on the upright piano – and thinking how mundane it all seemed.

How can I explain the unease I felt from the moment I arrived? Throughout dinner, I found it difficult to participate in the fashionable talk and realised with some distress that this was a world in which I was no longer at home; but nor did I long to return to my solitary evenings spent dining alone, served by Bill under the watchful gaze of Narcisse. After supper, I removed myself from the hotel company and its chatter, and wandered aimlessly around the streets of the town and the port. Outside the taverns, seamen and soldiers made merry, girls whom I supposed to be convicts on their arms. Several houses with red lanterns could be seen at almost every street corner. Any comfort here for my troubled mind would be short-lived, transient. Once again I fled the scene.

The meeting took place early next morning in the governor's office. Captain Rowlands was a small man, shifty and astonishingly ill-tempered. He scarcely greeted me and made it clear that he felt he was wasting his time. But his delicate relationship with Her Majesty's Customs and Excise left him in no position to dismiss me out of hand, which he would undoubtedly have done with great pleasure, had he been able.

Like all sea-faring men he proved to be taciturn, and the governor's presence together with the questioning from an unknown Frenchman did little to elicit confidences from him. It was not without many false starts that I managed to wrest from him the details I desired and to establish the following account:

"On the 19th February I had some repairs to make to the masts. I needed calm waters to send the carpenters to repair the upper rigging and I had heard of the bay in question on the north coast just south of Cape York. The *John Bell* entered the bay early in the morning and work began.

I gave permission to a few hands not involved in the repairs to go ashore. They did so and walked around on the beach for a while. From the top of the mast, one of the crew spotted some savages looking for shellfish on the rocks. He whistled to the men ashore to draw their attention to this, and signalled to them to go over and take a closer look.

It is always entertaining to see these infernal savages – and it makes quite an impression on the new lads. And if it so happens that a man isn't put off by the smell, or the colour of their skin, well I wouldn't stop him going into the bushes for a romp with one of their women. You take what you can get, don't you agree?

So off they went. As my men drew closer to the savages they saw a white man in their midst, stark naked and covered in tattoos. When they asked what he was doing there, the man didn't understand and answered in the savages' gibberish. They couldn't even get him to tell them his name.

The men's reaction could not be faulted. They immediately realised that he was a castaway, and without a moment's hesitation, they decided to bring him aboard. The question was, how to go about doing so.

The man was nervous and agitated; he kept on coming up to them and touching them, and then going back over to the natives. They'd stopped their fishing and my men offered them tobacco, nails, beads, but they didn't seem interested and my men calmly headed back to the dinghy. The white man followed them, the savages behind him.

One of the men blew the whistle three times to give the alert. Seeing the strange procession I decided to take precautionary measures and gave the order to get out the rifles and prepare the armoured launch.

For the moment things were calm on the beach. There didn't seem to be any immediate danger, but you never know in a situation like that. I was informed that the repairs were almost completed and immediately gave the command to prepare to set sail with all haste, but to do so unobtrusively so as not to draw attention to our intentions. The naked white man carried on walking to and fro between my men and the group of savages who stood back about twenty paces away, not daring to come any closer. With the aid of the telescope, I could see that the group was made up mostly of women and children, but I checked to be sure they weren't carrying any sticks or clubs.

First one, and then another of my crew climbed casually into the dinghy. They made a friendly gesture to the white savage, who followed them into the dinghy and sat down on one of the thwarts. Without a moment's delay, the other crew members pushed off and rowed as hard as they could towards the *John Bell*. When the white savage stood up they forced him back down again.

When they drew up alongside the ship, they all hauled themselves up the rope ladder, the white savage proving to be quite adept at this. I stared at him in amazement. He looked around and sized up the bridge – with some emotion, it was clear to see.

With the second mate directing manoeuvres, the sails were loosed. A good breeze was blowing and as the sails billowed in the wind the trusty *John Bell* began to pick up speed to leave the bay. The white savage realised we'd set sail and became extremely agitated, jumping up onto the gunwale and running around all over the place. It looked like he was going to hurl himself overboard and I was ready to tie him up: I was afraid he might provoke an incident, disturb the setting of the sails, or perhaps attack one of the crew.

Once we were out at sea however, he calmed down, found a spot to sit, parked himself there and didn't move an inch, all the time burbling something or other in that gibberish he speaks. I sent someone to go and find him a loincloth and something to eat. He let himself be covered up without making any attempt to resist. Then he sniffed gingerly at the soup but didn't touch a drop of it, much to the annoyance of our cook. He showed no more interest in bread or ale, and even refused one of our few remaining bananas. When evening came, I brought him a blanket, which he used neither to cover himself with nor to lie on. He just slept where he was, sitting upright.

He stayed there, not saying a word and hardly moving a muscle until we got to Sydney. After we docked, I went to tell the whole story to the gentlemen of the Admiralty. I had to keep him on board for one more night – I can tell you, my men aren't usually expected to act as prison guards. The next day, a detachment of soldiers came to take him off my hands."

That was all I could extract from this unpleasant man. The governor dismissed him and he left without bidding me farewell.

It was also on this occasion of my brief visit to Sydney that I was to appear before the Colonial Court judge in order for him to give me official responsibility for Narcisse.

I was ushered into the chamber where the portly bewigged judge was seated at his dark wooden bench, ostensibly asleep. I can make no sense of English law at the best of times, and in the colonies it seems to be even more incomprehensible. I was expecting to find advocates, witnesses, a prosecutor and court officers, but of these there were none. The affair was concluded in a matter of minutes. The judge gave the official report a cursory reading, after which he asked me to give my name and confirm that I agreed to become Narcisse's guarantor. Without even listening to my answers, he signed the document drawn up in advance, handed me a copy, and left.

In the dinghy on the way back, I read through the ten pages of script, written no doubt in the hand of a convict employed as a clerk, and understood more or less that I was now the guardian of the "unidentified person known as the 'white savage', who disembarked in Sydney on the 25th February 1861". The governor had kept his promise.

When I arrived back at the residence, Bill was waiting for me at the landing stage with the news that Narcisse had disappeared. It seemed that on the day of my departure, he and Bill had dined together, or rather side by side, and since then, Narcisse had not been seen. There had been no sign of him the next morning. Bill claimed to have become more and more concerned with every hour that passed, although I found this difficult to believe. Anxious to avoid a reprimand, he insisted that I had not asked him to guard Narcisse, and I reassured him on this point and told him he had done well not to inform the guard at the gate.

Narcisse must have been gone for several hours: I surmised that he had left at dawn, or perhaps even the night before. Why had he fled? Where had he gone? I was at a loss to explain this mysterious turn of events.

I wondered what course of action to take. Should I raise the alarm, call the soldiers camped at the end of the road and send them to patrol the area? I had no reason to assume they would do as I requested, and I doubted they would be able to catch up with an experienced bushman like Narcisse. A thorough and widespread search, possibly lasting several days would be required. Narcisse already had a considerable lead, and he was surely capable of concealing himself. The soldiers could walk right by without seeing him. And when convicts escaped, dogs were employed, animals trained to hunt down runaways and attack them with great savagery. Was this the price I wanted to pay to see Narcisse brought back?

No, he has returned to the forest. I feel strangely hurt by this departure and realise that I am beginning to become attached to this young man. But what right do I have to prevent him from doing as he wishes? Bill has been nosing around everywhere and informs me that Narcisse discarded his clothing before disappearing. By running off completely naked into the wild, has he not indicated his desire to return to whence he came? Could he make it any clearer that he does not wish to live as we do?

His family have long believed him to be dead, I have no means of finding them without a surname, they will never know that he is alive and has no wish to return to them. What purpose would it serve to search for him at great expense?

Narcisse is a free man, at liberty to do according to his will. He disappeared while I was absent. Is it possible that my absence was a cause of his departure? Did he think I would not come back? Does he feel any friendship or affection for me?

My only obligation is to the governor who conferred upon me the responsibility for Narcisse. I know full well that if I were to tell him that Narcisse had died, he would make no attempt to express any regret. As far as the governor is concerned, Narcisse is no more than a source of annoyance and trouble. It is my responsibility to inform him, but if I am not too hasty, I can give Narcisse the chance to disappear, if such is his wish.

I feel it is reasonable to wait until tomorrow morning. By

the time the dinghy has arrived and taken me to the governor's office, almost two full days will have elapsed before the search begins. If there is to be a search. And with this much delay, it will have little chance of success. This will be my parting gift to Narcisse.

All day long, my mind was filled with these dark thoughts. I took my lunch late and ate with little appetite. Bill served me as usual, aware that with Narcisse gone, he would surely be returned to hard labour. But my only concern is Narcisse's future. Will he encounter other savages in the bush? Will he be welcomed by them? Will he speak their language? Will he have the strength to go through the experience of accustoming himself once again to tribal ways, three or four hundred leagues to the south of his former clan's home?

I shall never know. The adventure on which I embarked two months ago ends thus, an ultimately insignificant event with no conclusion. My speculations as to how the adventure might develop have all come to nought.

As I was recording these reflections, I was interrupted by a horseman bearing a despatch from the governor, informing me that he had learnt of Narcisse's departure. There was no indication as to how he knew, but I suspected that Bill, thinking of his own future, had disobeyed my orders and prevailed upon the linen girl, or the skipper of the dinghy, to deliver a message. The governor informed me that he would not try to recapture Narcisse from the dense forests that covered the area all around Sydney. He noted somewhat coldly – or perhaps to be humorous – that Narcisse was a French subject, in possession of no documents and without the right of abode in the colony. Although Narcisse was in breach of the law, the governor did not feel that this in itself was grounds for a manhunt. Narcisse had come from nowhere and thence he had returned. The case was closed.

I perceived with astonishment that I was quite distressed by this. The messenger enquired as to what he should do next, and accordingly I sent him off to spend the night with the soldiers in the encampment just outside the grounds of the residence. This would afford me until the next morning to compose a response. All I had left of Narcisse were some sketches of his tattoos. I needed time to reflect.

And so ends my already overly lengthy epistle. I leave you to draw your own conclusions on this matter. Was this task that I accepted so readily too onerous for me? Would it have proven so for anyone in my position? Was I mistaken in my approach to Narcisse and in my chosen methods of inculcating him once again with our ways? What exactly did I do wrong? What did I neglect to do? What was the meaning of his resigned indifference towards our world?

The experiment has failed – it little matters for what reason. Narcisse has chosen. I shall return to France, occupying myself on the return voyage in the composing of a report on this venture, which I shall submit to the Geographical Society Review. I ask you in advance not to judge this piece too harshly and to moderate your judgment of my endeavours, which have the bitter taste of being unfinished.

I remain your faithful servant...

Post Scriptum

It is now dusk, and as I come to the end of this missive, Narcisse has returned. He has no notion of the dismay his absence has engendered, and is proudly carrying a beast that resembles a large fox by the tail.

My first instinct was to reproach him sharply. But I am neither his schoolmaster nor his sergeant – it is not my place to castigate him and he would not understand my remarks. He would see only my anger and would not have the means to fathom its cause.

Narcisse is squatting on his heels, clothed once more, watching his game roasting in the fire that he has dug near the river and covered with flat stones. Seeing that Narcisse has rejected his cooking for this evening, Bill is aggrieved and plagues me with his prattle. He complains that he will have none of the meat from this beast he believes to be some sort of cat or polecat.

Our singular family has been reunited.

4

The day dragged on. The savages had lost interest in him. They'd attacked him and mutilated his ear, and now they were ignoring him.

He spent the morning in dejected vigil on the other side of the water hole – not that the stagnant pond would provide any means of defence, but at least he'd be able to see them coming. At this distance, he felt less ashamed of his nakedness. Sitting on the muddy red earth he ran his left hand mechanically from his temple to the back of his neck in an unthinking gesture that calmed the stabbing pains from the wound. At least the bleeding had stopped, thanks to the old woman's ointment.

He started to feel hungry again, and headed back over to the burnt-out embers of the fire. Walking still with his right hand shielding his groin, his left on the injured ear, he eyed the few remaining bones where ants were feasting on the tiny scraps of meat still clinging to the bone. A pregnant young woman was lying under a nearby tree, weaving a length of vine into a kind of strap, humming quietly to herself. She paid him no attention as he picked up the bones.

His meagre feast over, he looked around. A group of about ten women and children had gathered and were starting to walk through the trees, in the same general direction the old woman had taken when she'd gone off with his clothes and his knife. Hoping to get a chance to retrieve his possessions, and having nothing better to do, he decided to follow at a distance. No one spoke to him. The group moved forward slowly, the pace set by the youngest of the children. Walking along in silence gave him a chance to reflect, to build up his hopes, even though he knew it was futile: perhaps they were making their way to a real village with a sizeable population and solid cob houses, or even just mud huts. They'd make him feel welcome, their chief would look after him. A village with a native who could speak a few words of English and could lead him to an outpost of the white man's world: an isolated farm, a landing stage, a mission perhaps.

But there was no village. And no sign of his clothes.

An hour later, the women stopped by a fallen tree that must have been dead for some time. Using small stones picked up off the ground, they scraped away the bark of the rotting tree and cut through to the sapwood to reveal a network of winding tunnels, each with a yellowish larva squirming deep within. With great delicacy, they poked a twig into each tunnel to pull out the grub. The children waited patiently for their turn, gulping down the fruits of this harvest with obvious delight.

Narcisse kept his distance from the group, not wanting to draw attention to himself. No one offered him any of the grubs and he was spared the need to refuse. Feeling discouraged and with no plan in mind, he lay down on the sparse grass, his ear still hurting, and watched them enjoy their snack. Here in this part of the forest, he could feel a hint of humidity in the air, and it seemed less alien to him.

Why had he imagined there would be a village? Why did the absence of such a village cause him so much distress? Why did he grasp at the smallest of threads, let hope rise up in him again like the tide, ebbing and flowing, like a wave breaking on a rock, pulling back, swelling again, only to crash as before?

He needed to take stock, to think and decide. If he carried on like this, tossed around by events and by the incomprehensible whims of the savages, he would go mad. He had to come up with a plan to save himself, to get back to the coast and be rescued.

He'd never needed to make any decisions before. He was always told what to do, at home, at school, in his father's workshop; he was expected to obey quickly with no questions asked. At sea, all that was required of him were strong arms and skilful hands for manoeuvring the sails and holding the tiller steady, a lithe body for slipping through the rigging, a good ear and a sharp eye on watch. It wasn't his job to think of ways to solve problems; he and his shipmates had only to obey orders, the timeless commands aboard ship, fixed and immutable from one ship to the next, from generation to generation.

Nothing in his past had prepared him for an ordeal like this. The tales he'd heard aboard ship, the humorous accounts, the tragedies, were no use to him now. What wouldn't he give to put himself in the hands of an officer, or a more experienced seaman? He'd been cast into utter isolation, thrown completely on his own resources. In this game that seemed to have no rules, every moment of the day, every choice he made, however insignificant could determine his chances of survival, the possibility of a successful return.

He had to hold firm. Hold firm and not give way to fanciful imaginings. There was no guarantee that the *Saint-Paul* would come back after Java. And if the ship were to arrive in the bay, his chances of being there at the right moment were small. He knew nothing at all about the area, he couldn't be sure there were any white men living in these parts. He had no way of knowing whether or not these savages had had any contact with white men before him. If by some chance the schooner were to come back, and if he happened to be at the right beach at that moment, it would mean he'd end up spending about two weeks among the savages. It could be longer than two weeks, much longer.

Much shorter too, if they were to kill him, or if he died of hunger or thirst, of sickness or poisoning, or of despair. And then he made himself a promise, a solemn, absurd vow: he didn't know how long this experience would go on, but he would come out of it alive. The force of this idea stunned him. Yes, he would survive!

Feeling somewhat calmer, he stood up, and with the trees around him for witnesses, he proclaimed: "I am Narcisse Pelletier, seaman on the schooner *Saint-Paul*."

The women woke up from their long siesta and began to dig around in the ground, collecting tubers. Then, as the sun began to sink, they set off back through the forest. He followed them. His ear still hurt; he was beset by shooting pains and a stinging sensation all over one side of his head. He kept rubbing his temple, trying to allay this feeling.

Back at the clearing, the young men had dug a pit, and lit a fire of twigs and small branches. They covered the glowing coals with flat stones, on top of which the women arranged a bed of leaves. The bulbs they'd gathered earlier were arranged on the leaves along with a few small animals: birds or bats perhaps. Then they placed more leaves on top of these and covered the whole thing with earth.

How many of them were there? They all looked so alike: short, stocky, dark-skinned, curly haired; he found it difficult to distinguish any individual characteristics.

There was the old woman, of course. And the group of women, or rather mothers. They were eight in number, nine counting the pregnant woman. The youngest of them was breastfeeding her baby. He counted fourteen children under about ten years of age. They always played together, rarely venturing too far away from the women.

He counted seven men. The oldest, a man of about sixty, the one Narcisse had spoken to when they arrived, had spent most of the day beside the fire. He decided to name him Chief. The others seemed to be about thirty to forty years old, as far as he could tell. Narcisse recognised the one who'd come up to him when he was washing himself off at the water hole. He seemed sturdier than the others, more determined. He decided to call him Quartermaster on account of his build.

The men and women spoke little. The group of young people, whose ages were anything from twelve to twenty-five, made more noise. They didn't mix with the children and stayed away from the adults. There were ten boys and six girls, but they didn't all stay together the whole time. At times, the boys would go off to one side and play jacks; sometimes they would pair up for a game or to do a job of some sort, sometimes one of them would go off alone into the forest. A boy and a girl were sitting under a tree together, openly touching each other. Narcisse blushed when he saw the girl stroking the boy's leg, her hand creeping up his thigh.

Nine women, seven men, fourteen children, sixteen young people: forty-six of them in all. He'd have to observe them carefully, work out who was in charge, understand the relationships between the men and the women, between brothers and sisters, fathers and children. It might be useful for him. He counted them up again on the sand, using twigs and stones. Even with the various comings and goings, he still arrived at the same total.

Chief, Quartermaster... he had to recognise them all individually. Thinking of names for them passed the time: he'd call this one Scarface, and that one would be Show-off, Broken Nose, and there was even one he'd call Kermarec after his shipmate on the *Saint-Paul* because of the way he walked. He wouldn't worry about naming the women. But when the men went away, talked among themselves and came back, he was no longer very sure of who was who.

It was getting dark when a young savage came running out of the forest. He wasn't sure, but he thought he hadn't seen this one before. The new arrival didn't even look at him, and went over to join the young people, even though he was clearly older and more broad shouldered than them. The boys gathered around him as he began to tell a story, punctuated with cries of surprise and approval. Kermarec and Quartermaster came over to listen too. The young man seemed, for all the world, like a wanderer returned from his travels, enjoying recounting his adventures. Will I have the same reception when I get back to my village? Narcisse wondered ruefully. He certainly couldn't imagine himself naked, sitting in front of an audience of naked listeners telling his tales. He added another stone to his tally. With the arrival of Wanderer, that made forty-seven in the tribe.

The old woman came scurrying over to him, and gestured to him not to move. With small, precise gestures, she removed the salve from his ear, spat some water from the gourd onto the wound, and applied a new layer of ointment.

The young men went over to open up the pit that served as an oven, just as they had the night before. The men were the first to eat, and again when Narcisse tried to join them he was met with a sharp rebuff. In the gathering darkness he felt less embarrassed at being naked. Or perhaps he was just becoming used to it. He made another attempt, but this time, Wanderer, himself among those who hadn't yet been served, stood in his way, giving him a menacing look. Narcisse didn't have the energy to get involved in a fight; he knew what the outcome would be anyway. And who was there to stand up for him? He turned around and waited. After the men and women had eaten, the old woman brought him a piece of the meat. It was almost black; smaller, drier and tougher than the meat they'd eaten the night before. Afterwards, he was free to go and help himself to some of the charred tubers he'd eaten before in the forest. The meagre meal did little to stem his hunger and his ear was still painful.

The savages sang for a while – although he wasn't sure their monotonous chanting could be called singing. It was a strange incantation, intoned in quavering voices, the strains punctuated with clicks of the tongue or jaw, the reedy voices of the women cutting through the men's growling. Then, when it was time to sleep beneath the ink-black sky, they bedded down under flimsy shelters of foliage, one or two women and a clutch of children to each man, the youths and older girls a little further off in the forest.

He found the tree he'd slept under the previous night and lay down on the ground. The unexpected sensation of the light evening breeze all over his body was a reminder of the loss of his clothes. He broke off a few small branches and palm fronds and used them to cover himself. Because of the wound, he had to sleep on his right side, curled up in a ball. A feeling of being completely alone overwhelmed him. He felt himself begin to cry, gently, without a sound. The flow of tears soothed him, helped him to bear all the losses and misfortunes he'd suffered since arriving on the beach. It was the first time he'd cried since he was a small child – his father would beat him even harder if he ever showed any sign of weakness. But what blows could be harder to bear than this long ordeal, sufferings endured with no understanding of what was happening to him? No one heard his lamentations, as he moaned and sniffed like a small, wounded, abandoned animal. And as he wept, he drifted off to sleep.

He woke up shivering violently, his teeth chattering. He felt devoid of strength. He tried to get up, but dizziness overcame him and he had to lie down again. The pain in his ear had subsided, he didn't feel hungry but he was cold and clammy with sweat, in the grip of a fever. Was it the water he'd drunk? The wound, or the salve the old woman had applied? Or was it the effect of black despair?

Curled up in a foetal position, he adjusted the fronds that were his only blanket and lay there trembling from head to foot. There was no one to help him.

The sun rose higher in the sky, but the rays that filtered through the branches did little to warm him. If he had fallen sick aboard the *Saint-Paul*, he would have dragged himself to the gangway to declare himself to the ill-tempered second mate. How he would have loved to hear the foul-breathed second mate uttering one of his nasty remarks, or declaring in his gravelly voice: "If you can walk as far as here, you're fit to work," a favourite dictum of his. The tactic of staying in the hammock and waiting for someone to come and get you was scarcely more effective: he'd witnessed the mate tossing an old hand out of his hammock and forcing him to go back to his post. He'd make allowances for the injured, but never the sick. And if by chance a sick man were to be granted a day or two's rest, the second mate had little to offer in his medicine chest: a few bottles of powders from which he'd make his selection – at random some said – and mix up a vile potion. Narcisse fell into a restless sleep, hoping he'd wake up and find himself on the 'tweendecks.

It was mid-morning as far as he could tell when the old woman came to see him. Did someone care about him after all? She applied some more of the ointment to his ear with a few deft gestures, as before. Then she spread her fingers and passed her hands, palms turned down, over his body from head to foot, muttering indistinctly under her breath. Finally she picked up a handful of the sandy earth and let it run between her fingers spreading it all over his body. She repeated this several times, until his skin, glistening with sweat, was evenly coated with a fine layer of dust.

With half-closed eyes, fighting against the waves of fever that pounded against his temples, he made no effort to resist and let the old woman do as she wished.

She brought the gourd to his lips and he forced himself to drink. Then she spread a few more branches over his chest and legs and left.

He fell asleep again, the layer of earth covering his body affording him some protection against the sensation of cold.

The old woman was sitting beside him again, calmly weaving leaves together to make some sort of cage or helmet. Satisfied with her handiwork, she put it over his head like a tent that made no contact with his skin. He was grateful for the protection it gave him from the sun's heat.

Touching a branch to some embers she'd brought over, she set it aflame and passed the burning leaves over the sick man's body, humming softly. The flames died and were replaced by palls of thick grey smoke. She held the branch close to his shoulder and let the breeze carry the smoke into her woven construction. He breathed in the hot, acrid smoke as it accumulated inside the helmet. It was bitter and astringent, bringing tears to his eyes. He began to cough, pushed away the smoke trap and lay down again.

The old woman persisted; she put the contraption back in place and brought the smoking branch towards it. Inhaling the fumes, the smell of a forest burning, feeling the heat on his cheeks and nose, he wondered if this could cure him of his fever. He forced himself to go along with it, to let the remedy enter into him.

When she came back, she made him eat some small bits of meat and drink from the gourd. Then she resumed the smoke treatment. No one else came to see him. He tried to get up, but he was no match for the dizziness and shivering that engulfed him. The raging fever prevented him from thinking straight. He remembered vaguely that he had important decisions to make, but moments of lucidity gave way to the desire to surrender completely, to burrow into his bed of leaves and dust, and let himself fall asleep to the rhythm of the waves of fever.

The old woman was making him drink. She was tending to his ear. Smoke was getting into his nostrils. The shivers were beginning to subside. He slept again.

Darkness fell abruptly, with the suddenness of the tropical night that always unnerved him. She offered him a piece of grilled meat: the rest of the tribe must have been sharing the evening meal of the latest kill. He made a herculean effort and managed to swallow a couple of mouthfuls. The meat reeked of burnt grease. He drank some more, closed his eyes and lay back again.

For five days, Narcisse was ill, and for five days the old woman fed him and gave him water to drink. She tended to his wound, covered him with earth and leaves, made him breathe the smoke from the leaves. Dimly, he felt himself getting weaker. Was this how he would end his days, lying here on the ground like a dog, surrounded by savages who would leave his body to be torn apart by wild animals?

On the fourth day, he was shaken by a blast of wind, harsher and more violent than the wind of the night when he was abandoned. Low grey clouds raced across the sky with alarming speed, leaves flew about in all directions, torn from the trees by the powerful gusts. Trees creaked and swayed. A few drops of rain drummed on the ground. Towards evening, the temperature dropped sharply. Narcisse shivered uncontrollably, his body wracked by convulsive shaking as he tried to dig himself into the ground to give the wind as little purchase as possible.

Suddenly, he felt a body next to his. The old woman had lain down right up against him and was wrapping her short arms around him. On his chest, her black wrinkled hand. A naked woman, lying right next to his own naked body. That smell of grease and sweat. A feeling of warmth on his back, his buttocks, his legs, protecting him from the biting wind. Her breath warm on the back of his neck. Two bodies locked in an embrace – where was the whore from the Cape, the vigour and laughter of that night? How obscene, he thought through the fog of the fever, an old black woman and a young white man, embracing.

Then he surrendered to the embrace, and in it, he found refuge.

LETTER IV

Sydney, 5th June 1861

Monsieur le Président,

I had initially believed that bringing Narcisse back into our world would be a simple matter: a slow process perhaps, but one in which he would nevertheless progress gradually along an unwavering path. His task would be to climb back up the hill he had already scaled as a child and from which he had descended during the period of his exile.

But the reality has proven to be more complex. Narcisse has a will of his own, and it has become apparent to me that there are some lessons he refuses to learn. I am at a loss to understand why this is so.

My attempts to teach him to write serve as an example. He had surely learnt his letters as a schoolboy – I could scarcely countenance the notion that this sailor was completely illiterate – and I desired to give him back a skill he once possessed.

I wrote our names in capital letters on a sheet of paper and followed along with my finger as I read them aloud to him. He understood what I was saying, but made no connection between the words I spoke and the marks on the paper. I wondered what a village schoolmaster would have done. I pointed to my name as I said it again and then handed him the pencil and the sheet of paper. He grasped them and looked at me as if to make sure that he had understood, held the pencil poised, and waited. Very gently I said:

"Now you. Write Narcisse."

Without further ado, he began to make marks on the paper. Alas, these were no clumsy half-formed letters, but a series of precisely drawn zigzag lines, circles, spirals and dots. Concentrating intensely and drawing rapidly, he gradually filled the page with a series of geometrical shapes in which could be discerned patterns of strange, abstract symmetrical forms. His work was a design of astonishing complexity, similar in style to the tattoos he sports. But yet more extraordinary was the manner in which he completed the design: he did not begin in the centre of the page with the principal figures, but rather he started in the bottom right hand corner, covering the page with a mass of details and ending in the top left hand corner. Not even Raphaël or Poussin could have executed a sketch in this manner. Narcisse never faltered in his composition and must have conceived the entirety of this primitive image in his head before beginning to draw. The curious result of his labours conveyed a mysterious sense of balance. I thought what a sure hand he had, and how well he seemed to understand the principals of design.

In no more than ten minutes, Narcisse had filled the page with his hieroglyphs. Then he put down the pencil and, apparently satisfied with his handiwork, displayed no further interest therein.

In language, he advances more rapidly, rediscovering each day further words of his forgotten vocabulary. His pronunciation too is improving and he now enunciates all the sounds of our language more or less correctly. Gone are the strange hissing noises and clicks of the tongue that marred his speech scarcely one month ago. He continues to lend a rhythmic sing-song quality to his pronouncements, with the result that he sounds like an Italian speaking our language.

One could scarcely describe him as talkative. I wonder if he is laconic by nature, or whether it is difficult for him to find the right words to express what he feels. Or does he simply have nothing to say?

The correct usage of verb tenses still eludes him, and he struggles particularly with the future. "The sun will rise tomorrow," is a mere conversational nicety for him, since the truth of the statement is self-evident. "Tomorrow, we will go and bathe in the river," means nothing to him. He understands each of the words, but imagines that we are going immediately to the riverbank.

When he expresses a personal opinion, even on the most anodyne of subjects, he prefaces his remarks with a solemn, "I say." No doubt, this is a rhetorical element that persists from the language of the savages, or perhaps a form of courtesy in their idiom: "I say: Bill's dinner is good."

But now that we can speak to each other with some measure of success, he still refuses to tell me anything about his life among the savages. When I question him on the subject, he seems to understand what I am asking, but no matter the approach I adopt, my attempts to elicit a response are always met by his silence. I know no more today about his experiences than I did on the day I met him.

Without this information from Narcisse, I cannot commence my report on the natives of north-east Australia, and yet it was in the hopes of carrying out such a study that I agreed to burden myself with the responsibility for Narcisse.

Does this mean that I have failed, that I shall not succeed in my project? I cannot say why, but I do not believe this to be the case. Narcisse's progress bestows other lessons upon me. At present, I can only sense this vaguely and am unable to bring any order to my thoughts on this matter. Perhaps I shall never learn anything about these Australian negroes, but the steps that Narcisse takes along his path convey intimations of another kind to me, and which I believe to be no less significant.

There is yet another possible explanation for these apparent failures. Narcisse has been unsuccessful in learning to write, in conceiving of the future and in recounting his past. When this experiment began, I saw his mind as a blank slate on which my lessons would be engraved, or as malleable wax on which I would make my imprint. But it cannot be denied that there are certain matters he refuses to countenance, and in these I can make no headway. The image I cherished of Narcisse progressing towards our world, emerging from Plato's cave and walking towards the sunlight of the nineteenth century, is erroneous. There are within him two distinct individuals: a sailor struggling to emerge from the dungeon in which he has been shut away for many years; and a wild creature battling every step of the way to prevent that happening. For the most part, it is the sailor who has the upper hand, but the battle is hard won.

Just as his skin will be engraved with tattoos to the end of his days, so will his spirit remain marked by all that he has endured. Perhaps he will never free himself completely of those experiences. It is strange indeed to think of a man in whom two opposing warriors struggle for dominion, but I can see no other way of trying to understand it.

I am persuaded that the time has come for us to take to the seas once more. There is nothing to prevent us leaving and I must confess that I was beginning to tire of our life of voluntary seclusion. I have not made another visit to Sydney, for fear of provoking Narcisse into disappearing once more. Our lessons keep me busy and I am gladdened by any progress my pupil makes, but I cannot deny that his company offers me few distractions.

I have written to the governor to inform him that our stay in the colony will be coming to an end, and he has promised us a passage next week on the *Strathmore*, a clipper recently constructed in the shipyards of Bristol. God willing, we shall be in France by mid-August, where I shall make haste to immediately introduce you to my protégé upon our arrival.

I received your letter of the 16th April in which you replied to my first missive. I am much affected by the compliments you pay me, all the more so since I have never viewed my adventure with Narcisse in the manner you describe. Indeed, you are too generous, sir. I have never seen myself as the Good Samaritan on whom you lavish such praise, nor do I desire to be such a one. Narcisse is indeed an endearing young man, and he has endured terrible hardships. But my only motivation is to conduct scientific research. I wish first and foremost to describe as comprehensively as I can the changes undergone by a white man who, having become a savage, returns once again to civilisation.

You have provided me with a list of questions, the importance of which I cannot deny. Alas, Narcisse stubbornly refuses to speak of his time among the natives and I am therefore unable to provide answers to any of your lines of enquiry. When I question him on the subject, he says nothing. He smiles but gives no explanation for his silence. He is similarly mute when asked to speak of the manner of his arrival in Australia, or of his life before the shipwreck. Nor does he speak of his youth. Indeed I cannot even be certain that his name is Narcisse: perhaps there was a misunderstanding and he has accepted this name as a shared convention between the two of us.

I must now tell you of an incident that caused me to reflect deeply on certain matters; I wonder what you will make of my musings.

I had retired to my chamber and was perusing my notes when I heard a woman scream. This was followed by a muffled thump and the sound of hurried footsteps. Recognising the linen maid's voice I quickly went outside and searched round the house only to behold the astonishing spectacle of Bill and Narcisse fighting. Or rather, of Bill trying to fight Narcisse, assailing him with punches and kicks, none of which attained their target. Narcisse was holding his ground, scarcely moving, evading every blow with a skilful feint and resuming his stance without ceding an inch, leaving Bill with arms and legs flailing in the air. Only an experienced fighter with a sound understanding of wrestling could remain so still, waiting until the very last moment to avoid the blows. I noticed too that he made no attempt to strike Bill, who would have made an easy target, thrown off balance as he was by the failure of his fairground brawler's punches to strike home.

With a shout I ordered them to desist, placed myself between the two men and made them stand well back from one another. I asked the reason for their altercation. Narcisse did not understand what had happened, and neither Bill nor the linen maid would say anything other than garbled nonsense. I was constrained to remind them that they were convicts and that

I could have them clapped in irons again. After interrogating each of them separately, I managed to establish the following account.

Twice a week the dinghy puts in at the landing stage, where it remains for several hours. On this occasion, Bill and the young woman made use of this time for an assignation in my servant's quarters where they disported themselves in amorous frolicking. That this was not the first time was of little concern to me. No doubt Bill realised that his position was precarious: he had secured the favours of the linen maid with the aid of a few coins, which could only have been procured by illicit means and at my expense. Fearing charges of theft and procurement, and imagining himself felling trees in the terrible penal colony of Port Arthur, Bill confessed all to me and implored me to show mercy.

The amorous pair repaired to Bill's straw mattress where they embarked upon their homage, if not to Venus, assuredly to Eros. In the throes of passion the linen maid happened to look up and was aghast to see Narcisse standing at the window. Arms folded on the window ledge, he was smiling as he gazed upon the wanton spectacle of the two servants cavorting in the heat of the afternoon.

The girl screamed. Bill was stunned and then enraged at having been thus interrupted. He jumped up, ran to the window and delivered a violent punch to Narcisse, who was taken completely by surprise and had no chance to evade the blow. Bill adjusted his dress and ran into the garden ready for a fight, an enterprise that met with little success, as I have already described.

Perhaps you consider this tawdry anecdote unworthy of your attention, but I urge you to allow me to persuade you otherwise.

Both Bill and the linen maid, when questioned separately, gave me the same description of Narcisse watching them: he was smiling. Not with the lascivious grin of a voyeur, savouring a forbidden spectacle, and risking being discovered and shamed; but with the candid smile of one who is witnessing an agreeable display, enjoying it with the participants. Narcisse is without any sense of shame.

I tried to explain to him what had transpired. Beneath his right eye, he had an impressive bruise, and he was fully aware that my servant had struck him because he had seen him with the linen maid. But he was at a loss to understand why this should be so. Such was the substance of my uncomfortable exchange with Narcisse. He held no grudge against Bill, and once again, he was baffled by our customs but accepted them with equanimity.

This discovery seems to me to be of major importance. In Narcisse's tribe, men and women must make no attempt to conceal their amorous activities, displaying their passion for all to see. Our temple of Venus is within our own house, between the sheets in the bedchamber where no candle burns. Even persons of the lowest order such as Bill and the linen maid, disporting themselves on a straw mattress in the full light of day, conceal themselves behind closed doors, away from prying eyes. Only with the greatest embarrassment can one imagine being watched in such circumstances; and who but the most inexplicably depraved would choose to watch? A sense of decorum has prevailed throughout the ages in all climes. And yet none of this has any meaning for Narcisse whose innocence has allowed me to glimpse something about which I would never have thought to ask him. As a result of Bill's corruption, scheming and subsequent rage, Narcisse has imparted to me a precious gem of information.

Alas, such innocence is lost as soon as it comes to light. If I had so wished, I might have staged a repetition of this scene. I could easily have offered a soldier and a girl from the port a few coins in exchange for allowing themselves to be surprised in a similar situation. But I had no desire to play the matchmaker for such a singular enterprise, nor would I be able to draw any conclusions from Narcisse's reaction to the charade. He will have learnt from the blow delivered by Bill and will think twice before watching at the window again. Never again shall that benign look of innocence be seen on his face, that smile beheld only by the linen maid and her paramour.

Narcisse is changing. With each day that passes, he comes closer to us and moves further away from the depths of the Australian bush. No sooner has he perceived our customs than he adapts to them. The breeches he wears, the words he succeeds in saying, the relationship he has established with me, all these bring him closer to us while hiding within him that which I seek to learn.

As I ponder this incident, I see that Narcisse bears a message. But like words traced with a fingertip on a pane of glass, the message vanishes as the mist evaporates from the glass. His secrets are lost forever. I must therefore make a record of all that I learn, for it will surely all melt away. With every day that passes, Narcisse will lose something of his purity – but not of his own doing. A chemist can repeat the same experiment a hundred times in order to validate his results. Narcisse's voyage back into our world will happen only once, and in one direction only. To record that journey will be my duty.

With such musings, I was able to counter the disharmony in my household and bring calm to my spirit. I instructed Bill and the linen maid to leave the premises and to depart with the dinghy: I could no longer retain in my service a convict who had raised his hand against my countryman.

There was one further lesson to be derived from this incident. When Bill had struck out at Narcisse the second time, Narcisse had parried the blows, but made no attempt to deliver any of his own. He had reacted spontaneously as a Christian should: I grant that he did not turn the other cheek, in strict accordance with the Bible's teaching, but he did demonstrate a forbearance of which few among us, having been struck once, would be capable. A dog bares its teeth when beaten, a child tries to scratch when scolded. An eye for an eye, a tooth for a tooth. To suppress the urge to return the attack and defend oneself only by evading blows requires exceptional mastery of the passions and the will.

But what does this mean? Must we recognise as civilised the primitive customs that Narcisse manifests at every moment? This cannot be. And yet, as I write these lines this evening, I do not know what to make of his gentle nature. One conclusion cannot be avoided. In this distasteful altercation, Narcisse, the white savage, showed himself to be more civilised than Bill, the convict.

Where will this conclusion lead me? I believe the time has come to take to the seas once more.

I remain your faithful servant...

5

When he awoke the next morning, the old woman was no longer lying beside him, the storm had passed and with it, his fever. He still felt weak, but his head was clear, his body calmed. Hunger gnawed at him again and he felt strangely reassured by the return of the familiar pangs. The throbbing pains in his ear had gone.

He stood up steadily, no longer shaking with fever, and took a few steps. Two women walked past and he instinctively brought his hands to his groin, conscious once more of his nakedness. The dust and earth the old woman had covered him with had mingled with the sweat from his fever and hardened to form a crust that hindered his movements. His face itched from the stubble that covered his cheeks and chin. He'd never gone so long without shaving or trimming his moustache. He'd been so proud of his moustache, tending it carefully whenever time allowed, relishing the swash-buckling air it gave him. And now, it was probably indistinguishable from the rest of his unshaven beard.

He reached the pond and immersed himself in water up to his waist, doing what he could to clean himself up. The cool sensation of the water was soothing, and he scrubbed at himself for a long time with his bare hands, cleaning himself thoroughly as if to erase the past. As he went through the motions unthinkingly, his hand brushed his left ear. With a shock, he realised that something was wrong. He felt his other ear whilst searching in vain for his reflection in the ripples on the surface of the water. With no mirror of any kind, he had only his sense of touch to rely on. His fingertips left him with no doubt: his left earlobe had been almost completely torn off.

They had mutilated him. For the sake of his gilt earring, the tribesmen had done this to him. And yet, the old woman had taken care of him. She was one of the tribe too, and she had nursed him and watched over him. She'd kept him warm, given him food and water. Her incantations and fumigations may not have had much effect, but there was no doubt that she had done all she could to tend his wound and calm his fever. But there had been no sign of compassion or pity for him in her ministrations. It was as if she were merely fulfilling a responsibility that fell to her; there was no emotion involved. But through her, the tribe was watching out for his health, in its own way. They did not wish to harm him – or at least not right away. If they were keeping him alive to eat him, they'd have to fatten him up a bit to be able to feast on him. Narcisse had never had much fat on him and now he was gaunt from hunger and sickness. And there was always a chance, he told himself, that they didn't eat human flesh after all. There was hope.

He walked slowly over to the fire and sat down. An animal the size of a calf had been cooked there the night before, while he'd been trembling with cold as the storm raged. A few bones lay scattered around in the sand, ribs with scraps of meat still clinging to them. The old man he'd decided to call Chief was dozing next to the fire. Narcisse picked up a bone, brushed off some of the dust and began to eat. The meat was stringy and cold and tasted strongly of smoke. He scraped and gnawed on the bone and managed to tear off all the bits of sinewy flesh. A young boy squatted down next to him and watched him, not saying a word.

Narcisse spent most of the morning eating. After drinking from a discarded gourd, he slept in the shade all afternoon. He listened to the chanting around the fire in the evening, and ate again when the old woman served him. That night, for the first time since he'd been abandoned, he felt a little less unhappy.

The next morning, as the tribe rose in their usual way, getting up one by one as they awoke in their own time, Narcisse noticed a change in their activities. Instead of spending the morning playing games, going for walks, having naps, they were busy and active. They all seemed to have a task to perform and were calmly going about their work. But what was it all for? He watched them gathering into small groups for quick discussions; what were they talking about? And why did that branch have to be moved? Why were they weaving vines into baskets, covering the dead coals with stones?

Before the sun was at its highest, the women and the children formed into a group. The old woman walked up to Narcisse and held out two water pouches, signalling to him that he was to carry them. He hesitated for a moment and eventually took hold of them. They were not heavy, but there were no handles or cords to hold them and he found it awkward. What was he doing agreeing to carry them? And who was she to give him orders?

The old woman rejoined the group as they started to move deeper into the forest, the adolescents following behind the women. No one made any effort to communicate with him, and Narcisse was left wondering what he was supposed to do.

Looking at the now almost deserted encampment, he thought how dismal it seemed. The makeshift sleeping shelters were scarcely visible, the branches used to build them almost indistinguishable from the surrounding vegetation. And now the men too were coming together into a group, each one of them carrying something: stones, a basket, an animal skin, a water gourd. From the clearing could be heard the sound of melancholy chanting.

One by one they began to walk towards the forest in the same direction as the women and children, setting off at regular intervals in seemingly random order. The tribe was abandoning the encampment by the water hole.

Should he stay here? He knew he wouldn't survive by himself, that he'd soon starve to death. And he didn't have the strength to endure the crushing solitude of those first few days again. He was better off in the company of these people, in spite of the absurd sufferings and the pain they'd inflicted on him. Better that than face the certainty of his imminent demise alone in this barren forest.

Picking up the two gourds the old woman had entrusted to him, he started off in the same direction as the group. He stopped at the edge of the forest and turned around. Kermarec and Wanderer still hadn't left. Were they waiting to bring up the rear? Were they making sure no one was left behind?

The whole tribe was leaving. They had stayed here at the encampment for the four days he'd been in the grip of the fever, and they'd waited another day while he recovered his strength. Did this mean they'd delayed their departure on his account? Had they been waiting until he was back on his feet?

He began to walk, carrying the two water pouches. They were probably made from the organs of some animal, the bladder most likely. Helping the tribe seemed like the natural thing to do: they were feeding him, it was only right that he should make himself useful. Was this what his future held in store for him? Being a porter, a slave for a pack of savages? And his life at sea? His decision to become a sailor had been easily arrived at. As the second son, he could not count on work in the family workshop. He could go to sea, or spend his life in the village where he was born, working as a farmhand, never marrying. The choice had been easy; he'd opted for the seafaring life. And now here he was, a servant, a water-carrier for an old woman. Addressing the trees around him, he murmured: "I am Narcisse Pelletier, seaman on the schooner *Saint-Paul*."

The forest was cool, even in the middle of the day. He tried to work out which direction they were moving in. They seemed to be walking more or less towards the north, as he'd done the previous week with the old woman. He'd never really paid attention to the maps on board the *Saint-Paul*, but he could just about remember that the coastline ran north-south for a considerable distance. So at least their route was not taking them further away from the sea.

The group of men, with Narcisse following them, caught up with the women and moved along at their pace. There was no path, no trail to guide their steps.

They stopped in a scarcely distinguishable valley where the bushes grew a bit thicker, and spent the hottest part of the day in the welcome shade. The exhausted children drank from the water pouches and fell asleep immediately.

In the mid-afternoon, they set off again, the men and younger adults moving gradually ahead of the women. They carried on walking in the same direction until the evening when they arrived at a low hill and stopped. Some of the men spread out in the forest to hunt, while the young people arranged branches for the shelters and prepared the fire. After a while, the hunters came straggling back, some with game and others, empty-handed.

The meal was short, served in the same manner as before. The old woman brought Narcisse a roasted bird complete with its feathers, which he pulled to pieces carefully before sucking on the bones. The walk had done him good, but his appetite had returned with full force since his recovery and this meagre meal did little to appease his hunger. Afterwards, he spent a long time massaging his left ear before he closed his eyes and dropped off to sleep.

The next day, they walked all morning, stopping only for a brief pause to let the children rest. The old woman took the two water gourds from him and rationed out the water for the children. Narcisse felt weak and oppressed by the heat in the humid, still air.

And then he saw the sea.

The forest stopped abruptly in a perfect curve, framing a sandy beach, as wide as the beach where he had landed. But it wasn't the same one. They hadn't retraced their steps, and many of the features of this bay were different. A lone rock, the reef visible above the water, the slanting trees, and no cliffs. And this bay was completely closed in by an impenetrable reef, broken only by three small islands, covered with scrawny bushes. Waves broke on the reef; it would be impossible for a dinghy to find a passage. No sailor would ever land here. The names 'North Bay' and 'Bay of Abandon' sprang spontaneously into his mind. How far away from here was the 'Bay of Abandon'? Two days walk, at the most.

How long now had he been ashore? He counted off the days on his fingers: four days completely alone; two with the old woman; two by the water hole before the fever; five days ill and recovering; two days walk to here. Fifteen days in all on these shores, if his calculations were correct. It would take the *Saint-Paul* a week to sail to Java, then two days to get the sick men ashore and prepare to set sail again, another week to sail back here. Any day now, the *Saint-Paul*, or perhaps another ship sent to rescue him, would weigh anchor in the 'Bay of Abandon'.

Of course, he couldn't be sure. The crossing might take longer if they encountered stormy weather. It could take longer than two days to load up with supplies and take on new hands. But with any luck, the rescue ship would make an appearance within a few days. He had to find some food and a water pouch. He had to get away. If he kept to the coast he would eventually arrive at the 'Bay of Abandon'. He'd be found, naked and exhausted, his ear torn off. He'd be the butt of his shipmates' jokes, but he would be alive. He remembered the promise he'd made to himself. Whatever happened, he would come out of this ordeal alive.

The tribe stopped at the edge of the forest. The mothers and babies stayed in the shade with the pregnant woman, while the young people assembled branches into shelters and the men went off to hunt. The women waded into the sea to collect white clams and fat, dark green mussels, the children playing in the waves and helping to find the shellfish. Narcisse could not swim and was afraid of the water. But here, on this gently sloping beach, he felt more confident. He waded into the sea, and still feeling self-conscious, walked past the women and children until the water came up to his chest. He was taller and could go well beyond where they were standing without being out of his depth. All around him were rocks covered with shellfish that were out of the reach of the others. He started to pick the shells off the rocks and when he could hold no more, he walked back towards the beach where a woman held out a basket to him. He took the basket, put his crop in it and went back out to the rocks. Before long, he'd filled the basket and given it to the women, who gave him another empty basket to fill. Heedless of the sun beating down on the back of his neck, the dazzling reflections of the sun on the water, he was happy to have something to do. He carried on working industriously, filling a stream of baskets with clams and mussels, the women supplying him with empty baskets as fast as he filled them.

Meanwhile, on the beach a fire had been lit, a large flat stone laid across it supported by a ring of smaller stones. Here and there, shellfish were piled up on the sand. Someone called to the women, who came out of the water and walked over to sit down around the fire. With the last of his baskets filled, Narcisse joined them along with the children.

The women arranged the mussels and clams on the hot stone, picking them off a few moments later to eat the barely cooked flesh. The flat stone, constantly replenished with a supply of uncooked shellfish, soon became the focus of a veritable seafood feast. After watching for a while, Narcisse understood what to do. He tried placing a handful of mussels on the stone. Seeing that this provoked no response, he carried on, picking the cooked mussels off the stone to enjoy his share of the feast. No one seemed to mind. In the noonday sun, with no breeze to cool the air, the intense heat from the fire was overwhelming. The women and children ate their fill, and so too did Narcisse, savouring every mouthful of salty flesh. After so many days of eating only plain unseasoned meat, charred by hot coals, he relished this feast of shellfish with its taste of the sea, and felt reassured by the inexhaustible abundance of the harvest.

Narcisse and the women slept for a while in the shade of

the trees. He'd seen these same trees everywhere he went, but he still couldn't identify them. After his nap, he went back into the sea to bathe and cool off. The little boy who'd watched him for so long two evenings ago came with him, playing next to him, jumping up and down, turning round and splashing him, shrieking with laughter, then running away and coming back again. This was the first time since Narcisse had been with the tribe that any of them had shown any interest in him. He thought of his cousins and his playmates from school, the hours they'd spent playing in the river or at the village wash house. How far away it all seemed.

With one final leap, the child stopped and stood, gazing intently at Narcisse. Placing his hand to his chest, a serious look on his face, he said: "Waiakh." Then, extending his right hand, his palm turned towards Narcisse, he added: "Amglo."

Narcisse decided to go along with this new game: "Waiakh? That's your name? Waiakh. Amglo. Waiakh. Amglo. And my name is Narcisse."

The child seemed stunned to hear his own words coming out of Narcisse's mouth. "Waiakh," he said again, repeating it several times, before running off to tell his mother and some of the other children about this exchange.

Late that afternoon, the shellfish collecting resumed. The young men emerged gradually from the forest each carrying one or two fine looking fish, placing them on the hot stone over the still burning fire. At dusk, the hunters returned bearing lizards, birds, bats and small furry animals that looked vaguely like cats.

This time, the meal was eaten with no regard for the customary formalities, all the members of the tribe serving themselves as and when they pleased, without waiting their turn as they usually did. Narcisse walked over to the fire and helped himself to one of the fish, a blue specimen with large scales and a prominent snout. No one made any attempt to stop him. He went to sit down a little way away from the group, savoured half of the fish, and hid the rest in some dry leaves. He went back over to the fire and ate his fill of shellfish, and then tried what looked like a pigeon with rather greasy meat. The last of the hunters had arrived and placed their kills on the stone. The old woman provided some water gourds that were passed around from one person to the next. Where had they found the water to fill them? When Narcisse was handed one that was almost full, he took a small sip and went to hide it with the uneaten half of his fish. No one paid any attention and he resumed his place by the fire to eat his fill of shellfish. He managed to sneak away a lizard that he took to hide with the rest of his supplies.

The copious meal raised the spirits of the whole tribe. He'd never heard them laughing and singing like this before, their talk so animated. One couple after another drifted off to walk on the beach. As the last glimmers of light faded into darkness, Narcisse glimpsed two black figures tumbling down to frolic on the sand.

He awoke before dawn. The sky was black, but the darkness was no longer impenetrable. He could see depth and texture in the void. At sea he'd spent many an hour on watch, gazing at the night sky waiting for daybreak. He knew that this quality of translucence heralded the dawn; the first glimmers of light would soon pierce the darkness to the east.

He got up and groped around to find his cache of supplies, and stumbled off into the forest, tripping on unseen obstacles. The tribe were all still sleeping.

When he estimated he was far enough away, he stopped and ate the piece of fish, struggling to keep it from slipping through his fingers. To get to the Bay of Abandon he'd have to follow the coastline. Rather than walking along the beaches and having to negotiate all the inlets, he thought it might be better to climb up on the plateau that rose to a height of about twenty metres and ran parallel to the sea. He could make out individual trees now as the forest became gradually suffused with daylight.

He set out at a good pace, the water pouch in one hand, in the other, the lizard. Beneath him, North Bay gave way to a rocky ridge and then a flooded plain, and then another bay where blocks of coral studded the beach. He had chosen his route well, even without a path to follow. Walking was easier now that there was more light. The tribe would be waking up, they must have noticed that he was not there. He wondered what they would do. Would they realise that he wanted to go back to the spot where he had first set foot in their world. Kermarec, Wanderer and Scarface were probably fast runners. Would they go to the trouble of trying to recapture him? Would they punish him for running away? And what kind of barbaric punishment would they inflict on him?

He would have to pick up his pace if he wanted to get to the Bay of Abandon in time to be there when his rescuers arrived. He knew it was a long way, but how long exactly? The low ridge he'd been following since he left had flattened out and gradually disappeared, to be replaced by the same flat, colourless forest where it was all too easy to get lost. The sea, visible through the trees, was his only means of orienting himself. Cautiously, he made his way towards the coast.

He kept cutting his feet on the blocks of coral that littered the ground. The heat intensified, bringing with it the clouds of flies. He allowed himself a brief pause, drank sparingly and set off once again. How many more hours of walking were ahead of him? And what would he do when he arrived at his destination?

After the interminable forest, he came to a bare, white limestone hill, shaped like the back of a giant tortoise. Looking out from the top of the hill, he saw an unchanging landscape in every direction, indistinguishable from the path he'd just trod. Creeks, low ridges, sunken forests, and far off on the horizon, towards the interior, a line of low blue ridges snaking parallel to the sea and marking the boundary of the coastal plateau.

Not knowing whether he was chasing an illusion or a realistic hope, Narcisse walked on valiantly. The sun was still climbing in the sky when he reached the top of another hill, this one higher and well covered with trees. With mixed emotions he recognised the Bay of Abandon in the distance, with the rock-strewn cliff to the north. No sign of a ship, no sail to be seen either in the bay or out to sea.

The *Saint-Paul*, or any other rescue ship should have been there by now. Had he miscalculated the time it would take them to get to Java and back? Or the amount of time spent preparing for the new crossing? Or had they already come and gone the day before?

He ran to the beach and paced up and down, turning this way and that. Nothing had been left there, no message, no sign of any kind.

Think. He had to think. In the shade of a tree – the same tree that had sheltered him that first day – he forced himself to eat the lizard and drink some water. Should he wait there? He could hold out for three or four days. But if no ship appeared, he would have to go back to North Bay. Would he have the strength to make his way back there? And what if the tribe had left and gone off somewhere else, God knows where.

Should he just go straight back? The two bays were closer

than he had imagined. He could be back by nightfall, eating fish, clams and mussels, pigeons. And drinking, drinking, drinking his fill of water. All day, he'd seen no sign of fresh water; the old woman hadn't shown him where she'd filled the gourds. But what if his shipmates arrived tomorrow? He had to leave a message. The savages were a long way off, they wouldn't see it, and they wouldn't be tempted to come and destroy it as they had his giant stone arrow. There was a large boulder in the middle of the beach. It was a prominent landmark, well above the line of high tide. That was where he would need to write his message. He'd use pebbles this time; he'd write his initials, N. P., and the date. That way, his shipmates would know he'd survived. What day was it now? He'd been abandoned here on the 5th November. He worked out the number of days since then and used pebbles to form a second line of writing: 21st November, followed by an arrow pointing towards the north.

Perhaps they'd see this message tomorrow. They'd know it was only recently written and they would set off to look for him. The *Saint-Paul* would patrol up and down the coast. He would see the sails, he'd light a fire in the forest to signal to them where he was.

When he'd finished his message he started on his route back. He walked for six gruelling hours, the sun high in the sky. He arrived exhausted, parched, not knowing whether he'd made the right decision, wondering how he would be greeted.

No one took any interest in him. He ate some mussels and small fish to replenish his strength and went into the sea to relax. Waiakh followed him, frolicking at his side. That evening the meal was less gargantuan than the previous night's feast, but he managed to grab a large fat pigeon and two bats. He finished eating and within an instant was overcome by sleep.

LETTER V

Monsieur le Président,

Little did I imagine that I would pen my next letter to you aboard ship, but I must now tell you of our crossing from Sydney as passengers on the *Strathmore*. True to his word, the governor, who was only too happy to be relieved of his responsibility towards Narcisse and me, purchased two tickets for the voyage to London. At my insistence, Narcisse was to travel with me in first class, and not, as the officials, ever mindful of making economies, would have had it, in third class.

Not only was this arrangement a matter of principle for me, it was also a practical necessity. Narcisse had begun to make astonishing progress, and every day spent at sea was needed for the continuation of our work. I was concerned too about the effect Narcisse might have on others: so strange were some of his reactions to events, I preferred to be able to observe him at all times.

We bade a hasty farewell to the governor, who scarcely recognised the clean-shaven, modestly dressed man at my side as the creature he had entrusted to me a mere three months earlier. The once naked savage was now attired in grey trousers and a loose white shirt, a blue cravat and a cap of the same colour. Our leave taking completed, we embarked on the *Strathmore* and set sail that evening.

The first days of the crossing were uneventful, with calm seas and fair winds. The first-class passengers began to make acquaintance with one another. Among their number I noted a few officials and members of the civil service returning home after completing their term of duty, a cotton merchant, an English lady on her way to meet her brother in San Francisco and a couple of Scottish missionaries. (Wherever I go, I seem to encounter British missionaries, one or two on every ship. Are there really so many of them?) Narcisse and I mingled little with our fellow passengers: we were the only Frenchmen on board and we had much to do.

Narcisse spent the first morning strolling about on deck, engrossed in observing the ship and its crew. He examined the rigging, the boom and jib and watched intently as the crew manoeuvered the sails or the cabin boy scrubbed the decks. He gazed at the ordinary seamen, the officers and the captain in his gold-braided jacket, and stared out to sea at the wind on the waves. Such close attention did he pay to all these details, that I was provided with further proof, if such were indeed required, of his seafaring past.

But of what he saw, he said nothing. I enquired as to his sentiments upon finding himself on board ship once again, but Narcisse never speaks of his feelings or emotions. I can never be sure, on such occasions, if he has really understood my question. Perhaps he is loath to share his thoughts, or cannot find the words to express himself. Or perhaps he simply has nothing to say.

One afternoon in the deckhouse, the English lady happened to walk past and glance at Narcisse who had rolled up his sleeves to the elbow. Seeing his tattoos, she uttered a cry of astonishment. Having noticed that I spoke English, she asked me about these strange markings. I replied, somewhat brusquely, that my friend had lived on an island in the South Pacific for a number of years and had decided to have himself embellished in this manner. Realising that we were talking about him, although not understanding the precise nature of our exchange, Narcisse smiled at the lady.

The next morning, he joined me in the dining room for breakfast, and informed me excitedly: "I shagged the English woman last night." As if to be sure he had made himself clear, he grasped the crotch of his trousers in a lewd gesture.

Surprised and shocked as I was, I almost burst out laughing and explained to Narcisse that it was not seemly to boast of one's exploits in such a way, nor to make such an uncouth gesture. He was disconcerted by this new rule:

"I must not speak of it?"

"One does not flaunt one's conquests in such a manner. Ladies prefer such things to remain private. You must be discreet."

"I can speak of it, but I must be discreet?"

"Yes, but you do not have to mention it at all. With one's close friends one can discuss such matters. Sometimes it is better, more amusing, not to divulge one's secrets. One should not make too much of these things."

"What do you mean?"

"Well, for example, instead of the gesture you made, you can wink, or just raise your thumb. That is all you need to do."

I winked at him to show him what I meant, and he tried it

himself before asking:

"What about you? Did you shag in Sydney? Or on the ship?"

I beg you to forgive me, Sir, for repeating Narcisse's words in all their coarseness. You instructed me to make a note of everything – scientific enquiry should never be compromised by mere notions of good taste – and, if you will indulge me by reading my missive to the end, you will understand the significance of his choice of words.

I explained to Narcisse that one did not ask such direct questions and that I preferred not to give him an answer.

"But we are friends, close friends?"

Dismayed to see that he had misunderstood, I smiled and reassured him on the subject of our friendship. Sensible of my reticence, he showed remarkable tact and did not press me any further on the subject. He then announced: "In Sydney, I didn't shag. Didn't want to."

What did he mean by this? Had the linen girl propositioned him? I was unable to restrain myself from asking him to clarify this.

"In the house. Bill signals to me to come into his room. Then he puts his hand on my belly, and lower down. I ask him why. He shows me he wants to shag me. I say no. I leave the room."

I was completely taken aback by this confession. I had rescued this convict from the penal colony, given him my trust and employed him in my service. He had taken advantage of that trust to indulge in the basest of his vices under my roof and had singled out Narcisse as the least likely to offer any resistance. One can imagine what depravity must be rife in the penal colony, but I was nevertheless astounded by the depths of this scoundrel's ingratitude. I reproached myself bitterly for having left Narcisse open to such abuse. Every day that passes brings further confirmation of the extent of my obligation towards this young man. This incident reminded me yet again that I alone am responsible for Narcisse.

Bill's vile overtures called for a long explanation, but nothing would have made me more uncomfortable than a discussion of this subject. Without pausing to weigh up the most appropriate response, I said simply: "You acted correctly."

So shocked was I to learn of the convict Bill's degenerate nature, that I did not immediately perceive the most important element of this conversation. Narcisse's very words were: "I shagged the English woman."

Where had he learnt this obscene word? Certainly not from me. And on board ship, as in Sydney, he heard no French from anyone but me. Could it be that his new lady friend had taught him this expression?

At the risk of making a scene, I resolved to clear up the matter. Some time later, I passed the lady in question on the gangway. I greeted her in French with a courteous *"Bonjour, madame,"* and in the same conversational tone one might adopt to exchange pleasantries, I enquired : *"Alors, vous avez baisé avec mon ami?"* repeating the very words Narcisse had used. But she registered no understanding of my impudent question, and I was neither slapped nor castigated for my insolence. She merely asked me to repeat in English what I had said. I excused myself for my momentary lapse into French, uttered an appropriately banal pleasantry, and continued on my way, satisfied that this woman had played no part in the conundrum before me.

I perceived that the only possible explanation was that Narcisse had spontaneously recovered this lewd expression.

He had no doubt uttered it frequently during his seafaring days, when he must have played his part in the daily round of swearing and bragging with his shipmates. Proud of his recent amorous exploit and wishing to tell me about it, he had summoned up the expression from the depths of his memory. Perhaps there had already been other less striking words that he had recovered in a similar fashion. I began to see that in his lessons with me, he was not merely learning French; he was rediscovering it, often quite independently of my efforts, and with a rapidity that would have been truly astonishing had he indeed forgotten it entirely.

Imagine, if you will, that his knowledge of our language remains frozen within him, bound in ice, and that it has not simply disappeared from his mind like a page of writing dissolved in water. Our conversations are like warm breezes wafting over the frozen block; from the moment I began to read Racine's verse to him, the ice has been melting, slowly at first, and then with gathering speed. And as it does so, the language locked inside gradually emerges from the frost that binds it. I am reminded of spring in Iceland, visions of snowdrops piercing through the snow as the meadows are released from their winter wrapping. And I had that English woman to thank for having enabled me to see this.

In the days that followed, this same lady would often retire to her cabin in the afternoon complaining of seasickness. Narcisse would disappear a few moments later. And the next morning in the dining room, he would wink and give me a thumbs-up gesture.

Three days before our arrival in Valparaiso, we were taking the air on the poop deck, conversing about nothing in particular. To say we were conversing is perhaps a little misleading, since our dialogue was largely confined to my efforts to engage Narcisse on all manner of subjects. He listened and occasionally, all too rarely, responded with a few words. I reminded him that upon our return to France he would be able to continue with his old life and we would go our separate ways. Sad as I would be to bring to a close our singular adventure, I would accept that this was the appropriate course of action. I added, half to myself: "*C'est la vie.*" He asked me to repeat what I had just said, a request he had never yet made until this moment. I did as he asked, and carefully enunciating every word, repeated that we would go our separate ways, adding as before: "*C'est la vie.*" Narcisse then said quite clearly: "Vie... Vie... Gil... Vie."

He did not usually make spontaneous associations between words, and "Gil" was a new addition, as new as the vulgar expression on the subject of which I have already importuned you too much. I was taken aback by the solemn air of concentration Narcisse adopted as he continued to mutter: "Gil... Vie... Gil."

Was the word "*vie*" itself reviving a vague memory of another life? And who or what was this "gil" or "gilles"? Prompted perhaps by the sight of the sea and the waves, my thoughts turned to a small fishing town in the Vendée, Saint-Gilles-sur-Vie. Without wishing to exert undue influence on Narcisse's ruminations, I suggested:

"Gilles-sur-Vie?" Narcisse responded immediately with "Saint-Gilles-sur-Vie," a look of astonishment on his face. We were both taken aback by his prompt completion of this name.

"Are you acquainted with the town of Saint-Gilles-sur-Vie?"

"I don't know."

He repeated the name several times, as if to savour its sonorities, or perhaps to summon up further sounds or more precise memories.

"Narcisse, do you come from Saint-Gilles-sur-Vie? Did you live there? Are your parents there?"

He did not reply, but went aft to stare into the water and contemplate the ship's wake. What were his thoughts as he gazed at the line carved by the ship in the water, a line that led directly to Australia? In deference to his desire for solitude, I left him alone.

As I pondered the significance of this spontaneous recall of the town's name I wondered if Saint-Gilles-sur-Vie was indeed the place of his birth. Was this his childhood home, the scene of his schooldays, his earliest games? For what name other than that of his childhood home could spring forth with such force from a memory as shattered as his?

No longer a man with no identity, the white savage now has a name and a place of origin: Narcisse from Saint-Gilles-sur-Vie.

I wrote a letter to the Mayor of Saint-Gilles-sur-Vie, asking him if a son of the town had disappeared ten or twenty years before during a long sea voyage.

With every passing day, as we come closer to Europe, I begin to take stock of what awaits Narcisse, and of the experiences to which I shall be exposing him.

Our next port of call was Valparaiso, where we made a brief stop. The captain did not wish to make landfall for fear of losing members of his crew to the gold fever that was laying waste to ships' crews faster than an epidemic of cholera. Men were flocking to California from all over the world, eager to join the gold rush and seek their fortune. We therefore remained at anchor in the bay while the dinghy went ashore carrying the mail and with it the aforementioned English lady, still complaining of seasickness. As soon as the dinghy returned, loaded with fresh supplies for the ship, the captain was eager to depart.

We set sail that very afternoon, our course set for the south.

Before long the weather turned foul and a storm was soon upon us. The next week was spent in a prolonged battle to round Cape Horn, where the notorious winter passage proved equal to its reputation. I hardly need to describe to you the raging seas and louring green-tinged skies we encountered, nor the ever-present dangers of icebergs and monstrous waves, or the spectacle of albatross and giant petrel, those great seabirds, borne aloft and buffeted by the winds. You are well acquainted with it all.

I was quite undone by the pitching and rolling of the ship, as were most of the other passengers. Gigantic waves crashed against the hull. At night my bunk was tossed around with the heaving of the ship; sleep was impossible, dreams mercifully denied. Eating was out of the question. I lacked the strength even to pay attention to Narcisse, let alone to engage him in conversation.

Seemingly unaffected by the storm, Narcisse kept his sea legs and maintained a healthy appetite. After three days of idleness, he was bored and expressed a wish to help manoeuvring the sails. Unable to dissuade him from his plan, and in a rare moment when the turmoil of my stomach allowed, I informed the captain. I stressed that this was not a mere whim and that my friend had considerable seafaring experience. The captain of the *Strathmore*, no doubt imagining that Narcisse was no more than an amateur yachtsman, responded with a polite refusal: it was out of the question to send a first-class passenger into the rigging at the height of a storm. Only in the most extreme circumstances would he consider such a thing, and the ship was certainly in no danger of sinking. Furthermore, Narcisse would be unable to understand the orders shouted to the crew in English. I concurred on this point but asked that he be permitted to take the helm.

Weary of arguing, the captain gave his assent and authorised Narcisse to double up at the helm with the man on watch. He wagered a bottle of port that my friend would not last the hour.

The bosun provided Narcisse with the necessary attire: a jacket and trousers of quilted oilcloth, a hat and some woollen gloves, and a pair of boots which Narcisse declined to wear, preferring to stand and face the snow squalls in his bare feet.

He steered the ship all day. Long forgotten skills came back to him and within a few minutes of taking the helm Narcisse was guiding the ship through the waves as it surged through the troughs and crested the waves. Keeping the stern starboard to the wind, he held the *Strathmore* on course. The crew said nothing to him: their voices would have been drowned by the howling of the wind and the hammering of the rain glancing off the desks. Even the sailor assigned to the helm with Narcisse was satisfied to watch in mystified silence, grateful for the respite from his task.

At the end of the watch, Narcisse refused to be relieved, and declined the food and restorative tea offered to him. The first watch was replaced by a less experienced helmsman who was happy to let Narcisse take command. Towards three o'clock, the man was thrown by a huge wave and banged his head on a piece of copper fitting, gashing his brow and forehead. Blinded by blood and knocked almost senseless, he went inside to have his wounds tended. I do not know if the watch officer was aware of his absence, but in any case, he was not replaced.

After the sun went down, Narcisse finally left his post and went straight to his bunk to go to sleep, without eating or removing his soaking wet clothes. I made the effort to go to dinner with the intention of trying to take a little soup, and the captain acknowledged that he owed me a bottle of port wine. I urged him to give it to the crew once we were out of these treacherous waters.

The next morning, I learned that Narcisse had awoken around midnight and returned to lend a helping hand to the helmsmen on successive watches until dawn – a dawn that in these climes is marked only by the moment when a cold silvery light begins to filter through the dense clouds, revealing the grey foamy seas that soon become one with the clouds.

For the next week, Narcisse would spend eight to ten hours at the helm and only three or four hours sleeping. He ate nothing but a piece of bread, which he kept in his pocket and nibbled slowly. The other passengers were too sick to notice any of this, but the officers and deckhands expressed both their admiration and their appreciation.

Finally, as the *Strathmore* rounded the Horn and set a course for the north, we sailed into the Atlantic. Violent stormy conditions and crashing waves gave way to mere bad weather and deep but regular swells. Narcisse left his post, removed his waterproofs and left them in the gangway, went to bed and slept uninterrupted for three days and nights.

Thus, he who had not sailed since he had been shipwrecked many years before, had recovered the essential skills of his calling during the storm. His memory is coming back in stages: in addition to words, names, and the memory of his place of birth, there are also the innate skills of a sailor secure in his seafaring knowledge.

When he had rested and recovered, I asked him why he had put himself in this position: the ship was not in any danger and he could have stayed in the warm and waited for the storms to abate.

"The men were finding it difficult. I had to help them."

This was all the response he gave. When the captain came to thank him he was no more successful than I in eliciting a more elaborate response.

Nevertheless I now had three pieces of information about the white savage: his Christian name, Narcisse; his occupation, sailor; and the name of a significant place: Saint-Gilles-sur-Vie. Will this be enough to restore him to his old life? And to ascertain the circumstances of his shipwreck?

A week after the end of the storm, one of the crew of the *Strathmore* came to see me, cap in hand. He informed me that the men were very grateful for the assistance my friend had afforded them and wished to make him a small gift. I translated this for Narcisse, who responded with a broad smile. From his hat, the sailor produced a miniature ship's hull on which were engraved the words: "Around Cape Horn" and the date of our passage. He proffered it to Narcisse who received it with an air of earnestness and gravity that more than compensated for words. Then he turned to me and said:

"They have given me a gift. I must give them a gift."

I had spent enough time in the South Pacific to know something of this form of courtesy. Turning my mind to the question of what we could give in exchange, I decided to send for another bottle of port wine. Narcisse presented the gift to the English sailor with an air of grave solemnity. Indeed one might almost have thought one was observing two ambassadors in the Sublime Porte of the Ottomans or the Imperial Court of the Emperor of China, so great was the seriousness with which the gifts were exchanged.

Since that moment, Narcisse has kept this small wooden token with him at all times.

I watch Narcisse as he gazes at the sea. We have now spent four months constantly in one another's company. No longer the terrified, mute white savage, the once alarming figure has become a smiling, reserved travelling companion who attracts little attention.

And I wonder if I too have been transformed by this adventure. The observations that I have made have begun to undermine the certainty of my beliefs. What exactly does it mean to be a savage? Had Narcisse indeed become truly savage and if so when exactly did he become civilised once again? At what time, and on what date? What does the manner of his learning teach us about the very act of learning itself? And which of us is the pupil, which the teacher?

I have no answers for these questions. I can only be sure that Narcisse's story is more than a mere footnote in history. I have learned much in the course of my life. I studied at the lycée in Grenoble, I have read widely, I have made visits to the Geographical Society, and my travels in Iceland and in the Pacific granted me insights into myself. All this has been a preparation for my encounter with Narcisse, but no part of it has given me the means to understand him. I have no tools with which to analyse what his transformation teaches us. And so, I am beginning to understand that I will have to forge those tools myself.

When we arrive in France, my mission will not be complete. How could I just abandon him on the quay? If I am successful in finding his parents, Narcisse will continue with his life in the bosom of his family. And if not, he will be settled by me in a place where his future will be assured. But my notes from months of continuous observation of him must form the basis of a vast enquiry of which I can scarcely yet discern the rudiments. I do not know if I will have the strength or the courage to bring this to fruition. The tale of Narcisse is more than the story of the man himself: any theories derived from his experiences will extend beyond his own personal story. And the anecdotes generated by his eventual return to France, the variety and appeal of which I can well imagine, will not be mere distractions. They will be obstacles in my path to understanding. I must not forget this.

I shall require your assistance, Sir, in attaining my lofty ambition. I can sense, at last, the direction that my life may take, if I do indeed manage to keep myself on this course. I wonder what Narcisse's future will be. Will the coming years be any more remarkable for him than for me?

I look forward with great anticipation to reading your wise counsel in the letters which I hope will await me upon my arrival in the Azores.

I remain your faithful servant...

6

After the day's long march, he awoke the next morning to renewed pangs of hunger.

Something had changed in the life of the tribe: no more laughter and games, no more wandering about in groups. The natives were muttering and seemed worried. At first he was afraid it might have been because of him and his escapade to the Bay of Abandon, but their indifference towards him remained unchanged.

The pregnant woman was lying on the ground a short distance from the group, moaning. The old woman squatted at her head, burning herbs. Scarface sat at her feet. Narcisse supposed he must be the father of the child.

No one was preparing any food. He walked down to the sea and since he still could not see any signs of a fire being lit, decided to eat as many mussels as he could find, right then and there. He thought he heard a dull, low sound, like a canon being fired in the distance. The *Saint-Paul*? Or was it just a tree falling in the forest? With great difficulty he resolved not to let himself give way to hope, and returned to his meal. There was no repeat of the sound and he found this strangely reassuring.

All day long, the pregnant woman writhed in agony, by

turns groaning, crying out in pain and moaning. Around her sat all the mothers, softly intoning an ominous-sounding chant. The men and boys kept their distance, conscious of their inability to help. Chief went back and forth between the two groups, making brief speeches and waving his arms about.

She died as the sun sank behind the trees. Her departure was hailed with cries and sobs from the women, while Scarface rejoined the men, devastated. The mothers collected up the children and headed into the forest a few minutes later. Waiakh, followed by the old woman, and lastly Quartermaster came and signalled emphatically to Narcisse to follow the group. He did as he was told.

They marched on through the forest, joylessly and in silence until the dead of night. Then, their bellies empty, they all simply stopped where they were and went to sleep. At daybreak, they took up their march again, arriving around midday at a new bay that Narcisse decided to call Round Bay. Walking at a good pace in a straight line, it couldn't be more than three hours from Round Bay to North Bay. This meant that it was nine or ten hours to the Bay of Abandon. But what good did it do to draw maps in his head? It had been easy to escape the first time, but in the end, he'd had to go back. Did he really want to set off again on an even more back-breaking walk, and risk having to turn round and come back once he reached the Bay of Abandon?

Waiakh came back over to him and said the two words again: "Waiakh. Amglo." But Narcisse did not respond to his overture. To keep himself busy, he set about building a shelter out of branches wedged between two bushes and a rock. Tonight, instead of digging himself into the sand like a dog, he'd sleep in his make-shift little house.

Constructing this shelter gave him another idea: perhaps

he could build a raft, a canoe, or a crude skiff and escape by sea. Staying close to the coast he'd probably be able to get to Sydney in two weeks. Why two? He didn't really know but he stuck to this estimate. At sea, he might encounter a ship that could rescue him.

He was completely naked of course and he didn't have his knife. What exactly would he need to build a boat? Wood, and fire to harden the logs, binding to secure them together. He had none of these things, and no idea how to go about building a vessel, but just having a plan filled him with joy. He wouldn't get any help from the natives, but they paid no attention to him anyway and wouldn't stand in his way. Their constant moving about would be a problem, but perhaps they would camp for more than just a few nights by the sea. When that happened, he'd have to be ready.

What sort of wood should he use? The trees in the sandy forest were all of the same kind. But there were the mangroves too with their twisted trunks. He broke off a few branches of different sizes, and picked up some fallen branches. Choosing a rock that jutted out, he set out his selection of sticks and hurled them one by one into the sea. The green and grey branches sank quickly and were soon dispersed by the current. But he wasn't discouraged: he'd need to try other things, char some of the branches over a flame. By experimenting like this, he'd find the best material.

But building some kind of floating vessel was only the first hurdle.

He'd have to find a way of propelling the boat, by sail or by rowing. He'd have to navigate carefully, hugging the coast, and come back to land at night. The greatest danger was of being carried out to sea and having no more landmarks. And he'd have to watch out for sheer cliffs, tidal streams, wind shifts, powerful waves and other hazards.

What would he live on? He knew he wouldn't be able to go more than four or five days without eating, and given the way the tribe seemed to live, he couldn't see any way he'd be able to build up a supply of food. And what about water? It hadn't been hard to steal one or two of the drinking gourds, but to take the tribe's whole stock?

His skiff would have to be equipped with some sort of chest for supplies. And a keel of sorts to be able to steer a steady course. With a paddle to propel the boat, a pole to use in the shallows and a stone to act as an anchor. Bit by bit, a basic canoe was beginning to take shape in his mind.

If he were to leave, it would be all or nothing. There would be no turning back – who knows what the tribe would do if his attempt were to fail? His plan would be to head south, towards Sydney or the first white settlement he came to.

Of course, he was without any of the things he needed for his escape, and he had no idea how to go about making them. But rather than just waiting to be rescued by a passing ship, or helped by the natives themselves, he would concentrate on patiently learning how to do what he needed. He would devote himself to making preparations, to tirelessly checking every detail. When the opportunity arose, he'd be ready to take his chances.

He knew what dangers awaited him at sea, but on dry land there were hidden dangers that he knew little about. Wild animals, impenetrable swamps, poisonous insects, tribes more savage than the one he was with. Escape by land or by sea? Which should he choose?

There was no reason to make a rushed decision. No reason at all.

He had plenty of time. Coming back to the group of women, he saw that the men and boys had still not joined them. They had probably stayed behind at North Bay for some kind of funeral ritual. He was alone with all the women of the tribe.

How many hours had he spent on the forecastle, talking and joking about just such a situation? How much time spent imagining a place far removed from the cold and wet, away from the cramped life on board ship with orders being shouted day and night. Alone on a far-away beach, lying idly beneath the trees, surrounded by naked women. They all knew it was just a fantasy. It had been all too easy then to while away the time waiting for their turn at the watch, regaling each other with obscene tales, boasting of improbable amorous exploits. The older men with their talk of ports of call in the tropics, fleshed out with lewd details, the younger men dreaming of women with burnished skin and long black hair. None of it would ever be real.

And yet here he was, naked and alone, surrounded by naked women. But this was a waking nightmare. The irony was not lost on him. He thought of his shipmate Kermarec, the biggest braggart of them all on board the *Saint-Paul*, and sighed: "Well, Kermarec, old mate, what wouldn't I give to change places with you now."

He was startled out of his gloomy reverie by a flurry of activity among the women. They were hurrying towards the sandy point at the northern end of Round Bay. Waiakh was calling to them, shouting gleefully. He'd found a turtle on the sand. The women joined him, and using sticks to lever it they turned the creature over on its back, and dragged it back to the camp on a bed of hastily woven branches.

Reaching the camp, where Narcisse, the old woman and

the mothers and babies had remained, they built a fire. Using a pointed shell, they cut the turtle's throat, and took turns to drink the blood as it flowed from the neck. They cut up the still warm carcass and placed the pieces of meat on flat rocks wedged against the fire. The strips of white meat began to sputter and brown, giving off a faint smell. Cautiously, Narcisse took a strip, cooked it for a moment on the other side, a finishing touch not copied by the others, and stuck it in his mouth. He bit happily into the meat, thinking it tasted a bit like veal. Now he understood why the old hands on the *Saint-Paul* spoke so highly of turtle meat. The women ate heartily too. He took another piece and sprinkled seawater on the still uncooked strips, to salt them. After so many days of surviving on shellfish, bits of fish and tough under-cooked meat, he felt his mouth water in anticipation of the taste of the grilled meat.

The men had still not come back, and the women had eaten their fill and gradually moved away to sleep under the trees. Only the night before, their sister or their cousin had died, and yet they had devoured their food and eaten as much as they could. Narcisse carried on cooking and savouring his turtle steaks, less greedily now, sensing his strength gradually coming back. He was starting to feel fit again, fit as he had been before the march to the Bay of Abandon, before the fever, before the hunger of his first days here, and before the fatal crossing from the Cape. Licking his greasy fingers, he forced himself to take yet another piece, telling himself that any meat left over would only rot in the sun, but he couldn't eat another mouthful. When would there be another feast like this? He walked back to his hut and went straight to sleep.

Later that afternoon, when the heat had gone out of the day, he began to wake gradually from his slumber and realised his hand was on his cock. He pressed a little harder and felt it stiffen in response. A shiver of well-being coursed through his body and he felt himself swell with pride. Sheltered from prying eyes in his make-shift hut, his eyes half-closed, he carried on. After all, what was he doing? Only what he used to do on board ship, at night in his hammock, when he wasn't too exhausted, and when he couldn't wait any longer for the next round of shore leave pleasures. Before the whore in the Cape, there had been the one in Bordeaux, a large placid woman plying her trade in one of the port's whorehouses, where he and his companions had celebrated being paid just before they left for China. And before Bordeaux, there was Nantes, and others before that. But he couldn't recall any of them in detail. Only the woman in the Cape, barely seen in the dim light of a candle. The fifteen minutes he had spent with her came back to him.

As his hand moved up and down, he saw himself again in his hammock on the *Saint-Paul*, returning excited from his visit to the tavern in the African night. The small courtyard with the shack, the straw mattress – he saw himself being careful not to move about too much under the covers, not wanting to draw attention to himself and become the butt of his shipmates' jokes. Since his arrival here, he had been living among these naked black women, but he did not think of them as women. He felt no desire of any kind for them, they seemed to belong to another species. That was why he had grown used to living naked in their midst so quickly. He and his shipmates used to make jokes and claim they were capable of having sex with just about any kind of creature. Some of them would still refuse the "black stuff" in the whorehouses of the Cape, but not him. The women of the tribe, though, these women who did not cover themselves at all, who lay down with men without any attempt to be discreet. No, he could never think about it.

So long as he was here, the only possibility was abstinence – or this solitary pleasure he had become used to. He moved his right hand, provoking familiar sensations, instinctive and pleasant. Ever since he had been stranded here, he had known no pleasure at all. Only fear, hunger, pain, thirst, boredom, fatigue, despair, bitterness, misery. One after another, and sometimes mixed up together. Never a moment of joy. And now, with this pleasure he accorded himself, he was filled with a feeling of satisfaction: putting all his cares out of his mind, he concentrated on obeying the burning demands of his flesh.

What was there in this to feel proud of? And why could he not take himself back to that straw mattress in the Cape, his body moving urgently against the woman's black body? Try as he could, all he could remember was the night one week later, when they had finally reached the temperate latitudes again after the squalls and snow flurries since the Cape. Demands on the crew were lighter, and he had finished his watch and gone back to the crew's quarters in the 'tweendecks. Taking off his clothes, he hung them on a nail and groped his way towards his hammock where he lay down under the meagre covers and touched his hand to his drawers. Listening attentively to his own breathing and the creaking movements of the ship, he was transported once again to the whorehouse in the Cape to take his three guinea's worth a second time from the woman whose services he had paid for. And now, lying in the hollowed-out sand that served for a floor in his makeshift hut, he saw himself again in his hammock, completely absorbed in his solitary pleasure, trying not to wake the others.

He closed his eyes, spread his legs, and with bated breath, emptied his mind of all else.

Afterwards, curled up into a ball and back again in North

Bay, he began to cry. The tears flowed freely, and just as he had earlier surrendered himself to pleasure, now he wept with abandon. It was as if the tears running down his cheeks were carrying all the helplessness he felt: his inability to live with the tribe and the impossibility of living without it. He had gradually become accustomed to the physical suffering, the uncertainty of his fate, to his nakedness and the revolting food. But immeasurably more painful than any of this was the absolute isolation: he realised that he was condemned to live utterly without human relationships. Friendship, companionship, love, understanding, respect, seduction, sex, the whole range of human emotions; from now on they were beyond his reach. And there was no one to share his experiences – that was what caused him the most profound despair. In these tears of self-pity there was some comfort to be had.

The village curate used to tell the boys that doing bad things at night in their beds would make their guardian angel cry. Well, let the angel cry then! Let him cry too. Or else, let him come and save Narcisse instead of staying up there safe and sound in heaven.

Not once had he seen any of the savages in the tribe crying. No, he had nothing in common with them. He wanted nothing to do with any of them, their women, their daughters. He would remain alone, with his solitary pleasures, his lonely musings, his worries, his plans and his memories.

The tide was coming in and he got up and went to wash himself off in the waves. Waiakh came over to him, wanting to play, but he refused to acknowledge the boy and carried on walking into the water until Waiakh could follow him no further. He went deeper, until the water came up to his chin. In the distance, the waves were breaking on the reef, fragile white hills disappearing and re-emerging on the horizon. A frigate bird hovered up above, only to be joined before long by a second bird in an elegant dance in the sky. What if he just stayed here and waited? He could not swim. The water would come up slowly, it would reach his mouth, his nose, his eyes. Just a small amount of courage and determination, that's all it would take. To wait until the warm sea engulfed him, set him free.

A wave came up and filled his mouth with seawater. He spat it out, turned round to face the horizon and murmured: "My name is Narcisse Pelletier. I am a sailor on the schooner *Saint-Paul*."

LETTER VI

Monsieur le Président,

Your letter of the 25th July was awaiting me at the hotel. I must protest, sir, you are too generous with your praise and that I am undeserving of the compliments you pay me for the progress Narcisse has made in Australia. My more recent letters will have given you invaluable information on this subject and will, I hope, have addressed some of your questions and suggestions. I am deeply grateful to you for your part in this dialogue conducted across the oceans, and I look forward to our correspondence being conducted henceforth with greater ease now that the vast distance that separated us has been so much reduced.

These three days in London have passed like lightning, amid much confusion.

We disembarked from the *Strathmore* early in the morning and travelled by carriage from the docks to the Savoy. Narcisse gazed at the warehouses, the factories and smoke, the parks and blackened buildings, the palaces, the dome of St.

Paul's Cathedral, the grey skies, the crowds, children, horses, women in their hats, the crossroads, constables, horse-drawn carriages, shops, tree-lined avenues and gentlemen dressed in black. This spectacle of a capital of Empire seemed to plunge him into a stupor. I had to take him by the arm and lead him out of the carriage and into the hotel, and then across the great hall and up to his room, where he went over to stand by the window. He remained there, standing motionless and silent all afternoon, watching the street scenes.

For in truth, what does he know of our world? An isolated house at the end of a sound, a clipper, and a glimpse of the small town that is Sydney? And now to find himself here, in what is perhaps the world's largest and most modern city. I had not previously given this much thought, but even so, what could I have done?

While Narcisse was gazing at London, I made arrangements for our journey to France, on the new railway from London to Dover, and again from Calais to Paris.

Within the pile of letters handed to me by the concierge was an envelope marked from Saint-Gilles-sur-Vie. I picked it up, my heart in my mouth. I trust that you will understand why I opened this missive from the mayor of that town before I turned my attention to your own letter. The mayor wrote:

"*Monsieur le Vicomte,*

Your letter posted in Valparaiso on the 22nd June has reawakened sad memories. The person whose past you seek to establish is most certainly Narcisse Pelletier, born on the 13th May 1825, the youngest son of a shoemaker of excellent repute in this town. He enlisted as a sailor at around the age of fifteen, and sailed first as a cabin boy and then as a sailor on various ships. With the fearlessness of youth, he signed on willingly for a series of long voyages, finding the time occasionally to return to the embrace of his parents, brother and sister between voyages.

He embarked in Bordeaux on the schooner *Saint-Paul* bound for China and perished at sea between the Cape of Good Hope and Java on the 5th November 1843. The date and the circumstances of his demise are recorded thus on the death certificate.

His whole family and all of Saint-Gilles were devastated at the loss of this fine young man who left only good memories of his all too brief life. His parents have never fully recovered from this loss; they feel it keenly even now, eighteen years later. The birth of grandchildren, of whom one is named Narcisse, has done little to ease their suffering.

I therefore did not wish to speak to them of your singular request, the motive for which I have not managed to fully grasp. I fail to understand why this tragic event from so long ago should be revived. I beg you to explain to me the reasons for your enquiries and entreat you not to undertake anything ill-conceived. We must avoid inflicting further unnecessary suffering on this unfortunate family. If, as I imagine, you have gleaned some information on Narcisse's last moments from someone who was witness to the event, I urge you to inform no one but me and to accept that I should be the sole judge as to whether or not the Pelletier family should be informed.

I appeal to your humanity, and in the hope of receiving further explanations from you,

I remain..."

Upon reading this, I felt an urge to throw myself upon Narcisse, to give him back his name, his age, his past, and let him know that his parents are still alive. But I restrained myself, and forced myself to reread the letter and reflect upon it. Why had the mayor used the words "perished at sea"? Both the governor and I had always assumed that Narcisse was the sole survivor of a shipwreck – or that he was the only one to have survived a sojourn among the natives. The mayor implied that he had died of illness or as a result of an accident aboard ship and that the ship had continued on its journey. The captain had made a report, noting the exact date, and had completed all the formalities. A sailor who perishes aboard ship is buried at sea. How could Narcisse have survived? Something was amiss here and I could make no sense of it.

If he was born in 1825, Narcisse must have been eighteen when for some reason as yet to be discerned, he ceased to be a seaman aboard the *Saint-Paul*, and was cast adrift in the wilds of Australia. He must have spent eighteen years living among the savages. Eighteen years! Some unknown drama had cut his life into two halves of equal length. Two halves that each ended in the same sudden and brutal change from one life to the other. Twice he had had to make the leap between ignorance and civilisation. Eighteen years! How could a man stand such a degree of isolation? Impossible even to imagine it.

I replied immediately to the mayor of Saint-Gilles, explaining to him briefly how I had met a citizen of his administration in Australia: a sailor by the name of Narcisse who had spent many years living amongst the natives, and had forgotten everything of his past. I concluded my account with a brief description of Narcisse, not mentioning his tattoos. I begged him to inform Narcisse's parents of his imminent return, approaching the matter with all due sensitivity as befits the announcement of such unexpected happiness. I stressed that it is, of course, essential that Narcisse be returned to his family. Once all the preparations were made for the prodigal son's return, the mayor could then inform us in Paris, and I would bring Narcisse to them without further delay.

"Sees-Ti-Ay-Oo-Pawl." Now I understood the meaning of those inarticulate cries uttered by the white savage in the first days of our acquaintance. Those meaningless syllables that had puzzled me so much were none other than the words: "Narcisse Pelletier of the schooner *Saint-Paul*." These fragments of words, their meaning lost to him, were the last thread linking him to his past, a final mark of identity to which he had clung.

No sooner had I finished penning this letter to the mayor, than I was informed that a journalist from the Daily Mirror wished to speak to us. I went down alone to receive him in the reception area. The young man in question informed me, somewhat nonchalantly, that he had learnt of Narcisse's story. When I asked him how he had done so he replied that an English lady, recently arrived in San Francisco from Sydney, had recounted the story to her brother in California. Silently I cursed the woman, this unscrupulous adventuress and her thoughtless chatter. I listened with mounting irritation to the fatuous questions of this ignorant scribbler who was undoubtedly incapable of finding Australia on a map. Was Narcisse a cannibal? Were his extraordinary tattoos a record of the enemies he had killed in battle? Had he married the chief's three daughters? Why had he attacked the sailors who rescued him, leaving the ship's captain no choice but to use a fishing net to capture him? I calmly disabused him of all this nonsense and did my best to give an account of Narcisse's gentle nature, his rapid progress in regaining his French and his manners. I was careful to avoid mentioning the failures and misunderstandings, the episode with the so-called English lady and his refusal to divulge any information about the time he had spent among the savages. And of course, I said nothing that might reveal his identity. The journalist took notes, only half listening to what I was saying, and said that he wished to speak to Narcisse, to which I said no. Perhaps I was wrong to do so, but the journalist did not insist and left without further ado.

Scarcely had I returned to my room and sat down at my desk than Narcisse burst in, his clothing all awry and with an expression of confusion that I had not seen in him before. He simply said: "Come," in a tone of voice that brooked no opposition and went back towards his adjoining room. There I beheld a serving woman from the hotel, in her underskirts, adjusting her bodice and muttering insults under her breath. I asked her what had happened and she replied in the appalling accents of the lower classes of London:

"Your friend there, wot don't understand a word of English. 'E was quite 'appy to come on all luvvy-duvvy and get me into 'is bed. But now 'es got wot 'e wanted, 'e won't give me my little present."

It took only a few shillings to persuade the girl to leave. I then had to try to explain to Narcisse what had happened. It is incomprehensible to him that the act of love should be purchased. It appears that for him, love between a man and a woman is justified in and of itself. He cannot conceive of seeking to derive any benefit other than the immediate pleasure bestowed by the act itself. And whatever the peculiarities of this particular commercial transaction, it is merely one manifestation of a wider reality that Narcisse understands even less: the question of money. He cannot eat the coins that I place in his hand, he cannot warm himself with them. They serve no purpose. I have failed utterly in trying to impart this dual lesson.

We continued to discuss this for almost an hour. To an observer, our exchange might have seemed quite scurrilous at times, at others, frankly comical.

I now understand how naïve I have been. Narcisse may wear trousers and drink from a glass, but does this mean that he has returned to our world? Narcisse, who is so far removed from us and from the fundamental principles of our societies, imitates what he can of our behaviour. I may think that I am leading him along a straight and well-marked path, but he is undoubtedly lost in a dense forest where all is strange to him. Am I simply taming him as one would an animal? A performing dog who does tricks? A mere illusion? I perceive that with every step he takes towards more civilised behaviour, Narcisse still remains implacably beyond my grasp.

Have all the inhabitants of London conspired to disturb me? Now the local detective constable has come to see me saying that he has been informed of the presence of a Frenchman not possessed of the requisite documents. I showed him the statement from the colonial judge in Sydney to satisfy him on this point, but he still wished to see Narcisse to ask him a few questions. I translated for Narcisse who did his best but had great difficulty following the constable's enquiries. Eventually, he appeared satisfied and left us alone.

In the evening I was able to peruse at leisure the appendix to your letter, in which you replied to a suggestion I had taken the liberty of making to you three months ago. In particular, I thank you for the research into published reports of survival tales from sailors shipwrecked in hostile lands.

I must exclude accounts of those unfortunates who were nevertheless blessed in having companions. Even if there were only two survivors in the group, they would derive strength and courage from each other and would have the advantage of speaking their mother tongue daily, all of which were denied to Narcisse. Similarly, I must exclude any modern Robinson Crusoe cast away on a desert island. I do not wish to imply that their sufferings were not as great. But the trials of those whose only adversary was nature itself cannot be compared to the travails faced by Narcisse.

The only cases that remain are those of lone sailors among native peoples. The majority of these were deserters. The attractions of a tropical island and the prospect of an idle and carefree existence, with smiling women and fertile soils have often proved too much of a temptation for sailors, especially for those disreputable individuals only too happy to escape the discipline of life aboard ship. Ensconced within the tribe, and having usually taken a wife and put down some roots, they generally become involved in trading, facilitating negotiations between passing ships and their adopted family. Some of them, living in the islands of the South Seas rich in sea cucumber and sandalwood have secured advantageous positions. Having never forgotten the life they have chosen to leave, these men are intermediaries between two worlds, and know how to negotiate to their own best advantage.

We must also consider as unique the situation of missionaries, both Catholic and Protestant. The strength they derive from their devotion to the service of God is unequalled. Deserters and missionaries alike may indeed live alone among natives, sometimes among the most terrifying savages, but they have chosen to do so.

After this sifting of accounts, we are left with seven

recorded cases of lone sailors washed ashore into the arms of some tribe or other. I note, however, that according to these precious records, they were rescued after a sojourn of three to twenty months. A period of time, impossible to know in advance, that must have seemed terrifying to them. But nevertheless, I cannot accept that they would have been as profoundly affected as Narcisse. I do not wish to diminish their suffering or their courage, but I must stress that Narcisse endured a sojourn more than ten times as long, and that this difference in length of time must surely change the nature of the experience.

There is one more factor that is perhaps significant: of all these unfortunates whose stories we know, the youngest was twenty-six, in other words, an adult. When he arrived among the natives, Narcisse was only eighteen, still a child, or very much a youth. How important was this? Did he perhaps, because of his young age, succumb more easily to the pressures that were exerted upon him, whatever they were? I do not know.

There were other accounts, no doubt. Shipwrecked sailors, picked up by natives, who survived hoping to be rescued, and who succumbed in the end to the blows of life's vicissitudes. Perhaps they died of hunger, sickness, sorrow or old age, after one year, five, twenty or thirty years, without ever setting eyes on a white man again. We cannot know. Such tragedies will remain forever forgotten, their only legacy the occasional blond or redheaded native on some far-flung shore, testament to the presence of a sojourner from northern shores a few generations earlier.

The next morning, the hotel manager sent the Daily Mirror up to me at the earliest opportunity. The story of the "white savage" took up half of the front page. I will not do you the disservice of sending it to you or of providing a summary of the report. Every sentence is a lie, every detail an invention, apart from the fact that the man in question is a Frenchman. I received this journalist in order to prevent him from writing such nonsense, but I was wasting my time. I folded the newspaper and tried to put it out of my mind.

Alas! All of London had already read the article and I received a stream of extraordinary and astonishing letters throughout the day. A missionary society wished to meet us in order to discuss a Pacific ministry; a lady desired to take tea with the unfortunate sailor; a renowned writer begged me to provide him with all the details of the story for his next novel; an obscure scholar invited me to comment on the validity of his theories, with which I was no doubt unfamiliar, and so on.

The French Ambassador asked me to come and see him in order to clarify the position of this compatriot of ours. Constraints upon my time made it impossible for me to accede to his request.

One request for which I was to make an exception was the invitation proffered by the President of the Royal Geographical Society: both his friendship with you and his position as an associate member of our Society recommended him to me. Furthermore, I surmised that he would not be susceptible to the inventions of the press and that he was genuinely interested in our friend. Vanity too played a part: I was flattered to be invited to dine that evening in the company of a group of highly eminent British explorers, and willingly accepted the invitation. The President of the Society tactfully left it up to me to decide whether Narcisse should be included. I informed him that Narcisse would not be coming. I gave as my reasons Narcisse's extreme shyness and the fact that he spoke no English; I did not add my true reason, which was that the Geographical Society in Paris should take precedence over the Royal Geographical Society in London.

Later that morning, I was busy dealing with my voluminous correspondence, when the manager of the hotel came to see me in my room. He led me over to the window, and looking out, I beheld a crowd of several hundred people jostling on the pavement and contained with some difficulty by the police. Who were these onlookers? What did they want? To see the white savage for themselves? Would Narcisse have to appear on the balcony? No, that was out of the question. Word of the spectacle would travel and attract an unceasing host of people drawn by idle curiosity. No, we would have to remain hidden, not go out, and ensure that Narcisse did not get caught up in a crowd. It was a regrettable situation, and one that was disturbing and worrying for the other guests. Before he had time to let me know that our presence was unwelcome, I ushered the manager to the door and reassured him that we would be taking our leave the next day.

That afternoon, Narcisse and I made our escape by a back door and went for a long walk. I did not burden him with commentaries on what we beheld: I wanted above all for him to look around him, take notice of what he saw and be immersed in the life of the city. He walked along looking unhappy, constantly jostled by people hurrying by, sighing every time he looked up at the buildings four and five storeys high. As we walked through Hyde Park, he seemed to become less agitated and trod the grass with obvious delight.

At the corner of Regent Street leading into a small dark alley, a red-haired beggar of indeterminate age, bearded and dressed in torn clothing, was holding out a hat to passers-by. Narcisse stopped abruptly in front of him and stared, whereupon the beggar began to grumble, muttering under his breath in the Irish tongue and only ceasing when I dropped a coin into his hat.

"Well, Narcisse? Shall we continue?"

He thought for a long time before answering: "All the people in London run. This man stands still."

How could I explain to him that he was entirely wrong? And what was there to be gained in pressing home to him that he understood nothing of what he saw?

Upon our return, I found several dozen letters waiting for us. I had not the heart to open them all and after tea, to which I had now become accustomed, I left Narcisse in the hotel and hailed a carriage to take me to the Royal Society.

The majestic setting is familiar to you, as are the president and the majority of the members, all of whom hold you, Sir, in the highest esteem, regarding you with great respect and admiration. As I mounted the steps I thought of all those who had gone before me into this temple of British power and boldness. I was received with great warmth and the utmost cordiality. The evening began with a lecture on that still unresolved question, the subject of the sources of the Nile. A light supper was then served, during which I set out the most noteworthy aspects of the white savage's adventures. My hosts listened in respectful silence and asked a few pertinent questions that testified to the quality of their attention. Finally, a speaker brought us up to date with the latest findings with regard to the North West Passage, bringing to a close a re- markable evening.

These four hours passed like a dream. Every one of these gentlemen – merchants, officers, missionaries, captains of ocean-going vessels – had earned their place in this circle by exploring a dangerous and unknown region of our planet, and all of them considered me their equal that evening. But my only contribution had been to make known the story of Narcisse: it was only because of him that I was able to say something about the north east coast of Australia and the nomadic tribes who wander there. I had no new discoveries to impart, and I asked more questions than I answered. Was I worthy of the compliments I received?

This morning, before we left to take the train to Dover, in which I am finishing this letter, Narcisse told me of yet another misadventure that had occurred during the course of the previous evening. I was immediately on the alert; this was the first time I had gone out and left Narcisse to his own devices. While he was dining in the restaurant he had exchanged glances with a young woman at the adjacent table, a German woman travelling with a brother and an uncle. They chatted for a few minutes with Narcisse in French. I know nothing of what Narcisse said to her, but she repaired to his room a little later. You can well imagine what followed. Undoubtedly the revelation one by one of Narcisse's tattoos only added to the lady's transports.

When events had run their course, Narcisse did as I had done the day before with the chamber maid. He searched in his pocket and gallantly presented the lady with the few coins I had taken the precaution of supplying him with. Scandalised, the German woman threw them back at him and rushed out of the room cursing him in her own language.

"Is it right to give money afterwards or not?"

I reassured Narcisse but made no attempt to explain the misunderstanding. I wondered what to make of his feminine conquests. He is certainly a well-built man, at thirty-six in the prime of his life, but one could not call him handsome. There is nothing remarkable about his general appearance or his rather mournful face, and his timidity could hardly work in his favour. Indeed, only a woman would be able to say wherein lies his charm. The only characteristic I can suggest is perhaps one that I find somewhat unsettling: his steady and unflinching gaze. He looks directly, and with a most unusual intensity, into the eyes of the person addressing him, and maintains his unswerving gaze, in utter silence. Perhaps it is this resolute attitude, at once promising and elusive, that fascinates women.

But there were other matters more important than these gallantries. For two days, I had been reluctant to inform Narcisse of the news I had received from the mayor of Saint-Gilles. But it was important to stop equivocating: Narcisse had to know who he was before our return to France. And so, while we were seated in the drawing room of the hotel, I began the conversation I had already put off too long.

"Narcisse, do you remember Saint-Gilles-sur-Vie?"

He nodded in affirmation. I knew that this gesture was more an indication of his complete attention than a sign to show he agreed with what was being said.

"I wrote to Saint-Gilles to find out if a sailor had disappeared ten or twenty years ago. I received a reply to my question. Your name is definitely Narcisse Pelletier."

"Narcisse, or Pelletier?" he asked.

"Both," I replied. "We have two names. The first is chosen by our parents and second is passed on through the father to his children."

"Narcisse, son of Pelletier?"

"If you like, yes. You were born in Saint-Gilles on the 13th May 1825. You were a sailor on the schooner *Saint-Paul*."

"The schooner *Saint-Paul*," he repeated in a pensive voice.

I let him absorb these names, an echo of his, "Sees-Ti-Ay Oo-Pawl." of five months earlier. But he made no comment.

"Your parents and your brother and sister are still living in Saint-Gilles. I have told them you are coming back. You are going to see your mother and father again."

"My mother is dead."

"No, Narcisse. She is expecting to see you."

"My mother? She's not dead?"

"Your mother and father are both still alive. Your father is a shoemaker in Saint-Gilles."

In a gesture I had never seen him make before, Narcisse pressed his clenched fists to his temples, as if to calm an inner storm, and closed his eyes. He was overwhelmed with emotion at the prospect of returning to his family home. At least, this is what I supposed. But then, without moving, he murmured as if speaking to himself: "My mother... she's dead. I saw her. She died. I was there."

His mother? Who was he talking about? Was it possible that he was talking about some sort of adoptive mother, some native woman who had looked after him? He had never spoken of any ties made with the people he lived amongst; nor had he ever spoken of how they regarded him. Had he been a son to them, a servant, a simple-minded soul? Or had they seen him as a prophet, or an exiled Prince, or a monster? On all of this, his silence was absolute, either because he did not wish to speak of his Australian years, or because he could not find the words to describe the trials he had endured. It was of the utmost importance not to rush him.

"Narcisse, your mother in Saint-Gilles is still alive and is waiting for you."

He remained in the same position, withdrew into himself and said slowly, as if speaking to himself: "My mother is dead.

She was ill for several days. Much heat. Too much heat, inside. She died."

Still a prisoner of his trials, Narcisse was unable to return to us. Surely my task was not merely to record his memories and the process of his transformation. It fell upon me to help him too. I tried to find the right words.

"You are a white man, like me. Your father is a white man. Your mother is white. They are both alive. I do not know who this woman is that you speak of, the woman who died. A black Australian woman cannot be your real mother. If she showed you some affection and helped you while you were over there, you may call her your adoptive mother, or if you like, you may say 'my native mother'."

At these words, he gave me a look full of fury, of hatred even. I was taken aback and thought for a moment that he was going to hit me. I had never seen him in this state of mute, barely contained rage, of which I seemed to be the object. I was at a loss to understand. He turned to look away, as if he could not stand to look at me, or as if this was his only alternative to physical violence. I remained speechless, not moving, unable to comprehend what was happening or what it was I had said to upset him so much.

Then, he buried his head in his hands and began to cry, long silent sobs. These tears that I had unwittingly provoked caused me much more pain than any blows he might have inflicted on me. What could I say without adding to his distress? I waited.

After a short period that seemed to me interminable, the concierge came up to let us know that the hansom cab to take us to the station was waiting. To see us there, Narcisse weeping, and my sombre expression, he must have thought that we had just learnt of the death of a loved one. And yet the truth was we were grieving for a native Australian woman, of whom I knew nothing, be she living or dead.

Why does Narcisse never speak to me of the years he spent in Australia?

I remain your faithful servant…

7

Where did she go to find water?

No stream flowed through Round Bay or North Bay, and yet the old woman always came back to the encampment with the water gourds filled. The only water he had seen in his wanderings with the tribe through this dry flat forest had been the stagnant waters of the pond. The water in the gourds was slightly muddy; it left a sharp, flinty aftertaste of dust in the mouth. Did she scratch at the soil with her bare hands or did she use a stone or a stick to coax water to well up from under the earth?

Water. Water was the key to everything. He would simply have to snatch it from the old woman.

He spent two days watching her continuously. She went off into the forest about twelve times a day. Sometimes she wasn't gone for long, and came back with herbs, bulbs or a lizard. If she took two gourds with her, she was gone for more than an hour.

He was not so interested in knowing where to find water within half an hour's walk of Round Bay. What he really wanted to find out was whether or not there was any fresh water within striking distance of the coast. In this eternally unchanging landscape, he had to know where to go to find water.

Seeing the old woman pick up her empty gourds, he began to follow her, staying a few paces behind her. She seemed unaware of his presence. They walked in what seemed to him like a straight line through the rows of identical trees for at least a quarter of an hour. And then she sat down on the ground. Keeping at a distance of about ten metres, he sat down to wait until she decided to set off again. In the silvery half-light of the undergrowth, he watched her, never taking his eyes off her.

Water. All his troubles had started with the water shortage, the ruined barrels on the *Saint-Paul*. Water was the reason they had sailed along this coast of Australia. In Java, which they must by now have left to come and find him, his shipmates would have regaled themselves drinking bad wine, Dutch beer, coconut water, juice from the fruits of every colour that he'd seen in the markets of the Cape or Ceylon the year before. But it was not the varied flavours of all these drinks that he longed for. It was only water he craved. Water, fresh and clean. At home, the family's well gave them water all year round. The bucket, the rope, the pulley... he pictured the tranquil scene, saw himself as a boy, proudly bringing his mother the few litres she needed to prepare supper and clean up afterwards.

A few moments later, he became aware that the old woman had disappeared. He must have taken his eyes off her for just a few seconds, and she'd left. She couldn't have gone very far. Jumping up, he ran about aimlessly in every direction. Try as he might, however much he swore, however frantically he beat around in the bushes, he could see no sign of her and not the least indication of the presence of any water. After wandering around in vain, and coming to the realisation that with all this milling about he would end up completely lost, he made his way back, somewhat sheepishly to Round Bay and the encampment.

The old woman was sitting there, her water pouches filled beside her. She seemed not to notice his arrival.

He followed her three more times, changing his tactics with each foray. Three times she vanished before his very eyes.

He tried to convince himself that these two days had not been wasted. He had found out how far away the water was. And he knew now that the old woman, for some reason he did not understand, did not want to show him where she found it.

That evening, collecting shellfish in Round Bay with Waiakh, who was always at his side now, he ate a few raw oysters before the fire was lit. Finding an irregular white pearl in one of the oysters, he washed it and gazed at it with conflicting emotions. It was not a priceless specimen, but it was big and white and well-formed enough to be worth something. With it, he'd be able to negotiate a good price in any port in the world. Two months earlier, he would have appreciated this unexpected bonus. He'd have slipped the pearl into his pocket and kept it there until the next port of call. But here… he had no pockets, he was naked, and there was no prospect of finding anyone to negotiate with. The rarest of pearls was worthless here. Even the most enormous of gold nuggets would have no value in this place. No savage would accept the pearl in exchange for a piece of meat, no woman here would think of wearing it as jewellery. It was nothing more than a growth in a shell, a plaything for Waiakh. Bitterly disappointed, he threw it down on the sand, as far away as he could.

Five minutes later, he was running to and fro like a madman, desperately searching for the discarded pearl. By a stroke of luck, he found it half buried in the sand. Throwing away the pearl would mean he'd given up hope. But help would come, he would have the pearl with him when he boarded ship. He'd have more pearls too. There would be others concealed within the oysters in the bay. He would have to search for them, keep them in a safe place. He pictured himself building up a cache of pearls in each of the bays so that wherever help arrived for him, he wouldn't go away empty-handed. When the time came for him to escape, by sea or on land, he'd take the pearls with him; they'd weigh virtually nothing.

In the middle of the beach in Round Bay stood a huge boulder, its shape reminiscent of a small chapel. Examining it carefully on all sides, he found an indentation on the surface that faced the sea and the waves, big enough for him to sink his fist into. He gathered some small rocks and tufts of dried grass, placed them in the niche in the boulder and set the pearl on top. This would be his strong-box. Waiakh copied him and found a hole in the rock he could easily reach, into which he solemnly placed some pebbles.

A pearl… a pearl necklace perhaps? He imagined thirty or forty perfectly formed identical white pearls in his cache, pearls destined to grace the neck of a Princess. But no. It could never happen. How many oysters would he have to open? How many days and weeks spent camping at Round Bay? Every pearl would mark an eternity, the slow passage of time, grains of sand running through an hourglass…

No, there would only ever be one pearl: the *Saint-Paul* would reappear within a few days at the most. He would board the ship with his pearl. He wouldn't sell it, he'd have it set in China or in Aden, mounted in silver on a leather cord, he would take it home for his sister. In his trunk aboard ship, under his clothes, he had stored a length of purple moiré fabric, threaded with gold. He'd bought it in the Cape from an Indian trader.

How pretty his sister would look wearing this shawl and the pearl pendant. How proud he'd be of her. Suitors would vie for her attention, and when the time came, she'd say yes to a respectable young man and live happily for the rest of her days. She would wear the mysterious pearl around her neck and no one would know where it came from.

The cloth from the Cape was aboard the *Saint-Paul*, and he was here on this beach. When a sailor perishes at sea, his shipmates divide up his meagre possessions. Had they already opened his trunk? Had they set his belongings out on the 'tweendecks, his seaman's slops, his hat and socks, his comb, his pewter mug, his razor? Had they already chosen what they wanted, the old hands taking first pick? And after one of them had unwrapped the tissue paper and shown his Cape purchase to admiring eyes, which of his shipmates would have claimed the purple cloth?

LETTER VII

Saint-Gilles-sur-Vie, 16th August 1861

Monsieur le Président,

Upon my arrival in Paris, I found your note informing me that you had been called away to the provinces to settle a matter of family business and that you would be away for some ten days. I extend my best wishes to you and trust that you will succeed in resolving the matter to your satisfaction. Narcisse and I are of course disappointed at this unexpected delay, but since it is now five months since our work began, an additional wait should be of little consequence.

A second letter, from Saint-Gilles, informed us that the whole town was eagerly awaiting our arrival and had been anticipating that day ever since the mayor, reassured by my explanations, had imparted the glad tidings to the family. I therefore decided to modify our programme and begin by taking Narcisse home to his family.

But first, I must tell you about our journey from London. For much of the day, Narcisse remained downcast and lachrymose, saying nothing. The silence weighed heavily on me as the train sped through the English countryside. It was raining in Dover, and in spite of the rough seas, Narcisse insisted on standing outside on deck for the duration of the crossing. I felt duty-bound to stay with him, all the more so since I was momentarily struck by the distressing notion that he had perhaps chosen this spot in order to be able to throw himself into the sea and find eternal oblivion. Even to entertain this dread possibility was to acknowledge that he might consider his life with me to be worse than anything he had endured in Australia. And if he had really resolved to take his own life, what right did I have to stop him from doing so? Who was I to take it upon myself to prevent him from exercising his free will? Just as Socrates resolved to drink the hemlock draft, Narcisse must be at liberty to choose his own path. My sole and fervent desire is that he will be able to find some pleasure in returning to live among us. And with such sombre musings, buffeted by the rain and high seas, we crossed the Channel and arrived in Calais soaked to the skin, but somewhat mollified. I have often perceived that when Narcisse is troubled, contact with nature and the elements provides a powerful antidote to his malaise. A meadow, a river, a park, an estuary, and most of all the open sea, have the power to soothe and calm him.

He was much in need of that equilibrium in Calais where a suspicious and blinkered police inspector insisted on conducting a thorough examination into Narcisse's situation. Brushing aside disdainfully the document from the colonial judge in Sydney – an English judge could have no jurisdiction over the legal status of a Frenchman – he announced triumphantly that Pelletier the sailor, having not completed the voyage on which he had originally embarked, and being unable to present his papers, was in a most irregular situation and was liable to a substantial fine. Moreover, what proof did he have that this suspicious looking individual in dripping wet clothes was indeed the said Pelletier, and not some imposter? I explained, calmly at first and then in a more light-hearted fashion, that having survived a shipwreck on hostile shores and been taken in by savages amongst whom he had lived for eighteen years, Narcisse had been somewhat preoccupied with matters other than his civil status. As for his precious papers, they had long ago been devoured by fish. To which the dullard responded by demanding to see the consul's statement confirming the loss of the ship. And furthermore, he added, who was I to speak for Pelletier the sailor, or indeed for the individual claiming to be Pelletier? The affair was none of my business and I should extract myself from the matter forthwith. The suspect would have to accompany him to the station and remain there until his situation was clarified. The security of the Empire could not be compromised; on no account could he permit this individual to enter France on the strength of such a ridiculous fable.

Pelletier the sailor followed this exchange in wide-eyed silence – I hoped against hope that he understood little of it. The discussion became more heated, the inspector invoking obscure regulations which I countered with mention of my contacts in high places and by alluding to the fundamental principles of human rights. Other travellers clustered around us, amused by the spectacle, interjecting disparaging comments. I was determined not to cede any ground: I would either enter France freely with Narcisse, or we would both be clapped into handcuffs. Finally, the Calais Chief of Police, alerted by the commotion, summoned us to his office. He listened to our tale, read the letters from the mayor of Saint-Gilles, and issued a pass for Narcisse allowing him to travel freely in France.

We booked into the Grand Hotel in Paris for three days. After an absence of more than three years from my native land

I had pressing matters of personal business to attend to. Once this was accomplished, I organised our journey to Saint-Gilles.

We travelled to Orleans on the new railway, which had not yet been constructed when I was last in France, and thence by diligence as far as Poitiers. From there we took a smaller, less comfortable horse-drawn conveyance and arrived in Saint-Gilles on the appointed day.

I shall not trouble you with a lengthy description of the celebrations held in Saint-Gilles, although they certainly lacked neither pomp nor noble sentiments. But those details – the archway garlanded with leaves, the mayor's speech, the bonfire, the emotional crowd, the applause, the tears, the singing by the whole commune – tell us more about the honest natives of the Vendée than about Narcisse himself and his adventure; were you or I to entertain the fanciful notion of undertaking a study of the people of this region, all this would be of greater import.

As the celebrations and reunions continued that afternoon and evening, I kept my distance. The mayor, an astute and efficient official, had made arrangements for me to be lodged with the curate. This proved to be eminently practical since the Pelletier household was already quite crowded, accommodating as it did the eldest son, his wife and their three children, in addition to Narcisse's parents.

Desirous of making a good impression, and not wishing to be suspected of having neglected my protégé, I had dressed Narcisse as a gentleman about town. Perhaps I should have been less extravagant in this choice of attire, for I perceived that while Narcisse, the shoemaker's son, was elegantly shod in leather boots, all around him were wearing wooden clogs.

Presented with this well-dressed stranger, the family showed some surprise: it was almost as if they had been expecting to see a youngster of eighteen years old. But it was not long before his mother gathered him into her arms amidst floods of tears, and Narcisse was recognised as the youngest son of the family.

I soon observed that Narcisse was sharing neither in the general delight nor in the emotional transports of his family. I was hardly surprised at his detachment: he participated to be polite, to play the part expected of him. He would have responded in much the same way to the embrace of any matronly woman presented to him as his mother. Memories of childhood seemed to elude him: the names of his brothers and sister, the disposition of the rooms in the house, the myriad family anecdotes. He did not throw himself enthusiastically into the open arms of those who welcomed him and responded laconically when addressed.

All of this began to engender a barely discernible sense of malaise, to which the mayor responded by choosing this moment to introduce me to the family. He reminded them of my role in the affair, upon which the curiosity of the family and the villagers turned towards me and I was assailed by hundreds of questions. I confessed that I knew nothing of the circumstances aboard the *Saint-Paul* and very little about Narcisse's life among the savages. I might have embellished my responses with tales of the South Pacific, but to what end? How much would they have understood of life in Fiji or Espiritu Santu and what would they have made of such accounts?

Narcisse had now been returned to the bosom of his family; his time of suffering and exile was over and he was back among his own people. I took my leave, as did the mayor and curate, and we left the Pelletiers to themselves.

The next day, being Sunday, a mass and *Te Deum* were to be offered in Narcisse's honour. The church was full to overflowing as the curate solemnly displayed to the faithful the baptism register opened at the page where Narcisse's baptism thirty-six years earlier was recorded. Seated with the family in the front row was a beribonned matron, Narcisse's godmother. But his godfather, the uncle who had regaled the young Narcisse with his tales of the Napoleonic campaigns and given the boy a taste for travel, was not beside her, having long since departed this world.

In his sermon, the curate took up the parable of the prodigal son – a tale to which I myself had on occasion had recourse – to obviate any comparison with Narcisse. He reminded the faithful that the prodigal son of the parable had impulsively claimed his share of his inheritance, squandered it of his own accord, and returned penniless to throw himself at his father's mercy. In spite of this profligacy, his father had forgiven him and killed the fatted calf to celebrate his return. For God is merciful: his mercy is greater than all our sins. Narcisse, by contrast, had shown nothing but courage. He had left his home to embark upon the life of a sailor; he had confronted storms and been separated from those he loved. God had placed formidable trials before him: he had endured eighteen years of exile among fearsome savages. But he had never lost heart; he put his fate in the hands of the Lord. Who could reproach him for having forgotten the words of the Lord's Prayer and the Credo? He had borne his cross in every sense of the word. And God had not forgotten his child, lost at the ends of the earth. He had reached out to him with His merciful hand and had brought him back to the bosom of his family, and here today to the church where he was baptised.

I cannot say what was the provenance of the curate's spiritual reflections; I had not dared to tell him that Narcisse probably had no understanding of who this priest was. He had conducted two long conversations alone with Narcisse, and I did not doubt that Narcisse's part in those dialogues had been to say what he believed the holy father wished to hear; he has the ability to reflect the image that each individual expects of him and does so spontaneously and entirely without malice.

The mass was followed by an outdoor feast in which most of the population of Saint-Gilles participated. Narcisse continued to give the impression of being present and yet absent from the proceedings.

Three of his childhood friends came over to congratulate him, admiring his tattoos and recalling the days when they had been a band of four wastrels, recklessly raiding apple orchards and hunting thrushes. But who were these men to Narcisse now, this Julien, Mathieu and Pierre, these married men following their fathers' professions? Narcisse consistently refused the glasses of wine they continued to press on him, thus causing further consternation.

After the feast, the villagers surrounded Narcisse and led him home to the accompaniment of the strains of a violin and a clarinet.

As a result of the afternoon's events, there ensued much diplomatic manoeuvring between Narcisse's father, the curate, the mayor and your faithful servant. At times, two or three of us would organise a *tête-à-tête*, at others, we met in ostensibly chance encounters to discuss what would become of Narcisse. The talks culminated in a discussion around the table after dinner with the curate. I was initally flattered to be included for I had no official relationship to Narcisse. The mission conferred upon me by the governor of New South Wales was coming to an end, my duty fulfilled once I had brought Narcisse to Paris to present him to you.

After much prevarication, and circumlocution, and with many repetitions, veiled allusions and references to sayings and proverbs, I was given to understand that the parameters of my mission might perhaps be adjusted. The protracted nature of these pronouncements was all too familiar to me from my dealings with the peasants of my estate in Isère: insisting on further clarification at this point would have been fruitless. I too wondered what kind of a life there would be henceforth for Narcisse in Saint-Gilles. All concurred that his position in the family was no longer what it had been. Of course there would always be a place for him at the family table, a bed to lie on in the barn. But how would he earn his living? His father and brother eked out a meagre living from the shoemaking workshop. And as it was, his brother relied on the small patch of land he farmed, the sheep and the cow he kept to supplement that living. Narcisse no longer knew how to use the cobbler's awl. He had forgotten how to milk the cow and shear the sheep. He had no facility with a hoe and could neither till the soil nor prune the vines. Who would have the time to teach him all these skills again? And the family holdings were too modest to support even one farmhand. Marriage with a local girl was out of the question, for who would want such a man with no property to call his own. Interest in him would soon begin to fade. He would risk becoming dependent on public charity, a most undesirable eventuality.

When all of this had more or less been made clear, I interjected, perhaps a little too light-heartedly:

"Well what should he do? Go back to sea?"

My suggestion was met with a general consternation, which

I believed to be quite sincere. If Narcisse were to remain in Saint-Gilles he would not starve, but it was a paltry existence that awaited him. At thirty-six, he displayed the naivety and ignorance of a child. What could be done with such a child? And at forty and fifty years of age, what lay in store for him? Narcisse's future no longer lay in Australia or at sea, but nor could it be here in Saint-Gilles.

My interlocutors were careful not to press their arguments any further and I surmised that this meeting had been carefully prepared in advance by the three interested parties. As befitted the tenor of the exchange, I took my time to absorb the implications and did not offer an immediate response. The curate went to the cabinet to select a bottle of liqueur and we joined together in lamenting the fate of the unfortunate Narcisse.

When I had finished my drink, I ventured a cautious suggestion; it was not rejected and the discussions were deferred for the evening, to be concluded at a more convenient time. My hosts understood that I had discerned their meaning: they wanted Narcisse to leave with me.

He would of course always be welcome in Saint-Gilles, as would I. Old Monsieur Pelletier was careful to stress that Narcisse would naturally be entitled to his share of the family inheritance.

In any case, there was no need to make a decision immediately. We would have to wait and see how matters evolved: it had been a mere five months since Narcisse had returned to the white man's world, a week since his arrival in France and he had only been in Saint-Gilles for one day. The important presentation of which I had informed them, and of which they felt great pride on Narcisse's behalf, meant that we would soon be leaving for Paris. There was no pressing need to come to any decisions.

Although initially unconvinced, I found myself in agreement. For eighteen years, family life had continued without Narcisse. He had been pronounced dead and all had grieved for him. The cycle of the seasons had passed many times in his absence. The child that Narcisse had been, the three year old who spent most of his days in his uncle's arms, meant more to Narcisse's father than this grown man returned from beyond the River Styx.

We parted on friendly terms and I stepped outside to enjoy the soft night air and take a turn around the sleeping village. The crescent moon was rising above the church. I walked as far as the river and on my way back, as I approached the church I came upon Narcisse, kneeling in a ditch, weeping and vomiting. He told me, between sobs, that he had gone with his three childhood friends to the café where he had finally accepted the glass of wine they had been pressing upon him since that morning. And then he had accepted another and another, he'd lost count. The three revellers had tired of Narcisse's reticence, finding him no more communicative even when in his cups and had gone off in search of wine elsewhere, leaving him alone and before long, sick. I helped him to get up and clean himself off and tried to console him. But he did not need consoling; as far as I could tell, he was not feeling any shame or regret. Such sentiments were entirely foreign to him. He wished only to understand what had happened and I explained to him as best as I could. The others were drinking wine, enjoying it in great quantities, but Narcisse was unable to tolerate it. For him, wine was akin to poison, and made his head spin. His old friends had not wished him any harm; they had simply not understood. He had a headache now, but it would be gone by tomorrow. Abstinence suited him and he should continue to abjure wine. My remarks seemed to calm him. I took him back to his parents' house, where they were waiting for him, and left discreetly.

Narcisse had been offered wine before, in the governor's prison by a soldier intent on making mischief. He had refused it then and I wondered if he remembered it now.

Last night, as I lay in bed in my modest quarters in the rectory, sleep eluded me for a long time. I pictured Narcisse being sick in the ditch outside the church, weeping for his adoptive mother that day in the hotel in London, repelling Bill's advances in our retreat outside of Sydney, escaping to the far side of the garden in the governor's residence in Sydney to catch a glimpse of the sea beyond the walls. An astonishing idea came to me: what if I had been wrong from the outset? What if the right decision would have been to hire a vessel, whether the governor approved or not, and return Narcisse to the beach where the whole affair had begun?

An absurd notion of course: who would be so hard-hearted as to return to his cell a man who has escaped from a prison so perverse and cruel that the prisoner no longer sees it for what it is. To send Narcisse back after these weeks spent in the white man's world would have been to plunge him for a second time into a world that was not his. Would he have been strong enough to forget the *John Bell* and the dinghy, the port of Sydney, my recitations of Racine, the European clothes and food? Would he have been able to return to life with the tribe, to become completely a savage once again? No, such cruelty would have been inhuman, barbarous. The path that Narcisse follows must be pursued in one direction only, upwards towards the heights. We must never forget that this is not an easy path and that Narcisse has nothing to guide him. Like Ulysses, he must overcome a thousand trials before his return to Ithaca. So it must be. Narcisse is not a child, and I had never promised him that his road would be easy.

He is suffering from a headache today, but what does this matter when weighed up against all that is at stake?

Next Tuesday, I shall introduce you to Narcisse Pelletier and you will be able to judge for yourself how much progress has been made.

I remain your faithful servant...

8

When he had first signed on as a cabin boy his father had gone with him to Nantes. It had taken them two days to get there, trundling through the countryside in an uncomfortable wagon. He'd spent most of that time staring avidly out of the window at the scenery unfolding before them, clutching his bag tightly with both hands. His father spoke little to him, and then only to repeat his advice to obey orders and work hard, or to wonder aloud about the price and quality of the various leathers he wanted to buy for the workshop.

His mother had made him a cake. It would keep for a while, she said, and he would be able to take a bite of it in the evenings when he felt overcome with homesickness. She had hugged him for a long time, something that he was not used to. His mind turned to the traveller's tales his uncle had told him: how he had been a grenadier in Napoleon's Grande Armée and walked across most of Europe before being injured in Prussia at the Battle of Eylau, and coming back to the village. Thinking of this only served to convince Narcisse that he had made the right choice. He was always arguing with his older brother, he had no desire to become a cobbler or a farmhand. There was no future for him on land.

They'd stayed with a cousin in Nantes. His father had given the cake to her, claiming that it would only have made Narcisse a laughing stock with the crew, the little cabin boy allaying his sorrows with his mummy's cake. There would be no comforts for him aboard ship and he might as well get used to it from the moment they set sail.

He gazed in amazement at the elegant houses and churches in Nantes, at the throngs of people and the ladies' dresses. But most of all, he marvelled at the spectacle of the port: ships as far as the eye could see, their masts as high as trees, carts, ropes, casks, hoists, porters, piles of merchandise and wood, sailors speaking in a babel of tongues, a black man, the first he had ever seen with his own eyes.

His father bought him a pair of trousers and an oilcoat from a second-hand-clothes merchant before taking him to be introduced to the captain of the brig *La Fidèle*. He was immediately handed over to the bosun, who was busy with preparations for the next day's departure and had no time for the clumsy cabin boy and his gauche father. He showed Narcisse his hammock, told him where to stow his effects and went off to oversee the loading of the freight.

Narcisse had been expecting to sleep that night at his cousin's house, but his father ordered him to stay on board the brig. He should spend his first night there, watching and learning. The earlier he learned to settle in the better. He embraced his son, and pulling a hat out of his pocket, placed it on the boy's head and walked away without turning back.

How different it all would have been if Narcisse had hit out at the second mate, or if he'd feigned madness, rolling his eyes, drooling and jabbering nonsense. What if he'd thrown himself into the Loire or fallen down in the 'tweendecks and broken his leg? If he'd come out in a rash and suddenly started coughing and spitting up green mucus, or if he'd broken in to the captain's cabin and helped himself to all the bottles of alcohol? Or if, snivelling and beset by dark forebodings, he'd simply turned round and left with his father, if he'd abandoned this ship and all that was to come after it...? But no, he'd done none of these things. Like a child discovering a new playground, he'd explored every corner of the ship. When the bosun saw him sauntering about with this hands in his pockets, he'd given him various small tasks to do – relaying an order, carrying a trunk, bringing a bucket and brushes, sweeping the bridge – he had ceased to be Narcisse Pelletier. He was the ship's cabin boy now. And like every cabin boy before him, he was castigated by the old hands for being caught out by the vast repertoire of technical sailing terms: was there ever such a numbskull for a cabin boy! But he knew this was par for the course. The afternoon passed in a flash and before he knew it the evening soup was being served. That first night in his hammock in the belly of the docked ship he slept a deep and dreamless sleep.

The next day the new cabin boy scurried around amidst all the excitement of the preparations to get the ship under way. The last of the sailors came aboard, some of them looking the worse for wear, with furred tongues and strained features. His father did not return. At three o'clock that afternoon, as the tide went out and a light breeze picked up, the captain gave the order to cast off from the moorings. The other more experienced cabin boy took the new lad under his wing and showed him the ropes.

And so the days and weeks went by – port after port, sailing to one after another.

He should have jumped ship in the Cape. With a bit of luck, a modicum of skill and a few years of hard work he'd have been able to open a tavern there. Before long, it would have become a favourite haunt for all the French seamen who put in at the Cape. Chez Narcisse, with its shady terrace, lanterns suspended from the branches of the trees, the friendly landlord always ready to answer questions, jugs of good wine, a few musicians. And in the courtyard, the huts, each with a mat on the floor, a bed, a basin and a candle. The other side of the Pelletier business. His girls would have been the finest in the Cape, beautiful creatures full of life and ready to give pleasure at any time of the day or night. In his left ear, he would sport an impressive earring of real gold. The red lantern hanging above the tavern door would soon be famed across the oceans. And even if he'd failed in all these plans, even if he'd spent a few months or years lurking around the port, earning the smallest penny wherever he could, offering his services for the most menial of tasks, a petty thief, sleeping in a straw hut, happy to gnaw on a crust of bread given to him by a charitable fellow countryman, even then, he'd still have been right to jump ship in the Cape.

After the Cape the *Saint-Paul* had sailed southeast and headed into snowstorms and monstrous waves; for the first time in his life at sea he had been truly afraid. Why hadn't he gone down to the hold at night with an auger, drilled holes in the hull and let the icy water come flooding in? He could have taken an axe to the rudder and smashed it. With the ship crippled, the captain would have had no choice but to turn back to the Cape. But the winds and the currents might have proved too strong and carried them further south towards those islands men spoke of in hushed tones. Treeless islands where giant birds nest and waterfalls tumble from basalt cliffs under leaden skies. They'd have struggled to run the ship to ground in some uncharted bay where they'd have built makeshift shelters with debris from the *Saint-Paul*. They'd have survived on what was left of the ship's provisions and the seals they hunted; no one would know that he had sabotaged the ship. They'd have endured some difficult months, but the thirty men, with tools and everything they'd managed to salvage from the wreck, would have survived, eking out their meagre rations and clinging together to keep warm. The spring would have come, heralding the return of the American whalers and sealing ships that were everywhere in the southern oceans. One of the whalers would have discovered them by chance while exploring new hunting grounds and rescued them. He and his shipmates would have worked their passage, slaving away for six months and more. And eventually they would have landed safe and sound in America, in Rhode Island or Connecticut. Yes, sabotaging the *Saint-Paul* would have been the right thing to do.

His father had warned him about life at sea. There would be no comforts for him aboard ship.

And so Narcisse whiled away the afternoon, playing with Waiakh skipping stones across the water, and musing on what might have been.

LETTER VIII

Paris, 3rd September 1861

Monsieur le Président,

I write these lines to you today with conflicting emotions. Permit me to begin by saying what a great joy it was for me to find myself once again before you in your study today. It was a pleasure indeed to hear the warmth in your voice as you welcomed us and reiterated your compliments to me. What happiness to finally introduce you to Narcisse Pelletier, to hear you speaking to him and asking him questions with all the acuity of your perspective and your experience.

Perhaps we seemed a little ill-at-ease. I cannot deny that we conducted ourselves somewhat tentatively: Narcisse because he is shy and retiring by nature; and I because I was honoured to be accorded such a reception. Like a disciple in the presence of the master, I was anxious to hear what you had to say. My initial reserve was perhaps excessive, but I believe that during the course of the long audience you granted us, I did gradually depart from that reticence.

The principal difficulty is one which you yourself experienced. How to prompt Narcisse to describe the tribe of savages amongst whom he lived for eighteen years? He does not respond to direct questions, for reasons which still confound me: he cannot have forgotten everything about the world he left only six months ago! It must therefore be either because he does not wish to speak of these matters or because he is not able to. Can he not find the words? Surely he would have no need of abstruse language to say something about the details of his everyday life, to talk of hunting, marriages, meals or celebrations. I am more inclined to believe that there is a complex feeling buried deep within him, which forbids him to speak, and which I am at a loss to understand. Indeed I have noticed that sometimes, particularly in the heat of emotion, he lets slip a few morsels of precious information, almost in spite of himself, or so it would seem. I make a note of each of these revelations and try to make sense of them. It is of course too early yet to say, but it is not impossible that all this laborious work will some day form the basis of an academic study.

You have congratulated me for the notebooks I have been keeping from the very first day and have said that my work is "worthy of praise". These notebooks will be testament to the fact that I have invented nothing. For the temptation to romanticise the life of this unfortunate soul could indeed be irresistible: imagine Narcisse's travails being turned into a musical entertainment for the *Opéra-Comique*!

The culminating event of these few days was the plenary session of the Geographical Society which took place three days later. I now reproach myself for not having prepared sufficiently for this occasion. I had previously attended several of these illustrious lectures, seated at the back on the benches reserved for associate members of the society, and had listened to the scholarly discussions that followed, even venturing to ask a question myself on one or two occasions. I believed I was sufficiently acquainted with this ceremony, its rituals and high priests. I knew too that under your wise presidency, the discussions would be of the highest order. I felt that Narcisse's presence could not fail to surprise or perhaps disappoint the audience. I was aware that he might himself be overawed by the solemnity of the lecture theatre. But being only too familiar with his taciturn nature, my greatest fear was that he would retreat behind a wall of silence. You and I prepared some questions, and both hoped that he would speak, albeit briefly but enough to flesh out the bones of his story. In short, I thought, somewhat naively, that I would merely have to step up to the podium and recount the tale, for the audience to be won over. I imagined myself acknowledging their applause and answering questions from admiring listeners.

You said nothing to dissuade me from harbouring these illusions; how could you have anticipated the turn the presentation would take? During our earlier meeting, we decided together what Narcisse would wear, rehearsed the ways in which we would prepare him to speak, and discussed when we should come to his assistance. We agreed on the maps to be displayed on the walls and on the length of my initial speech. You indicated to me that the singular character of this adventure would certainly attract a large and elegant crowd as well as several journalists. We were happy working together to make our contribution to a page that would surely be a notable one in the annals of our Society's history.

Word of the presence of the "white savage" spread all over Paris and reached the newspapers, none of whom managed to contact me – perhaps they did not even try. Indeed, why would they when it required much less effort to translate the nonsense from the Daily Mirror of one month ago. Our adventure was the talk of every Paris salon, and the echoes I heard of this gossip would have been enough to make a misanthrope of any explorer. When we arrived at the seat of the Geographical Society yesterday afternoon, the street had already been invaded by a crowd, which the constables were struggling to contain. The majority of these idle onlookers did not have a ticket to attend the lecture, nor indeed did they have any interest in geography. We were ushered in through the rear entrance by your secretary who let us know that never before had an event at the Geographical Society attracted such interest. I was beginning to feel that the affair had been taken out of my hands. For reasons I do not understand, Narcisse looked as if he was enjoying himself, which was a rarity for him. We were told that there were a number of well-known individuals present, among them Prince Charles-Augustus of Saxe-Weimar-Eisenach, the composer Mr. Rossini, Mr. Alexandre Dumas fils, the critic and man of letters Sainte-Beuve, and many society ladies whose names I do not recall, although I did get a good look at their impressive hats.

I must confess, Sir, that I was somewhat taken aback by the light-hearted tone of your introductory remarks and that I had been expecting you to address the audience with your customary gravitas. But, faced with such an unusually large audience and in the presence of so many ladies, you chose to speak on a lighter note in keeping with the best rules of rhetoric, and thereby succeeded in surprising your listeners and capturing the attention of all those present. You introduced Monsieur Pelletier, seated at the foot of the stage facing the audience. Attired as he was, he cut an unremarkable figure. Some were no doubt expecting to see him dressed in animal skins, or in an African mask or the feathered headdress of an Indian. Perhaps they were expecting him to be uttering inarticulate cries, or jumping about like a monkey. But his sober bearing set the tone of the proceedings: this was to be no fairground spectacle. The afternoon would be devoted to scientific enquiry.

I ascended to the podium like a preacher preparing to inspire the faithful during Lent. From the lectern, I was able to survey the hall in all its majesty. Seeing the people standing in the aisles I became aware of the size of the crowd. Until this moment I might have imagined myself to be at the theatre waiting for the matinée performance to begin. Now I imagined myself making a speech in front of the Chamber of Deputies, an idea that bolstered my courage. I thought briefly too of my brother Louis, whose ambition it is to one day be a member of the city council of Grenoble. I looked out at the audience waiting in absolute silence after your skilful introduction, and began to speak. Nature has endowed me with a voice that carries well; I was at last going to be able to give something back to the Geographical Society in recognition of all it had done for me.

I heeded your counsel and spoke without notes for almost an hour. I began by summarising what we know about the discovery of Australia and its geography, in particular the north-east and the mysterious tribes that live there; then I went on to discuss the white savage and his gradual return to civilisation. I spoke perhaps at too great a length about the rare intimations he had given revealing certain singular details about some of the practices of the tribe. I concluded with some remarks explaining how I had managed to establish his identity, and a few words on his return to his family in Saint-Gilles and to the embrace of his parents.

My presentation was greeted with sustained applause,

the ladies taking out their handkerchiefs, and I felt that I had succeeded in conveying the essential elements of this tale. I was barely able to see Narcisse Pelletier, who was seated two metres below me, immobile and perhaps smiling. You were gracious enough to speak again and announce that this venture qualified me to be promoted from associate to full member of the Geographical Society, at which the applause redoubled. I was taken by surprise, for you had given me no prior indication of this; it was not only as a result of the temperature in the hall that a flush rose to my cheeks.

With a smart tap of the hammer, you silenced the audience and opened the floor to questions. The first two were requests for me to clarify certain points about our stay in Sydney, and the governor's role in the affair. I gave my answer, somewhat disconcerted by the dazzle of the lighting on the stage, which made it difficult for me to distinguish the faces of my interlocutors.

The third question came from the Reverend Father Leroy, whom I knew only through his essays on northern Quebec and the Indian populations of that region. I scarcely need to remind you of the insidious nature of the attack he proceeded to mount. He began by congratulating me for having played the part of the Good Samaritan, and went on to say how sorry he was not to have heard this story from the lips of the individual concerned, who was himself present in our midst. Once more, I explained the problem that you, Sir, had intuitively understood: that Narcisse Pelletier has neither the desire nor the experience necessary to speak in such a setting. And then came the coup: how could the Society be sure that it was not dealing with an imposter? Father Leroy excluded me from this accusation and assured me that my good faith was not being called into question. But was this sailor not in league with the crew of the ship that claimed to have discovered him? Was he not indeed just a common deserter who had concocted an ingenious means of returning to France at absolutely no cost and absolved of all charges?

You too sensed the shiver that ran through the audience, who were enticed by the prospect of polemic and scandal. The question, offensive as it was to both you and me, was cleverly worded in such a way as not to seem insulting.

My answer was twofold: firstly, for a sailor, deserter or otherwise, to invent such a complicated story with so many people involved seemed most improbable. Who would risk so many uncertainties for such a meagre reward? And to successfully deceive not only the captain and crew of the *John Bell*, but also the soldiers, the doctor and Governor Young, without ever giving himself away? I reminded the Reverend Father that I have observed Narcisse continuously since the beginning of March and witnessed his struggle to learn to speak our language again. Had I too been deceived? I, who have observed that notions as basic as money and property remain completely foreign to him. Never has he given me the slightest indication of anything suspicious or untoward. The impressive tattoos and scarifications that cover almost all of his body alone would guarantee the veracity of his story.

This last remark was no doubt misjudged. Cries of "Show us his tattoos!" and "Take off his shirt!" rang out through the audience. Aware of the risk of allowing the plenary session to turn into a circus act, you called the trouble-makers to order, and threatened them with expulsion. Father Leroy appeared to be satisfied with my response.

Colonel Sebastiani's question about cannibalism came as no surprise. I freely admitted that I had no precise data on this subject, but expressed my conviction that Narcisse Pelletier was not at all aggressive and showed none of the characteristics of a warrior. The injuries to his left ear and right leg must have been sustained in a context other than battle. And above all, his calm, restrained character seemed to exclude any possibility of him ever having participated in tribal wars or in any form of barbarous feasting after victory in battle. I pointed out that when an Australian convict had raised his hand to him, Narcisse Pelletier had not sought to hit back but had evaded the blows. This was testimony to his gentle nature – I remembered the words I had used in an earlier letter to you – he had behaved with truly Christian forbearance. With this final point I turned towards Father Leroy and bowed ironically. The audience smiled. I did not realise then that I had quite needlessly made a lifelong enemy of this gentleman.

Monsieur Decouz – whom you had described to me earlier as a "generous patron and meticulous compiler of records, whose most exotic expeditions have never ventured beyond Clermont-Ferrand" – then opened the debate on an important question whose pertinence I acknowledge even though the conclusions I draw from it are altogether different. He began by acknowledging amicably that he did not doubt the authenticity of this affair and went on to draw attention to the youth and limited intellect of the sailor Pelletier. If the hero of this adventure had been a man of substance, an officer or some other person of rank, would he have forgotten everything of his past in the same way? Would such a man have sunk like this sailor to the level of the lowliest of savages? Would he not have found in the treasures of his intelligence and of his culture, as well as in the consolations of religion – and here he too bowed towards Father Leroy – would he not have found the strength to resist the moral abasement of which this sailor bore all the scars? A man of standing would certainly have survived in the midst of the savages, but he would have done so by reciting to them the most moving passages from the *Pontic Epistles* or from *The Odyssey*. He would have spent his time in exile in the company of Ovid and Homer.

I had, as you know, already asked myself this same question. To provide a definitive answer, I countered, would it not be necessary to conduct a scientific experiment? Would we not have to abandon an engineer, a master of the Sorbonne, a frigate captain on various far-flung shores? And return eighteen years later to see if they had successfully taught the savages their multiplication tables or the fables of Lafontaine? Formulated aloud from the platform, my question lost much of its incisiveness and conferred upon me an air of arrogance, entirely foreign to my intentions.

You interceded, skilfully moving the discussion on and enabling me to clarify my position. During his sojourn with the savages Narcisse Pelletier had lost not merely what he had learnt in his training as a sailor at fifteen years of age. He had lost the basic notions we acquire at ten or five years of age: the ability to talk about, to think about the future, to evoke the gamut of emotions, the vocabulary of everyday life. He had even forgotten the things we learn almost in the cradle: the names of his brother and sister, his mother's face, the fundamental elements of our language. I believe that a man's education can be likened to a house with many storeys; the knowledge to which Monsieur Decouz believed one could cling was the third story of that edifice, whereas Narcisse had lost the entire structure, right down to the foundations. My explanation seemed to make little impression and was apparently no more convincing than those I had postulated earlier. But the worst was yet to come.

The next speaker, whom I did not recognise, had read my modest work, *Scenes from the Pacific*. He complimented me on the book and remarked that in it I had described the Melanesian archipelagos, and that my only reference to Australia had been a description of the port of Sydney. I inclined my head in acknowledgement of this. Was he therefore to conclude that I have no knowledge of the savages of Australia? I could not but concur, and repeated that I do not claim to have any particular expertise. The speaker had made his point with great skill.

From the associate members' benches at the back of the hall, a voice with a marked English accent spoke up in my defence. The individual, whom I did not know, had been present at my appearance before the Royal Geographical Society on the 1st August. He observed that my presentation on that occasion, although less detailed than today's, and without the presence of the sailor, had been scientifically rigorous in every respect and had provoked much interest. I bowed in acknowledgement of this unexpected support. Father Leroy then pointed out that it was not customary for an associate member to be the first to report on the activities of a foreign society, even one as prestigious as the Royal Geographical Society in London. This rancorous procedural remark invalidated any credit the gentleman at the back of the hall might have brought to my case and alienated me from a section of the audience. Not wishing to become involved in controversy, I did not comment.

There was of course nothing to prevent you, as President of the Society, from taking a stand on this point, aware as you are of the circumstances under which I accepted this invitation.

Monsieur Collet-Hespas, who spoke next, had clearly had an excellent lunch. He began by recalling a previous occasion, some four years earlier, when he had interviewed me on the prospects for fishing in Iceland. I acknowledged that I remembered this. He then asked for your permission to address a question to "this fine young man". You will recall that we had anticipated this eventuality and had agreed that to refuse such a request would perhaps suggest that we had something to conceal. We would therefore grant the request but you would ask me to rephrase the questions as I saw fit. Not remembering to take this precaution, you invited the worthy ship owner to address his question to the hero of the day. Narcisse, who had revealed nothing of substance to me, and had intimated nothing further to you or to his parents in Saint-Gilles, would surely not impart anything to this man whom he was meeting for the first time in front of a noisy, curious crowd.

"Tell me, my good man, do the savages practise polygamy? Does each man have several women?"

"Yes... just like people here."

This remark was greeted with a clamour of objections and with much amusement. It was only later, when I discussed the exchange with Narcisse that I perceived the source of the misunderstanding. Narcisse explained to me that counting on his fingers, he had "had" several women: the English woman on the *Strathmore*, the chambermaid and the German woman at the Savoy, and three days ago, a new mistress in Paris, a liaison of which I had previously been unaware. Narcisse had given a candid response without understanding the reference to polygamy. But the audience had assumed that he had answered with an indecent witticism in order to avoid that very question – when in truth both repartee and the conventions of morality are a mystery to him.

I passed a note to you with the suggestion that we take a break in the proceedings or perhaps call a halt to the session altogether. But to no avail. Father Leroy had asked to speak.

"Tell us, my boy, what did you eat when you were over there?"

"Fish... meat... mussels... clams..."

"Very good. Very interesting. And tell me, what is the religion of these savages?"

I was somewhat alarmed to see the reverend father raise the subject of theology, but not daring to venture a reference to the sermon given by the curate in Saint-Gilles – it would have necessitated too much explanation – I muttered something about the question being too abstract for Narcisse. And indeed he did not say anything in response to the question.

"Let me put it more simply. Do they worship their ancestors? Spirits? The gods of hunting, rain, good health? The sun?"

For Narcisse, words such as "worship" and "religion" were equally obscure. Imagine my surprise therefore when he said, very slowly: "Sun..."

Sometimes, he repeats the last word said to him, in order to give some kind of response and as a courtesy to the speaker. But on this occasion, he repeated the word "sun" several times, with an unfamiliar intensity, as if he were elsewhere, not there with us at the meeting. Then he stood up.

The speaker too appeared somewhat surprised by the reaction he had elicited. Seated as he was in the front row he seemed afraid that Narcisse might raise his hand to him – even though I had repeatedly stressed Narcisse's gentle nature. Narcisse turned round, looked me directly in the eyes, and proclaimed in a loud voice: "Narcisse Pelletier... Sun."

What did he mean? What was it he wanted to say specifically to me?

You asked me what this meant and I found myself unable to conceal my bewilderment. My frankness provoked some sniggering.

Father Leroy then stood up too and addressed Narcisse: "Very good. Most interesting. But I fail to see what we can conclude from this. Let us try another approach. Tell us about the savages' dwellings. What are they made of? Do they build huts? Are they round, square? Are they made of wood, palm fronds, stone, cob? Is there one for each family or are the men separated from the women? Do they perhaps sleep in caves? Or in tents? Igloos?"

Such a torrent of questions could only have the effect of paralysing Narcisse. I was of a mind that Father Leroy was aware of this and was doing it intentionally. Narcisse remained silent. I was reluctant to intervene, fearing that I might add to his confusion.

"And the children? Who is responsible for their education? The father? The mother? The old women? Up to what age? Do they have any initiation ceremonies? What form do they take?"

Still Narcisse did not react.

The speaker spread his arms wide and spun round towards the audience, his cassock swinging out as he turned. Against all precedent for a session of this nature, he addressed the hall.

"I for one have heard quite enough. Or rather I have heard nothing at all. This man is clearly an imbecile. One can learn nothing from him. I fail to see what he can add to our understanding of Australia. During my time as a minister in Quebec, I produced a description of the curious practices of the natives of that region. I spoke every evening with elderly Indians and through the intermediary of a half-caste, wrote down all that they told me. Monsieur le Vicomte's contribution to the science of geography, his only innovation, is to introduce the singular notion of the researcher who has nothing to say. His introductory address was most exciting, but upon approaching the source of his study, I find that the spring has run dry, if indeed it ever flowed at all. We are told that the unfortunate individual before us today reveals his confidences exclusively to the Viscount. No doubt that gentleman brings talent and imagination to his interpretation of this man's grimaces and silence. But what is the good of bringing us here on this account? We are told that he is not an imposter. We are told that he has experienced terrible things and we are asked to accept that he does not wish to speak to us of these unfortunate events. Well then, I shall be happy to offer up prayers to God on his behalf, but I refuse to consider him as useful to the study of geography. And that, after all is the purpose for which we are assembled here today."

In the hubbub that followed this diatribe, applause was heard from many of the benches around the hall and everyone seemed to have something to say about the Reverend Father's philippic. You invited me to speak, but in the general confusion no one paid attention, all the more so since Father Leroy had launched into a loud discussion with several of his neighbours. Narcisse was watching the general confusion, his face set in the half-smile I know to mean he is bemused. I cannot but confess to you that I felt utterly despondent.

You called the meeting to order several times and calm was eventually restored. I responded to your reiterated request for me to speak, and appeared inevitably to be on the defensive. Indeed, the image of an accused man summoned to defend himself before a hostile and partisan audience comes to mind. I evoked yet again the circumstances of Narcisse Pelletier's return to civilisation. I spoke of the difficulty he had in communicating and the need to adjust to his limitations in this regard. One had to know how to listen attentively to what he said and learn how to extract the information he let slip in spite of himself, as it were. In the middle of my address, the Reverend Father stood up and left. Several other members of the Society followed suit as did some of the members of the public. My words were drowned by the sound of footsteps and chairs scraping against the floor. Realising that there was little point in continuing, I was constrained to radically curtail my remarks.

And with this you brought the session to a close.

I shall not dwell on the humiliation – it is not too strong a word – that I experienced, nor on the feeling of being supported by no one. Upon reflection, I wish only to underline that whatever might have caused Father Leroy to arrive at his position, his attitude does not seem to me to be scientific. And that alone should suffice to discredit it.

He claims that the rare statements offered by Narcisse are difficult to interpret, that he is not as forthcoming as the Indians of Quebec and there is no more to be said.

Let us consider Champollion, my illustrious fellow countryman. Would we know his name if he had merely learnt to read and write hieroglyphs at the dictation of an elderly Egyptian? It is precisely the difficulty of the enigma, impenetrable to all those who came before him, that is the basis of Champollion's fame. Narcisse is my Rosetta Stone. The fact that Reverend Father Leroy does not wish to make the effort to learn to read the stone's message proves nothing at all. I am engaged in deciphering it, patiently, slowly and with great difficulty. I am proud of this work.

It seemed necessary to inform you of my perspective on the events of yesterday. I trust that you will understand why I am sending a copy of this letter to the President of the editorial committee of our Review, to assist with the editing of the account of the session, which will no doubt appear in a future edition.

I remain, nevertheless, your faithful servant…

9

They used mussel shells for knives. He watched as the women cut up the fish with the sharp edge of the rounded blue-coloured shells, around the point where the two sides of the shell joined. They shaved the children's heads with them too, coating their skulls with paste made of loam and sand first.

They chopped off branches with another kind of shell: this one was white, elongated and shaped like a finger, with a bevelled edge. Grabbing the shells firmly in their fists, the women hacked at the branches with short sharp downward swipes. Even the thickest of branches yielded to their blows, and if the shells broke as they worked, they simply threw them down and replaced them.

And then there were the tiny white button-sized shells they used for cuts and grazes. Passing a shell lightly over the skin they made a small incision before cleaning and tending the wound.

He watched the women at work, trying to make sense of what he saw. At first, he simply wanted to trim his beard, which was beginning to grow thick and making his skin itch. On board ship he used to shave about once a week, and this feeling of having his cheeks covered with hair was new to him. Now he could see what kind of shell was best to use and what to do with it. He tried it out on his forearm a few times, experimenting with the consistency of the paste he needed to apply. He did not worry too much about grazing the skin a few times and eventually found a way to use his makeshift razor without hurting himself too much. No one paid any attention to him or to his experiments. When he felt he'd perfected the technique, he coated his face with damp earth and scraped his cheeks and chin slowly and carefully with the shell. There was a little blood on his hands, but he didn't seem to have cut himself any more than he would have done with a dull cut-throat razor. A quick dip in the sea was enough to clean the nicks and cuts and ensure that they healed.

He felt encouraged by this small victory.

It meant that he had an implement for cutting once again. It was obviously no substitute for his knife, which must have been discarded somewhere in the forest. He felt its lack keenly and missed it now more than his clothes. The knife was a gift from his father. He'd given it to him after his second voyage as a cabin boy to mark his passage into adulthood. The blade in its leather case fixed to his belt had never left him, on land or at sea, working or sleeping.

If he could cut things again, he'd be able to take some branches, shape them, secure them together with vines or pegs; he would become a ship's carpenter and make himself a canoe. He'd need some sort of grease for caulking, good strong wood for the paddle, a large rock wrapped in vines for an anchor: it'd be a perilous undertaking, navigating along the coast. There were a lot of questions still to be answered, he would undoubtedly have to endure many hardships, but he felt that he was making progress.

It was futile to cut himself off from the savages, sulking and nursing his wounded pride: he should be spending all his time watching them. He needed to see how they did everything, learn all their secrets. He was resourceful and resolute, and he was determined to get through this. If he could learn the savages' secrets, he'd be able to overcome the obstacles in the way of his escape. He would deal with them one by one. There was no point in being impatient, in trying to rush things. Time passed differently now.

It was boredom that had made him decide he needed to shave. That was why he'd worked out what they used for cutting things, and how they shaved the children's heads. From now on, he would have to dedicate all his efforts towards watching them constantly, observing every detail of what they did so that he could learn from them and acquire the skills he needed. Now he had something better than a goal: he had a plan of action.

Using the elongated shell by turns as an axe, a plane and an adze, he went to work. He cut down a branch, stripped off the bark and began to hew the branch into shape. The tool slipped and he cut his hand, but after three shells and an hour of hard work, he had managed to fashion a rudimentary plank. The ship's carpenter on the *Saint-Paul*, a taciturn sort from Dieppe, would have shaken his head in disdain and thrown this shapeless barely trimmed pole onto the scrap heap. But with these meagre tools, could the carpenter have done any better?

He started on a second piece straight away; with practice he was becoming more adept at this, working more efficiently. And besides, he had nothing else to do. He wondered if these three primitive planks were the first pieces, the beginnings of the vessel he'd construct. He gazed at them with pride. Not wanting to alert the savages to anything unusual, he decided to use them for his hut: it paid to be careful. He knocked down his shelter from the night before and began to reconstruct it. Using his three makeshift planks gave him more ideas. By anchoring forked branches to holes in the limestone rock, he managed to make a basic frame and create a space where he could almost stand up. With the materials from his original hut and some more branches and palm fronds he was able to construct the semblance of a roof and walls. They did little to keep out the sun and the wind, but still, he wasn't unhappy with his creation.

He felt reassured by the progress he'd made; the day meant something now. Waiakh had decided to build himself a small hut next to his and he helped him with it, after which they went to play in the waves. The child kept on saying: "Waiakh. Amglo" in a sing-song voice, waving his arms in the air and putting his hand to his chest when he said Waiakh. Narcisse realised that the tribe had named him Amglo. He made a funny face and said: "Amglo. Narcisse Pelletier, dubbed Amglo by the savages."

"Amglo," Waiakh repeated. He pointed to the sun, and stretching out his arm, made a sweeping circular gesture taking in first the sea, then passing over the top of his head and coming back down towards the tops of the trees. The child was indicating the movement of the sun. Was Amglo the word for the sun? Why had they decided to call him Sun? Because he was taller than they were? Because his white skin seemed dazzling in comparison to theirs? Was it because his ship had come from the east, appearing on the horizon at dawn? Or was it for some other peculiar reason?

"Amglo. You're calling me Sun…"

So now he knew one word of their language. He would

have to learn others, more of their gibberish. How did they say: "Where can I find water? Go and get me something to eat. Are there any other white men around here? Come with me to Sydney…?"

No. It was impossible. It would take him months and months to learn enough to be able to communicate with them. He had no desire to talk to them, and he had no intention of spending several months here. Either the *Saint-Paul* would come back, or he'd escape to the south.

He went back over to his hut, the child trotting along behind him. He found this display of loyalty exasperating: what good was it to him? He kicked at Waiakh's hut several times and knocked it down. The boy could go and sleep somewhere else! It was spiteful of him, and there was no reason to do it. But it made him feel better.

"What? What is it?"

The child was staring at him uncomprehendingly.

"You think I'm cruel?"

Narcisse laughed sneeringly.

"You're the cruel ones! The whole lot of you. Much worse than me. You're filthy, you smell. And look at you, you're so small! You're midgets, deformed. You're dwarves, you're ugly and horrible. You're hideous. Even you! You're like a monkey. Uglier. You're black. And not that beautiful shiny black of some of the men I've seen in Africa. They're big and strong. Their skin glows. But you, you're all covered in dust, your skin's dull, faded. It looks like withered cowhide. The skin of a sickly cow. You don't talk – you growl. You never smile, you don't laugh. You can't sing – you bark and click your teeth. You don't even walk properly, you scamper along. You're like, like gnomes, straight out of a nightmare. You're worse than a man's worst nightmares – you couldn't imagine a more horrible creature even in a dream. You're the devil's spawn, all of you, and you're torturing me. The things you eat are revolting, disgusting. You run around stark naked and you're not at all embarrassed. You've stolen my clothes. You ripped off half my ear so you could steal my earring. You're stupid, greedy, nasty and ugly as sin – uglier than all the seven mortal sins. A dog is capable of more love and affection than you. A pig, even! You're not men, you're less than human, there are no words to describe you!

You've made my life miserable every moment of every day. And how do you think this is all going to end? I'll tell you. The *Saint-Paul* will come back, but it won't be just with a crew of thirty men. There'll be other ships, merchant ships, fishing boats. And they'll all be ready to punish you for what you've done to me. And then the warships will come, French ones, English ones, Spanish and American. A whole fleet of ships. They'll seal off your coastline. Whole armies will come ashore and they'll all be white, like me. And then you'll really see what it means to be a white man! You won't act so clever then. You'll growl and bark and click your teeth and we won't understand a thing and it'll be our turn to laugh at your terrified looks. You know nothing about guns, you don't know what a shot is, but believe me, you'll learn soon enough. All those angry sailors and soldiers, they'll chase you into the forest, they'll trap you, surround you, pen you in, they'll beat you with cudgels and make you keep walking: you, the men, the women, the old and the children. We won't need you to find us water, the ships will have enough water for everyone to drink their fill, to wash from head to foot every day if they want to. But there won't be a drop for you! And then when you're all rounded up and tied up they'll start cutting off your left ears, all of you. With billhooks, bayonets, knives, daggers. They'll pile all those black ears up together and set fire to them. Then they'll kill you all, slowly, one by one, with no mercy. You'll get what you deserve, all of you, a hundred times over. They'll drive knives into your stomachs, and spread your entrails out on the sand and they'll leave you to bleed to death, and there won't be a single one of you left on earth, and none of your kind either. You'll be writhing in agony, you'll die slowly in the blazing sun! You'll be crawling and groaning and begging for mercy, and they'll kick you down. And just to make sure they've finished the job, the warships will bombard the forest, you'll see just how far they can fire, they'll keep firing right down to their last round of ammunition, until there isn't a single tree left standing. And when they've done that, they'll set it all on fire, a fire to end all fires, it'll consume everything in sight and beyond, a great bonfire to celebrate the end of the lot of you...

And I'll be aboard the *Saint-Paul*, standing on the poopdeck. I'll be dressed in linen trousers, a cotton shirt, a silk scarf, a felt hat – linen, cotton, silk, felt, you don't know what any of it is do you, little monster, son of a stinking black dwarf – and I'll be drinking good Cape white wine, wearing my smart new clothes, watching the soldiers kill you and set everything on fire, and I'll be applauding them and shouting 'hooray' at the top of my voice and I'll cheer them, I'll shout: 'Go on, lads! More! Don't let a single one get away! Don't give them an inch!' And when after three days the fire finally dies down and the smoke settles on your accursed land, it'll be burnt to a cinder and no one will ever know that anyone lived here, and we'll be able to leave in peace and we won't look back.

I'll go back to France and I'll never go to sea again. I'll go back home, I'll see my parents again, I'll look for work, and you'll see just how hard I can work! I'll settle down, I'll meet a pretty girl and I'll take her to the dance and I'll marry her in church – you have no idea what a church is, do you, you little black goblin – and we'll have a baby in no time at all, a little boy and he'll be all pink and plump, and I'll cradle him in my arms whenever she's not nursing him, and then we'll have more children, two or three at least. I'll play with them in the evenings when I get home, they'll come and jump into bed with us, and I'll tell them about my travels all over the world, but I'll never, ever tell them what's happened here. Never.

And the day I get home, you know what I want? I want my mother to make me my favourite stew. You obviously don't know what that is, you filthy little monkey. I'll go and get some of the best new potatoes from the cellar: I'll choose a nice crunchy green cabbage in the garden, a big firm cabbage; turnips, white and purple, sticks of celery, leeks. I'll get some nice fat round sausages from the salting tub, a hunk of lard, a pig's trotter, some bacon. I'll put it all out on the table, I'll help my mother chop the vegetables, and she'll put it all in the pot and stew it all afternoon on a slow fire. The whole house will be filled with the delicious smell and the neighbours will know what's simmering on the stove, and they'll stop in to say hello. And in the evening, I'll sit down to eat it, at the table in the garden if the weather's nice, and if not in the kitchen near the stove. And there'll be cheese too, several different kinds, and bunches of grapes, nuts, a jug of wine. And then when we've eaten all we possibly can, she'll produce a plum tart from the oven."

He'd never uttered such a long speech in his whole life. He'd spoken to hear the sound of his own voice, intoxicated by his own words, astonished at what he heard himself saying. And Waiakh had stood there, not moving, listening intently, not saying a word, watching with obvious interest, somewhat intimidated by the outburst. Narcisse took a deep breath. What was he doing, talking about plum tart to this boy, this black lizard-eating child?

LETTER IX

Monsieur le Président,

Who could have imagined that this adventure would lead to our being received at Court?

Upon his request, I went to see Count Marsigny, the Imperial Grand Chamberlain, who informed me that Her Majesty Empress Eugénie had learnt of the presence of a white savage and had expressed a wish to meet him. Rumours circulating around the city had reached her, as had the press reports although the Count made no mention of our Society and did not allude to the heated meeting of which I have already spoken. I bowed and assured him that Narcisse and I were entirely at Her Majesty's disposal.

"He is not," he hesitated, "shall we say, dangerous, is he?"

I had become accustomed to this question and replied by assuring him that Narcisse was the gentlest and most devoted of Their Majesties' subjects. Indeed the first word he had pronounced in Sydney, the word that had enabled him to be identified as French, was none other than the name of the noble founder of the royal dynasty. And furthermore, the Pelletier family were united in their reverence for Narcisse's uncle, a veteran of the Grande Armée, wounded at Eylau. The Grand Chamberlain looked at me as if to say he would like to take me at my word but that further guarantees would be required to secure Her Majesty's safety. I did indeed receive a letter from my brother a few days later informing me that the Prefect of the Isère had been instructed to gather information about me and our family, and moreover that this had been carried out without excessive regard for discretion. I can only assume that the enquiry had yielded results that were not deemed too negative.

The Grand Chamberlain continued to question me: "Where, in your opinion, should the audience take place? And how should it be conducted?"

"I would not presume to offer advice to either Her Majesty or her courtiers. I can only stress that Monsieur Pelletier is still somewhat shy and impressionable."

Never before had I, nor anyone else, referred to Narcisse as Monsieur. It was a strange sensation to hear this formal title coming from my own lips, as if a new being – no longer the white savage, no longer just Narcisse – was beginning to emerge.

"I fear that the pomp and ceremony of the court might intimidate him or render him completely mute. If he could be presented to Her Majesty in a more intimate setting with a small number of participants and a minimum of protocol, he would be more comfortable and better able to answer her questions."

"The rose garden in the Palais de Compiègne would perhaps be a more suitable setting than the state rooms of the Palais des

Tuilieries?" suggested the Grand Chamberlain. "And you say that he is capable of recounting his tale?"

"Monsieur Pelletier will be only too happy to satisfy Her Majesty's curiosity. He expresses himself in very simple language, and still sometimes struggles to find his words; I believe he has not yet fully grasped the extraordinary nature of his adventure. He does not speak of his experiences in the most skilful fashion, but he will answer all questions."

"And will his tales be of an appropriate nature to be recounted in the presence of Her Majesty and the ladies of the Court?"

"Monsieur Pelletier is no mere common seaman. He has returned from his ordeal with an astonishing simplicity of soul, a complete absence of malice or irony that is almost childlike. He is deeply honoured to be received by Her Majesty "

Narcisse is certainly not an accomplished storyteller: in six months I have learnt nothing about his sojourn in Australia. But how could I admit that his reticence might result in an audience that could well prove to be dull and uninteresting?

Our exchange was being recorded by a secretary seated at a table. After a few more questions, the Grand Chamberlain concluded: "We shall receive this Monsieur Pelletier."

One week later, we travelled by railway to Compiègne. A carriage transported us from the station to the château: we entered directly into the gardens without stopping at the main gate, and travelled along the alleyways to an elegant wooden lodge. It was a lovely early autumn afternoon. We were offered refreshments by a valet and as I sipped a glass of orangeade, I repeated my advice to Narcisse one last time on how to conduct himself, advice that I had not ceased to repeat throughout the journey.

I had been much exercised by the question of how he should dress for the occasion. Style and elegance mean nothing to him: he prefers to wear garments that do not bind around the neck or the waist, with ample sleeves. He would have been most uncomfortable dressed as I was in jacket, waistcoat and silk neck-tie. After having sought advice as to acceptable attire for an afternoon in Compiègne, I purchased a pair of white canvas trousers for him, a loose linen shirt with a scarf at the neck, a grey untailored jacket, and a black broad-brimmed hat. Thus attired, he could have passed for a gentleman with a taste for boating, a trader returning from a horse fair perhaps, or even a Balkan aristocrat.

We were greeted by an officer of the Hussars, a broad-shouldered giant of a man, who escorted us through the gardens. Narcisse walked along at a good pace, smiling as he is wont to do when he is surrounded by nature. Neither the hussar nor I paid any attention to the first of the autumn leaves underfoot, but Narcisse managed, without looking at the ground, to effortlessly avoid stepping on them.

The hussar led us to a copse, where the Empress was seated on a bench behind which two more powerfully-built hussars stood sentinel – the Grand Chamberlain had not wished to take any risks. Her Majesty greeted us with a smile. She was dressed in a green silk gown, a fine white shawl, and a charming ivory coloured cap. I came within three steps of her and bowed respectfully. Narcisse bowed too, but towards the lady seated on Her Majesty's right, whose blue dress embroidered in gold thread and wide-brimmed hat decorated with a pheasant feather had seemed to him to be the sign of a higher rank.

"Pauline, the Empress is eclipsed in your presence," said Her Majesty teasingly. The lady in question, whom I understood to be Princess Pauline von Metternich, realised

Narcisse's mistake and responded with a peal of laughter, leaving Narcisse nonplussed. I greeted the Princess and a rather stout elderly gentleman sitting in an armchair whom I recognised to be the writer Prosper Mérimée. The Imperial Prince was playing with a hoop under the watchful eye of his governess, Madame Bruat. Two ladies-in-waiting were occupied with their embroidery.

"Viscount," said Her Majesty, "I am most grateful to you for bringing Monsieur Pelletier here. I thank you for having escorted him back to France from Australia, and for conveying him here to us today in Compiègne."

"Which of the two journeys, Viscount," asked the Princess, "have you found the more remarkable?"

I was quite taken by surprise and was unable to utter any but the most dull and foolish of responses.

"It was my duty, Your Highness, to bring him back to France, but to be received in Compiègne with him is both an honour and a great pleasure."

Perhaps Her Majesty was displeased by my banal and ingratiating response, for she turned her attention away from me and addressed Narcisse.

"Tell me, Monsieur Pelletier, are you happy to be back in France?"

"Yes, Your Majesty."

My lessons in etiquette had made a greater impression on Narcisse than had my instruction in the art of conversation.

"Tell us how you filled your days during all those years over there."

"In the morning, the men hunt or fish. When it gets too hot, everyone sleeps. In the evening, the women prepare the meal. Later, they sing, or else everyone dances. Then at night, everyone sleeps."

This response, which owed little to Narcisse and much to my invention, had been well rehearsed. Narcisse played the part well: he had learnt his lines and his answer was well received.

"How I should have liked to lead such an existence!" Her Majesty remarked dreamily.

"And what did you eat?" asked the Princess.

"Fish, shellfish, snails, and… and…" he searched around for the word. "An animal that flies, in groups. It's green."

"Birds?" suggested the Princess.

"No."

The Imperial Prince had moved closer to hear the conversation and suddenly exclaimed:

"Mother, I'll go and get my picture book!"

As the young Prince ran off to find his book, the Princess remarked on his intelligence and presence of mind. Returning with the picture book, he gave it to Narcisse who turned the pages and eventually found the creature in question. The French word came back to him when he saw the illustration: the image had enabled him to remember the word. I alone realised this, the others all mistakenly believing that he was able to read.

"Grasshoppers."

This was met by an exclamation of surprise and disgust. Monsieur Mérimée made a remark that was both elegant and witty, the precise details of which I cannot recall.

"Was it cold?"

"No, Your Majesty. Only a little bit, between full moons and during the heavy rains."

"And what sort of clothes did you wear?"

"There were no clothes."

Her Majesty made sure that the Imperial Prince had not

heard this exchange, and indicated with a delicate smile that she did not hold the witness responsible for the improprieties revealed by his frank response.

"How many wives do the men have?"

"One, Your Majesty."

"Only one? And can they change wives?"

"When the wife starts to get a bit old, you can take another one. You have to continue to feed the first one."

I was astounded to see Narcisse willingly telling the Empress about life among the savages, when the questions I had asked him a thousand times had remained unanswered. With her natural goodness and simplicity, Her Majesty elicited far more information than had Monsieur Collet-Hespas the previous week.

"An Australian custom that seems to be practised in Court," sighed Her Majesty.

Judging my penance to have lasted sufficiently long, she turned to me and said:

"Viscount, tell us how you saved this unfortunate man's life."

I explained to her how the adventure had begun, stressing the role of chance as well as the part played by the governor of New South Wales.

"We must thank him for that. I shall write a letter to Victoria about this matter."

One of the ladies-in-waiting, no doubt the lady responsible for the royal correspondence, inclined her head in acknowledgement and wrote a few words in a notebook.

"But were you certain of the truth of the story from the very beginning?" the Princess asked. "Were you not worried that you might have been the victim of a malicious deception?"

"In Paris," declared Monsieur Mérimée, "one scarcely

dares to do anything nowadays for fear of being duped."

"The first time I set eyes upon this unfortunate young man in the gardens of the governor's residence," I replied, " he was dressed only in a loincloth. His tattoos all over his body spoke for him."

"Do sailors not routinely have tattoos?" interjected the Princess.

"That is correct, Your Highness. But these markings, together with the other symbols etched on his skin, are unlike anything previously beheld. Perhaps it would interest you to see them?"

A barely perceptible movement of the royal fan indicated that the offer had been accepted, and I asked Narcisse to remove his jacket and roll his right shirtsleeve up to the shoulder.

A line of scarring begins at the biceps, winding twice around the forearm and ending on the back of his hand. Beneath it is a tattoo, a long check pattern that seems almost to be churned up by the twisting lines of the scarification. In the remaining spaces are broken lines, circles, spirals, arranged in no discernible pattern. The motifs are etched in black pigment, outlined in red on the inner side of his forearm, and are perfectly executed. One has the impression that many, many hours of work were involved in the creation of these markings.

Her Majesty, and all of her entourage, including the officers of the Hussars, gazed in amazement at this entirely novel spectacle. Narcisse, who seemed only too happy to show off the markings on his skin, was slowly rotating his arm, opening and closing his fist to bring the strange designs into relief.

"I want one too, Mother. I want a drawing on my arm too!" exclaimed the young Prince.

Princess Pauline explained to the Imperial Prince that this would involve a thousand pricks with a very long, fat needle and the Prince's enthusiasm seemed to wane.

I signalled to Narcisse to roll down his shirtsleeve and don his jacket again. I hoped to avert any requests to see his other arm, his back, or perhaps even his legs, with the wound to his thigh. All these marks were merely the outward residue of what Narcisse had endured and I hoped that a new line of questioning would permit him to reveal other aspects of his experiences.

"And what of your family while you were over there?" asked Her Majesty.

Narcisse turned towards me and I replied for him: "His parents, his brother and his sister, all believed him to be dead. They received official notice of his death from the shipowner."

"Eighteen years..." said Her Majesty pensively before turning to her aide-de-camp: "Captain, make sure that the Minister of the Navy examines why this unfortunate man was abandoned and how it came about that his parents were falsely informed of his death."

Then, turning back to Narcisse, she asked: "Have you seen your parents again?"

"Yes, Your Majesty. The Viscount took me to Saint-Gilles-sur-Vie."

"How affecting those reunions must have been!"

I bowed in acknowledgement, not wishing to importune Her Majesty with the details of our visit to the Vendée.

"And while you were in Australia, how did you survive?"

"At first, I was like a child. I didn't know how to do anything. I didn't know how to speak, to hunt or to eat. An old woman looked after me. I stayed with her until I grew up."

"But how old were you when you were cast away on those shores?" asked the Princess.

Seeing that this question was beyond Narcisse and that he

was unable to answer, I spoke on his behalf:

"Eighteen and a half years old. I believe that the savages initially looked upon him as a child because he knew nothing of their ways."

"How curious!" exclaimed Her Majesty. "And the old woman you speak of, my friend?"

"She died."

"Oh, I'm so sorry. You must have felt alone all over again. And afterwards?"

The question related to any relationships that Narcisse might have formed subsequently, but he interpreted it in quite another manner.

"Afterwards, we left her under her tree. That evening, we left for another part of the forest."

"How so?"

"When death comes, we leave. It is forbidden to touch the dead person, his arrows, his baskets, his food. You must leave, otherwise, bad things happen. It is forbidden to return to that place."

How much invaluable information lay concealed in these few sentences! In his desire to please Her Majesty, Narcisse was revealing far more than he had throughout all my vain and persistent efforts to interrogate him. Her Majesty was of course completely unaware of this. I must confess that I was somewhat piqued. I see now that I was wrong to stubbornly persist with my questions, with my method and my principles of enquiry. As I write these lines to you, I begin to understand that Narcisse speaks when and as he pleases.

Putting this rather sad episode behind us, Her Majesty enquired:

"And me, my friend. Do you know who I am?"

"You are the wife of the big chief."

"That is not such a bad way of looking at it," sighed Her Majesty as she turned towards her friend and said in a dreamy voice, absently stroking an embroidered cushion: "Those eyes... never, since I have been Empress, has any man looked at me with such frankness, such force. I could not hold his gaze."

An awkward silence followed. Narcisse and I waited to be invited once again to participate in the conversation. What could one say after this admission? To break the spell, the Princess clapped her hands like a child and exclaimed:

"Let us play some music. Let us turn to the language everyone understands! Ladies, play something for us."

Two of the ladies-in-waiting lifted a brocade cover from a piece of furniture to reveal an upright piano standing upon a small platform. The youngest of the ladies drew up a stool upon which she sat and performed two Chopin preludes; she played with much emotion, perhaps a little too much.

Narcisse had already had occasion to hear our music: a trio in a café in Calais, the harmonium in the church in Saint-Gilles, a military band in a bandstand in Paris. I knew that he understood nothing of it and that he neither showed interest in nor derived pleasure from it. He listened politely, sensing that Her Majesty had not yet finished with him.

"Tell me, my friend, when you were in Australia, did you sing?"

"Yes, Your Majesty."

"Sing us one of your songs then, a tune from over there. It will make a change from our fashionable ditties."

I was alarmed by this unforeseen request. I had of course made the same request myself on several occasions, but always to no avail. We had not prepared anything and I did not know how he would respond. He bowed his head, gathered his memories, and began to perform.

How shall I describe the sounds that issued from his mouth? Never before had I heard their like, in the South Pacific or elsewhere. Whining and mewling, staccato repetitions of syllables, clicks of the tongue and teeth, syncopated grunts, whistling sounds, all of these bore no resemblance to anything taught in our conservatoire. No key signature, no arrangement of flats and sharps on the stave could ever convey this monotonous threnody. The strange, pronounced rhythm suggested that he was indeed singing. His voice had taken on a guttural, muted timbre. Something of the harshness of Australia, the solitude of its deserts, the burning heat of the sun on the cracked earth entered into the gardens of Compiègne, and I half expected to see specks of red dust settling imperceptibly on the Empress's shoulders.

Narcisse stopped abruptly, with no rallentando or cadence to mark the end of his song. A shiver ran through Her Majesty, and to lighten the mood, she said, without managing to smile:

"Well, Pauline, this is doubtless much more astonishing than the latest of Monsieur Wagner's innovations, of which you speak so highly."

Princess Pauline rescued the conversation from the lull that threatened to engulf it, and turning towards Narcisse asked:

"And what will you do tomorrow, my friend?"

This innocuous question threw him into profound confusion. I could see from the way he was twiddling his fingers that he was at a loss. He bowed towards the Princess, took a deep breath and ventured:

"Tomorrow, the sun will rise."

Her Majesty and the Princess went into raptures over the "oriental wisdom" of this response and could not have seen, in Narcisse's utterance, the evidence of my grammar lessons and my attempts to inculcate in him the very notion of the future.

"That," said Her Majesty, " is how I shall henceforth reply to all those who constantly importune me with questions about what the Emperor and I are planning to do."

I made no attempt to dispel the misunderstanding with regard to his response. It occurs to me as I write these lines that the entire audience was nothing more than one long misunderstanding.

"And do you not have a trade, a situation of some sort?" continued the Princess.

He lowered his gaze.

"And if the Viscount had not taken care of you, would you have starved to death?"

Narcisse was at a loss as to how to answer. Hypothetical reasoning was even more foreign to him than speculation about the future. His silence was taken as a sign of delicacy of feeling.

"Captain," Her Majesty commanded, "I want someone to find this unfortunate man some employment in government service. You will confer with the Viscount as to what might suit him. I want his years of wandering and suffering to end today."

She rose – the audience was finished. Her final words were for me: "Viscount, I intend to recognise what you have done. You have rescued this unfortunate individual even though you were under no obligation to do so. You have devoted your efforts to him, you have looked after him as a brother. You have brought him back to his country. Indifferent to gossip and glory alike, you seek no reward for your act of generosity. I do not know if the French people will understand your attitude; indeed, I believe that their opinion matters little to you. Your Empress salutes your generosity of spirit, be she the only one to do so."

I was surprised and moved in equal measure by these words from my sovereign, and I bowed deeply in response, preferring to remain silent rather than to utter a trite rejoinder.

"Take this ring as a token to remember me by. The colour of the stone will remind you of the sea."

Her Majesty removed a gold ring decorated with diamonds and a sapphire from her middle finger. As she handed me the ring, both she and the Princess seemed moved and subdued by the strange solemnity of the moment. Narcisse was watching a flock of birds fly south, the wind rustling the leaves of an elm tree.

The hussar came back over to me, a sign that it was time for us to take our leave. Her Majesty had turned away and the Princess was declaring with a charming peal of laughter that she intended to risk playing the piano.

As we were walking back towards the pavilion, we heard the strains of a polka echoing through the trees. Narcisse turned round as we were about to cross to the other side of the hedge, and looked for one last time at Her Majesty. She was standing, her head half turned over her shoulder, watching him walk away.

We were preparing to climb into the carriage when the hussar took me aside:

"Monsieur le Vicomte, how can we do as Her Majesty commands? What employment is this chap able to sustain?"

"I do not know."

"You cannot envisage him working for the government then, in the Council of State perhaps?"

"That would make him most unhappy."

The officer gave me a disapproving look, believing that he had detected a note of impertinence in my response to his ironic suggestion. But I had been entirely sincere in thinking only of Narcisse; I could equally have pointed out that he did not know how to read. I continued:

"He is still… unfamiliar with paperwork and the written word. He is uncomfortable in a crowd, as he is when he is required to converse, or simply to listen to others. Manual work, outdoors would suit him. I cannot imagine him in Paris or in a big city."

"Can he follow orders?"

"Perhaps not as a soldier should. But he is gentle, full of good will and he does what he is asked."

"A position in forestry perhaps?"

"He has always lived near the sea. If you could perhaps find him a situation that would allow him to live by the sea…"

"Her Majesty has given you her ring, and we must obey your wishes," concluded the officer with a curt movement of the head and a note of insolence that undermined his assertion.

While we were discussing the future, Narcisse was admiring the bay horses of the imperial carriage team. I wondered by what mysterious alchemy Her Majesty had obtained from him so many precious gems of information. As if without thinking and undoubtedly without realising, she had coaxed from Narcisse intimations that he had hitherto revealed to no one else. Ah, if only the sceptics from our session at the Society could have been present at this interview, how foolish they would have felt.

On the way back to the station, Narcisse asked me: "Will we see the Empress again?"

"I don't know. I think not."

It was the first time I had heard him use the future tense, the first time he had asked me a question or shown some interest in what was happening to him. He asked to see the ring, but the only light that filtered through the carriage's narrow windows was a dull autumn glow in which neither the gold nor the stones shone. He lost interest.

Should I relay to you what he had to say about this memorable day? I trust that you will keep this in the strictest confidence, and that you will remain sworn to secrecy in the name of science.

"The Empress is a beautiful woman. More beautiful than Princess Pauline."

I remain your faithful servant...

10

Throughout the days on the beach Narcisse had stayed in the shade as much as possible; he'd done all he could to protect his naked body from the sun. And yet this morning his skin was peeling. Burnt dark by the sun, it had blistered and was coming away in strips. The most painful areas were his shoulders, back, buttocks and thighs, the parts of his body that had always before been protected by clothes. And the new pink skin that emerged was even more sensitive, defenceless against the sun, sand, wind and salt.

His whole body was on fire. What could he do to soothe his burning skin? You could buy phials from the Chinese in ports all over the world, concoctions that gave protection against sunburn. But here? Plant sap or crushed leaves might work, but he knew nothing about any of these plants and he couldn't risk picking them at random. He tried using the traces of fat on the underside of the skin of a cooked fish, but it seemed to have no effect.

The old woman had seen the state he was in but she offered no relief. He watched with disgust as she picked up a scrap of dead skin from the ground, chewed on it, swallowed and spat it out. What did she think? That he was sloughing off his skin, like a snake?

He thought of snakes shedding their skin with the changing of the season, hares changing colour, birds replacing their plumage. Was he to be transformed too? What unimagined metamorphosis was in store for him? What was it that he would cease to be? And what would he turn into? A caterpillar does not choose to be transformed into a butterfly. Would he have any more choice than a caterpillar?

Later that morning, an old man emerged from the forest. As soon as they saw him the women stopped what they were doing and came running over. Others awoke from their sleep or came out of the water; mothers stopped playing with their children. They clustered around the new arrival, eager to touch him, be near to him, talk to him, sing him a little tune. He walked slowly over to a lone tree and lay down underneath it. The women brought him water, fish, shellfish and twigs to make a fire near where he was lying. They sat down with the children, surrounding him and chattering incessantly all at once.

Narcisse went over to have a look. The man seemed old beyond imagining. His wispy hair was the colour of snow – unlike the tribe's elder, the man he called Chief, whose hair was, if no longer actually black, still not completely grey. This man's face was furrowed with deep wrinkles fanning out in every direction, making his eyes seem deeply sunken in the sockets. Age had withered the muscles of his arms and legs, leaving the excess skin hanging off his bones like clothes a size too big. All tattoos and markings on the skin were lost, indecipherable in this ashen skin that seemed already to be dead. He was missing the little finger on his right hand, like the carpenter on the *Saint-Paul*, and in his mouth there remained only a few rickety teeth. Unlike the other men of the tribe, who were all completely naked, he wore a thin belt of woven vines around the hips, a miniature rose motif suspended from the front of the belt.

Who was this ancient being?

Narcisse watched as the women scurried around, striving not merely to obey the old man's wishes but to anticipate his every need, proud to be in his presence. It reminded him of the ladies of his church, those pious women thrown into raptures by the visit of an emissary of the bishop. The children, even those older than Waiakh, were carrying on with their games and paying no attention to the old man. He decided to follow their example and ignore him too.

In the afternoon, the old woman came to find him and signalled to him to follow her. She led him over to the old man who was still lying down, dozing lightly. Narcisse remained standing, revelling in his own size and strength as he looked down on the frail creature before him. The old woman intoned a short speech and he thought he caught the word "Amglo". Did local etiquette demand that he be formally introduced to this elder? He bowed mockingly and announced in a loud voice: "Greetings, oh filthy Prince of the savages. I am Narcisse Pelletier, sailor on the schooner *Saint-Paul*. Your people are incapable of speaking normal language, so they call me Amglo."

Something about the old man's penetrating gaze made him feel uncomfortable. Disconcerted, he turned away.

All day long, the women fussed over the ancient visitor. Narcisse did not want to pay any attention to him; what difference did it make to him, one savage more or less? The old man hadn't come here to see Amglo, to make plans for his future: he'd shown virtually no interest in him. Perhaps he was a shaman or a magician, come to console the women after the death of a woman in childbirth. Well, let them sing then, all of them! Let them sing their savages' requiem. It would keep him entertained for a while.

Then, as he sat sucking on the remains of a large fish with bluish scales, he was struck by something. If this old man had come specifically to mourn the dead woman, or to mark Amglo's arrival, or for both of these reasons, it meant that he must have been told about these developments in the tribe. Who had told him? And how?

He looked at the fragile old man; even the simplest movements seemed an effort for him. It was inconceivable that he could be living as a hermit in some corner of the forest. He would need other savages to help him hunt and find water. And with those small shaky steps, how could he have come here alone, walking for two, three days or more? There must be another group of savages with an encampment not too far from here, and he must live with them.

Narcisse thought back to Wanderer's arrival when they had been at the water hole. At the time, he had supposed that the young man had been hunting alone for several days. But perhaps he had gone to visit his cousins, to greet the chief, to take a message, to look for a wife, or who knows, to seek the blessings of an ancestor.

There must be savages everywhere in Australia: other groups wandering around all over the place, along the coast, in the forests and mangroves, in the endless wastelands of the deserts.

The southernmost tribes, near Sydney, must be in contact with white men.

Could he dare to hope that he might be led from group to group as far as the English colony, or to its furthest outpost?

Or perhaps he could send a message, from one tribe to the next, a message to his own kind, etched onto a piece of bark, alerting them to his presence?

He was jumping ahead of himself, getting carried away with a new plan, a wild hope based on two separate ideas. He had no means of fulfilling either of them; there would be no miracle. He must not let himself be duped. He had simply learnt that other tribes existed; they moved about, had contact with each other.

What if he were to go from one tribe to another? But even supposing all the savages were friendly, that they all welcomed him, how could he be sure that his new hosts would lead him in the right direction? Towards the south, yes, but did they move in straight lines?

Would it be safer to send a message? He tried using shells to scratch on a piece of bark and after many attempts, managed to etch a few lines. He would definitely write his name, but what else should he say, and to whom? He did not know how to explain where he was and the tribe kept moving their encampments. And even if he did manage to etch his name and an approximate map onto a piece of bark, with the idea of at least prompting a search, how could he explain the importance of this message to the savages? The urgent need to pass it from one black hand to another, until it reached a white hand? The bark on which he patiently engraved his name, carrying all his hopes, would it not just end up being used to light a fire?

LETTER X

Monsieur le Président,

Thank you for your letter of 10th September and for your explanation of the concerns uppermost in your mind at the plenary session. I fully understand that as chairman of the session you were of course subject to a host of contradictory considerations. Indeed, I am grateful to you for having taken the time to raise a matter that might otherwise have constituted a source of misunderstanding between us. The meeting occurred soon after the singular experience of those few days in Saint-Gilles and my view of the afternoon's events must indeed have been clouded by the intense emotions to which I was prey. No doubt my desire to protect Narcisse Pelletier played its part too, as did my lack of experience in such affairs. My letter to you was written in the heat of the moment and was indeed lacking in perspective. As you know, the meeting was followed by another momentous occasion, the audience with Her Majesty of which I have sent you a full report. After all of this, I had little choice but to leave Paris in search of peace and quiet.

My sister Charlotte, whom I had not seen for four years, was expecting us at the Château de Vallombrun. She was eager to meet Narcisse: I had informed her of the essentials of our adventure and she wished to make the acquaintance of the hero of my tale. As you will have gathered from my prolonged silence, now that I find myself in the tranquil setting of the Château de Vallombrun, I have taken the time to reflect upon matters.

We have installed Narcisse in a guest room. He takes his meals with us, and our staff treat him as they would any other guest. For the first few days here, he seemed content to savour the sights of the trees in their autumn colours, the meadows and hedgerows, the village fountain, the streams and the country paths. From some of the hilltops near the chateau, one can make out the snowy peaks of the Alps. I noted with some surprise that we are no longer separated from the mountains by the border of the Kingdom of Piedmont-Sardinia: our Empire has expanded and the border has retreated to the highest peaks, beyond the river basins of the Isère and the Arve. While I reflected upon all of this, Narcisse gazed uncomprehendingly at the white substance on the horizon.

Much as I had loved to walk when I was a young man of twenty, I cannot now afford the luxury of accompanying Narcisse on his daily expeditions: I have pressing matters to deal with, all the more so after such a long period of absence. I had seen evidence of Narcisse's excellent sense of direction in the forests around Sydney and later in the streets of Paris, and was confident that he would not lose his way. I left him to discover the area for himself.

He duly set off one morning at a good pace, only to return that evening with his jacket torn, his trousers spattered with mud, and his cap gone. I feared at first that he may have been involved in an unfortunate encounter, but this was not the case. Two leagues from here, he had come across some peasants unloading a cartload of logs for the winter. Spontaneously, and with barely a word, he "lent them his hand" as they say in these parts. Surprised, and no doubt somewhat scornful at first to see this strapping, well-dressed fellow carrying wood over to the woodshed, his new friends made the most of their good fortune. Narcisse remained indifferent to the fate of his smart new clothes and assisted with the two further cartloads of logs that followed. The peasants shared their bread, cheese and sausage with him, and together they finished stacking all the wood for the winter. Narcisse then returned to the chateau.

Days passed and he continued with his walks. On one occasion, he found himself in the company of a shepherd and his flock as they descended from their mountain pastures. His wanderings led him at other times to work at cleaning out manure from a stable, carrying barrowloads of earth from a building site, and digging out a blocked ditch. You would be mistaken to suppose that he set out in search of employment or physical exertion. He simply goes where his fancy leads him. When he encounters men at work, he acts as he did aboard the *Strathmore*: he cannot but offer his assistance.

I provided him with clothing more suitable for this strange pastime. I have recently become aware that there are mutterings among the villagers: they no longer find his unusual comportment amusing and sometimes take umbrage. They are spontaneously wary of such singular generosity. My staff are no longer certain whether to treat him as a guest or a workman – for Narcisse cannot let the coachman bring the hay out of the barn without assisting him, any more than he can desist from helping the cook to carry a crate of apples. And although my sister says nothing to me, I understand her consternation at having to dine every evening with a guest who remains silent at the table. I myself have learnt absolutely nothing new from him during these last few weeks and I find myself wondering where the limits of my responsibility towards my guest should lie. Narcisse is a fine fellow, but is this enough to entitle him to my hospitality indefinitely?

I also have reason to believe that Narcisse had a dalliance with a girl from the village. Both the father of the girl in question, and the curate have made it clear that they consider his presence undesirable.

In short, if Narcisse is not to live in Saint-Gilles, where is he to reside? Is there any more of a place for him here in Vallombrun?

I was pondering the nature of my relationship with Narcisse when I received a letter from the Minister of the Navy. Her Majesty's request had not been forgotten. The minister had asked Admiral Jurian de La Gravière to preside over an official enquiry into the events that had led to the sailor Pelletier spending so many years among the Australian savages. How had it come about that his death had been wrongly reported, and thus no search carried out? Behind the scenes, I was assured that disciplinary or penal proceedings had not been ruled out.

The owner and the captain of the *Saint-Paul* were found without any trouble; so too was the ship's journal. But the second mate, who had countersigned the report of the sailor's death on the 5th November 1843, had been stabbed in a brawl in Valparaiso in 1855.

The ensuing commission of enquiry convened in the splendour of the naval headquarters in the Hôtel de la Marine.

Captain Porteret, who had sustained a wound to the leg and was no longer at sea, had at first pleaded that he no longer clearly remembered this affair of long ago, and that he recalled nothing more than a difficult crossing from the Cape to China, with men falling sick, and an unexpected stopover. The reporting officer of the commission had studied the ship's log and pressed him with questions on his choice of tactics. Why had he chosen such a southerly route on leaving the Cape? Why had he then persisted on an easterly course, when he had logged the presence of several sick men, and could have made it to Reunion Island, Mauritius or Ceylon? Why this slow cautious course towards the west coast of Australia and thence around the north coast, punctuated with vain and half-hearted attempts to find water? Why had he waited so long to finally decide to make for the nearest port and abandon the effort to replenish the water supply?

With each question, the captain shrank further into his seat, mumbled something, and gradually remembered more details. His fragmentary, at times contradictory answers left one with a baleful impression of incompetence. I found it difficult to imagine that this elderly man had once been in command of a schooner on a long ocean voyage with a crew of thirty men.

A young officer then assailed him with questions about the maps they had been using to navigate in 1843. The captain no longer knew exactly which ones they had used. They were certainly old and of inferior quality: the owner was parsimonious and economised on everything, even on essential navigating equipment. Had they used maps from before the Revolution? Maps that predated Nicolas Baudin's expedition to Australia? Captain Porteret no longer knew, but he was certain that he had never had any English maps at his disposal.

It was the admiral who delivered the decisive blow: "How

many deaths did you sustain after the Cape?"

The captain, ashen-faced, was forced to admit that he no longer remembered.

"In that case I think it is time to adjourn the hearing and let you read your ship's journal once more. I trust that it will be of assistance to you as we continue."

A second advocate led the captain to an adjacent office while the admiral came over to us.

"Good morning, Viscount," he said. "Good morning, sailor. The next encounter promises to be most interesting; I am eager to see what it will reveal. I am not sure that this Captain Porteret has understood why he is here. He certainly made some poor navigational decisions, although for the time being, I cannot see anything improper. On the other hand, abandoning a member of the crew and making a false report of a death are crimes. The minister attaches a high price to the solving of this enigma." He turned to Narcisse and added: "It will all depend on your testimony, my good fellow."

The commission of enquiry proceeded to ask me about the circumstances in which the sailor Pelletier had been discovered. I reiterated my account of the events of February and March in Australia. One of the officers then asked me a question that had never occurred to me before: "The bay where the sailor was found by the English ship, the *John Bell*, cannot be described as *terra incognita*. It has been mapped and the anchorage is recorded in the official Sailing Directions. We are told that it is advisable to avoid it in an east wind or at high tide. But, it is the only bay in the sector. In short, this bay is regularly frequented. How can you explain the fact that in eighteen years, no ship noticed anything untoward? Or do you perhaps think it possible that the sailor chose to present himself on that particular day?"

I turned towards Narcisse, little expecting him to speak. He remained silent, and I was obliged to improvise:

"As far as I have been able to understand, the savages who welcomed Pelletier into their midst are nomadic: they divide their time between the coast and the interior, according to the seasons. It would be wrong to suppose that they camp permanently on those shores. I cannot tell you whether Pelletier sought contact with the white man, or if he fled from it. We must not forget that he was scarcely master of his own movements: he may not have been physically bound, but he had little choice but to stay with the tribe. When the English dinghy landed on the beach, Pelletier and a few of the savages continued fishing on the rocks. They neither fled nor tried to hide, and Pelletier made no attempt to single himself out from the others. The Englishmen only realised that there was a white man among the savages when they approached the group. As they drew closer, they could see that one of the men was taller, and clearly of the white race, despite his dark sunburnt skin. He spoke only the language of the savages. They gestured to him, inviting him to get into the dinghy. They did not use force, but when he found himself aboard the *John Bell* as it set sail, it was quite clear that he was greatly distressed."

"And why does he not tell us this himself?" asked the admiral.

Narcisse was gazing calmly at the uniformed officers, as if all of this was of no particular concern to him. I waited for him to respond. He said nothing. I opened my arms wide, as if to ask them to observe his attitude for themselves:

"I do not know. He has always refused, or I should say he has always refrained from answering my questions about what happened over there. I have of course asked him about the circumstances of his arrival on that coast. On this question, as on all the others, he maintains an absolute silence. I can do nothing about this. Her Majesty the Empress, alone, has been able to draw a few confidences from him."

I made this last remark with the intention of warding off any further questions about Narcisse's silence. My strategy was successful and the admiral continued: "Did the existence of this white savage come as a complete surprise to the English?"

"A complete surprise, yes. There had been no talk of it in any quarter: no tall tales told in taverns, no shipboard rumours, no mention anywhere of such a case."

"And yet," objected the admiral, "there have been other cases in the South Pacific of sailors who have, as they say 'gone native'." The admiral seemed to relish using the expression, commonly heard in those parts of the world, no doubt recalling the voyages of his youth.

"We know of a few similar cases of sailors who have deserted, or been shipwrecked. The Geographical Society gathered information on all such recorded cases, at my request. Of these men, none had remained completely isolated for eighteen years. And we are absolutely certain that none had adopted so completely the ways and language of the natives. This case seems to be wholly without precedent: nowhere in the records is there another account of a young white man forgetting everything of his origins and becoming so completely a savage himself."

I could have offered a more scientific analysis, one that I had been developing for myself, but I felt it unnecessary to voice my thoughts to the commission. We know of the savages brought to Europe who adapted to our way of life. One thinks of the remarkable case of Aoutourou, from Tahiti who came to France with Bougainville, to the court of Louis XV. Natives from the plains of America, the depths of Africa or the furthest

Pacific islands have adapted to life in Paris or London, whether they came of their own accord or were brought by force. And more remarkable yet, missionaries have succeeded in civilising savages in their own lands.

Thus, the savage who lives among white men adapts to our ways, while the white man who finds himself thrown among savages retains the beneficial effects of civilisation for many years. The only known exception to this rule is Narcisse, whose case is all the more fascinating for being unique. In all the other documented examples, we can clearly see the laws of attraction at work, always pulling in the same direction and confirming what common sense would suggest. What better demonstration is there of the superiority of the white man over the savage?

With the exception of Narcisse.

The admiral seated us near the door and called Captain Porteret back in. We were the only civilians in the room and the captain glanced at us as he walked past but did not register any particular interest. Nor did Narcisse seem to recognise him.

"So, Captain, have you remembered what happened on the 5th November 1843?"

"Yes, Sir. We entered the bay, which seemed welcoming enough, and I sent men ashore to search for water. They returned with the dinghy an hour later and informed me that Pelletier had disappeared. I sent them back ashore with arms and reinforcements and ordered them to patrol the coast and the adjacent forest. I instructed them to fire into the air to make their presence known. They walked for two or three leagues in every direction from the point where the sailor had last been seen. They found no footprints, no sign of him. Pelletier had disappeared, as if by magic. Every time I signalled to the dinghy I received the same response: nothing. The ship was not well positioned: the anchorage left much to be desired, the tidal current was strong and a storm was approaching. The sick men were moaning and groaning. The second mate was urging me to abandon the search, but I could not resolve to do this. At dusk however, I had to accept reality and call off the search. Despite the mounting seas, the men ashore managed to re-embark with the dingy and with great difficulty, we sailed out of the bay. I had given orders to leave some food supplies ashore together with a gun and some ammunition. If Pelletier was still alive, I wanted him to have every chance of surviving his night ashore. I was intending to return the next day to continue the search for as long as necessary. Dead or alive, a man does not just disappear without trace. But the storm raged for two days, carrying us a long way from the coast. I had to make a decision: should I turn back against the prevailing winds, or save the ailing men on board? After long discussions with the second mate, I made the decision, with a heavy heart, to head for Sidney. What else could we have done? Searching the bay and the surrounding area over and over again would have achieved nothing. Pelletier had not replied to any of our signals. Both the second mate and I were having second thoughts: he was probably dead, his body lying in some inaccessible place, in a cave or a swamp. What could have killed him so suddenly? A snakebite, heat stroke, a fatal fall? We'd have needed days and days, and a great deal of luck, to find his body. I believed him to be alive when we set sail from the bay, but as the hours passed, I came to the conclusion that he was dead. There were other men in my crew in need of water and medical attention. I made up my mind. Continuing to search in vain would have led to the death of the sick men.

And on top of all this, the second mate was now warning me of the possibility of mutiny."

The officers cast him a dubious look.

"There is no mention of any of this in your ship's log."

"It came back to me when I read it. The journal contains all the details required by the regulations, as recorded by the second mate on my instructions. Pelletier's death is logged on the 5th November 1843."

"But you had no proof of this! And according to you, it was not until the next morning that you came to this conclusion. Your journal is a fabrication."

"Forgive me, Admiral. The journal may be rather vague, but it is not false. I had every reason to believe that Pelletier was dead. When a man falls overboard, it's the same: no one sees his last moments, there is no corpse, but alas, the outcome is never in doubt."

This astute analogy lent a little more credibility to the captain's remarks. Not wishing to lose the upper hand, the admiral pointed to Narcisse and asked the captain:

"Do you recognise this man?"

"No, Sir."

"This man is Narcisse Pelletier."

The captain stared long and hard at Narcisse. He shook his head: "It was eighteen years ago. A young lad I'd taken on board two months before, one man in a crew of thirty. I don't know. I don't recognise him."

The admiral turned to Narcisse and asked him the same question. It came as no surprise to me that Narcisse did not recognise Captain Porteret either. Then one of the officer's spoke:

"Well sailor, you have heard the captain's account. Is this the way things happened?"

"Yes, Monsieur."

"Can you remember the moment when you were separated from your shipmates?"

"No."

"Did you look for them?"

"I don't know."

"Did you hear their shouts, the whistles, the gun shots?"

"Yes... no... I don't know."

"Did you find the food supplies left on the beach for you?"

"..."

You remember nothing of that day, the 5th November 1843?"

"No. Nothing... of the time before."

In the absence of any witnesses, the captain's account came to be accepted as the truth. At last I knew something of the events that had led to Narcisse's arrival in Australia, although there remained one mystery: why had he missed the dinghy's departure? How had he become lost? Had he lost consciousness? Or had the savages captured him and gagged him? We shall never know.

"But, my good fellow," complained the admiral, "if you no longer remember anything of that day, how can you confirm the truth of the captain's account?"

This remark implied that the admiral had his doubts, but chose not to express them publicly. He was visibly disappointed: the commission of enquiry was not going to throw any light on this forgotten drama, and there would be no sanctions for an act of deliberate abandonment. The commission's report would gather dust in a cupboard, the minister would inform Her Majesty in writing of its conclusions and there would be no cause to mention the admiral's name or his zealous pursuit of the truth. All interest in the case would be lost.

Sitting to the right of the admiral was a ship's captain, whom I had thought to be dozing until this moment. He spoke up and said in a faint voice:

"There is one thing I do not understand, Captain. You sailed across the Indian Ocean in adverse circumstances, men were dying or injured, your water supplies were low. You sailed along the west coast of Australia as far as the northernmost tip. You were not that far from Java. According to your ship's log, this was in fact your ship's destination when you left the Cape. Why then did you never head due north? Why did you sail along the coast of Australia, in the opposite direction from the Dutch East Indies? With every passing day you were going further away from your supposed destination?"

The old captain was visibly embarrassed by this question of geography. He was clearly unsure as to how to reply and eventually mumbled something about his ship being difficult to manoeuvre and his preference for a course with a wind from astern.

"You cannot mean that you were unable to sail on the larboard tack! I'm not talking about sailing upwind…"

"We are straying from the point," interjected the presiding officer.

"Forgive me, Admiral. One last question. After Pelletier's disappearance, with sick men on board and water becoming more and more scarce, you continued on to Sydney, the nearest port. After a short stop there, you set sail directly for China. You never went to Java. Why not?"

The captain was utterly at a loss. I was not in a position to appreciate the full import of this question, not having had access to the ship's log myself.

"Well, you see. The last time I'd stopped in Java, I'd had some trouble with the authorities there. I'd been accused of…

of fraud."

"Of contraband?"

"It was a long time ago."

"Of smuggling?"

"Of leaving without paying all the customs duties… some bills… I preferred to avoid Java. The Dutch don't forget. They give no quarter with matters of that nature."

"So, you showed no hesitation in choosing between the life of one of your sailors, and a fine?"

Captain Porteret bowed his head.

"If you had made a stop in Java, Pelletier would never have ended up alone on a beach in Australia."

The admiral was clearly losing interest. He left it to one of the officers to give the captain a lecture about keeping the ship's log and to raise the question of some form of censure. And with that, he brought the hearing to a close.

Two days later, I was received by Her Majesty's aide-de-camp. We had been corresponding on the subject of Narcisse's employment in accordance with the Empress' wish that a post should be found for Narcisse in government service. I had insisted upon the post being close to the sea, not too far from Saint-Gilles and had already refused a situation mending roads in Burgundy and one as gamekeeper in the Landes. But after all, who was I to make such decisions about his future? On whose authority? I could not refuse the third offer, which was probably the last before the officer of the Hussars ran out of patience. The candidate himself had no objections; as with all such matters, he left it up to me. The affair was concluded, the documents signed and Narcisse Pelletier was appointed storekeeper third class in the Lighthouse Service, for the Baleines Lighthouse on the Île de Ré. He was to take up his post on the first of the month. This left us sufficient time to thank the aide-de-camp and to go back once more to Saint-Gilles before settling Narcisse into his new life.

You will no doubt ask me if it is right to send him to the lighthouse at the furthest outpost of such a remote, impoverished island. Is this not just another prison, no bigger than that of the governor of New South Wales, and within three leagues of the infamous prison of Saint-Martin-de-Ré? His sole distractions will be shell gathering and walks along the shore. With the tedious nature of the work and only the monotony of the sea to gaze at, will he not tire of this existence? To this I reply that it is surely time for this fellow to find a stable situation, and that to this date I have found nothing more suitable.

His family seem only too happy with the arrangement. Our second visit to Saint-Gilles was shorter and less extravagant than the first. The family congratulated Narcisse on being appointed by imperial decree, privately nursing the unspoken jealousy felt by those whose future is always uncertain towards aristocrats and bureaucrats – whose privileged positions were being confirmed before their very eyes. All things considered however, Narcisse has been fortunate: his lodging is guaranteed, he will receive a monthly income, and at the age of thirty-six he finds himself in a position that many sailors of his age would envy. "All's well that ends well," is the conclusion expressed to me by the mayor and the curate. And as old Pelletier said, Ré is not too far and the family will be able to go and see him often, although one suspects that they will do nothing of the kind.

During a brief sojourn in La Rochelle I was able to call on the subdivisional engineer and introduce him to his new subaltern and explain to him why the appointment of a mere storekeeper third class had been signed by the minister himself and not by a divisional officer. Without going into unnecessary details, I explained something of Narcisse's life and of his singular character. The engineer discerned my meaning and assured me that he would faithfully maintain the interest taken by Paris towards this fellow.

We then embarked on a ferry to the Île de Ré, where a horse-drawn cariole took us to the lighthouse. The weather was calm and the landscape serene, but I thought how terrible it must be when storms move in from the Atlantic. The engineer's instructions to the chief officer of the station facilitated the process of installing Narcisse. He was given a room in the keepers' quarters, where he set out the few effects I had purchased for him, and affixed the model of the *Strathmore* to the wall.

His duties are simple: he is responsible for cleaning, oiling and maintaining the lighthouse equipment; for sweeping, tidying and maintaining the buildings; tending the garden, the vegetable plot and the stable, and helping in the kitchen as required.

The chief officer and his crew are all former sailors. Men of few words, they know that Narcisse has had some unfortunate experiences, and they have accepted him as one of their own. The novice storekeeper third class set to work immediately under the supervision of an old hand, and seems happy to be of use. I asked the chief officer to send me a monthly report on Pelletier. This good fellow agreed and refused the payment that I offered. He also offered to manage Narcisse's salary for him and make it available to him in a sensible and timely manner.

I took leave of Narcisse, wished him good fortune and assured him that I would come and see him once or twice a year. I have fulfilled my obligations towards him. He displayed no particular emotion when we parted; perhaps he had not fully understood.

On the way back to my inn at Saint-Martin-de-Ré, it became clear to me that I still do not understand Narcisse Pelletier. I know him no better today than I did on the first day of this strange adventure.

I remain your faithful servant...

11

The men were back.

For three days, the tribe did nothing but eat, drink and sleep, feasting on the small game brought back by the hunters. Instead of the usual mealtime rituals there was a continuous procession back and forth to the fire and hot stones, everyone helping themselves to as much as they wanted, relishing the change from their usual diet of fish and shellfish. Narcisse had no scruples about going back for more over and over again.

His belly full, he gave himself up to bitter-sweet nostalgia: he was alive, to be sure, just as he had promised himself he would be; he wasn't condemned to die of hunger. But was this to be his fate: weeks, months, years spent sleeping and eating on one beach or another?

On the third evening he noticed that the old man had gone. There was no sign of the one he called Wanderer either. He'd probably gone with the old man to some other family group. Narcisse was not exactly upset to see him gone. Wanderer was the one who never missed a chance to look at him askance and express his barely disguised hostility. Why did he hate him so? To hell with them, he thought, the pair of them. They could rot in hell for all he cared.

Dawn the next morning saw the return of a period of frenetic activity. Just as when they'd left the encampment by the water hole, the tribe were gathering up the few belongings they would take with them. The women set off at a steady pace, followed by the children and finally the men. Narcisse picked up the two water pouches the old woman had entrusted to him and followed the tribe into the forest.

The march was long and the smallest children found it difficult to keep up. It wasn't long before he worked out that they were walking almost due west, away from the coast: he knew they weren't far from the equator and he realised he was walking on his shadow in the morning with the afternoon sun in his eyes until sunset. How far had they gone? Three leagues, maybe four. Far enough to be out of sight of any rescue party that might come for him.

If the *Saint-Paul* did come back, or if another ship were to sail into the Bay of Abandon, they would find his message and head north. But there would be no more clues to point them in the right direction. Nothing to indicate what had happened to Narcisse Pelletier. They'd go back to their ship empty-handed, knowing he'd survived until the 21st November, the date he'd written on the beach with the rocks. But of what had happened after that, they would know nothing at all. What would the captain decide? If he were to spend a few more days searching the area, he would lose more time and risk the disapproval of the ship owner. And there was virtually no possibility of a team setting out in the right direction, venturing deeper into unknown country and ending up coming upon the tribe. It would be a big risk to take and the chances of success would be minimal. When they found no one on the beach, the captain would give the signal to set sail. No, it would be better if no one came looking for him now. He'd been concentrating all his energy on hoping for a ship to arrive, but now he focussed that same energy on wishing for a delay. And he had definitely given up the idea of striking out on his own, away from the tribe: he knew he wouldn't survive here.

They walked on all day through the barely changing landscape: the same colourless forest, the same eternally flat plateau, the limitless horizon. Sometimes the trees grew more sparsely on soil that was no more than sand and dust. In the still air, the day grew hotter. Clouds of flies, gnats and mosquitoes attacked him constantly, feasting on his pale flesh. He was completely exposed, his body naked and defenceless as he waved his arms about and slapped at himself in a vain attempt to disperse the insects. There was no offer of ointment from the old woman; the insects showed no interest in her. His only protection came from the layer of mingled sweat and dust on his skin that had formed a crust here and there. Realising this, he sprinkled handfuls of sand on himself in an effort to shield himself from the insects. But there was still not enough dirt on his body to ward them all off.

They walked without stopping until nightfall. Wanderer was waiting for them at the bivouac, a fire already lit. The old woman made no move to go and fill the empty water gourds. The hunters had little to offer, and just as during the first few days – or perhaps because they had left the beach – Narcisse was no longer permitted to go up to the fire and serve himself. He had to wait until the old woman brought him his meagre pittance. When she came back for the second time, Wanderer barred her way, took the small morsel that she was intending for Narcisse, swallowed it in one mouthful and looked Narcisse up and down. It was a look he knew well, the chin jutting forward, looking for a fight. This savage didn't scare him. He needed a good thrashing; that would soon show him who was stronger. He was playing a dangerous game, deliberately humiliating a sailor from the *Saint-Paul*. Narcisse would be only too happy to give this arrogant little fellow a severe punishment. He'd learnt plenty of moves in various ports. He knew how to throw a punch and it would give him great pleasure to use his skills to teach him a lesson. But it wouldn't be wise to make a show of his strength. He had no way of knowing how the tribe might react. What if they didn't approve of the punishment he meted out to Wanderer? If all the men were to come to Wanderer's defence, Narcisse would not be able to overpower them all. The only time he'd tried that, he'd been defeated by their sheer numbers, and had lost half his ear as a result. He had no desire to go through that again. He gritted his teeth and let the moment pass. The old woman did not come back with any more food for him.

He would have to use his intelligence to save himself, not brute force. He pondered his situation. Wanderer had left the night before with the old woman. Whatever he had been doing all day, he'd arrived at the designated spot for the encampment. So they must all have a map of the area in their heads, and maybe some sort of compass too. They could arrange to meet in specific places and get there following different routes. He would have to gain the same knowledge of the terrain to be able to get away when the time came. The more he walked about the territory with them, the better equipped he'd be to walk through it alone.

He also needed to work out just why Wanderer was treating him as he was. All the others seemed completely indifferent to him. When he fell short on respecting their strange customs, they would demonstrate what he was supposed to do: they let him know that he had to wait until the old woman gave him food after all the men had eaten, instead of helping himself to meat. But once he had shown that he'd understood and done what they asked of him, they paid him no more attention. They bore him no malice for his lack of knowledge of their ways.

But Wanderer's hostility was unrelenting; it was systematic and more marked now than during the first few days. If the tribe had decided as a group to make Narcisse welcome, to help him and feed him, to burden themselves with him, Wanderer's attitude must surely have seemed most disrespectful to the elders. Narcisse tried to imagine a similar situation in his village: if a stranger were welcomed by the mayor, the curate or some other pillar of the community, they would all be expected to treat him with courtesy. If one of the boys showed a lack of respect towards the stranger, his impertinence would soon be punished with a slap.

They seemed to be about the same age, as far as Narcisse could tell, although it was difficult to judge how old any of them were. Was Wanderer afraid he might provide competition? Did he see him as a rival with girls? That was impossible. Narcisse had never shown the slightest interest in any of the girls, and he didn't have to pretend either. Was it to do with the old woman then? Was Wanderer jealous of what she'd done for him? She'd looked after him, brought him food. He didn't understand why she'd done all this, but that hardly mattered. She knew what she was supposed to do. Did he feel threatened for some unfathomable reason?

What was Wanderer's relationship to the old woman? Was he her son perhaps, her grandson, a nephew, a godson? And who was his father? He had to work out the relationships between the members of the tribe and stop seeing them all as interchangeable. He tried thinking of the old woman as a Dowager Princess, Wanderer as a hot-headed Prince of royal blood. Was his position threatened by the arrival of a white man? Why? How could a white man's presence be such a threat? He had no way of finding answers to these questions. Not yet. But he would. He'd find answers.

He'd had plenty of opportunity to get used to the blows and rebuffs dealt out by a brutal and distant older brother at home and in his father's workshop. He didn't like the way his brother Lucien treated him, and he fought back. Wanderer was like Lucien's malevolent double, and he could no more avoid him than he could his brother before he left home.

If Wanderer wasn't his friend, so what? He didn't need friends, he didn't want to make any friends among these savages.

The hunger was back; the scrap of meat that Wanderer had stolen from him would have done nothing to satisfy it. He lay down in the dirt and did his best not to think about the copious meals they'd eaten on the beach. Here on the plateau with its sparse trees and scrub, the men must know how to unearth creatures like lizards and desert rats. He would have to learn the same skills so that he'd be able to feed himself when he escaped.

He'd make a friend of any hunter ready to teach him his skills.

LETTER XI

Monsieur le Président,

I have received the most recent edition of the Geographical Society Review with its two-page article on the plenary session of 2nd September.

I have done as I believe you would have advised and have waited for one week after reading the article before I put pen to paper. You had left me in no doubt that you considered my initial response to events of that afternoon to be unduly fervent and that I had reacted too hastily. I waited a further three days before beginning this missive to you, spending my mornings in walks through the still snow-covered fields around the castle, reflecting upon matters.

(I have of course disregarded the brief articles that appeared in the press in the autumn, which gave only a very poor idea of the importance of my presentation. One cartoon did however cause me to smile for a moment: a barbed caricature depicting the Duc de Morny suggesting to the white savage that he enrol in the duke's expedition to Mexico. Will this prove to be the abiding image instilled in the public imagination: the spectacle of a savage dressed in a grotesque fur cape and a feather headdress?)

I am still most irate. If you have been good enough to keep my letter of 3rd September, I ask you to read my account of the meeting once more, and urge you to bring to mind your own recollections of that afternoon. Is this the same session as the one described in the Review? Was the individual who penned those lines actually present that afternoon? Or does he mock me? In signing only his initials he adds cowardice to his treachery, although his identity is transparent to you and me alike.

My first thought was to cancel my subscription to the Review, but on reflection I perceived that in depriving myself of this incomparable source of valuable information, I would be punishing only myself.

I considered the possibility of seeking legal redress. But against whom, and for what crime? I went so far as to consult an advocate of my acquaintance and was persuaded that such a course would be most ill-advised.

Should I challenge the writer to a duel? But why should I put my own life at the mercy of his pistol? If anyone were to be injured or die in such a confrontation, it would surely be me.

It has not escaped me that according to the statutes of our Society, in particular article 24, the president of the committee responsible for the Review acts independently and is not subject to your authority. In addressing these remarks to you, I am not seeking your support, nor do I wish to place you in a compromising position: I wish only to keep you informed, out of courtesy for our long-standing association.

I am therefore addressing a note to the said president asking him to rectify all the errors in the unsigned account published in the Autumn-Winter edition of 1861. You will smile and point out to me that my nineteen-page response is considerably longer than the short piece it criticises. But I have no desire to choose which of the myriad nonsensical assertions printed in the Review to refute and which to disregard. The president of the committee will publish my letter in its entirety, in part, or not at all, as he pleases. For myself, I shall find out if I am dealing with an honourable man.

I am no less incensed when I consider that this constitutes all that will be known of the tragedy of Narcisse Pelletier: those who were not present at the session will think only of this caricature of a fairground side-show in which a skilfully disguised phenomenon is exposed to the prurient gaze of onlookers. This sneering and partisan account is an insult not just to my unfortunate friend and to me. It is an affront to you too: you are not the ringmaster of a circus. My remarks will redress all this and establish the truth of the affair.

I struggle to find words to express the extent to which this fallacious report wounds me. I have already given you my thoughts on the Society's plenary session: I had cherished the hope that it would go some way towards restoring the truth of this affair after the debacle in London. This was not to be. The editor of the Review has endorsed the lies, become party to a calumny and what is worse, displayed self-satisfied ignorance.

I must tell you that for more than a year now, all my efforts, my energy, my travels and – I cannot deny it – a part of my fortune have been devoted to Pelletier's travails. To see what is perhaps the greatest endeavour of my life reduced to… to this wretched account. This is not merely a personal injustice. It is a loss to science.

Will Her Majesty the Empress prove to be the only person to have understood the importance of this affair?

While certain small-minded individuals were occupied writing for the Review, Narcisse Pelletier, storekeeper third class at the Baleines Lighthouse, was demonstrating the kind of courage rarely seen among members of our Society. You will admonish me for this acerbic remark, but I must ask you to consider: who is more deserving of our admiration? Monsieur Decouz taking notes at a plenary session before an evening at the opera, or Narcisse Pelletier, at that remote outpost assailed by howling winds and pounding waves, with only the nearby saltworks or storms at sea to gaze upon? The Reverend Father Leroy, more oft plotting than praying, or Narcisse Pelletier, assiduously learning his new occupation, always smiling and ready to help his fellow workers? Monsieur Collet-Hespas, born with a silver spoon in his mouth, heir to a flourishing business created by his industrious father, or Narcisse Pelletier who possesses only the shirt on his back, and depends on the lighthouse keepers for his daily bread?

I am beside myself with rage. My ill humour renders me unable to think rationally. Surely it is I who am the injured party in this affair.

I could all too easily continue in this vein for many pages, at the risk of exhausting your good will. Rather than continuing therefore on this acrimonious note, I shall instead give you the news from the Île de Ré, whither I returned some two months ago.

The new storekeeper greeted me as if we had been parted for no more than a day, with the same smile and equanimity of mood that never leaves him – is this a sign of profound wisdom, or simply a mask? Harmony seems to reign with his fellows. They are appreciative of his pleasant disposition; indeed they burden him with perhaps too many lowly tasks, but Narcisse does not balk at hard work and all are satisfied.

He has revealed an unexpected talent for shore fishing using a small harpoon fashioned by his own hand. Whenever he has a free moment he is to be found barefoot on the shore when the tide is out, in all weathers, searching through the rock pools. He never returns empty-handed. The lighthouse master was most concerned when he beheld Narcisse on the beach at nightfall in foul weather. But Narcisse made nothing of his warnings and the men soon became accustomed to seeing him return at the dead of night, soaked to the skin, his bag filled with fish. He is equally skilled in collecting a great profusion of all kinds of shellfish, so much so that his fellows, who are mostly meat-eaters, tire of his offerings. When his harvest is refused, he goes into the village and distributes the contents of his basket to those who desire to avail themselves of his bounty.

Much to my surprise, I continue to learn new secrets of Australia.

Narcisse's lighthouse colleagues have spoken to me of his "cat's eyes", a phenomenon I had never had occasion to observe since we had always had the benefit of candlelight or gaslight in the evenings. On the Île de Ré, however, such luxuries are a rarity. Narcisse moves around in unlit corridors and in the darkest of huts without any difficulty, just as if it were full daylight. It is only when he is plunged into the blackest of nights, when there is not the smallest glimmer of light, that he begins to move gingerly and stumble over the furniture. This remarkable capacity to find his way in the dark can only have been acquired in Australia, perhaps during night-time hunting expeditions, or nightly vigils and bivouacs under the stars.

Permit me to give you another example of Narcisse's unusual skills. I accompanied him on one of his fishing expeditions at the beach. He equipped himself with his harpoon, a sort of spear which he wields with immense skill. Desiring to learn how he had made it, and knowing that an abstract question on this subject would go unanswered, I merely said: "Narcisse, I too would like to fish. Will you make one for me?"

Without a word, he went straight to work. He selected a woody, twisted shrub growing at the edge of the beach, broke off a branch and stripped off the twigs. The shape of the harpoon was vaguely discernible. Then he carefully chose a stone – which to my untutored eye looked no different from any other – and used it to shape the branch and sharpen the points of the fork at the end. Working, not as one can with a good knife, but with sharp downward movements of the entire right arm, he seemed almost to stroke the piece of wood as he shaved it down to the exact thickness required. Patiently and with perfect efficiency, he shaped the handle. Every blow struck home, none was wasted, the handle emerging as rounded as if it had been manufactured on a lathe and polished with sand paper. I gazed admiringly at his handiwork, but it was not yet finished.

Casting around again, he picked up a handful of lichens and fallen leaves from a hollow in the rocks and piled them up meticulously between three stones. Then, he took two pieces of hard wood and rubbed them one against the other, eventually producing some smoke, which he slid under the lichens. A small flame appeared, then another and his fire took.

He blew on it gently, added a few twigs and in no time at all we had a good fire. Then he carefully passed the sharpened tips of his harpoon over the flame to harden them. When they glowed red and were about to catch fire, he doused them in the sea, alternating hot and cold several times. Without showing any hint of pride in his work, he handed me the finished harpoon, as if this was the most natural thing in the world and he was simply doing what was expected. I was speechless. We proceeded to fish with the aid of our respective instruments, I without managing to catch a single fish and he soon filling his basket.

It was the ingenuity he displayed that impressed me most. Imagine, Sir, if you will, what would happen if any one member of our Society were to be left on a beach on the Île de Ré on a winter evening. Would he be able to fashion a harpoon with just what he is able to find on the beach, to light a fire, and catch a fish in under one hour? I trust you will concur that Narcisse's skills are indeed extraordinary.

You will say that he is merely demonstrating the knowledge he acquired from the savages. Undoubtedly. But this means that we must accept there is a store of knowledge among the savages. What kind of knowledge is it? And what further treasures are contained therein?

That same evening, another notion occurred to me as I awaited my supper, sitting by the fire in the dining area of the island's only inn. Three villagers were enjoying a drink at the neighbouring table, talking about this and that. One phrase stood out from the background hum of their indistinct chatter and made me sit up and listen.

"...I was walking home the other evening at nightfall and I saw that lunatic from the lighthouse on Conche beach. He was out there, still fishing!"

The 'lunatic from the lighthouse'; this is how the new member of the crew of the Baleines Lighthouse is known. It was said without malice, and I must confess that I have seen enough of Narcisse's eccentricities to hear it without taking umbrage. It is an epithet that is less cruel than some that have been printed, you will agree.

And when all is said and done, what if these good people are right? Is Narcisse mad? We know that excessive suffering and unhappiness can tip the most well-tempered minds into madness. Pelletier the sailor undoubtedly had some terrible experiences, and of these he never speaks. Either he has knowingly thrown an impenetrable veil over eighteen years of his life, or has unknowingly forgotten them. Is this a symptom of madness? Is it a particular kind of madness?

I was deeply troubled by this line of thought. If Narcisse is insane, he is in need of a doctor. My good intentions will have deprived him of the care required for his condition. And if he were indeed a madman, he would no longer be a resource for science – and I would have been wasting my time, as would you.

I was loath to accept this judgment and decided to seek a definitive answer to the question. I have no knowledge of such matters and I therefore made some enquiries after my return from the island. I was able to visit some asylums. Heaven preserve you, Sir, from the spectacle of the infernal scenes to which I was witness. My pen refuses to describe what I ascertained – the nature of madness, the many varieties of lunacy – and the methods that are used to treat the deranged, none of which offer any hope of a cure. I also had long discussions with several notable alienists.

I shall not venture to propose a general definition of

madness. But from what I have seen and understood, and from my discussions with the best specialists, I gleaned only that Narcisse is not deranged: he is not suffering, nor does he cause others to suffer; he does not refuse to engage with the world around him; he knows who he is. His silence on his years in Australia might, as one eminent specialist suggested, indicate a profound and inexpressible longing. Or perhaps it represents the stigmata of indescribable torments. Or – I venture to express a most singular notion to you – an intermingling of the two. For myself, I know what it means to experience at times that silent longing for the skies of the Pacific, and this does not make me a madman.

I trust that you will see, from these few haphazard notes that I have penned, how much Narcisse has brought to science. And that you will understand the extent to which the Review, in publishing only those two sorry and unworthy pages, has failed in its mission. I shall not forget the affront the Review has made to me, but to be frank, there are greater satisfactions for me elsewhere: in observing Narcisse and reflecting on his condition, I find fulfilment of an entirely different nature.

I remain your faithful servant...

12

·

They walked all day again the following day.

This time Narcisse was determined not to suffer as he had
the day before. Before they set off, he searched among the
ashes, picked out some charred bits of bone and feather and
crushed them between his hands to make a blackish paste.
He rubbed the paste all over his body and sprinkled himself
with sand. If anyone were to see him now, naked and bearded,
coated with sweat and dirt, spattered with grease and soot,
carrying two water gourds made from animal bladders, what
would they think? Would they recognise in this apparition the
dashing sailor from the *Saint-Paul*?

The forest quickly gave way to a sort of desert. No more
trees, not a single bush, only the odd tuft of dried grass. The
red earth lay like a shield over the land, its armour plating
pierced here and there by patches of red gravel. Rock
formations appeared, white stone streaked with grey. Now,
instead of the flat plain, they were walking over undulating
terrain, small valleys about ten metres deep, some of them
steep-sided, their walls like petrified high seas. At the crest
of each hill, there was only the next valley and the next hill
to be seen. Unchanging, difficult walking even for someone

equipped with a good hat, a sturdy pair of boots and a belly full of good food. For Narcisse, it was gruelling, his feet torn and scratched by the scorched ground. The children too were having difficulty keeping up the pace: they didn't cry – none of the children ever cried – they dragged their feet or got their mothers to carry them.

On they went, never wavering from their course, due west as far as he could tell. Were they going to cross the whole of Australia like this? And how would they survive in this godforsaken land devoid of any source of food or water?

By late morning, the tribe had stretched out into a long column, the weakest no longer able to keep pace with the men. They stopped at the foot of a huge lone rock, as big as a barn. Its shape was irregular with an overhang on one side. They took refuge in the shade provided by the overhang and shared out a few barely cooked lizards and the last of the water. Thankful for these few mouthfuls, Narcisse worried about what would happen now that the water was all gone. Forty or more people, with children among them, crossing the desert without any access to food or water.

Huddled in the hollow of the rock, they waited for the hottest part of the day to pass before setting out again. The men walked on ahead, soon disappearing from sight, leaving Chief to guide the rest of the tribe. Towards evening, the terrain flattened out, the exhausting march over hills and valleys giving way to easier walking on a plateau where the earth was still of the same red. The plateau ended as abruptly as it had begun, to be replaced by a landscape of sparse scrub with a few scattered trees. They stopped to make camp beneath some trees and soon the old woman was brandishing two full water gourds. She went off again – Narcisse was too exhausted to think about following her – coming back with more, replenishing the water supply.

At dusk, Broken Nose arrived carrying a hunk of meat in each hand; it looked as if it had been ripped from the animal, complete with skin and fur. Broken Nose said something to the group in general, put down his prize and started to walk away. The women bustled about lighting the fire and a few of the youths followed in the hunter's footsteps. Waiakh gestured to Narcisse and convinced him to go along with them too.

They walked for fifteen minutes before coming upon Kermarec and Scarface, who hadn't waited for reinforcements to arrive and were already busy taking apart the carcass. Narcisse wondered how the three of them had managed to kill an animal bigger than a man without any weapons to speak of – all they had was that stick, some stones and their darts. It was a strange beast: it had a small head, red fur and disproportionately large hind legs with a long, powerful tail. It must have weighed as much as a good-sized calf. The hunters had used stones to cut through the skin around the joints, twisting the limbs and tearing off pieces of meat or still smoking entrails. A smell of blood and death floated above the carcass, attracting clouds of voracious flies.

The beast was quickly cut up and everyone headed back to the camp carrying as much meat as he could. Only the feet, the spine and the ribs were left. It was a welcome bounty after the harsh crossing of this rocky desert. Broken Nose carried the head triumphantly, and swelled with pride when he saw the other groups returning empty-handed from their hunting forays.

Narcisse smelt the aroma of roasting meat before he got back to the camp and his mouth began to water. He knew he would have to wait until after the men had been served, but this time Wanderer would not be able to prevent him from claiming his share. The feast had been announced to the whole tribe.

They spent a full day at the camp, sleeping and devoting every waking moment to eating.

As the next day dawned, they set off and walked again all morning, still heading due west. Towards the middle of the morning, Narcisse saw what looked like a sand dune rising gradually on the horizon. As they approached, it began to take shape into a great rock, as high as a mountain and white as milk.

The rock was shaped exactly like an egg, lying on its side and buried up to the middle. It was smooth and pinky-white in colour, like a shell. There were no cracks or hollows for earth to take hold; no trees, no grass grew on its surface. A single groove snaked from the base to the summit and looked like it might be a path. Rising more than a hundred metres from the sandy red earth that bore it, the immense rock loomed like an alien, its outline unlike any other on the horizon.

For a man from the lowlands of the Vendée, it seemed immensely high. He felt that he was gazing up at a great steep-sided cliff. They had walked in a westerly direction for three days and had covered at least ten leagues. This mountain was marked on no map, nor was it visible from the coast. He would not have believed it possible, but now he felt even more lost than he had during those days and nights on the beaches.

It was evening when they eventually arrived at the foot of the mountain, in the middle of an arid plain dotted with scrawny bushes. They found a small hollow with a grove of imposing weeping willows, or their Australian cousins, that grew in a great oval, marking the edge of a meadow of thick green grass. With every breath of wind, the leaves rustled in a metallic murmur. It was in this strange place that the tribe chose to make camp. Narcisse noticed they were speaking in hushed voices and talking even less than usual. The children seemed particularly overawed, even the older ones like Waiakh.

The next day, Chief – why did he think of this old man as the chief? – spoke all day long. From the moment the sun rose, he sat cross-legged, muttering continuously: it wasn't a speech, but nor was he making it up. It was more of a recitation. The others would come and sit close to him, listen for a few moments, leave and come back again; there didn't seem to be any logic or pattern to their comings and goings. The bard continued, not stopping to drink or eat, even when the sun was at its highest, one phrase following another for twelve hours at a stretch, with not the slightest hesitation. He betrayed no emotion, no joy, fear, anger or surprise. Was he reciting the tribe's *Iliad*? Their *Odyssey*, or a list of ancestors perhaps, of events, names of places or animals? Narcisse remembered having to memorise multiplication tables, reciting a list of departments with their principal towns and sub-prefectures, intoning them in the same way. None of it had sunk in, despite the teacher's efforts to encourage them with whacks from a ruler.

As the sun slipped below the horizon, Chief stopped abruptly. And everyone went back to their ordinary evening chores.

When the darkness was all-enveloping, the women gathered the children together and shaved their heads, working more carefully than usual, in complete, contemplative silence. The old woman proceeded to shave Narcisse's head, running her

271

fingers over his shaven skull once she had finished, feeling for lumps and indentations.

He went to sit beside Waiakh, and without stopping to think, silently took the boy's hand in his own.

In the red glow of the firelight, the child's hand rested in the young man's. They stayed there silent and motionless, both of them seemingly at peace. In the half-light, the black hand in his own.

The whole of the next day was devoted to the mountain.

LETTER XII

Monsieur le Président,

I beg you to forgive me for imposing once again on your valuable time. This letter brings you news of my protégé, which I believe will be of interest to you.

As we had agreed, the master of the Baleines Lighthouse has been sending me brief monthly reports on Narcisse Pelletier. A man of few words, this excellent fellow informs me that he can find no fault with Narcisse's work as storekeeper. Narcisse does not simply obey orders, he applies himself to the task with enthusiasm. He is tireless and courageous, always good-humoured and a pleasant companion. Were he to recover the ability to read and write, his work would be exemplary.

As far as one can tell, Narcisse has adapted with relative ease to life on the Île de Ré. If there is a pressing concern, it is that he still does not understand the notion of private property. He gives away his hat or his jacket to anyone he deems to be in need of them, and avails himself of such items as he might require in a similar fashion. One cannot regard this as stealing:

273

he borrows without malice, and his companions have become quite used to this eccentricity. The lighthouse master gives him his pay once a week, holding back sufficient funds to cover his clothing and heating expenses. The few coins that Narcisse receives slip through his fingers at the village shop where he purchases colourful trinkets, sweets for the children and tobacco for his colleagues, whose fondness for the pleasures of the pipe he has noticed.

As for conquests among the local women, I do not know if he has equalled the success he enjoyed with the ladies in London and Paris. The lighthouse master makes no mention of the subject – far be it from me to read anything into this silence.

I returned in person to the Île de Ré in August 1862 and found Narcisse to be, if not exactly happy – how could I ever be sure of this? – undoubtedly calm and accustomed to his new life. Constantly under the watchful, paternal eye of the lighthouse master, he enjoyed cordial relations with the five other keepers. When I had seen him last, he was still all lean muscle and sinew, his skin burnt nut-brown by the sun. Seeing him now, restored to health and strength, his cheeks plump and rosy, I believed I would learn no more from him. There would be no more interviews.

The report I received in October mentioned that Narcisse was feeling somewhat sad "on account of the little ones". I was quite taken aback by this turn of phrase, and it was only after the exchange of several letters that I eventually understood – the lighthouse master had believed me to be better informed on matters than I was.

It transpired that one of the keepers had suffered the loss of his only son, a child of the age of three. Narcisse and his colleagues sat up with him during the vigil and offered condolences as befitted such an occasion. The grieving father had unthinkingly asked Narcisse a question:

"What about you? Do you have any children?"

"Yes, two."

"Boys?"

"A boy and a girl."

"How old?"

Narcisse did not give a direct answer, but indicated, by comparing them with the children around the lighthouse, that the boy was about eight years of age and the girl five. No one paid any attention to this brief exchange, and the vigil continued in silence.

For the next few days, Narcisse seemed melancholic "on account of the little ones".

I was struck as if by lightning by this news. Never had Narcisse made the slightest allusion to children in my presence. His silence with regard to his experiences in Australia has remained complete and unfathomable. It is only when he is in the grip of powerful emotions that confidences slip out: at such moments he seems unable to maintain the strict silence to which he has apparently sworn himself. His admiration for Her Majesty led him to sing a ditty from that world, and now, the misfortune suffered by his colleague had caused him to speak of his own children.

Why I was unable to foresee this eventuality, I do not know. I had referred to the discovery of certain half-caste children in my letter to you from London on August 2nd of last year. My reflections on the documents you had sent me led me to allude to such children as providing the only evidence of the survival of a forgotten castaway. Why had I not thought of this possibility in Narcisse's case? Had I raised the subject with him then, when his silence was less impenetrable, I might perhaps have been able to extract some definitive confidences from him. This was indeed a lost opportunity and one that will not present itself again.

It has been nigh on two years since he embarked on the *John Bell*, and in all that time he can have had no news of them. Nor has he received word of their mother, or their mothers, as the case may be. Not once has he complained of this – he never complains of anything – nor has he spoken of them or invoked their memory. At my request, the lighthouse master tried to speak to him of the children, with the intention of finding out their names at least. But his efforts were in vain. Narcisse smiles, but gives no answer. He will say nothing of the little boy and girl he has left behind over there.

You will not be surprised to learn that my thoughts immediately turned to seeking a way to reunite him with his children.

I considered going to Sydney at first in order to organise in person a search for the children. My sister, with her customary tact, promptly gave me her blessing for yet another absence, and one that might last for many months. I have sufficient means, I am yet in good health, and I have the time at my disposal for such a venture. Narcisse no longer needs me and there is nothing to hold me permanently in Vallombrun. I made enquiries about passage on forthcoming voyages to Australia and began to purchase books to fill the long hours at sea.

But the question arose of how I should proceed upon my arrival. Should I go to the beach where the *John Bell* had found Narcisse, and wait, perhaps for many weeks, in the hope that the savages would appear and present the children to me? But what if they believed that Narcisse had been kidnapped and were now afraid of the white man? The situation would necessitate mounting a veritable expedition, perhaps several. One would have to recruit a small group of steadfast men, sleep under canvas, explore and map constantly, penetrate further into the interior of unexplored territory, send out patrols in all directions and, always assuming that there were no hostile savages, interrogate any of them with whom communication was possible. I have no expertise in such ventures. I should be unsure of myself, lacking in experience, and no doubt a burden to an expedition in which each man must play his part in accordance with his appointed function.

If I am to undertake this venture, far better to make all necessary preparations and direct the expedition from a distance, from Sydney or even from Vallombrun, with a second in command in Sydney. My friend Harry Wilton-Smith, a well-known merchant in the colony seems eminently suited to the position. Indisputably one of the most well-informed individuals in Australia, he is accustomed to being in command of men of action. Efficient and precise he will be well placed to determine how best to find the children and repatriate them.

I have therefore written to him at length with the inclusion of a contract and a bill of exchange. My proposal, which I have every reason to believe he will accept, is as. follows: at my expense, a series of exploratory campaigns is to be launched, radiating in all directions around the beach where Narcisse was found collecting shellfish. Mr. Wilton-Smith will choose the leader of the expedition, and determine the number of men to be engaged. He will supervise the logistics, register the expeditions and repeat the searches as many times as necessary in different seasons. He will also make sure that all relevant information is sought and that any rumours of half-caste children are followed up, specifically those that pertain to a boy and a girl, aged approximately eight and five years.

The orders for the leader of the expedition are simple: to find these children who are French by birth (I underlined this), and to bring them back, of their own free will if possible, by force if necessary. The mother will be left among her own people, even if she exhibits a desire to accompany them. Any violence against her person should be avoided, especially within sight of the children.

How to be sure that such children are indeed Narcisse's? The captain of the *John Bell* had spoken frequently of his men's dissolute behaviour with the native women; a few children of mixed blood might indeed have resulted from those encounters. But a half-caste brother and sister of eight and five years old? Surely there could be neither error nor deception involved in this case.

My orders are that as soon as the children are found, they are to be embarked on the first ship leaving for Europe. I have insisted that they be spoken to only in English, and as little as possible. It is my intention to meet them in London and to be the first to speak to them in their father's tongue. These precautions are to ensure a truly scientific observation of the development of these two half-caste children.

Scientists have had much opportunity to study the mixing of races: the full spectrum of interbreeding between white and negro races can be seen in the mulattos and quadroons of the West Indies. Many examples of the offspring of whites and Polynesians can be observed in the South Pacific islands. But of the mixing of white races and the savages of Australia, very little is known. There are indeed a few such persons, unfortunate creatures leading a miserable existence in the backstreets of Sydney, but not one has been, to my knowledge, scientifically examined. These two children will thus provide the opportunity for an original study.

Like their father before them, they will progress slowly towards acquiring the benefits of civilisation: they will renounce their dietary practices, their language, their ways, and gradually, alas, all or almost all of their memories. My interest is not merely in creating two more French citizens, let alone persons of the lower orders. But to observe on a daily basis their transition towards a new condition, to record all that their babbling, their errors and their setbacks reveal about their previous state; this will be of profound interest.

In making the journey back towards the world of the white man, their father has not taught me as much as I would have wished about that other world which he inhabited for eighteen years. I do not begrudge him for this. But the children will arrive without preconceptions straight from their desert, with all the ignorance of their tender years, exulting in being reunited with their father. They will be a precious source of information.

One may even hope that once he is reunited with his children, Narcisse Pelletier will himself begin to speak the language of the savages again with them, and that he will at last yield some of his memories. The shock of the return of his children could well have this salutary effect. And it seems to me, although I cannot say why this should be, that he would be happier and freer were he able to tranquilly evoke his past. May his children be the first to hear those memories.

I have not forgotten the question raised during the Society's plenary session on 2nd September 1861 pertaining to Pelletier's intelligence. It was suggested that his undoubtedly limited intelligence had caused him to sink to the level of the savages, whereas an educated man suffering the same trials would not have abandoned his learning and culture. The more I reflected upon this notion the more it seemed to me to be erroneous; the children will provide the confirmation of this.

Imagine if you will, Sir, a new plenary session in which Pelletier, his son and daughter at his side, responds to the legitimate curiosity of our members, at long last breaking his silence to reveal all that he knows about north-east Australia. Who can doubt that he would then hold centre stage on the platform?

You will say, no doubt, that I am allowing my imagination to run away with me, and I cannot but concur.

I remain your faithful servant...

Post Scriptum

It will not have escaped your attention that the Review has not published a single line of my response in its Spring-Summer edition of 1862. I find it intolerable that those two pages of inane and sneering remarks should constitute the only record of Pelletier's tale. My own account of the affair, which I have begun to draft, begins with the facts. I have set them all out as accurately as possible and followed them with my remarks and reflections. I cannot yet say what form this work will take but it is my hope that interest in it will be stimulated by the children's arrival.

It is also incumbent upon me to inform you that the execrable article in the Review afforded me an abundance of correspondence in the months that followed its publication.

The majority of the correspondents write from all over Europe to congratulate me: for my work with Narcisse, for the advancement of the cause of science, and some in the name of morality or religion. I confess that my vanity has not remained untouched by this. For, with the exception of Her Majesty, who until now has sought to hail my actions? I have so often felt alone in this venture that I have begun to doubt the wisdom of my own actions. I have been much affected by these tributes (naïve though some of them are), more so than I would care to admit. Some letters were even accompanied by a banknote "for the unfortunate sailor".

Two or three small-minded individuals, still under the influence of the bitter words they had read, took violently against the "wretched imposter". I did not hesitate in consigning these letters to the flames.

Captain Varot, recalling his years spent sailing around the Pacific is preparing a scholarly paper on the tattoos of the Tahitians, Marquesans, Wallisians and Maoris. He begs me to provide him with a full description of Pelletier's tattoos, to assist him in classifying the various styles he has identified. This description is of course to be found in my notebooks, and I have sent him a copy of those notes.

I have also received from the eminent neurologist Professor Guarneri of the University of Bologna a summary of his work, citing the most notable of the cases that provide the foundation of his theories. Having thus introduced himself, he asks my permission to proceed with an experiment that could lead Narcisse to candidly reveal his memories of his time in Australia. The benefits promised are clearly considerable, but this cannot be said of the method he proposes. He wishes in fact to perform a trepanation and to remove a certain area of the right frontal lobe of the brain. The professor is sufficiently honest to point out that the operation is not without danger for the patient and that its success cannot be guaranteed, with implications for the patient's intelligence and indeed for his survival. I hesitated. I could not ask for the opinion of the subject himself, since he would have understood neither the procedure nor the purpose of the operation. Although I am neither guardian nor parent, it fell to me to make a decision on Narcisse's behalf. After much thought, and a discussion with a medical friend, I declined the offer.

I trust that you will now appreciate further what an opportunity has been so foolishly lost. If the Review had published an honest report in good faith, how many other readers might have taken up their pens? How many proposals and fertile hypotheses might have resulted from this! How much might the cause of science have been advanced!

13

At a bend in the dried up riverbed stand some tall trees vaguely reminiscent of oaks. Here in a rocky outcrop in the shade a few pools of water still remain; footprints in the sand mark the passage of animals that come to drink there.

As the tribe comes within sight of this small grove of trees, the only ones in the vast plain, Narcisse realises there is a group camping there already: a large family or maybe a small tribe. They look different, not so stocky, their skin colour a bit lighter perhaps. None of the savages seem to be in the least bit surprised, almost as if they have agreed to meet up. Five children come over to take a look at the white man and Waiakh gives them a good telling off. Narcisse can still make no sense at all of what is being said, but amidst the jumble of sounds he hears him say "Amglo" several times.

The two groups slowly began to mingle. The women sit down all together in a big circle under the trees talking animatedly leaving the children to run around all over the place.

Narcisse has known since the old man's visit that his forty-seven hosts are not alone in the immensity of Australia and he is not surprised to encounter another group. He wanders around aimlessly, searches for a spot where the muddy water seems relatively clear, and has a drink.

He is just about to settle down on the grass for a nap beneath a low branch, when the old woman signals to him and a group of children and leads them behind a pile of boulders. There in the vague shade of the rocks are a few stalks of a sickly yellowing plant that looks a bit like sorrel. They set about pulling up the fleshiest stalks, the ones with leaves that are already wilted, and sink their teeth into them. A warm slightly sweet syrup runs down Narcisse's throat. For the first time in his days as a castaway, he tastes sugar; he feels a jolt of pleasure, so powerful it brings tears to his eyes.

A well-built man of about thirty walks past him carrying a spear; he pays no attention to Narcisse. He has a determined look about him, and unlike the others who have their hair cut short, he has long hair. He wears it in a plait, tied with a piece of fine woven vine, and something else. Intrigued, Narcisse stands up and moves towards him to take a closer look, keeping a careful distance. And yes, there, wound into his hair is a thin band of checked cotton fabric that must once have been pink but now is grey and faded.

It is the first time in all his days here that he has set eyes on anything manufactured. He has no way of knowing how this piece of cloth left the white world to become an ornament in this man's hair: he'll never know how long it had travelled for, how many stages there were in that voyage, how many friendly exchanges were involved, if it was lost or plundered in an act of violence. All of a sudden, Narcisse is seized by the desire to make that journey back himself. Without stopping to think, he stands in front of the man and barks a few words at him, pointing to the scrap of material, making exaggerated gestures. Of course, no one understands a word, but maybe the man will see the link between the bauble in his hair and this white man, both of them visitors from another world. Perhaps he'll guess. Who knows, he might want to return the white man to his people in the hope of earning some more tokens to decorate himself with?

Narcisse cannot stop himself from making a move towards this scrap of cloth, almost as if to stroke it, not to make a grab for it exactly, just to make his meaning clear. Suddenly, the piece of faded cloth seems to contain all his hopes. If only he could touch it, imploringly, make it his talisman, his guide for the way back...

The man takes a step back, more surprised than frightened by this white hand reaching for the back of his neck. Has he forgotten that he has fixed this bit of rag to his plait. Will he be willing to part with it?

As if by magic the old woman suddenly appears and plants herself between the two men, as though they were about to fight, ready to separate them. She launches into a long speech, turning first to one and then the other, addressing them with short threatening commands. Then she takes Narcisse by the elbow and leads him away.

She has never treated him like this before. He follows her without putting up any resistance. For the moment, he will have to be satisfied with the proof of contact provided by this scrap of material. Like a prisoner receiving a message in the depths of his dungeon, he is overwhelmed by the importance of this discovery, although he cannot imagine yet how it will help him.

He goes back to sit under the tree, his heart pounding. The man with the plait has gone off to hunt and will soon be out of sight in the bushes. The other members of his family have mingled with the tribe, or else they are sleeping. Maybe they have something too? He has to find out. Narcisse gets up, strolls about in the middle of the groups to pick out the new faces, take a look at their hair, their wrists, their weapons, their baskets. Nothing, no glass, no metal, no cloth, nothing that could have come from the white man's world.

The hope engendered by the scrap of coloured rag wells up again. But why? What's the point? What difference would a second clue make? The piece of fabric in the hair is enough.

Is it? Enough for what? He doesn't know what to hope for any more, it's all too complicated. His trains of thought are all so fragile, but how can he stop himself from thinking? If he is to get out of this alive, as he's promised himself, he must leave no avenue unexplored.

If the man with the plait has been in contact, however indirectly, with people who possess cloth, some day surely he will cross their path again. Should Narcisse not then stay with him rather than with the tribe? But the tribe goes to the beaches, where his rescuers will come for him. How is he supposed to know? What should he do?

Later, after the afternoon siesta, the man with the plait is sitting with Kermarec, deep in conversation. Narcisse walks up to him, keeping his distance to make sure the old woman doesn't get involved, and says insistently to him three times:

"I am Narcisse Pelletier from the schooner *Saint-Paul*."

His fair skin, his height, the sound of this language so completely different, his appearance on the beach one day, the others must have told him about it... doesn't he understand? How can he not understand? Narcisse rubs his hand slowly over the back of his own neck, to suggest some sort of association between him and the scrap of material. Kermarec and the man with the plait watch him intently. They show no reaction, and when Narcisse eventually gives up and walks away, they go back to their conversation.

In the late afternoon the twenty or so youngsters from the two groups have all gathered. They are passing stones around from hand to hand, in a pattern that Narcisse can see is complicated, with strict rules, humming a little refrain. Every once in a while, they stop, and anyone left holding a pebble looks disappointed, as if they've lost. Narcisse doesn't even try to imagine what the rules of the game could be, if it is actually a game. He would have liked to join in. At last, some form of distraction. And just then, he becomes aware of the terrible boredom that afflicts him, a boredom he is condemned to by his inability to understand their language. He could sit down among them, take a stone and pass it on to his neighbour, imitating what he sees them do, like a monkey, without understanding what he's doing, with no strategy in mind, no conversation, no pleasure to be derived... but what would be the point?

Wanderer comes back over to the group of young people and talks to one of the girls in a solemn and commanding tone, very loudly so that all can hear. After his announcement, or maybe it was a warning, all the children gradually leave the game and move away silently, dragging their heels, leaving Wanderer alone with the girl. She wants to go too, and as she moves backwards without taking her eyes off him, he grabs her roughly by the wrist and forces her to turn to face him. It's all too clear what he wants.

Narcisse has often seen the teenagers flirting, ducking and running away, but never such obvious, rough gestures. The girl says something and Wanderer hits her in the face and knocks her down onto the sand. She tries to get up, he jumps on her, forces her down on her back. She tries to stop him and he slaps her again. She manages to get away by rolling onto her side, he grabs her again and crushes her into the ground with his full weight and hits her again. With his right hand, he holds both her hands over her head. She doesn't cry out, utters no protest, all the while struggling to get away from her attacker. With his knee and his other hand Wanderer forces her legs apart, lies down on top of her and rapes her.

Narcisse's first instinct is to go to the aid of the victim. How could he not react? A crime is being committed before his very eyes, a few steps away? And the thought of having it out with Wanderer once and for all is appealing.

Before jumping in, he looks around him. The women go on talking. The men have stopped what they were doing and are watching the scene without moving, showing no signs of disapproval. One or two of them make a few comments that cause the others to smile. It reminds Narcisse of when he saw a group of peasants commenting on a young bull-calf mounting a heifer. Quartermaster is watching the most intently, smiling and nodding, taking personal pride in what he sees. Is it possible that he approves of the rape? That Wanderer is his son?

Narcisse doesn't move. Wanderer is soon finished and uttering a few stifled moans, turns over and stretches out on the sand, making no attempt to stop the girl as she makes her escape.

LETTER XIII

Vallombrun, 13th February 1867

Monsieur le Président,

You do me a great honour in proposing me as a candidate for the vice presidency of the Pacific section of our Society, and I am most sincerely grateful for your generous offer.

I am however, unworthy of such distinction and must decline to stand. I do not say this merely to be polite, but for many reasons quite independent of any claim I might have to the qualities you attribute to me. In the first place, the office would require too many visits to Paris: my health is no longer what it was and travelling tires me. Furthermore, I have no desire to come face to face with either the Reverend Leroy or the gentleman who presided over the Review in 1862, and who did not even acknowledge my letter, let alone respond to my concerns. Finally, I must remind you that my knowledge of geography is meagre and my travels already long past. I cannot deny that the group you generously refer to as the "Academy of the Pacific" gathers regularly around my table. It is true that these dinners do indeed bring together missionaries, officers, scholars and poets, all of whom have recently returned from a voyage across the great oceans, or are about to embark on such a venture. But my role in these proceedings is merely to play the host.

What is more, I have only been a full member of the Society since September 1861, the time of that memorable session, and therefore do not yet have the ten years of full membership required for appointment to the committee. Your position would surely be compromised were I to stand as a candidate under these conditions. And what if the campaign were to result in failure? I would not wish to grant my adversaries the satisfaction that such a failure would surely confer on them.

No, I am by nature better suited to the silence and tranquillity of the mountains.

I surmise that you will respond by sweeping aside all my objections one by one: you will tell me that meetings are infrequent, that Paris is not too far away and that it lies on the route to the Île de Ré, that you have already counted the voices in favour, and that you will support my campaign and assure its success.

I bow in advance to your greater wisdom, but must nevertheless decline the offer. In truth, I am presently engrossed in another, more ambitious project.

You will remember Narcisse Pelletier with whose case I so importuned you a few years ago. If you will allow me to give you news of this fellow, I think you will agree that the vice presidency should be offered to someone more worthy than I. You will understand too where the aforesaid adventure has led me.

Pelletier still occupies the position of storekeeper at the Baleines Lighthouse and makes no further plans for his future.

He no longer resides in the lighthouse, having removed to a fisherman's cottage, where he has set up house with a local woman. Her husband, a butcher from La Rochelle, was said to beat her harshly. I was told that she was not of good repute and that her interest in her new consort could largely be attributed to the salary he receives. It is true that she is neither comely nor agreeable, fair nor dark and that she is of indeterminate age. But, like him, she has been shipwrecked as it were, and in their partnership, I see neither ill-will nor manipulation. She takes care of him, and he is no longer alone. She sells the fish and shellfish that he continues to catch with great success, she keeps their modest house clean, and tends a small vegetable garden, pleasantly embellished with a few flowering shrubs. This companionship has not rendered him any more loquacious. He seems to me to have put on some weight. Much to my surprise, he offered to open a bottle of wine, and then proceeded to do it justice, consuming more than his fair share, and certainly more than his companion, whose capacity proved greater than mine.

I continue to learn nothing new, and my visits to the Île de Ré have become quite infrequent.

Mr. Wilton-Smith accepted my proposal and undertook the searches according to my wishes with his characteristic efficiency and energy. He chose as expedition leader a veteran of the Indian Army, a seasoned adventurer whose exploits ranged from prospecting for gold to trafficking in sandalwood.

The sloop chartered in my name arrived at "Pelletier Beach" on the 1st February 1864, three years after Narcisse was found on the 3rd February 1861. Assuming that the savages move around according to a yearly cycle, it seemed expedient to begin the search here, in the not unreasonable hope that the nomads would be in evidence. There was not a soul in sight.

In the days that followed, a group of six sturdy, well-armed stalwarts set out in every direction to explore the area. The principal difficulty – besides the unrelenting heat and the insects, which the Australians are used to – was the lack, or I should say, total absence of water. Not one river, not a single water hole was discovered. Every man had to carry his own water supply at all times, a burden that limited any incursion to a maximum of four days. Maps were drawn up, of ever greater accuracy. A food cache was established, a pennant hoisted to identify it, and a few glass beads left to lure the savages, but still none came. After one month the explorers returned to Sydney, as I had instructed. Mr. Wilton-Smith sent me a brief report, followed three weeks later by a meticulously detailed account of all expenses. He had also offered, at his own expense, a handsome reward for any useful information. This thoughtful addition resulted in the appearance of many a fraud and necessitated much scrupulous cross-checking all of which yielded nothing.

Further searches were undertaken in October 1864, August 1865 and February 1866, leaving either from Pelletier Beach or from other docking points further north or south. The entire region has now been thoroughly explored: an area of about fifty leagues along the coast and fifteen leagues inland is no longer unknown territory. Until now, only the coastline of this arid region had been charted: now its dunes, forests and its few patches of mangrove hold no mysteries. Some modest seams of coal and a few prospects for iron ore have been identified. It seems to me that this methodical work qualifies my friend Wilton-Smith to become an associate member of our Society; I believe that he would be greatly honoured to receive this distinction.

A few tribes have been found and questioned with the aid of a savage from the north who speaks a little English and whose presence the expedition leader had requested. But no information was obtained about a white savage, or of half-caste children – although Wilton-Smith himself has expressed reservations about the competence and indeed the reliability of the translator.

I am not discouraged by the lack of results, nor do I regard this as a failure. My search continues. These children must be somewhere in the Australian desert. They are now thirteen and ten years of age. We will find them eventually.

Nor does their father's disregard shock me. I have spoken several times to Narcisse and have informed him of the efforts I am making on his behalf. I have told him of my sincere wish that he should find his son and daughter. He looks at me, smiles and does not answer. I know him too well to be deceived by this show of indifference. Australia renders him mute, this is the explanation. But if I were to arrive at the Île de Ré, with his children, if he could take them in his arms, what conversations I would witness! And how much the progress of these two young half-castes would say about the path their father had followed before them!

And yet, in spite of all my endeavours and my genuine concern for them, Narcisse Pelletier's children remained indistinct to me, blurred and faceless, as if veiled by a mist of sand. I finally perceived that these children were without names – their father resolutely refused to utter the names he had given them in the language of the savages. It fell to me therefore to once again act on his behalf and, if not to baptise them, at least to give them an identity.

Selecting a name for the little girl was straightforward: she would be called Eugénie. For the boy, I was at a loss, until the name Charles – in homage to Charles Darwin, an English scholar whose revolutionary ideas I have recently discovered – came into my head. The second part of their names will be those of my dear brother and sister, who I hope will one day become their godparents.

They also needed a date of birth. Narcisse had suggested their ages, the age they must have been when he was separated from them. I calculated the years of their birth to be 1853 and 1857. The actual dates were chosen at random. For Charles-Louis it will be the 2nd December, to honour the day in 1852 upon which our Emperor, his namesake, was proclaimed Emperor of France. I chose for his sister the date of my first encounter with their father in Sydney: 1st March 1861.

Charles-Louis Pelletier, born in north-east Australia on the 2nd December 1853, and Eugénie-Charlotte Pelletier, also born in north-east Australia, on the 1st March 1857, are the children of Narcisse Pelletier, born in Saint-Gilles-sur-Vie on the 13th May 1825 and an unnamed Australian savage. I drew up a letter to the Imperial Prosecutor in La Rochelle, which their father signed with a cross, requesting that his two children be entered in the official register of births.

Narcisse Pelletier has been back in the world of the white man for six years. Not a day has gone by when I have not thought of this matter. I no longer pity him, although I have not ceased to feel compassion for him. He has endured terrible ordeals, of this there can be no doubt. But of what use are emotions such as sympathy or horror in the face of suffering? I am a scholar, a man of science and I cannot be satisfied with mere sentiment.

It is my fervent wish that he will find some happiness. In

saying this, I confess that he must often have been unhappy since his return. And for all the privations and suffering he endured in Australia, I find myself wondering if he had perhaps managed to find happiness among the savages. An astounding notion indeed, but one which I now can entertain.

We will never know how Narcisse Pelletier, the eighteen year old sailor, became a savage. I have tried to understand the process by which Narcisse Pelletier, the thirty-six year old savage became a white man once more: how he learnt our language and customs again; how the various elements of his character came together to form his personality today; why he almost never speaks of his life in Australia.

For a long time, my reflections led nowhere. I could not find a way to order my thoughts, to find meaning in his reactions. What did I have other than mere anecdote to rely on? Only chaos.

Gradually, I began to see that I needed to distance myself from Narcisse Pelletier in order to gain a clearer perspective. And since science provided me with no key to understand this tale, I would have to construct such a tool myself – and perhaps, in so doing, lay the foundations for a new science.

I imagine your surprise at reading this Promethean declaration, and I beg you to grant me a little more of your time.

In truth, only an all-encompassing science can bring together the heretofore scattered fragments of understanding in the study of mankind. New terms have appeared of late: sociology, ethnology, psychology, anthropology. These disciplines are of great value and hold much promise for the future. They complement all that we learn from geography, ethics, pedagogy, grammar, politics and even medicine. They all address the question of man in relation to his fellow beings. But each of these disciplines exists in isolation, insensible to the discoveries of the other sciences: they do not listen to each other and refuse to learn from the discoveries of their counterparts.

I see them now as a series of chapels that together form a vast cathedral, whose architecture I can sense. After much reflection, I have chosen a name for this universal study of man, and of all mankind: Adamology.

I am currently sketching the following theory: all sciences that study man follow the same fundamental principles and have exactly the same structure. These points of convergence must be found and developed in order to make of them a harmonious ensemble. What one might call Vallombrun's theory came to me gradually during the long winter of 1866. Like Pythagoras, Aristotle and Fermat, I seek no glory beyond that of giving my name to a fundamental principle.

Allow me to explain by analogy. Since ancient times, the links between medicine and zoology, or medicine and botany have been understood. Each of these sciences has its own domain, but all obey the same fundamental principles of general biology. In the same way, astronomy and mechanics have shown themselves, since the time of Newton, to be sister sciences; with their cousins, electricity and optics, they make up the domain of general physics. Similarly, the science of Adamology would lay claim to unifying status.

The sciences that form its branches are not books of knowledge stacked next to each other on the shelves of an infinite library; rather they are bodies of knowledge that have much to say to one another. They enrich each other. They all flow from the same principles and belong to a greater family;

they are governed by the same laws.

But here the similarities end. If a blade of grass and a cow are governed to a certain extent by the same laws, we can study one while ignoring the other. All branches of Adamology are concerned exclusively with the human brain; it is here that they must inevitably overlap or at least influence one another. Who could refute the links between education and grammar? Between sociology and ethics, ethnology and politics? Surely we must henceforth search for these multiple resonances in a systematic manner. Are those resonances not as important as the bodies of knowledge they link? More important perhaps?

You will discern, I trust, the contribution that Adamology will make – and the magnitude of the task that awaits me. I am conscious of its ambitious nature and do not know if I will be equal to the task of conducting such a study. I am more inclined to travel than to bookishness, and shrink from the thought of shutting myself away in Vallombrun, labouring for many years to substantiate this theory.

I trust you will understand why this ambition renders it absolutely impossible for me to accept the nomination for the Vice-Presidency of the Geographical Society.

There is an architecture to the cathedral of which I have spoken, but the architect's plans are as yet only sketches. My task will be to provide the solid foundations. What I envisage is an entirely new set of annotations, a system of commonly accepted abbreviations and symbols, a compendium of signs that will enable every idea, in every branch of study to be identified and linked across the disciplines. Adamology studies will be printed in columns, with two columns on each page: one for the text and the other for the stars, triangles, capital letters and oblique lines. New type will be developed to enable the printers to typeset the symbols.

A musical score is made up of different staves, with staffs for the voice and piano, and a line of text for the words. If one element is removed from the score, the music makes no sense. In the same way, Adamology will set out in one column the linear progression of an idea within one branch of science, and in the other column, the network of links to the same idea in sister sciences. My contribution will not be to present the ideas as such, but to present them within a network of correspondences, parallels and resonances – which in turn spark further links. And in this structure, the only system that allows us to fully understand the richness of an idea, do we not see a mirror image of the functioning of our own brains?

An adventure that began on a faraway beach in Australia has led us to fundamentally rethink our conception of Man.

I remain your faithful servant...

14

For two days Narcisse has been thinking about death.

It started with the old woman killing a snake. She'd grabbed it by the tail as it was sleeping under a stone near the camp. Holding it at arm's length, she beat it with a stick before crushing its head with a rock. One minute, the creature was wriggling around all over the place trying to break free, baring its fangs and spitting. And the next, it was nothing but a lifeless object, thrown aside ready to be served up for the evening meal. Whatever its life may have been in the dumb world of reptiles, it all came to an end there, its skull ground into the dust. That was it, the end.

Narcisse had thought again of the cabin boy, the lad from Quimper, and how he'd suffered in his last days. Becalmed in the Indian Ocean, the ship drifted, deserted by the winds. Lying at the foot of the mainmast, the boy had wept and prayed, groaned and vomited all week long. One Sunday at noon he stopped breathing. And that was it. Two hours later they said a hasty prayer, cast his body into the sea and left it at that. What more could they have said? That they wished he'd been kept alive for longer by the second mate's potions? That his agony had been prolonged? He would never have made it as far as Australia. There was nothing more to be said.

Is he any better off than that boy? What difference is there between his fate and the cabin boy's? Their parents would all be sent the same letter, share the same pain. The boy's body lies at the bottom of the ocean, but until Narcisse finds a way to get back to civilisation, he might just as well be buried in the desert sands. He is alive, but somehow, in a way he cannot quite understand, he knows he is dead. And death no longer seems strange to him. He is less afraid of it now.

He is dead too on the night of the new moon, when Chief and the old woman spend what seems like hours chanting and blowing smoke at him before Quartermaster and Scarface signal to him to come over to the fire. The whole tribe looks on attentively as Scarface takes a long thorn that has been coated with a blackish substance and passed through the fire. Quartermaster chants, his voice rising on the night air, intoning a refrain three times. He points to Narcisse's left shoulder and Scarface pierces the skin several times with the spike to form a line of dots.

He grits his teeth and makes no sound. The pain is bearable, so too is the smoke in his nose from the old woman's fumigations. His tattoo is just a simple design, like Waiakh's and the other children's. The older boys have tattoos covering their arms and thighs, the men over most of their bodies.

It seems right that he too should be tattooed. Not for him the tattoos of a sailor. It is not his flesh being pierced with this thorn; he is beyond the reach of Quartermaster, Scarface and all these savages. He is dead. He must be. Sitting there among them in the dust and sand of this never-ending forest, he can only be dead.

He thinks about death in the evening, when the sun disappears behind the trees, sinking fast, as it does only in the tropics. The sun, his name in their language, the sun that melts away to be replaced by fear and nothingness. He has a dim memory of the bosun telling him that the sun rises on the other side of the world in Saint-Gilles just as it is setting here. But he cannot fly across the sky with the sun as if it were a hot air balloon. All he can do is gaze as it disappears from sight every evening, its abrupt demise leaving him so unsettled. Nor does he find solace in the knowledge that just as surely, another day will dawn. The evening colours will soon fade and only the improbable red glow of the fire will linger in the shadows. He wonders what kind of beacon shines on in death.

He thinks about death at midday, when everything dissolves in a haze as the crushing heat rains down from above. The vague trees, the outlines that shimmer in the baking air, this difficulty in breathing, the flickering thoughts that drift randomly around in his head, this oppressive weight of the body, inert and ineffectual. Isn't this what it feels like in the next world? Or in those last moments, leaving this life, when everything gradually fades to nothing and all the senses shut down one by one, like the gunports of a fighting ship as the cannons are withdrawn.

He thinks about death at night, for hours on end, as he lies curled up in a hollow in the sand, not moving.

He thinks about death in the morning when another day of unceasing emptiness and loneliness looms over him, every day the same as the one before, crushing him. What reason is there to hold on? What is the point of bearing it day after day?

And again at midday. And again in the evening.

And if death persists in sending him welcoming signs but still refuses to come to him, must he seek it out? He does not know if he has the strength to go in search of death, nor how to go about it. To stop eating or drinking demands courage that he does not possess. He dreams of a rapid journey, a voyage of no return.

He could climb to the top of a tree, or find a rock high enough to throw himself off, head first into the void. Yes, he can picture it: he steps lightly like a dancer and launches himself, arms outstretched to embrace the sky. Let the old woman try and put the pieces back together then with one of her potions! Let her try and understand the smile on his face as she gazes in surprise at his wide-open laughing eyes, eyes that will never again look into hers!

But what if he misjudges the height? What if the ground is too soft? What if his efforts fail and he has to spend the rest of his wretched days a cripple, dragging himself around, limping along behind the tribe.

No, he'd have to do it right. A plant with poisonous sap, a fish with a lethal barb? He doesn't know of any yet, but he will find them. Eventually he'll learn to identify the plants they take away from careless children. And when the right moment comes, he'll make himself the sweetest of all desserts.

But why wait so long? He could sit down under a tree, open the veins in his wrists with the small bluish mussel he's learnt to use for slicing fish open. A small cut at the base of the palm, just below his right hand, then the left, and his life would flow slowly out onto the sand. He would go to sleep; he might feel a bit cold, and that would be it. So long as they didn't find him, the savages would assume he'd fled.

Or perhaps his destiny was to die at sea after all. He could walk into the sea, just as he's done so many times before, give a friendly wave to Waiakh, walk until he was out of his depth, move his arms and legs about like a dog heading out to sea, feel first one wave and then another break over his head, and go proudly forward towards the shadowy outline of the schooner, its two masts just visible at the entrance to the bay.

LETTER XIV

La Rochelle, 13th December 1867

Monsieur le Président,

I fear I do not have the fortitude to bear the realisation that these last ten years of my life have led only to the bitter certainty of failure, that all my travels have been in vain.

I have striven to put in order my thoughts on what I have termed Adamology and perceive that it was naïve, nay, imprudent of me to inform you of its provenance. I have read widely, written extensively and cast much into the fire. A thousand theoretical and practical difficulties confronted me, and I felt that I was seeking to scale a mountain of great height, my way barred by raging torrents and impenetrable glaciers.

From the terrace at Vallombrun, as I contemplate the mountains on the horizon, the rudiments of Adamology seem to me no more accessible than those inviolate peaks.

My first error was to misjudge my own character. I am not a man at ease with ordered systems. I have not succeeded in converting my intuitions and enthusiasms into solidly supported scientific certainties. I leave it to others to take up that mantle and find the paths to conquest and success.

Can I hope at least to be remembered as the man who elucidated the mystery of Narcisse Pelletier? Alas, no.

In continuing the research that you had commissioned on similar cases, I uncovered a few other forgotten dramas, not of castaways from shipwrecks, for which your records proved to be complete, but of individuals kidnapped on dry land, seized by raiding parties. In the plains of Patagonia and of North America there are a number of white men who have been taken in this way and who have lived among the natives. In a few cases, those abducted as young children have adopted Indian ways completely, having lost all memory of their life with their parents. Others have kept alive the memory of our civilisation throughout their sufferings in captivity, until the longed for day of their deliverance.

But none has twice undertaken the voyage from one world to another as Narcisse Pelletier has done.

I have observed much, but what, if anything, have I understood? The enigma remains as impenetrable as on that first day. What began in Sydney has now ended in La Rochelle. Should I have spoken to him differently during those days in Sydney? Should I have found another way to approach him upon our return to France? At what cost did I persist in the face of his silence? How heavily did my words weigh on that silence?

It is my duty to bring to an end this narrative and I must now tell you of our last encounter.

Having received the final report of the four expeditions conducted in Australia by Mr. Wilton-Smith in search of Charles and Eugénie Pelletier, a copy of which I have submitted to our Society's archives, I decided to make a comparison between the findings of the report and the recollections of Narcisse Pelletier, its principal subject.

I made the journey to La Rochelle, whither the subdivisional engineer was kind enough to summon his lighthouse store-keeper, thus sparing me the rigours of the winter storms of the Ile de Ré. At the appointed hour, Narcisse came to my hotel from his temporary lodgings at the naval barracks. I showed him the maps of Wilton-Smith's expeditions and repeated to him the explorers' tales from their various forays. I wondered if talk of that landscape, the mangroves and sand dunes, the islets along the coast, the vast flat colourless forests would inspire him to reveal any confidences. Would the tales of bivouacs, of encounters and occasional exchanges with savages arouse any emotion in him? Alas, no. He listened politely and uttered nothing in response. I cannot deny that I was scarcely surprised at this.

Narcisse Pelletier's refusal to speak of his years in Australia remains absolute. The silence he keeps is as impenetrable as it was when we first met in Sydney in 1861.

The next day, I summoned him again. This time I had my Australian notebooks with me and tried another approach: I told him his own story.

"You were in the gardens of the governor's residence, you were dressed in a loincloth, guarded by two soldiers. A group of gentlemen came to observe you and speak to you in different languages..."

As I read him the account of those events, which I reported to you at the time, embellishing it with all the details I could recall, he was as if transfixed. He remained absolutely still, listening with inexpressible attentiveness, almost frightening in its intensity, a pearl of sweat on his forehead. I finished telling him about that first day and continued:

"Before that. You were on the *John Bell*, you were terrified, crouched against the guardrail, for ten days, refusing to eat anything…"

Silently, I gave thanks to that scoundrel Captain Rowland, whose account given in the office of the Governor of New South Wales enabled me to evoke for Narcisse those first days at sea.

"Before that. You were sitting in the dinghy. The dinghy was rowed out to the ship, you climbed up on a rope ladder…"

Narcisse had begun to cry and was looking at me imploringly. I carried on mercilessly.

"Before that. You were collecting shellfish with the tribe on the beach, a day like any other. Your children were beside you. You saw the *John Bell* sailing into the bay. The sailors came up to you and you felt no fear…"

Narcisse was in a state of utter confusion and despondency. Only the stoniest of hearts would not have been moved by his suffering and tears. Undaunted, I persevered: "Before that, Narcisse?"

I could see that my question filled him with terror. What was going on in his head? He made no attempt to leave the room, but begged me by his mute silence to put an end to this torture. I persisted regardless. There would be time later to console him.

"Before all that, Narcisse? What happened?"

He stood there, wringing his hands, ashen-faced. And as I stared at him insistently, driving home the question with my searching look, it was as if all our previous conversations, all my failed attempts to make him speak had led to this moment.

"Before… before. That was not Narcisse…" he muttered

in a heartrending voice. What did he mean by this strange confession? In an effort to get to the heart of the matter I went back to the day when he was lost, November 5th 1843.

"That was not Narcisse, before? Tell me then, what happened the day that Captain Porteret sent you to look for water, when you lost your way and did not get back to the *Saint-Paul*? What happened after that?"

This continuing torture made him tremble in every fibre of his being, and I thought he would surely faint.

"After that, you were alone on the beach, the ship had left without you and you did not know if it would return..."

"After... after... that wasn't Narcisse," he managed to utter in one gasp.

I took a deep breath to muster the strength to continue, to try and find the smallest crack in the constancy of his refusal, and finally get to the truth.

"After, it wasn't Narcisse. Before, it wasn't Narcisse. But in between, when you were over there? All those years? Who were you then?"

And then, like a prisoner begging for mercy, who finally silences his interrogator by revealing the secret that will condemn him, he uttered what sounded like a word of two syllables. It was whispered under the breath, but I thought I heard something that sounded like "Ango".

"What did you say?"

Without repeating his confession, his secret, he broke down, his head in his hands. But I did not relent.

"In between this before and after? Who were you then?"

He looked up, his shattered face bathed in silent tears, and finally said in a deathly whisper:

"Speaking is like dying."

I harassed him further – I tormented him cruelly with

questions for many long minutes only to be greeted by silence, weeping, or the mysteriously repeated phrase: "Speaking is like dying."

At length, I took pity on him. At a loss as to how to comfort him, I went to find him a glass of water, intending to calm him and beg him to forgive me for the harsh treatment to which I had subjected him in the name of science.

When I came back into the room he was gone. Sensible of what I understood to be his need for solitude, I decided to leave him in peace for the rest of that day. How mistaken I was.

The next day, he did not appear for our meeting. I sent someone to search for him at the naval barracks only to be told that he had not returned to his lodgings there. He was avoiding me. He had fled. I sent a telegraph to the lighthouse and learned that he had not been seen there, nor had he returned to the little house that had become his home.

Increasingly concerned, I extended my search to the hospital, the prison and the morgue. There was no sign of Narcisse Pelletier. He had vanished, taking with him nothing but the clothes on his back. Where should I look for him?

I informed the police of his disappearance and was required to state my relationship to him. Friend of the family seemed the least false description. The inspector listened to what I had to say and assured me that a search would be conducted. I also alerted the mayor of Saint-Gilles.

I had no clues to follow. And besides, why should I pursue him? To beg his forgiveness? To question him further? To keep him under my control? For science?

It is now one week since he disappeared. Strangely, I am not concerned that he may have ended his days. I know that he is somewhere out there, beyond the reach of all questioning. Neither white savage nor lighthouse storekeeper, he is just another wanderer, a man with no past and no future.

Before leaving La Rochelle to return to Vallombrun, as I waited for news that did not come, I reflected on his attitude.

His agony seemed to begin as soon as I questioned him on those two moments when he had been propelled against his will from one world to the other – and the closer my questions came to that tipping point, the more troubled, torn and broken he had seemed. His mind, his whole body fervently refused to remember. It was not a question of consciously willing. He was in the grip of some unknown force, a state that I had already perceived in 1861 in Australia, and which I had likened, in one of my letters, to a struggle between two distinct characters within him: a sailor in a dungeon who perceives the door to be open a crack, and a demon that prevents him from leaving. That demon, or rather an obscure and overwhelming force has prevailed.

His tears are testimony to the violence of this struggle. The tears he shed that day in London, when I pointed out to him the impossibility of his being the son of an Australian negress, issued from the same source. We must look upon Narcisse as a battlefield. The smoke from the cannons has dissipated, the armies have moved on, and all that remains of the once rich farmland is the mud-strewn plain, studded with ravaged trees. This is Narcisse's soul.

My only key to unlocking the enigma is the dictum that is perhaps his parting gift: "Speaking is like dying."

To speak, to put into words all that is indescribable about those days over there, to articulate the memories that I unceasingly solicited, memories stamped forever as forbidden. Responding to my questions would have meant placing himself in mortal peril. Not of death in the physical sense, but of dying to himself and all those other people. Dying of being unable to conceive of the two worlds at one and the same time. Dying because of being unable to be simultaneously both white man and savage.

Twice he has made the impossible crossing from one world to the other. In order to live with the savages, he must have had to forget everything of his life as a sailor – at what cost to him we shall never know. Returned once more to the world of the white man, he instinctively refused to endure again a similar ordeal, and sought refuge in forgetting. To answer would have meant lowering the drawbridge of his fortress and allowing the sailor and the demon to face each other in mortal combat. His sanity would not have survived.

Her Majesty had been able to open a postern and catch a glimpse of what lay on the other side: perhaps this was because her power and status made her seem unreal to him. And in his compassion for his workmate's suffering at the loss of his child, Narcisse let down his guard for a moment and let slip a fragment of his Australian tale, the existence of his two children. But it was only the intensity of these emotions that freed him to speak of these things. I have been questioning him for six years and he has confided nothing to me. Silence is the key to his survival.

And now I begin to wonder what would have become of him if Wilton-Smith's expeditions had succeeded in bringing his children back to him. Would he have been carried away by the joyous emotion of the reunion? Would he have been overwhelmed by the intrusion of his Australian past into his new life here? To what unsuspected hazards would my naïve desire to do good have exposed him? Would he have found the words to say to his children: "Speaking is like dying?" And in which language?

He could neither answer my questions nor leave them unanswered. And so, he has fled.

I sense that we will see him no more. Neither the police, nor the mayor of Saint-Gilles have received news of him and nor indeed has anyone else. I am much affected by this dramatic turn of events and am returning to Vallombrun, where I hope to be able to confirm what I believe I have understood.

Among all the questions which I now know he will never answer is one in particular that causes me great pain. His attitude towards me has always been genial but reserved, never revealing anything of his deepest emotions. What have I been to him all these years? A friend? An older brother, albeit one who is a mere four years older than he? A mentor? A persecutor? An instrument of fate, devoid of meaning? All of these things at the same time?

All that is left for me is to pray that Narcisse Pelletier finds peace and tranquillity, and an end to his tribulations. And to ask that he never again has to utter those terrible words: "Speaking is like dying."

May God come to his aid.

I remain your faithful servant…

15

Narcisse was a boy of eight when his uncle died, and he no longer remembered him very well. But he hadn't forgotten the short walk to his uncle's small house at the edge of the village and the countless adventures to which it opened the door. Narcisse's parents and other relatives had never travelled; they knew only of life in the Vendée. But his uncle had once been a grenadier; from the windows of the house at the edge of the village, Narcisse could see beyond the surrounding farmland to distant battlefields and German forests. The old grenadier liked to tell of his campaigns, and the boy would listen avidly as his uncle talked of taking the enemy by surprise, of fording rivers and entering victoriously into towns whose names they never knew, of young generals reviewing the troops, of the heady thrill of battle, the smiles of the girls serving in the mess and of the camaraderie in camps a world away from Saint-Gilles.

The child listened with rapt attention to the grenadier's tales: he heard of a duke's palace sacked in Pomerania, of surgeons tending the wounded in the baroque splendour of a Bavarian monastery, of dark days spent crossing mountains deep in snow, of a bivouac beside a town in flames, the town destined to fall the next day, of cannons wrested from the enemy. His uncle talked of the forever-deferred dream of invading England, of the heavenly sight of bell towers with their blue and gold curves, of trumpets and fifes sounding the charge, the smell of powder, the fury of hand-to-hand fighting – and then of being wounded, lanced by an uhlan's sabre slicing deep into his right arm, the arm that now hung limp and useless... he had no regrets. Sometimes he would brandish his boots and sing their praises, as if he had worn only that pair to trudge across half of Europe and bear arms in the name of the Empire for five years – and the child believed it all.

Grenadier Pelletier's favourite memory was of a reconnoitring exercise in Bohemia with three comrades. Cutting through the woods, as they rounded the bend of a sunken lane, they came face to face with a carriage drawn by four horses. The grenadier had the presence of mind to take aim at the postilion, who stopped his team, and fearing his last hour had come, fled into the forest. A face appeared at the window of the carriage, a terrified young woman wrapped in a capacious blue coat, pleading with them in a language they did not understand. Then, a boy of about ten, her brother probably, poked his head up, making a brave show to demonstrate that the young woman was not alone. With no orders for such an encounter, the soldiers decided to escort their captives back to camp. Pelletier installed himself as postilion and forbade anyone to climb in with the prisoners as he drove them the two leagues to their camp. The colonel was dining in his tent when the carriage drew in. Hearing the commotion he came outside and gallantly offered his hand to the young woman. And then, before inviting her and her brother to dine with him, the colonel publicly congratulated Pelletier for his audacious actions.

"Just imagine it, lad! I stopped her from running away. A countess. Her life changed for ever, and all because of a young chap from Saint-Gilles-sur-Vie!"

And as the old soldier's tales unfolded, Narcisse thought of his father, always grumbling about the poor harvest and the lack of business in his workshop.

Narcisse had always known that he would travel. At twelve, when he'd wanted to sign on as a cabin boy, his father had said no, and again at thirteen and fourteen. At the age of fifteen, Narcisse convinced his father to let him go. And since then he'd seen Nantes and China, Aden and Bristol, Ceylon and Barcelona, the Cape and Bordeaux. He'd travelled to more lands and crossed more oceans than his uncle had ever dreamt of seeing.

If it hadn't been for that countess in a sunken lane in Bohemia one autumn evening, a blue coat, a terrified woman pleading for mercy in an unknown tongue at the hands of Napoleon's soldiers... Narcisse had heard this story so many times that he felt as if he'd been there himself, as if he'd been one of the grenadier guards fighting alongside his uncle, or the boy, his frightened face barely glimpsed, determined to hide his fear and protect his sister.

What did he know of that evening in Bohemia? Everything. He could conjure every detail: the smell of the horses, the fainthearted coachman, the countess with her dishevelled blonde curls, her perfume, the rustling of her silk gown, the sniggering uncertainty of the French soldiers at a loss for what to do, the mud-spattered uniforms, the little boy's proud expression, the colours of the fallen leaves, the tolling of a bell in a nearby village, and that anguished voice imploring the soldiers to show mercy...

315

Who could have imagined that a sunken lane in Bohemia would have led him to this remote desert at the other end of the world?

He could not deny that the immensity of Australia filled him with dread. But he had wanted to travel; this was the life he'd chosen. He'd lost part of one earlobe, but his uncle had lost an arm in his campaigns. He'd walked barefoot across the desert, but how far had they actually gone? Probably not even as far as from Nantes to Saint-Gilles. Grenadier Pelletier had marched across Europe for five years and he certainly hadn't had a comfortable bed to sleep in every night and three square meals a day.

Narcisse tried to see himself as an old man, telling tales of his voyages some day in Saint-Gilles. What would he say about this moment? Would he admit that he was terrified every day, every minute, and hope that the children didn't believe him? Would he make a joke of it, find the humour in these dark days and nights: "Stark naked? Yes, naked as the day I was born, the whole time!" Or would he hide it all away for ever, bury all that he'd endured in a well of terror and anguish never again to penetrate its depths?

As a child he'd never thought to ask his uncle what became of the countess – nor even how he'd known that she was a countess at all. In the story, she simply disappeared at dusk on the arm of the colonel, into his tent, with her brother as chaperone. Had Grenadier Pelletier set off the next day to cross the Elbe or the Danube? Had the colonel sent the young woman back into her caleche on a secret mission, or dispatched her to some wretched dungeon? In his childish imagination, he'd give different endings to the story, changing it depending on how he felt.

The countess appears at the window of her carriage wrapped in her blue coat. She looks at the grenadier who has taken aim at her coachman. The coward flees but the grenadier doesn't fire. She gazes intently at the French soldier and speaks to him, terrified, knowing that he will not understand, pleading for her life.

And she will always remember it as the best day of her life, that day in Bohemia, in that sunken lane.

Narcisse listens.

Waiakh interrupts his reverie and hands him a bundle of sticks. Together they scrape off the bark and Narcisse shapes them into points with a sharpened rock. They have spent the whole morning hunting lizards and now they are tired and resting. Their catch was meagre: two lizards for Waiakh, none for him.

Bohemia recedes into a dreamland. He tries to conjure another pleasant memory, the image of the whore in the Cape. But he cannot summon it. He can no longer remember her face, her warmth, the pleasure it gave him.

Has he forgotten everything? He tries to recall the names of his shipmates from the *Saint-Paul*, but his memory refuses to yield them. The larboard watch? Surely he can remember them. There was a Pierre, Yvon. And the other one? The little one with a good voice? He doesn't know. He can't remember. How many were they?

He can't remember the sailors from the *Saint-Paul*, the whore from the Cape. The Bohemian countess is still there somewhere, a vague presence. In his uncle's memory or in his own? They are all shrouded in mist, wrapped in the same fog. He gives up trying.

Half-remembered images coalesce, dissolve and vanish, scrambling his past. He is losing his memory. He has no will, no strength to fight it. Like a vast wave, the tide of forgetting rises from the depths of a wide, steep-sided bay and he feels no anguish. Only indifference. What good are memories of the 'tweendecks, the Cape, Saint-Gilles or Bohemia? They are nothing but old tales, merging and fading, barely discernible in the swirling grey mists where dreams arise.

A countess in a blue coat at the window of her carriage.

A girl sitting on a coral block, dipping her finger in red clay and drawing semi-circles on his face and chest.

A shell on the sand, tinged with orange.

LETTER XV

Letter from Charlotte de Vallombrun to the President of the Geographical Society.

Vallombrun, 7th March 1868

Monsieur le Président,

It is my sad and painful duty to inform you that my beloved brother Octave de Vallombrun has been recalled to God.

After his last visit to La Rochelle, he came directly to our brother's house in Grenoble. There we celebrated Christmas together. Upon his return to Vallombrun he continued to take the long walks he loved so much in spite of the January cold and wintry showers. A chest infection set in upon his return from one such walk and the next day he was feverish. He struggled valiantly for three days, received the consolations of religion and gave his soul up to God on the 20th January.

He lies in the family tomb in the cemetery of Vallombrun.

For more than ten years, since before his sojourn in Iceland, I have witnessed the admiration and respect he held for you. Your correspondence, of which he was rightly proud, continued without interruption and he would often invoke your wise and kindly face in the course of our conversations. Of all his titles, the one of which he was the most proud was that of member of the Geographical Society.

Maître Vion, our advocate in Grenoble, presided over the reading of the will. Since I do not know if Maître Vion has been in contact with you, I am enclosing a copy of Octave's last will and testament, which I beg you to read before continuing with my letter.

Last Will and Testament of Octave de Vallombrun

I, the undersigned Octave de Vallombrun, being sound in mind and body, in the presence of Messieurs Poullier and Dufourg, gentlemen of property, declare this to be my last will and testament and hereby revoke any previous will and testament.

I give and bequeathe:

1. To my coachman, Firmin Delessert, the sum of twenty francs, in addition to my clothing so long as the said Firmin Delessert shall be in my employment at the time of my decease.

2. To Félicie Sorel, who much more than a cook has been the soul of the château for half a century, the sum of sixty francs. No conditions are attached to this bequest.

3. To the curate of the parish of Vallombrun:

– the sum of fifty francs for the establishment of a perpetual mass to be sung with the children of the choir on the day of the anniversary of my death for the remission of my sins and that my unfortunate soul may rest in peace if God so wills it.

– the sum of fifty francs for the maintenance of the church and the presbytery

– the sum of fifty francs to offer succour to the poor of the

parish, to be spent as the curate sees fit with no one family to receive a sum that exceeds five francs.

4. To be placed in the charge of the curate of Vallombrun, the sum of one hundred francs to provide a dowry for four or five virtuous and impoverished girls of this parish, the recipients to be chosen by the curate in consultation with the mayor.

5. To Monsieur Narcisse Pelletier, storekeeper at the Baleines Lighthouse on the Île de Ré (Lower Charentes) the sum of eight hundred francs. The sum to be placed in the charge of the master of the said lighthouse, for him to disburse to the interested party in the form of an allowance in such increments as he sees fit, taking into consideration Monsieur Pelletier's needs and his other sources of income.

Should Monsieur Pelletier predecease me, and should he leave heirs, the remaining sum shall be distributed in equal parts between his children upon their reaching the age of majority.

6. To Charles-Louis and Eugénie-Charlotte Pelletier, the sum of two thousand five hundred francs. This sum shall be disbursed annually in tenth parts to Mr. Wilton-Smith, merchant of Sydney (Australia) for him to finance expeditions in search of the said Charles-Louis and Eugénie-Charlotte Pelletier, and if necessary to repatriate them to France. Mr. Wilton-Smith shall be required to present an annual accounting of the manner in which the funds have been used.

If the allotted sum is not spent in its entirety (as a result of the death of Mr. Wilton-Smith or in the event of his declining to undertake the said expeditions, or for any other reason) the remaining funds shall be apportioned as in 5.

Once the children have been found, the remaining funds shall be placed in the charge of my brother, Louis de Vallombrun, for him to provide for the needs and education of these children until the age of their majority. The remaining capital shall be used in one half to establish Charles-Louis in a profession of his choice, and the remaining half to provide a dowry for Eugénie-Charlotte.

7. To the Geographical Society of Paris, the sum of two thousand and two hundred francs for the Society to undertake and finance within ten years one or several exploratory expeditions in north-east Australia, within the area outlined in the attached map. As an absolute condition of this bequest, the reports written by leaders of the expeditions shall be published either as articles in the Geographical Review or in book form, according to their length.

8. To Mr. Wilton-Smith, merchant of Sydney (Australia), the portrait of me that hangs in the library, unless my sister Charlotte exercises her right of option on this item at the time of the reading of the will. The portrait was painted by Aristide Verne, an associate member of the Geographical Society, in the spring of this year and shows me in three quarters bust, holding in one hand, a six-holed native flute, in a rocky landscape of red tones evocative of Australia.

The rest of my movable and immovable property shall be divided in equal parts between my brother Louis and my sister Charlotte, who are equally dear to my heart.

However, the Château de Vallombrun, with all the land and furnishings at the time of my death, shall fall to Charlotte's share. The same shall apply to the ring which I had the honour of receiving from the hands of Her Majesty. If as a result of this Charlotte's share should be greater that Louis', so be it. No compensation shall be due.

Finally, I wish my tomb to be inscribed with the dates that mark the boundaries of my life and the single line: "Octave de Vallombrun, traveller".

May God have mercy on my soul.
Written and signed at the Château de Vallombrun on this day, 22nd February 1864.

Octave de Vallombrun
(Countersigned by Messieurs Pouillier and Dufourg)

My brother, the Viscount Louis, who is in full agreement with me on every point in this letter, is as surprised as I by these terms.

In particular, points 5 and 6, concerning Monsieur Pelletier and the search for his hypothetical children, at considerable expense, are entirely unreasonable.

My late brother showed great generosity of spirit in taking in this fellow and bringing him back to France. As if this fine gesture did not in itself suffice, he then obtained by imperial favour a position for Pelletier in government employment. This was admittedly a modest position, but nevertheless one that far exceeded the candidate's qualifications. Having thus assured Pelletier's future, my brother then proceeded to finance, entirely at his own expense and at extraordinary cost, four expeditions to Australia, which were by any account a wasted investment.

Pelletier spent almost one month in Vallombrun at the end of 1861. This sailor's countenance bespeaks a lack of intelligence; he utters few words and has nothing to say. Degenerate by nature, he takes for granted all that is done for him, shows no gratitude whatsoever and seems not to know his place. One cannot but ask oneself if he is simple-minded. Or was he playing the fool in order to exploit Octave's excessive generosity? I would prefer to believe this man to be simple-minded and naïve rather than calculating, but I have alas several times had the occasion to observe his surly and manipulative character.

My late brother's patience and generosity may not have been exhausted, but I have certainly been driven beyond the limits of forbearance, as has the Viscount Louis. The vain efforts and fruitless waste that ensued from Octave's benign whims cannot be allowed to continue beyond his lifetime. Must I add that my late brother's kindness towards this man gave rise to the most scurrilous of rumours with regard to the nature of the interest he showed in the sailor. Not only has Pelletier compromised my brother's fortune, he has also besmirched his reputation.

It is therefore our intention to contest this will and render it null and void. We shall cite our late brother's occasionally excitable and fanciful temperament, and we are confident as to the outcome. The matter is in the hands of the lawyer and we shall proceed in accordance with his advice. However, nothing would be more distressing – or indeed more contrary to my late brother's wishes – than to find ourselves before the bench in confrontation with you. At the sound of the clerk of the court calling the affair of "the Vallombrun heirs versus the Geographical Society", Octave's eternal slumber would surely be wretchedly disturbed.

For this reason we feel it is preferable to approach you for a settlement. As you will have gathered, you are prevented from enjoying the full benefit of my late brother's legacy to you by the condition imposed in the will: the extravagant obligation to finance further expeditions to north-east Australia, expeditions that have already been undertaken in every direction on four occasions during Octave's lifetime, and always in vain. Too much time, money and energy have been squandered heretofore. Furthermore, the obligation to publish the results, (or the absence thereof) can only serve to tarnish your Society's image.

Octave was as if bewitched by this affair, but we could not tell him: our affection for him was too great. Alas, the time has now come to break the spell.

Not wishing to see our brother's legacy dissipated in the financing of further absurd expeditions, we feel it is more salutary, and indeed more faithful to Octave's memory, to make a payment to your Society. While the sum would be more modest than the amount stipulated in the will, it would come free of all conditions, for you to spend as you see fit: on expeditions to the pampas of Argentina or the steppes of Kamchatka perhaps? The acquisition of a collection of books? Repairs to your headquarters? Who better than you, Sir, to make such decisions?

We therefore wish to propose that you renounce my late brother's bequest. Louis de Vallombrun and I would make a gift to the Geographical Society with no conditions, of a sum of five hundred francs, for example. These points would be agreed in the presence of a lawyer.

(May I take the liberty of adding not a condition, but a humble request? That Octave's name should be inscribed on a plaque placed in a location of your choice within the walls of your headquarters. We would of course take full responsibility for all costs.)

We have presented this proposal to the other beneficiaries of the will: the curate of Vallombrun, the mayor, Monsieur Firmin Delessert and Madame Félicie Sorel, and they are in full agreement. I have exercised my right of option on the portrait of Octave. I should add that the witnesses to my brother's handwritten will, Messieurs Pouillier and Dufourg, are prepared to testify to my late brother's exaggeratedly fanciful state of mind when the will was written in February 1864, at the time of the first expedition.

If all parties are in agreement, Pelletier's opposition would be the only obstacle to declaring the will null and void. I must tell you that he seems to have disappeared quite suddenly following his last conversation with my brother in La Rochelle. His inexplicable defection affected Octave profoundly. If Pelletier's whereabouts remain unknown, the case against him will of course be greatly strengthened.

Must I also point out the will is dated February 1864, before Pelletier disappeared? How can one be sure that these would still have been Octave's final wishes after Pelletier had acted in such a cavalier and unworthy fashion towards his protector? Had Octave lived a few more weeks, would he not have rescinded, with one furious and richly justified stroke of the pen, the benefits he intended to bestow on this ingrate?

These are all the reasons that have led us to propose this simple compromise, a solution that could be both rapidly executed and mutually advantageous. Our peace of mind depends on your response: a quick and successful case against Pelletier, or may God forbid, a long and painful legal action against your Society.

If I may once more presume upon your good will Sir, I would also like to mention Octave's papers.

I have had the sad task of sorting and classifying these documents. While Octave was alive, I never set foot in his study. But he was meticulous, as I have always known, and I had no trouble making an inventory of the contents of the various drawers and cupboards.

I ask your opinion on a geographical matter and seek your opinion on two types of papers.

Firstly, there are three notebooks on Pelletier. The notebooks contain a daily record of my late brother's singular encounters with him in Sydney in the gardens of the governor's residence. The notebooks begin on the 1st March 1861 with the record of the initial encounters followed by notes on further meetings, and by my late brother's personal musings. There is nothing definitive here, nothing that could be considered ready for publication: rather the notebooks form a diary, a record of Octave's thoughts on the affair.

Secondly, there is a box bearing the inscription "ADMLG". This title means nothing to me. Octave said nothing that might throw any light on this. Inside the boxes are twenty-five files, with the headings "Introduction I, II and III", and "Volumes 1 to 22". Each file contains three to ten pages. On each page are three, four or five lines of inscriptions, some with only one word, others with geometrical shapes, diamonds, stars and squares. His hand here is smaller. It is distended and unlike his usual hand. I find it quite impossible to decipher.

He had sometimes in the course of the last two or three years alluded to a great work in progress. His tone was ironic at first, but this became increasingly sardonic as he began to doubt his ability to complete the work. Because of one or two allusions he made, I understood his efforts to be in some way related to geography. Yet he said that he had distanced himself from your Society and from geography, a state of affairs which he manifestly regretted.

As you will have surmised, we have no use for either these notebooks or the box of jottings. The papers are carefully stored in the attic, and are entirely at your disposition, whatever may be your decision with regard to the will.

I am deeply grateful to you for your kind attention to our affairs and beg you to accept my humble thanks in memory of our beloved brother, Octave de Vallombrun.

My brother Louis sends you his respects.
   I am your humble and most devoted servant,

   Charlotte de Vallombrun

16

The rains have ceased. The land is carpeted with lush green grass, studded with white flowers. The colour of the trees has softened too, their green less metallic. A barely perceptible aroma of honey floats on the air.

For the thousandth time that day he waves his right arm to swat away the flies. And then, perhaps because of the look Waiakh gives him every time he does this, he sees the futility of the gesture. The flies will come back whatever he does, whether he swats them away or leaves them alone. Watching them as they buzz around and land on him again, he decides not to move, to resist the urge he's been giving into, and just accept their presence. The flies roam about on his skin, take off, come back again. He no longer cares about them.

The hunters have done well, and everyone has been able to eat their fill, and more. In the evening, the men draw close to their wives, the young become amorous.

The children play and run around all over the place, teasing and taunting each other, tussling and fighting, breaking off without waiting to declare a winner. He doesn't join in these activities, but he too feels lighter, tranquil almost.

They are camped at the foot of a small hill, and after the midday rest, he climbs to the top to make the most of the almost imperceptible breeze. Beneath him, the grey plane, dotted with clumps of trees, stretches as far as the eye can see in every direction.

Between two rocks, he spots an outcrop of yellow earth, rich and lumpy. He puts his finger in the earth and runs it over his thigh: a clean line appears, as if drawn with charcoal. An orange tinted line on his tanned skin.

He sits down and dips his finger again in the yellow earth. He traces a circle on his chest, beneath the right breast, then another on the left side. He dips his finger in again to draw a circle under his navel and one above it, and one more under his left shoulder. It gives him a subtle and indefinable pleasure to decorate himself like this, drawing whatever patterns take his fancy. Once more he takes some yellow earth on his finger and slowly traces a series of broken lines on his thighs. He looks at his arms and is pleased with the contrast between their unmarked skin and his painted legs and chest.

Then he goes back down to the tribe.

"Amglo!"

The old woman calls out his name and extends her arm towards him. She shouts a short phrase, very loudly, several times, as if to call to the tribe.

He is immediately alert, not knowing what he's done, which rule he's infringed. He knows instinctively that his drawings are the cause of this upset.

They all come running up, forming a circle around him, looking at what he cannot hide.

The old woman says a few more words. Then, unable

to speak any more, she splutters, her shoulders shake, a few inarticulate sounds escape her – yes, the old woman is laughing, she's convulsed with laughter, she laughs until she cries.

The other women start to laugh too, then the children and the men. They all roar with laughter, shouting out jokes, slapping their thighs, rubbing their eyes and bursting into laughter again.

He was expecting an unpleasant surprise, to be shouted at, beaten. He's disconcerted by all this hilarity: he has never seen them come together in enjoyment like this before. He doesn't understand what is so funny about his paintings.

He wonders what to do. And then he takes a deep breath, spreads his arms wide, does a few improvised dance steps, a sort of gig to accentuate his muscles and display his decorated body. He jiggles about, waiting to see how the tribe will react.

Gales of laughter break out once more in the group. The children roll on the ground waving their legs in the air, the women gasp for air and laugh till they cry, the men clap their hands and shout gleefully. It seems as if this general hilarity will never end. Whenever the laughter starts to die down, someone cracks another joke and off they go again – even Waiakh chimes in with a quip of his own.

Soon he starts to smile and then he too joins in the laughter. He doesn't know why he's laughing, if it's at his own misfortunes, at seeing them laugh, at being on display like this – he laughs with them and it's like a drug flowing through him, a pleasing warmth, an escape to dimly perceived moments of happiness, a way of sharing the tribe's good mood.

He places his hand on his painted chest and announces proudly: "Amglo!" And then he starts to laugh again.

LETTER XVI

From Charlotte de Vallombrun to the President of the Geographical Society.

Vallombrun, 8th April 1868

Monsieur le Président,

Viscount Louis joins me in conveying our heartfelt gratitude for your kind words of comfort in your letter of 25th March. Your sentiments bring solace to our troubled spirits, saddened as they are by the premature death of our brother Octave.

It was most courteous of you to send us the text of the obituary prior to its publication in the Geographical Society Review; we thank you for this. The complimentary portrait you paint of my late brother and of his work is in every respect faithful to the man he was and to the memory we preserve of him. Our only request is that you remove the paragraph on the white savage. This Pelletier affair must surely be regarded as no more than an act of personal charity; it has been of no benefit to the Geographical Society.

We have also taken note of the fact that the governing body will soon be considering both your favourable report and our proposal for an agreed solution to matters arising from the will.

We await the formalisation of this agreement with confidence and look forward to signing the notarised documents in your presence.

Two years ago, Octave donated the majority of the artefacts brought back from his travels to the Museum of Grenoble. Two trunkfuls of these objects, carefully inventoried by Octave, still remain in the attic. If the Society is interested in any or all of these artefacts, I shall be happy to send them to you.

One of these trunks is a sailor's chest of studded leather containing an assortment of oiled wool garments for protection against cold and rain, including gloves, hats and scarves. Most of these items are old and patched at the elbows and knees. The chest also contains a bible in Icelandic with a dedication written in German by the pastor in whose house Octave sojourned; knives, needles of all sizes, chess pieces made of ivory from the teeth of I know not what marine beast; a rag doll; a pair of snow shoes; a metal harpoon with barbed spikes.

The second trunk is larger and of inferior quality. In it are woven skirts and belts made of sturdy leaves; a puzzle; a coconut shell sculpted into the shape of a hut; twelve long necklaces of small white and yellow shells; a grotesque mask in black wood with splashes of red paint, its lips set in a grimace with the tongue half exposed; three digging sticks; a "black wood fork with three bent prongs known as a cannibal's fork"; five wooden statuettes vaguely human in form; eight black or green "magic stones"; a "Kanak coin"; a cloth bag containing an assortment of strange seeds; a headdress of birds' feathers which is already crumbling away.

Finally, I found among Octave's papers a note that had previously escaped my attention, much of which I could neither read nor understand, but which contains a reference to your Society. I cannot imagine that Octave would have wanted this rudimentary draft to be disseminated. However, since fate denied him the opportunity to bring order to these reflections, the fruit, as it were, of his deliberations shortly before his death, and bearing in mind your position and the relationship he enjoyed with you, I thought that these jottings might perhaps be of use to you. I have accordingly made a copy of the note for you to peruse. You will see that it has harsh words to say about a gentleman by the name of Leroy: I rely on your tact with regard to this.

I remain, Sir, your most humble and devoted servant,

Charlotte de Vallombrun

FOR/AGAINST THE GEOGRAPHICAL SOCIETY

The Geographical society is mistaken because it is right. It is mistaken in that it tries to understand savage peoples – we can never understand them; in observing them we change them: such curiosity is therefore impossible to satisfy. It can only lead to illusion – but it is right to try and be the first there. All things considered and since the white man will assuredly travel to the ends of the earth, better that the first contact be with a man of science than with a reiter (illegible)or a pastor or a merchant hungry for profit. Or all three of them together.

The forests will never be dense enough, the deserts never dry or frozen enough.

What is important is Peace. And Peace lies in Escape.

Read in the latest edition of the Geographical Society Review a long essay by Leroy on the Indians of Northern Quebec. Leroy, king of the imbeciles! Those cynical savages answered all his questions but told him a pack of lies. He clearly missed the point. He repeats their tales without ever stopping to think. Repeats parrot fashion.

The Indians talk to Leroy. Their lies are their salvation, their only means of escape. NP escaped. NP's children have escaped. I am left alone.

(Three illegible lines, except for the word Australia)

A savage among savages. Savage for the savages.
In the governor's garden, from the highest point, over the walls, he would gaze at the sea.

Movement more important than vision (mission? Unclear word)
NP escaped in search of peace. NP's smile throughout the plenary session of the Geographical Society.

What is a savage's peace? What does it mean?
NP is not (4 indecipherable words)
Monsieur le Président, I have been the first to land here on the far shore of human knowledge. I am not sure if I can discern you yet.

NP's flight is a personal failure, a scientific fact.
For me, NP's flight is a betrayal, a vow, a promise, a sign of confidence and friendship; alas, what does scientific success matter.

17

He looks at the two islets in the middle of the bay: one is covered in luxuriant vegetation with lustrous green palms swaying in the breeze; the other, utterly sterile, nothing but a pile of sand reflecting the dazzling light.

Waiakh gathers shells. He signals to him with a wave of his hand. Around his left ankle, the tattoo no longer troubles him.

Now, he knows some words.

Quartermaster gave him the word for the Sun. His own name. The East. East wind.

The old woman gave him the word for Water. Water pouch. Tears. Pool of water standing in the bend of a dried up stream.

Waiakh gave him the word Ant. His name.

The old woman has given him the words for Good-to-eat and Not-good-to-eat.

The old woman has given him the word Fire. Campfire. Wood for rubbing together. The tree the wood comes from. Feverish rash.

Wanderer gave him the word Dislike-and-Despise. Words

to be whispered at nightfall to ward off evil creatures of the night.

Waiakh gave him the words Come and Wait.
    The old woman gave him the word Silence. Her name.

The old woman gave him the word Hunting. The leaping animal that stands on its hind legs, leaning on its tail.
    The old woman gave him the word Dreamless-sleep.

In his head other words slumber, words of no use to him.
    Narcisse. Pelletier. Schooner. *Saint-Paul*.

Quartermaster gave him the word Spear. His name. Southern Cross, fixed body in the southern sky.
    The old woman has given him the word Singing-together. Clapping the rhythm with your hands. Banging a rock with a stick to keep time. Murmuring softly. With the others. With all the others.